THE MURDER OF THOMAS CARDWELL

THE CASEBOOK OF BARNABY ADAIR: VOLUME 11

STEPHANIE LAURENS

ABOUT THE MURDER OF THOMAS CARDWELL

THE ELEVENTH VOLUME IN THE CASEBOOK OF BARNABY ADAIR NOVELS

#1 NYT-bestselling author Stephanie Laurens returns with a perplexing case in which her favorite sleuths must untangle a web of interconnected motives to identify the man who killed Thomas Cardwell.
When Thomas Cardwell, an upstanding man-of-business, is murdered, Roscoe enlists the aid of the best investigators in London – namely Barnaby and Penelope Adair and Inspector Stokes of Scotland Yard – to solve the puzzle of why anyone would want to kill a man as honest as Cardwell.

Dispatched by Roscoe, London's gambling king, to learn what "nefarious activity" an upstanding man-of-business has stumbled upon, Jordan Draper—Roscoe's own man-of-business—arrives at Thomas Cardwell's office to discover Cardwell very recently murdered.

Soon, Jordan finds himself working alongside the Adairs and Inspector Stokes as they search for clues as to why anyone would kill a man as unthreatening as Cardwell. Unexpectedly, Jordan finds himself drawn to Cardwell's family, especially Thomas's sister, Ruth, and as the investigation progresses, the greater Jordan's compulsion to find the murderer and bring the family resolution and respite grows.

Clue by clue, motive by surprising motive, the investigators seek to identify Cardwell's murderer and, along the way, uncover the "nefarious activity" he'd sought to bring to the authorities' attention. But in a case cluttered with intertwined motives and a web of potential suspects related to each other as well as the victim, finding the kernel of truth amid the chaff is no easy matter. Only through enlisting the help of the investigators' wider circle of supporters do they make any headway, and on the heels of uncovering a cascade of crimes, they finally—*finally*—close in on the man who murdered Thomas Cardwell.

A historical novel of 77,000 words interweaving mystery, crime, and a touch of romance.

PRAISE FOR THE WORKS OF
STEPHANIE LAURENS

"Stephanie Laurens' heroines are marvelous tributes to Georgette Heyer: feisty and strong." *Cathy Kelly*

"Stephanie Laurens never fails to entertain and charm her readers with vibrant plots, snappy dialogue, and unforgettable characters." *Historical Romance Reviews*

"Stephanie Laurens plays into readers' fantasies like a master and claims their hearts time and again." *Romantic Times Magazine*

Praise for *The Murder of Thomas Cardwell*

"Inspector Stokes and the Adairs are once again called upon to solve a baffling mystery—a quest that will lead them from the heights of society to the depths in pursuit of the killer. A touch of romance adds spice to this engaging tale set amid the timeless elegance of the Regency era." *Irene S., Proofreader, Red Adept Editing*

"London financial manager Thomas Cardwell contacts well-placed friends for advice regarding some 'nefarious activity' he's come across, but before Thomas can hear back from them, he's murdered in his own office, stabbed with a letter opener. Part-time sleuths Barnaby and Penelope Adair are quickly called in to join Inspector Stokes of Scotland Yard. With suspects aplenty, this Regency-era mystery is one readers will enjoy trying to solve." *Angela M., Copy Editor, Red Adept Editing*

"Readers who love historical fiction, mysteries, and a touch of romance will enjoy this latest book from Stephanie Laurens! Both new and familiar characters work through the twists and turns of a murder investigation and ultimately uncover more than they expected." *Kristina B., Proofreader, Red Adept Editing*

OTHER TITLES BY STEPHANIE LAURENS

Cynster Next Generation Novels
The Tempting of Thomas Carrick

A Match for Marcus Cynster

The Lady By His Side

An Irresistible Alliance

The Greatest Challenge of Them All

A Conquest Impossible to Resist

The Inevitable Fall of Christopher Cynster

The Games Lovers Play

The Secrets of Lord Grayson Child

Foes, Friends and Lovers

The Time for Love

The Barbarian and Miss Flibbertigibbet

Miss Prim and the Duke of Wilde

A Family Of His Own

Lady Osbaldestone's Christmas Chronicles
Lady Osbaldestone's Christmas Goose

Lady Osbaldestone and the Missing Christmas Carols

Lady Osbaldestone's Plum Puddings

Lady Osbaldestone's Christmas Intrigue

The Meaning of Love

The Casebook of Barnaby Adair Novels
Where the Heart Leads

The Peculiar Case of Lord Finsbury's Diamonds

The Masterful Mr. Montague

The Curious Case of Lady Latimer's Shoes

Loving Rose: The Redemption of Malcolm Sinclair

The Confounding Case of the Carisbrook Emeralds

The Murder at Mandeville Hall

The Meriwell Legacy

Dead Beside the Thames

Marriage and Murder

The Murder of Thomas Cardwell

The Curse of Ill-gotten Gains (October 16, 2025)

Bastion Club Novels

Captain Jack's Woman (Prequel)

The Lady Chosen

A Gentleman's Honor

A Lady of His Own

A Fine Passion

To Distraction

Beyond Seduction

The Edge of Desire

Mastered by Love

Black Cobra Quartet

The Untamed Bride

The Elusive Bride

The Brazen Bride

The Reckless Bride

The Adventurers Quartet

The Lady's Command

A Buccaneer at Heart

The Daredevil Snared

Lord of the Privateers

The Cavanaughs

The Designs of Lord Randolph Cavanaugh

The Pursuits of Lord Kit Cavanaugh

The Beguilement of Lady Eustacia Cavanaugh

The Obsessions of Lord Godfrey Cavanaugh

Other Novels

The Lady Risks All

The Legend of Nimway Hall – 1750: Jacqueline

Medieval (As M.S.Laurens)

Desire's Prize

Novellas

Melting Ice – from the anthologies *Rough Around the Edges* and *Scandalous Brides*

Rose in Bloom – from the anthology *Scottish Brides*

Scandalous Lord Dere – from the anthology *Secrets of a Perfect Night*

Lost and Found – from the anthology *Hero, Come Back*

The Fall of Rogue Gerrard – from the anthology *It Happened One Night*

The Seduction of Sebastian Trantor – from the anthology *It Happened One Season*

Short Stories

The Wedding Planner – from the anthology *Royal Weddings*

A Return Engagement – from the anthology *Royal Bridesmaids*

UK-Style Regency Romances

Tangled Reins

Four in Hand

Impetuous Innocent

Fair Juno

The Reasons for Marriage

A Lady of Expectations An Unwilling Conquest

A Comfortable Wife

THE MURDER OF THOMAS CARDWELL

This is a work of fiction. Names, characters, places, and incidents are either products of the writer's imagination or are used fictitiously and are not to be construed as real. Any resemblance to actual events, locales, organizations, or persons, living or dead, is entirely coincidental.

THE MURDER OF THOMAS CARDWELL

CHAPTER 1

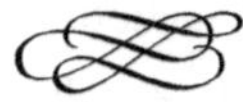

MARCH 1, 1841. DOLPHIN SQUARE, LONDON.

Jordan Draper's life revolved around figures; numbers were life blood to him. As the third son of a provincial man-of-business, he'd been exposed to the calculus of various types of enterprises from an early age. Consequently, it had surprised no one when, after completing grammar school, he'd taken to the business of accounts and estate management like a duck to water.

Then, utterly unexpectedly, for excellent and, indeed, commendable reasons, a scion of his father's premier client family, the Delbraiths, who held the dukedom of Ridgware, elected to leave behind his life of dissolute comfort to become, of all things, London's gambling king. The absurdity and the challenge appealed to Jordan, and he followed Neville Roscoe to London, becoming Roscoe's man-of-business and, in all things managerial, Roscoe's right-hand man. As such, Jordan watched over all the accounts pertaining to Roscoe's vast entrepreneurial empire.

Despite there being more than a decade between them in age, Jordan and Roscoe had always got on. They understood each other at a level that meant that, in any situation, Jordan instinctively knew what Roscoe would want done. Over the years, the day-to-day excitements and never-ending challenges had ensured Jordan remained engaged and involved in the constantly evolving business that fell under Roscoe's hand. That invariably, Roscoe stood on the side of justice and fairness made Jordan's work considerably easier than might have been supposed.

Now, decades after Roscoe's arrival in London, the authorities were entirely content to have the upper stratum of gambling establishments in the town firmly under Roscoe's control.

With his position at Roscoe's side assured and all running smoothly, Jordan found that his life had grown pleasant and comfortable, but rather less exciting and challenging.

There were times he wasn't entirely sure if that was for the good.

On the first afternoon of March, toward the end of a rather dreary day, seated behind the desk in the accounts office in Roscoe's sprawling mansion in Dolphin Square, Jordan was finalizing the last of the day's correspondence when Mudd, one of Roscoe's bodyguards, tapped on the open door.

"Boss wants to see you in his office," Mudd rumbled.

Jordan nodded, tucked his pencil behind his right ear, and pushed back his chair. "Any clue as to why?"

Mudd stepped back and waited for Jordan to join him in the corridor. "Some letter that just came. Seems it's a mite puzzling."

Intrigued, Jordan walked beside Mudd, a hefty ex-bruiser closer to Roscoe's age than Jordan's and also one of the trusted few who made up Roscoe's inner circle, down the elegantly appointed corridor to Roscoe's large office.

The door stood open, and Jordan and Mudd walked in to find Roscoe, a dark-haired, elegantly handsome gentleman whose face testified to his aristocratic lineage, sitting behind his large mahogany desk and faintly frowning at the sheet of paper he held in one hand.

Leaning on one of Roscoe's broad shoulders and also avidly scrutinizing the letter was Lady Miranda, Roscoe's wife.

Another man, even taller and heavier than Mudd, stood before the curtained windows, attempting to look inconspicuous and failing. As Jordan crossed the thick carpet toward the desk, he grinned and tipped his head to Rawlings, another of the inner circle.

Both Roscoe and Miranda looked up as Jordan neared.

Miranda straightened and smiled, the gesture warming her pretty face.

Jordan smiled back, then met Roscoe's eyes, which continued to hold a frown. "You wanted me?"

Roscoe's gaze returned to the letter. "Remember Thomas Cardwell, Hemingway's man-of-business?"

Jordan nodded. "We dealt with him in negotiating the Hemingways' contract."

Hemingways' Linens supplied the linens to all of Roscoe's various clubs. As far as Jordan was aware, the firm had always been reliable with no issues at all.

"Correct." Roscoe held out the letter. "This just arrived, and I'm not sure what to make of it. What do you think?"

Jordan took the letter and quickly scanned the neat, businesslike script.

Thomas Cardwell had written:

Dear Sir,

I've stumbled upon a nefarious activity that I believe needs to be brought to the attention of the authorities. However, the situation is sensitive, and I have no connections in that sphere and do not know how to proceed. I am hoping that you might advise me as to what the best approach would be. I will be in my office from eight in the morning tomorrow or will willingly travel to Dolphin Square should you or one of your advisors be available to discuss the matter.

Yours sincerely, Thomas Cardwell.

"Nefarious?" Jordan could see why Roscoe was puzzled. "He could have been a trifle more forthcoming."

"Indeed. That was my immediate reaction," Roscoe confessed. "What on earth could Cardwell have stumbled upon?"

Still studying the scant lines, Jordan offered, "I assume labeling the situation 'sensitive' means this discovery involves one of his clients."

"Possibly," Miranda said, "but who's to know?"

"Only one way to find out." Jordan looked at Roscoe. "Do you want me to go to his office tomorrow and learn what this is about?"

Roscoe considered the question, then glanced at Mudd and Rawlings. "Have we heard anything about Hemingways' recently?"

Both large men shook their heads.

"Not a peep," Mudd confirmed. "Far as we know, they're carrying on as usual with no dramas."

Roscoe tapped one long finger on his blotter, then returned his gaze to Jordan. "One never can tell. Best you go and see Cardwell and find out what he's uncovered."

Miranda added, "We don't want to suddenly discover the clubs are short on linens. And"—she caught Roscoe's eye—"just in case there's more to this than meets the eye at first glance, you might take Gelman with you."

Gelman was in training to eventually assist Mudd and Rawlings with their duties.

Rawlings was quick to support Miranda's suggestion. "The lad needs to get out and about and learn more of what the business covers."

Mudd tacked on, "What he might be called on to do. He needs experience if he's to step up to our level one day."

Struggling to rein in his grin, Roscoe nodded to Jordan. "Yes, take Gelman with you. It won't hurt for him to be put to wider use."

Jordan folded the letter and slipped it into his pocket. "Gelman and I will head over to Cardwell's first thing tomorrow."

At eight o'clock the following morning, accompanied by John Gelman, Jordan left the big white mansion on the north side of Dolphin Square, hailed an idling hackney, and set off to cross London to Thomas Cardwell's office in Broad Street, just north of the Bank of England.

Gelman was an average-sized man in his mid-thirties, perennially neatly and quietly dressed and keen to prove himself worthy of inclusion in Roscoe's innermost circle. Like Mudd and Rawlings, he'd been a guard at one of Roscoe's clubs and had shown himself to be a sensible man who understood the value of restraint and of using common sense to defuse fraught situations. He could be intimidating when required but also knew when to stand back and let the promise of his presence do the talking. Unlike Mudd and Rawlings, who with their crooked noses and cauliflower ears bore the signs of their previous lives in their faces, Gelman possessed an unremarkable appearance, which made him an excellent choice for this excursion.

In common with all of Roscoe's men, Gelman wasn't a natural chatterer, and Jordan spent the journey to Broad Street mentally constructing possible scenarios to account for Thomas Cardwell's appeal.

The hackney drew up opposite Cardwell's office. With muted eagerness, Jordan opened the door and stepped down to the pavement. Gelman followed and paid the jarvey.

When the carriage drew away, Jordan remained on the pavement and studied the three-story building across the street. It was typical of the area, having a wide façade with a central door that would give access to stairs leading to the apartments on the upper floors. The ground floor played host to two offices, each reached by doors flanking and at right angles to the central door, which was set back a yard or so from the pavement so that the three doors formed a rectangular alcove. Both offices had wide bow windows fronting the street, and above the window on the right, a discreet gold-lettered sign declared it to be the premises of Thom. Cardwell, Business Agent.

Jordan stepped onto the cobbles and, with Gelman at his shoulder, crossed to the opposite pavement and led the way to Cardwell's door. Given it was half past eight, Jordan was unsurprised to find the door unlocked. He opened it and walked into a neat and welcoming office.

Three comfortable chairs arranged about a round table occupied the area closer to the window, while farther back, a wide solid desk sat squarely across the rear of the room. The three interior walls were lined with shelves holding account ledgers and books about accounting practices.

In one sweeping glance, Jordan took all of that in and found nothing out of place.

The sight that jarred him and brought him to a halt two paces beyond the door was the younger gentleman with his pale, slack-jawed face and horror-struck expression who was standing stock-still behind the desk and staring downward in utter shock.

Slowly, as if the movement required great effort, the younger man dragged his gaze from its fixation, looked at Jordan and Gelman, and, ashen-faced, stammered, "I... I didn't..." He swallowed and blurted, almost on a wail, "I didn't do it!"

Freed by the sound, Jordan swiftly went forward.

Gelman closed the door and followed.

They rounded the desk and halted, looking down at a sight that explained the gentleman's distress.

A dark-haired man in a neat suit lay sprawled on his back, with blood seeping through his waistcoat from where the hilt of a letter knife protruded from his chest. With a sinking feeling, Jordan recognized Thomas Cardwell. Cardwell's eyes were wide open, and his expression was one of surprise and shock. Judging by the position of the desk chair, Cardwell had been sitting in it when he was attacked and had subsequently fallen off to one side.

Jordan and Gelman both softly swore, and Jordan crouched and set his fingers to Cardwell's neck to check for a pulse. There was none, but from the warmth of Cardwell's skin and the still-oozing blood, he'd been dead for mere minutes.

Absorbing that fact, Jordan raised his gaze to the unknown younger man.

The man rushed to declare, "I only just got here! I arrived a bare minute before you two."

Gelman stepped back to stand against the wall closer to the door. "No signs of a fight that I can see."

Jordan returned his gaze to the body, then he straightened and looked more closely at the other man. Jordan suspected he knew the answer even though he asked, "Who are you?"

The younger man was having trouble breathing. "I… I'm his brother." He hauled in a tight breath. "Thomas's younger brother. Bobby Cardwell."

The resemblance Jordan had observed borne out, he asked, "Why are you here?"

"I came to speak with him." Bobby's eyes were drawn once more to his brother's corpse. "I got here just before you two, and I found him"— Bobby swallowed and gestured wildly—"like that!"

"He was already dead?" Jordan glanced around the area. As Gelman had said, there was no sign of any struggle.

"Yes!" Bobby calmed a fraction. "I checked, like you did. He was already gone."

The door opened, drawing the three men's attention.

A lady somewhere in her thirties carrying an armful of ledgers came bustling inside. She was of average height, slender but with well-formed curves filling out the dark-blue jacket and full skirt of her outfit. Her sable hair was gathered in a bun at the nape of her neck, and her black bonnet framed an oval face with large periwinkle-blue eyes, a straight nose, and a determined chin. She set the ledgers on the round table and blinked at Jordan and Gelman. Her lush, blush-pink lips formed a silent "Oh."

Then her gaze passed on to Bobby, with his pale face and stunned expression, and puzzled concern infused her features. "Bobby? What are you doing here?" Her gaze flitted back to Jordan and Gelman. "Where's Thomas?" When no one immediately answered, she focused on Bobby and, frowning, started for him. "What's wrong?"

Both Jordan and Gelman shifted, their instinctive impulse being to block the lady's sight of the slain man, but unsure who she was, both hesitated.

Then she neared Bobby, and he drew in a shuddering breath and pointed down behind the desk. "He's dead!" He gulped and almost on a sob continued, "Oh God, Ruthie! Thomas is dead!"

"Wha—" The lady's exclamation cut off as she reached Bobby and, with her gaze, followed his pointing finger. Her face drained of all color —every last vestige—then she made an inarticulate sound, pushed Bobby aside, crouched by the body, and as Jordan had, searched for a pulse.

When she found no trace, she slowly rocked back on her heels. Her hand rose to her throat. "Oh Lord. Who…?" Then her gaze snapped to Jordan and Gelman, and she rose. Her eyes full of suspicion, she demanded, "Who are you?"

Calmly, Jordan replied, "We came to keep an appointment Cardwell made. He invited us to call."

Her eyes narrowing, she tipped up her chin and declared, "I know all my brother's clients, and he didn't mention meeting any new ones."

So she was Cardwell's sister. His older sister, Jordan suspected. Keen to see what she would make of it, he drew Cardwell's letter from his pocket and held it out.

Ruth Cardwell seized the letter and read it.

Bobby had recovered somewhat and gathered his wits enough to say, "It's true, Ruthie. They arrived just after I did."

Watching a frown of even greater puzzlement invest Ruth's face and deducing that she had no more notion of what had prompted her brother to write the letter than Jordan did, he reached over and filched the sheet back.

She frowned vaguely, but let him have it.

Bobby went on, "I got here just a minute or so before them and found Thomas"—Bobby's breath hitched—"like that." He looked at Jordan and Gelman and, unprompted, went on, "I came in, and I couldn't see him. I looked around, then called his name as I came to the desk…" His memory rolled on, and his complexion lost what little color it had regained.

Jordan merely nodded and focused on Ruth Cardwell. Although white-faced and clearly deeply shocked, she appeared more in command of her faculties than Bobby. "When does Thomas normally unlock his door?"

"Eight o'clock, on the dot." Ruth glanced at Jordan, but then her gaze returned to the body of her brother.

In a quiet voice, Bobby added, "He always said it was important for his clients that he was punctual."

Jordan nodded, but his attention was on Ruth Cardwell's face. She was staring at the body, sorrow filling her large eyes, but she was biting her lip, and even though grief was already etching her features, there was an element of concern in her expression that Jordan couldn't quite reconcile.

"Is the letter knife his?" he asked.

She nodded. "It was usually lying on his desk." She glanced at the desk and pointed at the top-right corner of the blotter. "Just there. He always kept it there."

Jordan studied brother and sister. "Thomas had met me through the business of one of his clients. He knew I work for Neville Roscoe."

Both Ruth's and Bobby's eyes widened. As Jordan had anticipated, even these innocents knew of Roscoe at least by name and reputation. He went on, "Thomas sent Roscoe that letter asking for advice about some particular activity he'd uncovered that he, Thomas, believed needed to be brought to the authorities' attention." Jordan arched a brow at Ruth and Bobby. "Do either of you know why your brother appealed to Roscoe for advice?"

Both remained deeply puzzled and shook their heads.

Ruth directed a frown at Jordan and Gelman. "Thomas never mentioned any dealings with Neville Roscoe."

Suspicion was, once more, back in her eyes.

"It was Hemingways' Linens," Jordan said. "Roscoe has a large contract with them."

"Ah. I see." Ruth relaxed somewhat, which told Jordan that she did, indeed, know her brother's clients.

Gelman shifted and glanced at Jordan. "So what now? Want me to fetch a bobby?"

Jordan considered the situation—in all its puzzling aspects—and shook his head. "Given Cardwell contacted us, this might be more than the local police can handle." He looked at Ruth and Bobby. "We'll arrange for Scotland Yard to be notified." With a wave, he encouraged the pair to the door. "Until they send someone to take charge, Gelman will remain on guard to ensure nothing is touched or tampered with."

Gelman inclined his head and stepped back against the wall.

Jordan had to physically crowd Ruth Cardwell to get her moving, but underneath her outward façade, she was shocked, shaken, and grief was quickly rising, and when Bobby took her arm, although patently reluctant to leave their dead brother, she went with Bobby to the door.

Jordan followed. "Your address?" When Ruth glanced blankly at him, he added, "The police will want it."

Rather numbly, she said, "Number twenty-nine, Finsbury Circus. Just south of East Street."

That was a pleasant area populated by the gentry.

Jordan nodded. "I'll pass that on."

He got the Cardwells out of the office and onto the pavement.

Bobby drew in a deeper breath and looked at Jordan. "It's not far. We always just walk."

Jordan watched as Ruth took firmer hold of Bobby's arm, and together, walking slowly with their heads bowed, they set off for Finsbury Circus.

Once they'd turned down a side street and passed out of sight, Jordan hailed a passing hackney and ordered the jarvey to make for Dolphin Square with all speed.

CHAPTER 2

On returning to the mansion that dominated the north side of Dolphin Square, Jordan went straight to Roscoe's office.

As usual, the door was open, and Jordan strode inside.

Roscoe was lounging behind his desk and discussing something with Mudd, who was standing to one side of the mahogany expanse.

Both men glanced expectantly at Jordan. At the sight of his grim expression, Roscoe sat up, and Mudd came to attention.

"What's happened?" Roscoe demanded.

Jordan halted before the desk. He nodded to Mudd, then reported, "Cardwell's dead. Murdered. Stabbed with his own letter knife just before we got there." Briefly, Jordan described the scene as he and Gelman had found it.

"So this brother," Mudd said. "Could he have done it?"

On the journey back, Jordan had pondered that at length. "Unlikely. He was badly shaken, and frankly, I don't think he would have the spine for it."

"You left Gelman on guard?" Roscoe clarified.

Jordan nodded. "Given that Cardwell wrote that he'd found evidence of some nefarious activity that needed to be brought to the authorities' attention—and by that, I assume he meant authorities higher than the local police—and then, before we can speak with him, he's murdered, I thought you'd want to handle this by going directly to those higher authorities."

Roscoe inclined his head. "Good decision. I agree this calls for involvement at a more elevated level." He tapped his pen on the blotter while he thought, then he looked at Mudd. "Go to Scotland Yard and speak with Stokes. Specifically Stokes and no one else. Tell him all that Jordan's told us and that I've sent Jordan to wait for him at Albemarle Street."

Mudd saluted, turned, and left.

Jordan frowned. "Albemarle Street..." Then he remembered. "Ah." His expression cleared. "The Adairs."

"Exactly. Number twenty-four, Albemarle Street." Roscoe continued, "I don't have a clue as to what Cardwell found, but he reached out to us, and we didn't get there in time. It appears that Cardwell tried to do the right thing and paid a heavy price for it. He deserves the best brains on his case, and indubitably, that means the Adairs."

Jordan couldn't agree more.

After a moment of thinking, Roscoe said, "Take the letter and go to the Adairs. When Stokes arrives, tell them all you know and then go with them. Follow the investigation. By all means, tell them that's by my order, but I doubt they'll argue. They'll recognize the value in having your expertise to call on. From our point of view, I want to know what got Cardwell killed." Roscoe met Jordan's gaze. "Until this case is solved, you're relieved of all other duties."

When Jordan allowed his uncertainty to show, Roscoe smiled and added, "I know you're protective of your books, but in this instance, for the next week or so, Miranda can keep an eye on things while you concentrate on seeing justice done for Thomas Cardwell."

In Jordan's mind, the fleeting image of Miranda working on his accounts—and he knew very well she was more than capable of managing for a few weeks—was, to his surprise, supplanted by a vision of Ruth Cardwell and the sorrow and uncertainty that had filled her face.

There was something there—something more troubling—and to Jordan's surprise, he wanted to help her resolve whatever the problem was.

"Right," he heard himself say. He refocused on Roscoe and snapped off a salute. "I'll head for Albemarle Street."

"And," Roscoe said as Jordan made for the door, "keep Gelman with you. Use him for guard duty or whatever other tasks seem appropriate. The experience will stand him in good stead."

Jordan glanced back. "Will do." With that, he quit the room and headed for the stairs. He went out of the front door, strode to the street, and cast about to find another hackney, as Mudd had commandeered his.

It was past ten o'clock when Jordan reached Albemarle Street. He had the jarvey let him out on Piccadilly at the end of the street and, after paying the man, started strolling up the pavement toward Number 24.

At that time of day, there were a goodly number of people around, both staff from the town houses lining the street as well as their masters and mistresses setting out for the day. With his well-cut coat and conservative attire, Jordan raised no eyebrows, and few took note of him as he strode along.

Looking ahead, he saw a small procession walking down from the far end of the street. A tall, elegant gentleman in hat and coat was walking beside a petite lady in a fashionable purple redingote and matching bonnet, who was ushering two young boys before her. One young lad was managing a hoop, while the other, rather younger and not so steady on his feet, was attempting to lead a black-and-white spaniel on a leash.

In reality, the lady was the one restraining the dog, which, given the beast's exuberance, was just as well. As a further precaution, an attentive nursemaid and a watchful footman followed close behind the group, ready to lend assistance if required.

Jordan smiled at the sight. Over recent years, courtesy of Roscoe and Miranda's brood, he'd grown accustomed to having young children around and secretly enjoyed the unexpected amusement he derived from their antics.

Nevertheless, not knowing how the Adairs viewed their family and, therefore, uncertain of his welcome, he slowed his pace so he approached the steps leading up to the door of Number 24 just as the door opened and the children and dog were ushered inside.

Pausing on the porch after ushering Penelope and the children through the doorway, Barnaby Adair saw Jordan halt at the foot of the steps. Barnaby recognized Jordan instantly and inclined his head to him, then waved the maid and footman—who had also seen Jordan approach and hung back—into the house.

Once the pair had slipped past, Barnaby gestured to Jordan to join him. When Jordan did, Barnaby offered his hand. "It's been some time since we last met."

"Indeed." Jordan gripped the proffered hand and shook it. "I wasn't sure you would recognize me."

Barnaby smiled. "I rarely forget useful people."

Jordan grinned.

Penelope stuck her head outside, clearly wondering what had delayed her spouse. She saw Jordan, and her face lit. She bustled out and gave him her hand. "Mr. Draper." As he straightened from his bow, she eagerly went on, "Dare I take it that Roscoe sent you?"

"He did." Jordan glanced at Barnaby, then returned his gaze to Penelope. "A man has been murdered, and I've been directed to wait with you until Stokes arrives."

"Excellent!" Penelope's expression grew even more delighted. "Well," she corrected herself, "not about a man being murdered, but do come in." She beckoned Jordan and Barnaby inside. "The children and dog have been suitably exercised and have retired for naps upstairs, so we can settle in the drawing room, and while we wait for Stokes, you can tell us all."

Faced with the prospect of having to repeat his information twice, Jordan was relieved when, virtually as soon as they'd sat—him on one long sofa and Barnaby and Penelope on the sofa opposite—the doorbell pealed, and seconds later, the drawing room door opened, and Inspector Basil Stokes strode in.

Jordan got to his feet, and after Jordan had shaken hands with Stokes, who also remembered him, they all sat, and at Stokes's instruction to "Start at the beginning," Jordan commenced, "Yesterday, in the late afternoon, a letter was delivered to Roscoe at Dolphin Square."

He drew the letter from his pocket and handed it to Stokes. Stokes unfolded the single sheet, read it, then huffed and passed the letter to Barnaby, who scanned it and handed it to Penelope.

"As you can see," Jordan went on, "the request was for advice on how to contact the authorities about some nefarious scheme Cardwell had uncovered. Roscoe sent me and another of his men, Gelman, to meet with Cardwell this morning, but when we arrived, we found Cardwell stabbed with his own letter knife and already dead."

"What time did you get there?" Stokes asked, already taking notes.

"Eight-thirty," Jordan replied. "More or less on the dot."

"Was there anyone else there?" Barnaby asked.

Jordan nodded. "Cardwell's younger brother, Bobby, was standing over the body, staring down at it and, it seemed, in deep shock. Neither

Gelman nor I believe he was the killer—once you meet him, you'll think the same—and by his account, he arrived only a minute or so before us."

Stokes paused, then instructed, "Start from the moment you walked into Cardwell's office. What did you see?"

Jordan dutifully described the scene and what they'd observed and said and heard, all the way to ushering Ruth and Bobby Cardwell out of the office and leaving Gelman on guard before heading to Roscoe to report.

Stokes pulled a small face. "I would have preferred you'd come straight to the Yard, but…as it is, we haven't wasted much time."

"And Gelman is on guard," Barnaby mildly observed.

"Indeed." Penelope flourished the letter she'd continued to study. "It's really most vexing of Cardwell to have given no clue at all as to who is behind these nefarious activities or what they are."

Stokes waggled his fingers, and Barnaby took the letter from Penelope and returned it to Stokes, then Barnaby asked Jordan, "Did you know Cardwell?"

"Not well," Jordan replied. "We were acquainted through having to negotiate the contract for supplying linen to Roscoe's clubs. Cardwell was the agent for the linen suppliers."

"So," Stokes observed, "not a deep or close acquaintance."

"But"—Penelope fixed her dark gaze on Jordan's face—"you would have formed an opinion about Cardwell, at least as far as his duties as an agent went. So what did you think of him?"

Looking down at his clasped hands, Jordan took a moment to review his memories, then offered, "He struck me as honest and hardworking. Upright, with a decent backbone and a clear sense of right and wrong. He kept excellent records and, I feel, would always—rigidly so—do the very best he could for his clients." He met Penelope's gaze. "That's how he appeared to me, but I only interacted with him on three occasions."

"Well"—Stokes waved the refolded letter before tucking it into his notebook—"he clearly understood where the line between right and wrong lay with whatever it is he uncovered."

Penelope was frowning. "You said that when the sister—Ruth—came into the office, she was carrying a stack of ledgers." When Jordan nodded, Penelope asked, "Why did she arrive just then? And why was she ferrying Cardwell's ledgers?"

Jordan raised his brows and admitted, "I don't know the answer to either question."

"Obviously," Stokes said, tucking away his notebook, "our first act must be to go to Cardwell's office and get an update there. I've sent down my team to take charge, and by the time we get there, with any luck, the medical examiner will have arrived as well."

"As I mentioned, I left Gelman on guard." Jordan rose as Stokes got to his feet. "We didn't want to disturb the body or anything else by hunting around for the key."

"Good." Stokes eyed Jordan. "Am I right in thinking you've been told to stay with us?"

Jordan smiled. "Given the boss was the one Cardwell appealed to for help, he now feels he has an iron in this fire."

Stokes inclined his head. "No saying but that you and your boss's resources won't come in handy."

Jordan's smile deepened. "That's what he said you would say."

Stokes huffed and looked at Barnaby and Penelope. "Well, then, we'd best be moving. Let's go."

Stokes turned and led the way out, and the other three readily followed.

With Barnaby at her heels, Penelope followed Jordan and Stokes into Thomas Cardwell's office on Broad Street. She didn't know the area well, but the location was considered highly respectable, being quite close to—within easy walking distance of—the Bank of England and all the financial offices that clustered around that edifice.

After crossing the threshold, Penelope stepped away from the door and paused beside the round table situated to make the best of the light that shafted through the large bow window. Blocking out the activity occurring about the large desk at the rear of the room, she scanned the space, hoping to get some sense of the deceased from his chosen surroundings.

She took in the books and ledgers, neatly set upon the shelves and obviously in good order. There was nothing ramshackle about the place, and as she trailed the others as they approached the desk, she noted that the general tidiness extended to the desk's surface, where an ink set was placed above a pristine blotter in the perfect position for effective use. There was no dust anywhere, and the furnishings were in good condition.

All in all, Cardwell's office reflected a personality much as Jordan had described—an honest man with a deep sense of integrity and a devotion to doing the right thing by his fellow man.

Inwardly, Penelope acknowledged the unfairness inherent in it being a man of Cardwell's character who had been slain.

Then she blinked and focused her attention on the short, rotund man crouched over the body.

Having rounded the desk and seen the man, Stokes grunted and said, "Findlay—despite the circumstances, I'm glad to see you're on the case."

Findlay looked up, amusement glinting in his eyes. "I think you mean *because* of the circumstances." He rose and nodded to Barnaby, Penelope, and Jordan. "And I'm here because I was the closest, and the examination was deemed urgent." Curiosity welling, he asked, "Who are your friends?"

Stokes introduced Penelope, Barnaby, and Jordan. "Findlay's the medical examiner for the River Police."

"Ah," Penelope said. "The Sedbury case."

"Indeed." Findlay acknowledged them with a half bow, but didn't offer to shake anyone's hand. To Jordan, he said, "I met your friend, Gelman. Good thinking, leaving someone on guard. Even in this neighborhood, there's no telling what might have been nicked or rifled if you hadn't." Findlay looked down at the body. "I haven't moved him yet—I thought you'd want to see this one in situ."

They all stared at Cardwell.

"The face," Stokes said.

"Yes. His expression is telling, I think." Findlay looked at Jordan. "According to Gelman, the expression was even more pronounced when you first saw him."

Studying the corpse, Jordan nodded. "Yes. It was even clearer that he'd been taken by surprise."

"Utter surprise, by the looks of it," Barnaby said.

"So he didn't expect to be murdered," Penelope concluded, "and consequently, he wasn't on guard." She glanced around. "That's why there's no sign of a struggle."

"Indeed," Findlay said approvingly. "There's not a hint of a struggle anywhere here. And then there's the physical evidence—the layout, so to speak." Findlay stepped back and studied the scene. "I believe the attack came from over the desk."

He looked at Jordan. "When you were here earlier, did you see anyone move that chair?" With his head, Findlay indicated the chair facing the desk.

"No." Jordan considered the chair, which sat a little back from the desk. "It looks like someone was sitting there and suddenly stood up."

"Exactly." Findlay pointed at the letter knife. "Gelman told me the sister said that the knife was lying on the desk."

"She did." Jordan pointed at where Ruth Cardwell had said the letter knife had lain. "Just there."

Findlay nodded. "So what I think happened was that Cardwell was discussing something with someone he saw as no threat at all. And without any warning whatsoever, that someone stood, grabbed the letter knife, lunged across the desk, and stabbed Cardwell in the chest. Subsequently, Cardwell fell out of his chair, pushing it to where it currently stands."

They studied the position of the chairs and the angle of the knife.

"That's why," Barnaby mused, "the knife went in at a slight downward angle. The attacker was essentially standing, albeit leaning over the desk, while Cardwell was still seated."

"Yes, and sadly for Cardwell," Findlay said, "that's what made the attack so lethal. The knife went through the heart at a downward angle. No hope of surviving that, even for a short time."

"Could the killer have been a woman?" Penelope asked.

Findlay considered that, then shook his head. "Highly unlikely, I would think. The blow was delivered with considerable force. It had to be —letter knives are not generally the sharpest of implements."

Busy making notes, Stokes grunted. "What's your official time of death?"

Findlay grinned. "For once, I can be remarkably definitive." He nodded at Jordan. "Thanks to Mr. Draper here, we can say Cardwell was killed before eight-thirty. And as we were summoned so soon after death, by the temperature of the body, I would say he was killed no earlier than seven-forty-five."

"Forty-five minutes?" Stokes looked incredulous. "I don't think I've ever had such a short window for a murder."

Findlay nodded, transparently pleased. "It's quite a landmark in my experience as well."

Stokes looked energized. "I'm going to set my men to canvass the area. With any luck, someone will have seen something useful."

Jordan moved to accompany Stokes. "If you're agreeable, Gelman can assist." With a smile, he added, "He's with me to gain experience, or so I've been told."

Stokes grinned. "Always pleased to have extra men."

Findlay called after them, "I'll be finished here shortly. Is it all right to transfer the body to the morgue?"

Halfway to the door, Stokes halted and looked at Barnaby and Penelope. "Anything else we need from the body?"

Penelope looked down at the corpse. "The key to the office?"

Barnaby added, "And anything else he was carrying on him."

Findlay nodded. "I was just about to search his pockets."

After a key ring with two keys, a coin purse, a billfold, and a clean, folded handkerchief had been found and surrendered to Stokes, Penelope and Barnaby left Findlay to his examining and ambled about the office, idly looking at the contents of the shelves. Eventually, they joined Stokes and Jordan about the small round table at the front of the office, where the pair were discussing what other steps they might take to further the investigation.

All were contingent on what Sergeant O'Donnell, Constable Morgan, and Constable Walsh—a recent addition to Stokes's team—learned from the shopkeepers manning the various establishments surrounding the office.

Penelope sat in one of the chairs and, letting the men's rumbling voices pass over her head, looked out of the window and across the street.

She saw Morgan, accompanied by another man she assumed was Jordan's Gelman, come quickly out of the baker's directly opposite. With barely a glance up and down the street, the pair came hurrying across the cobbles.

Taking in their excited expressions, Penelope rose. "I believe we have news."

Morgan led the way inside, with Gelman on his heels. Morgan saluted Stokes. "Sir. The baker opposite has a direct view of the front door over here. He says he was going back and forth from his ovens to the shop, so he might have missed something, but what he did see was a gentleman loitering about the pavement in front of Cardwell's door."

"This was before Cardwell arrived for the day," Gelman put in.

Morgan nodded. "So sometime before eight, according to the baker. He said Cardwell was regular as clockwork, and sure enough, he turned up at eight on the dot, just like he always did."

"Cardwell's siblings confirmed that," Jordan said. "He took pride in being on time."

"Right," Morgan said. "So according to the baker, Cardwell seemed to recognize the gentleman. They shook hands, then Cardwell opened his door, and they went inside."

"Description of this gentleman?" Stokes demanded.

Morgan grimaced. "Not all that helpful. The baker labeled the man as a gentleman because he was wearing one of those long dun-colored coats that are all the rage." Morgan nodded at Barnaby. "Like Mr. Adair here. The baker says the man was of average-ish height, perhaps a touch shorter than Cardwell, who was medium tall. The man was wearing a black top hat, just like other gentlemen favor. Other than that, the baker said the man was just a gentleman, the sort you pass by on the pavements around here all the time."

Stokes sighed. "Well, at least we've got that much, for which, apparently, we're supposed to be grateful."

Gelman shifted and offered, "The baker had to return to baking and his oven, so he didn't see what happened over here until he came out into his shop again later."

Morgan went on, "He was away for at least twenty minutes, he says, so when he returned to the front of the shop, it would've been a few minutes before eight-thirty. At that time, he glanced over here and saw the younger Mr. Cardwell—"

"That would be Bobby," Gelman put in.

Morgan nodded. "Seems like. The baker said as this younger Cardwell went in, and then just a minute or so later, he saw you and him"—Morgan nodded at Jordan and pointed at Gelman—"arrive and go inside. Then about five minutes later, our baker saw Miss Cardwell come along with ledgers in her arms and go in."

Stokes had been busily scribbling. "Oh, for such an accurate and knowledgeable witness to every murder." He glanced at Morgan. "I take it this baker is sure who he saw?"

"He said he knows the Cardwells well," Morgan replied. "Apparently, Cardwell has had this office for years, and all three of the Cardwells he saw this morning buy buns and cakes and bread from him, so he's sure."

"Blessed be," Stokes murmured, jotting that down. Then he looked at Morgan and grimaced. "I take it our wonderful baker didn't see the gentleman who met Cardwell on the doorstep leave."

Morgan shook his head. "He mentioned that he hadn't seen the man come out, but then he was off tending his oven for those twenty minutes."

"He did wonder if the man had left the back way," Gelman added. "If so, he wouldn't have seen him anyway."

Penelope, along with Barnaby, Stokes, Jordan, and even Findlay, stared at Gelman.

"The back way?" Stokes turned to look at the narrow panel set into the wall at the rear-right corner of the office. "I thought that was a closet."

O'Donnell, who had returned from his own canvassing and was standing with Walsh by the front door, listening to Morgan's report, stated, "We looked, sir. It is a closet."

Findlay beat everyone else to the panel and opened it.

Looking past Findlay, Penelope saw a gentleman's brown coat hanging on a hook.

Findlay huffed. "Looks like Cardwell's coat."

Jordan was standing beside Findlay. "There's a draft." Jordan reached past the coat and gently pushed on the panel at the closet's rear. The panel swung away on hinges, revealing a narrow corridor beyond.

"Stand back," Stokes ordered, and when Findlay and Jordan complied, Stokes stepped forward and slid sideways into the "closet," past the hanging coat and on into the corridor beyond.

Penelope leapt to follow. Unimpeded by the narrowness, she trailed Stokes along the corridor and into a small storeroom-cum-kitchen at the rear of the building.

A single solid wooden door was set into the rear wall. A large bolt could secure it, but was presently drawn back. Stokes reached out a hand and pushed the door, and it swung slightly open.

Stokes grunted. "Left swinging, not even properly closed."

"That would be the source of the draft. It seems our murderer left in a rush." Penelope crowded behind Stokes as Barnaby, followed by O'Don-nell, Morgan, and Jordan, shuffled into the limited space. "What's beyond the door?"

The answer was a narrow lane that ran along the rear of the buildings on that side of the street.

Penelope stepped back and let the men exit into the lane. She watched from the doorway as Stokes, Barnaby, O'Donnell, Morgan, and Jordan looked around. After glancing back and forth along the largely empty lane, she suggested, "The murderer saw Cardwell hang up his coat, and I suspect the panel at the rear of the closet space was normally left wide open. Why would Cardwell shut it?"

"It wasn't latched when I pushed it open," Jordan said. "It swung freely."

"So after killing Cardwell," Stokes said, his expression grim, "the murderer didn't want to risk being seen on the street, leaving the scene of the crime."

"He came out this way," Barnaby concluded, "and unless we're very lucky, he wouldn't have been seen by anyone."

Stokes grunted in resigned agreement. "O'Donnell. Morgan. Take Walsh and Gelman and knock on the rear doors of the premises along this lane to either side and see what you can turn up."

O'Donnell and Morgan snapped off salutes, and Penelope turned and led the others back along the corridor to the office.

When, after Stokes had sent Walsh and Gelman to help O'Donnell and Morgan, Barnaby, Stokes, and Jordan rejoined her, she was standing at the round table at the front of the office, busily flicking through the ledgers stacked upon it.

"Anything there?" Stokes inquired.

She shook her head. "Nothing obvious in these, but as I understand it" —she glanced questioningly at Jordan—"these weren't here when Cardwell was killed."

Sliding his hands into his trouser pockets, Jordan confirmed, "They weren't. Ruth Cardwell, the sister, brought them when she arrived."

"So they're likely not linked to Cardwell's death." Penelope shut the topmost ledger and patted the cover approvingly. "They're very neat."

While they'd been in the lane, two of Findlay's men had arrived with a stretcher, and Findlay had directed them in placing the body upon the canvas and covering it decently with a sheet.

Now, the men hoisted the stretcher and made for the door. His black bag in one hand, Findlay followed, dipping his head to those at the table as he passed.

With Stokes, Barnaby, and Jordan, Penelope watched in silence as Thomas Cardwell's remains were ferried away.

Once the small procession had departed, Jordan exhaled. "The senseless ending of a life."

Stokes glanced at Jordan, then gently said, "There will have been some sense to the killing—there always is. It's up to us to learn what that was—why someone thought Thomas Cardwell had to be killed—and that will lead us to his murderer."

"Indeed." Barnaby had been studying the shelves of account ledgers. "To that end, what can you tell us of Cardwell's business?"

Jordan grimaced. "This is purely from what I gathered through my limited interaction with him, so it might not be the full sum of it. I understood the bulk of his business lay in acting as a financial manager, in the same way a man-of-business does, for small- and medium-sized enterprises. For instance, the linen supplier that was the reason I met Cardwell is a long-established medium-sized business, but I sensed they were among Cardwell's larger clients. Most would have been smaller than that —shopkeepers and the like." Jordan nodded through the window. "You might even find the baker was a client."

Penelope nodded. "So Cardwell got to know you and Roscoe because of the linen supplier's contract." She turned a questioning gaze on Jordan. "If we accept that Cardwell had uncovered some nefarious undertaking that he felt he had to bring to the attention of the authorities, why did he turn to Roscoe for advice?"

"Had he and Roscoe met?" Stokes asked.

Jordan shook his head. "Cardwell had only met me and Rawlings. I handled the negotiations, and Rawlings was there as either he or Mudd usually are."

Barnaby's gaze had remained on Jordan. "So why did Cardwell contact Roscoe? Could it have been because Cardwell's concerns arose from the linen supply business, and therefore, Cardwell felt Roscoe would want to know?"

Jordan thought about that for a moment, then slowly shook his head. "I seriously doubt Hemingways' Linens would give rise to concerns about nefarious activities. They are simply not that sort of business. They're family owned and operated and very well run." He paused, then added, "My only guess as to why Cardwell chose to contact Roscoe is that, as we all know, Roscoe's reputation is legendary. He's widely known for running his gambling businesses with an iron fist and insisting every last little part of them is entirely legal. For those like Cardwell, with no real experience of the underworld, Roscoe figures as an authority on how to successfully walk the difficult line between criminality and legality."

Understanding the point, Penelope added, "They see Roscoe as knowing how to deal with criminals on the one hand and the authorities at all levels on the other."

Jordan nodded. "Just so."

Stokes grunted. "All right. That's a believable explanation. So what's our next move?"

"It should be noted," Penelope said, "that courtesy of our observant baker, the window for the time of death has narrowed even further. The baker saw Cardwell and the unknown gentleman go into Cardwell's office at eight o'clock on the dot."

Barnaby nodded. "And Jordan and Gelman arrived at eight-thirty to find Cardwell dead." He looked at Stokes. "Half an hour is a very short period."

Stokes grunted. "Long enough, apparently."

Footsteps heralded the return of Stokes's men and Gelman. They filed into the office, and smiling, Constable Walsh, younger than the other three and plainly eager to prove his worth, saluted and brightly reported, "Found one sighting, sir. A maid tossing slops into the lane at the far end." He tipped his head toward the north. "Said she saw a gentleman coming up along the lane. According to her, this would be about twenty or so minutes past the hour. She couldn't be more exact, but she was sure it was before eight-thirty. She said the geezer was just an average gentleman, black top hat and the latest fashionable coat, nothing else to remark about him, but she was surprised to see a gentleman in the lane, so she took note. She said he had his head down and seemed in a hurry."

Walsh grimaced slightly. "She turned back to her door before he reached her, so she didn't see any more detail than that."

Stokes sighed but tipped his head. "Even so, good work. At least we now know in which direction he went."

Barnaby concluded, "So our murderer met Cardwell on the street, came in through the front door, spent perhaps fifteen minutes in discussion with Cardwell, then killed him and left via the back door and the lane."

Stokes looked at everyone, then returned his gaze to Barnaby. "He has to be our murderer."

Penelope stated, "Unless there's some reason our unknown gentleman left by the rear door, and someone else, unseen by anyone, whipped in and stabbed Cardwell…" She looked around the circle of faces. "I admit I just can't see that."

No one else could, either.

Stokes tapped his pencil on his closed notebook, then shoved the book into his pocket. "Right, then. We have what seem to be sightings of our murderer, but sadly, the description we have thus far fits half the gentlemen in town."

CHAPTER 3

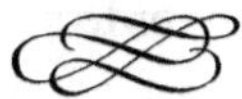

"*R*egarding the reason Cardwell was murdered," Barnaby said, "the one real clue we have is the letter he sent to Roscoe."

Stokes obligingly drew out the letter and read it aloud. He looked at Jordan. "We've already discussed why Cardwell might have chosen to appeal to Roscoe, and you feel it's more to do with Roscoe's reputation and assumed knowledge about dealing with the authorities rather than because of some specific issue with the one business Cardwell represented that Roscoe has a contract with."

Jordan nodded. "The more I think of it, the surer I am of that. I truly doubt there's anything nefarious going on at Hemingways' Linens."

Stokes inclined his head. "Be that as it may, we need to check on that business. However, before we start chasing hares, we should call on the Cardwells. I want to meet this younger brother. We need to be sure we're not overlooking something there. He might not be our unknown man, but Bobby Cardwell might yet know something pertinent about why his brother was killed."

"Well," Penelope put in, "we don't actually know that Bobby *didn't* meet the unknown man here—whether before or after Thomas was murdered."

Along with the other two men, Barnaby pondered that scenario and had to admit that his wife was correct. Thinking further along those lines, he suggested, "Could Thomas's murder, possibly in front of Bobby, have been intended as a warning to Bobby?"

Penelope opened her eyes wide. "At this stage, who can say?"

"Which only underscores our need to interview the Cardwells." Stokes looked at Jordan. "Did you get the address?"

"Twenty-nine Finsbury Circus," Jordan supplied. "Ruth Cardwell said the house is just south of East Street."

"If you're free," Penelope said, addressing Jordan, "I think you should come with us to pave our way."

Jordan smiled fleetingly. "My orders are to do whatever I can to help solve this case, so consider me at your service."

Stokes dispatched O'Donnell to check that the rear door was bolted, and when the sergeant returned, they left the office and gathered on the pavement outside.

Stokes locked the office door, then turned to Walsh and handed him the key. "I want you to remain on guard here and watch for anyone who might be interested in the contents of Cardwell's office. It's also possible we might need to return and retrieve something from inside. Try not to be too obvious—amble up and down the street as if you're just a bobby on the beat, but keep this place in sight. If anyone turns up to see Cardwell, take their name and direction. I'll send someone to relieve you later."

Walsh pocketed the key and saluted. "Right, guv."

Stokes looked at Morgan and O'Donnell. "You two can search for any other sightings of our unknown man. We know he came out of the rear lane at the northern end. See if you can pick up a trail around there." Stokes glanced at Penelope and Barnaby, who were chatting with their coachman. "Give us an hour, then meet back here."

"Aye, guv." Both men saluted.

Jordan turned to Gelman. "It might be useful if you follow us to the Cardwells, but hang back and see if anyone shows an interest in our doings."

Gelman nodded. "Will do."

Having overheard, Stokes inclined his head approvingly. "Good thinking." He looked at Jordan. "Are you familiar with this area?"

Jordan nodded. "Finsbury Circus is only a few minutes' walk away." He tipped his head down the street. "This way."

Assured that the distance wasn't enough to be bothered with their carriage, Barnaby and Penelope joined them, and Jordan led their group of four—with Gelman trailing unobtrusively behind—south along Broad Street, then turned right at the next intersection, and a block later, they were crossing a street and entering East Street, one of the four short streets that gave entry to the inner circle of Finsbury Circus.

Barnaby took note of the surroundings. The area was distinctly well-to-do, and the Circus itself exuded an air of quiet, stable gentility. The circle of neat, well-kept terrace houses was divided into quadrants by four short streets, unimaginatively named North, South, East, and West Streets, with a cobbled circular carriageway sweeping around the pavements before the houses. In the center of the area, protected from the carriageway by an iron-railing fence, a circular park played host to mature trees, well-tended shrubbery, neat gravel paths, and manicured lawns. Barnaby thought it likely that the majority of the families in the terrace houses had been occupants since the terraces were built more than twenty years before.

It was that sort of neighborhood. An air of respectable prosperity blanketed the locality.

As they approached Number 29, Penelope glanced back toward Broad Street. "Cardwell didn't have far to walk to his office."

"No surprise, then," Stokes said, "that he could be so punctual and regular in his habits. Easy to know what time to leave home so as to be at the office door at bang on eight o'clock."

Stokes paused in front of the three steps leading up to the porch of Number 29. The knocker on the door was already swathed in black crepe. Stokes sighed, glanced at the others, then mounted the steps and knocked firmly on the door.

A minute passed, then the door was opened by a sad-looking maid. She hiccupped. "Y-Yes?"

Stokes introduced them. "We appreciate that this is a difficult time, but we need to speak with the family. All of them."

Penelope stepped up beside Stokes. "We wouldn't intrude if it wasn't important. I'm sure everyone here wants the police to catch whoever killed Mr. Cardwell."

The maid's eyes had widened, and plainly recognizing Penelope's station, she bobbed a curtsy and opened the door wider. "Yes, ma'am. If you'll step into the drawing room, I'll tell the mistress you're here."

They allowed the puffy-eyed maid to usher them into a well-appointed drawing room, then the girl whisked off, and they heard her footsteps hurrying up the stairs.

As Penelope drew in her skirts and sat on the sofa, she looked at Jordan. "She said mistress, not master. Is Cardwell Senior still alive?"

"I don't know." Jordan glanced around as if searching for some hint and not finding anything. "He might have passed already."

"We'll have to ask." Stokes drew out his notebook.

Several minutes passed before heavy footsteps came slowly down the stairs.

They got to their feet as a lady of thirty or so, presumably Ruth Cardwell, helped an older woman, transparently bowed down with grief, into the room.

Ruth's gaze swept their group and landed on Jordan. Her lips tightened, and she nodded fractionally, then helped her mother to the chair beside the hearth.

Mrs. Cardwell was a faded beauty, her dark hair now streaked with gray, and the lines in her soft face were made more prominent by obvious grief. Her large eyes were darkly shadowed, and she'd obviously been weeping, but her lips were set, and, Penelope judged, she'd already reached the stage of wanting justice for her slain son.

After settling the older woman, Ruth Cardwell straightened. Pressing her palms together, she moved to the chair opposite her mother's and faced them. "Good afternoon. We understand you need to speak with us. We'll try to answer your questions as best we can."

While outwardly, Ruth appeared calm and in control, Penelope noted her fingers twisting tight and the slight—very slight—quaver in her voice. Ruth was putting on a brave face as women of her station always did.

Gravely, Stokes inclined his head. "Thank you, Miss Cardwell." He bowed to the older lady. "Mrs. Cardwell. We would like to offer our condolences on the family's recent tragic loss. We truly appreciate you giving us your time at this difficult juncture. I'm Inspector Stokes from Scotland Yard. Mr. and Mrs. Adair"—he gestured at Barnaby and Penelope—"are here as official consultants. They are called in to support the force on cases in which their insights are likely to help in solving the crime. As I believe you're already aware, Mr. Draper was called in for advice by Mr. Cardwell—Mr. Thomas Cardwell, the deceased—and is also assisting the police in an advisory capacity."

Penelope noted that Ruth's gaze had returned to Jordan, and she'd paid particular attention to his reason for being there.

Quickly approaching footsteps drew all eyes to the open doorway. Looking distinctly pallid and not a little disheveled, a younger gentleman paused on the threshold and stared at them. Then he swallowed and croaked, "I'm Robert Cardwell. I found the body—Thomas's body."

Stokes inclined his head. "Please join us, Mr. Cardwell. We need to speak with you."

Ruth waved vaguely. "Please, sit, and we'll endeavor to answer your questions."

Swiftly assessing the younger Mr. Cardwell, Penelope judged him to be in his mid-twenties. He came in and chose to sit, rather gingerly, on a straight-backed chair a yard from the one Stokes had claimed and opposite where Jordan was seated.

Stokes caught Penelope's eyes, and she accepted the unvoiced invitation to open the questioning. She fixed her gaze on Mrs. Cardwell. "Our first questions relate to the composition of your family. Is Mr. Cardwell, your husband, still with you?"

"No." Mrs. Cardwell's voice was hoarse, and she gripped a damp handkerchief in one tight fist. "My husband passed on more than ten years ago." Her gaze drifted to Ruth, then diverted to Bobby. "It's just the four of us who live here now. Me, Ruthie, Thomas, and Bobby." Her voice hitched, then in fading tones, she added, "Just the three of us now…"

"I see." Penelope allowed sympathy to color her tone. "Now, we understand that Thomas arrived at his office at his customary time of eight o'clock this morning." She glanced at Ruth and at Bobby. "Was there anything—any hint, any comment—that gave you cause to think that something might be wrong?"

Ruth drew in a tight breath and replied, "Initially, it was just Thomas and me at the breakfast table. Mama takes breakfast upstairs. Bobby came down as Thomas was leaving."

"And," Stokes asked, pinning Ruth with his gray gaze, "did you feel Thomas was at all uneasy or tense?"

Ruth frowned. "No. He was…exactly as normal." Her voice caught, and she swallowed, then she looked directly at Stokes. "There was nothing, nothing at all, that was out of the ordinary. Thomas was as he always was. We chatted about the usual things we spoke about most mornings. Then he left for his office at the usual time."

Bobby cleared his throat and quietly added, "I passed him in the hall. All we said to each other was good morning." He hurriedly added, "That wasn't unusual."

Penelope refocused on Ruth. "We understand that you brought several ledgers to Thomas's office later, a little after eight-thirty."

Ruth stared rather blankly at Penelope, then slowly nodded. "Yes. I…

realized that Thomas had left them here, and I thought he might need them. He doesn't often leave accounts here, at the house."

"I see." Penelope wondered why she didn't quite believe that eminently straightforward explanation. She changed tack and, with a glance at Stokes, elected to reveal, "We now know that there was a man, a gentleman, judging by his attire, waiting for Thomas when he arrived at his office. Thomas recognized him and greeted him, then took him into the office. Do any of you have any idea who that man might be?"

Their expressions were answer enough. They had no notion. Bobby, in particular, looked totally confused.

Ruth faintly frowned. "Thomas didn't mention any morning meeting." She colored faintly and glanced at Penelope. "Over breakfast, he often went through which of his clients he was expecting to see or, more often, visit that day, but as far as I know, he intended to work in the office on the accounts for various firms today. There were no meetings that he mentioned."

Stokes was nodding. "The description our witness gave of the interaction outside the office is consistent with Thomas not having expected the man to be waiting on the doorstep." Stokes arched a brow at Bobby. "I take it this man wasn't still in the office when you arrived?"

"No." Bobby appeared utterly mystified. "There was only Thomas…"

"Was that man the one who killed Thomas?" Mrs. Cardwell's hoarse voice reminded them she was there.

Stokes exchanged a glance with Penelope, then stated, "It's possible, but at this point, we can't be certain."

Barnaby asked, "Did Thomas mention any client with whom he'd recently had a disagreement or difficulty?"

A pause ensued, then Mrs. Cardwell replied, "Thomas never discussed any details of his work with his clients. Indeed, I would be hard-pressed to name any."

Penelope took note of the glance that, while their mother was speaking, passed between Ruth and Bobby. Penelope inwardly frowned but could think of no way to pry. Not at that time. "Perhaps," she said, looking at Stokes, "if you three would read the letter Thomas sent yesterday to Mr. Draper's employer, it might spark some connection."

Stokes drew out the letter, smoothed the sheet, and handed it to Mrs. Cardwell. She took it with a shaking hand, read it, and frowned. "Nefarious activities? What on earth had he found?"

She held the letter out to Ruth, who took it, briefly glanced at it, then said, "I read it earlier, at the office." She rose and crossed to hand the letter to Bobby.

He accepted it and read it while Ruth returned to her armchair.

On reaching the end of the short missive, Bobby, too, frowned. "I say. This sounds serious." He looked up. "I mean, is this—finding out about these nefarious activities—what got Thomas killed?"

Barnaby responded, "It's tempting to think so, especially considering the timing of the murder, but at this stage, we can't be certain even of that. It's possible that the reason behind Thomas's death was something else entirely."

"Until we know more, we can't say," Stokes stated.

"Speaking of knowing more," Penelope said, "was there anyone— anyone at all—with whom Thomas was on poor terms? Anyone at all who might have wished him ill?"

The three Cardwells exchanged glances, but then, as one, shook their heads.

Mrs. Cardwell clutched her handkerchief tightly. "No one springs to mind."

Ruth Cardwell offered, "Thomas wasn't a difficult—argumentative— sort. He generally got on well with people."

Penelope noted her careful phrasing, but couldn't see any way to probe further, not without being insensitive in the extreme. She looked at Stokes and fractionally shook her head. She had nothing left to ask at that time.

She glanced at Barnaby and saw that he, too, was doubtful that they'd managed to extract all these three knew but accepted that they'd gone as far as they could that day.

Stokes duly shut his notebook and rose. As Penelope, Barnaby, and Jordan came to their feet and Bobby Cardwell belatedly got to his, Stokes turned to Ruth and Mrs. Cardwell. "Thank you. We know this is a dark time for the family and appreciate your forbearance. If you should think of anything—anything at all—that might have a bearing on Thomas's death, please send word to me at Scotland Yard."

Ruth inclined her head. "Thank you, Inspector."

Penelope assured both ladies that they could find their way out, and as they left the drawing room, the little maid came sniffing and hurrying to open the door for them.

Penelope led the way out of the house.

She waited until the others had joined her and they'd walked to the corner of East Street before pausing and glancing back at the Cardwell residence. "I accept that those three truly are grieving Thomas's untimely death, but I'm also convinced they're not telling us all they know."

"Or," Barnaby added, "that they suspect."

His hands in his pockets, Jordan was frowning. "I definitely got the impression that they were…hiding something."

Stokes nodded. "Skirting around some subject. What subject is anyone's guess."

"It might even be several somethings," Penelope stated. "A different secret for each of them."

Stokes sighed. "Even if they are concealing something, there's no saying that it will have any bearing whatsoever on this case."

"Sadly, that's true." To Jordan, Barnaby added, "When it comes to murder, people hiding things is no help at all."

"Yet when faced with a murder, nearly everyone does it." Penelope shook her head.

"One point I think we can agree on," Stokes said. "I believe we're on solid ground in thinking that Bobby Cardwell had no idea there had been a gentleman in the office before him."

Barnaby nodded. "That was the one certain piece of information we gleaned."

They spent the walk back to Cardwell's office discussing their next move.

"It's really not helpful," Penelope stated, "that the family know so little of Thomas's work—how he interacted with clients, that sort of thing. Ruth might have known he had no meetings planned for today, but did clients ever turn up on his doorstep as our unknown man did? Was that a common occurrence?" She paused, then went on, "I also find it odd that, given Thomas lived in the same house as Ruth and shared something of his timetable with her—and she thought to deliver his forgotten ledgers this morning—that he hadn't mentioned to her, at least, anything about stumbling across the nefarious activities that pushed him to seek advice from Roscoe."

Penelope glanced at Jordan. "We know that Roscoe's a gentle soul, but for most people, taking such a step would be a major decision."

Jordan briefly smiled. "Just as well. I don't want to be inundated with pleas for help. However…I have to agree that Thomas not telling Ruth seems strange."

"I suspect they're much of an age," Penelope said. "If anything, I think she might be older, and she's the sensible sort that a cautious man like Thomas would likely confide in."

"Yet," Barnaby said, "I truly don't think she knew of the letter."

"I agree," Jordan said. "She had no idea the letter existed until I showed it to her."

Stokes sighed. "You're forgetting something. Thomas was the man of that household—the oldest male. He stumbled on what, to him, were nefarious activities. Of course he wasn't going to tell his older sister."

"Ah." Jordan nodded. "You're right. He would have wanted to shield her from anything potentially dangerous."

Penelope harrumphed. "Yes, well. There was his first mistake. If he had told her, we'd be much further on in the matter of catching his killer."

None of the men ventured a response.

They turned onto Broad Street and were within sight of Cardwell's office when Stokes stated, "I believe our next port of call should be the linen supplier's. That's the simplest explanation for why Thomas chose to contact Roscoe—because in Thomas's eyes, Roscoe is already involved via his contract with that business."

Jordan pulled a face that stated he thought investigating the linen supplier would be a waste of time.

Accurately reading the expression, Stokes declared, "Regardless of how unlikely it seems, we have to eliminate the linen supplier as the source of Thomas's concern."

With that, they all had to agree.

They reached the office and went inside. Jordan and Penelope hunted through the business ledgers and soon located the set for Hemingways' Linens, then they sat at the round table and rapidly scanned the entries.

Penelope shut the ledger she'd studied and looked at Barnaby and Stokes. "Everything seems to be above board with their day-to-day accounts."

Jordan closed the ledger he'd examined. "Likewise with their capital investments and major expenses. I can't see any sign of financial stress in the business." He, too, looked at Stokes and Barnaby. "Nothing to excite any suspicion of nefarious activities."

"Maybe so," Stokes said, "but given the connection to Roscoe, we still need to investigate the firm. It's possible the activity Cardwell stumbled upon was not financial, at least not directly. Not something in the books but something he became aware of by some other route." Stokes pulled a face. "It's a stretch, but it's possible someone let fall something in Cardwell's hearing, and it led him to his disquieting discovery."

Jordan sighed. "I have to agree there's a chance, so I assume we're heading to Battersea."

"Is that where Hemingways' is?" Penelope got to her feet.

Jordan nodded. "On the river, not far from Vauxhall Gardens. The company that manages the booths in the gardens is another client of theirs." He rose, collected the ledgers, carried them to the shelves, and slid them back into their proper places.

About to follow Stokes and Penelope out of the office, Barnaby noted a faintly puzzled expression on Jordan's face. "What is it?"

Jordan focused on him, then shook his head. "Something's niggling at my brain—as if I've seen something but not yet realized what it is I've seen—but the harder I try to think of what it is, the further into the fog it slides."

"Ah." Barnaby smiled. "That sort of feeling. Stop thinking about it, and it'll suddenly pop into your mind, crystal clear."

Jordan nodded. "Sound advice," he said and followed Barnaby out to the street.

CHAPTER 4

They took the Adairs' carriage and traveled in comfort to Hemingways' Linens, which was located in buildings that hugged the east bank of the Thames just north of Gunners Stairs.

As Barnaby followed Stokes and Jordan onto the pavement, then paused to hand Penelope down, he took stock of the business's façade. It appeared to support Jordan's assertion that Hemingways' was a well-run enterprise. The site stretched along the river, facilitating access to the water, and black-painted wrought-iron railings separated the long, low buildings from the pavement.

Steam gushed in clouds from the rear of one of the three brick buildings, and in the forecourt before the central building, several wagons were being loaded with packages of folded linens ferried from inside a warehouse-like section by porters using handcarts.

Jordan glanced at Stokes, Barnaby, and Penelope and tipped his head toward the central building. "This way."

He led them through the main gates, which had been set wide to admit the wagons. From the gravel forecourt, a paved path led to what was plainly the business's main door.

Jordan opened it and walked inside, and Stokes, Penelope, and Barnaby followed.

They found themselves in a small well-lit foyer. Pictures apparently depicting the business over the years hung on the cream-painted walls.

Two doors, presently shut, were set into the wall facing them, and another two, also shut, were on their right.

An opening in the wall on the left connected the foyer with a small office, and a young man appeared at the counter between. "Can I help you?"

Jordan looked at Stokes, who stepped to the counter and declared, "I'm Inspector Stokes of Scotland Yard. We need to speak with…" Stokes rolled an eye at Jordan.

"Mr. Hemingway," Jordan supplied. "Actually, both Mr. Hemingways, junior as well as senior."

The clerk was studying Jordan. "You're Roscoe's man."

Jordan nodded. "But today, I'm here helping the police. Nothing to do with the Dolphin Court account."

The clerk looked relieved, yet still a trifle uncertain. "I'll see if I can find the Hemingways for you."

Jordan added, "Tell them Roscoe would appreciate them assisting the police."

The comment seemed to reassure the clerk, and he departed through another door that presumably led to the business's inner workings.

Not two minutes later, one of the doors in the rear wall opened, and an older man of average height with a shock of white hair, beetling brows, and a craggy yet well-worn face strode through, followed by a gust of warm, moist air that carried the faintest hint of lavender. The man wore a coarse white linen shirt and thick trousers held up by suspenders. His expression faintly curious, he halted and nodded at Jordan. "Mr. Draper." His sharp gaze shifted to Stokes. "You're the inspector?"

Stokes introduced himself and added his usual explanation of Barnaby and Penelope's presence. "I take it you're Mr. Hemingway Senior, owner of this business?"

"I am."

Stokes continued, "We'd like to speak with you about Thomas Cardwell."

"Cardwell?" The surprise on the man's face was entirely genuine. "A good man. We've never had any difficulties with him. Does his job well and doesn't charge the earth."

A second, younger man came rushing through the door and, at sight of them, abruptly halted. That this was Hemingway Junior barely needed to be said. The resemblance to his father was marked.

"There you are. All right with the steam, then?" Hemingway Senior asked.

His son nodded. "Just a stuck valve. It's working now."

"Good. Well"—Hemingway Senior waved at Stokes and the others—"seems these people want to ask us about Cardwell."

"Thomas?" The puzzlement on the younger Hemingway's face was plain. "Why?"

"I haven't yet heard." Hemingway Senior's gaze shifted to the counter behind which the young clerk, who had returned, now stood. "Whatever it is, I suggest we go to the office and hear about it there."

Stokes, who had also noticed the clerk's return and his keen attention, agreed. "That might be best."

"This way." The older Hemingway turned to a door in the right-hand wall, opened it, and led the way into the bowels of the building.

Stokes followed Hemingway Senior, and Hemingway Junior fell in beside Jordan at the rear of their small procession. In the middle, Barnaby and Penelope, neither of whom had ever been inside a linen supplier's premises, looked about with avid interest. The area through which they were led was given over to the sorting and packing of freshly laundered linens of all types. Women in neat aprons stood at long benches and flicked and folded and stacked, while men, also wearing clean bib aprons, shifted the stacks onto sturdy carts and ferried them to another area where they were packaged in brown paper and tied with different colored tapes.

"Presumably, the color of the tapes identifies different orders," Penelope whispered.

Barnaby was taking in the ambiance. "Everyone here seems quite content." Although the workers' hands were constantly busy, there was laughter and conversation being traded back and forth. He also didn't see any unnecessary activity. "It all seems very smoothly run."

"Very sensibly organized," Penelope agreed. "Now I think of it, I recall hearing that many of the senior hostesses—those who host massive events during the Season—as well as Almacks get their linens from Hemingways'."

Behind them, the younger Hemingway had been quietly quizzing Jordan regarding any difficulties with the Dolphin Court account, and Jordan had reassured him, reiterating that the reason they were there had nothing to do with Roscoe's clearly highly valued contract.

They progressed through several packing stations and eventually reached an office tucked into the corner of the building. Its one wide window looked out over the river and admitted a stream of soft diffuse light. The Hemingways quickly organized chairs for their visitors, then Hemingway Senior sat in the large chair behind the massive desk, and his son claimed the chair that was plainly his usual seat behind his sire's right shoulder.

"Now." Clasping his hands on his blotter, Hemingway Senior fixed an almost challenging gaze on Stokes. "What's this about Cardwell, heh?"

Stokes paused, then said, "I'm sorry to have to inform you, sir, that Thomas Cardwell was murdered this morning."

"Murdered?" The depth of shock on both Hemingways' faces was impossible to manufacture. "Where?" the older Hemingway asked.

"In his office." Stokes paused while the Hemingways digested that.

It was the younger Hemingway who, with a frown forming on his face, asked, "But why are you here?" He grimaced and added, "I'm sure you're not visiting all of Thomas's clients to inform them of his death, and we haven't seen him since last quarter day, when he came in to go over our accounts."

Stokes studied father and son, then said, "Yesterday, Cardwell sent a note to Roscoe, asking for advice on how best to bring certain nefarious activities he'd uncovered to the authorities' attention. That's what led to Mr. Draper's involvement. Unsurprisingly, London's gambling king wishes to know why someone asking him for advice should, soon afterward, wind up dead. That connection also explains why we're here, as Hemingways' is the only business Cardwell represented with a contract with Roscoe's enterprises."

From both men's expressions, it was plain they were following the links and were beginning to realize that they and their enterprise were under suspicion. Before they could grow too defensive, Barnaby asked, "Has Cardwell visited in the past few weeks?"

Both men shook their heads.

The younger added, "As I said, he hasn't been here since…well, it would be around the beginning of January. We weren't due to see him again until after the end of this month."

"What about the usual reports?" Jordan asked. "All up to date?"

The younger Hemingway nodded. "He did them at the close of the year, and we finalized everything when he came in January."

His father nodded. "We signed off then. Cardwell was always prompt with everything. He never let anything slide."

Jordan caught Stokes's eye. "That's what I would have expected of an agent as careful as Thomas appears to have been."

The older Hemingway nodded. "Aye, he was that—careful and precise. He'll be missed and not just by us." He glanced at his son. "I suppose we'll have to find someone else, now."

The younger Hemingway didn't look enthused.

The father returned his gaze to Stokes. "I don't see what more we can tell you, Inspector. We know nothing about nefarious activities and would challenge anyone to find anything amiss with our practices."

The last was said with a hint of rising ire.

Jordan stepped in to say, "We've looked through your accounts—the ledgers Cardwell kept on the business—and found nothing whatsoever amiss or in any way suspicious."

Hemingway Senior responded, "That's because there's nothing to be found."

Stokes inclined his head. "This visit is purely because Cardwell left no clue as to which of—or, indeed, whether any of—his clients' businesses were involved in what he uncovered."

"We had to check, you see," Penelope put in. "To convince ourselves that there isn't any problem here and that we need to look elsewhere."

The Hemingways exchanged a long look, then Hemingway Senior returned his attention to them. His gaze shrewd, he eyed them for several seconds, then stated, "Our business is an open book, at least to the authorities. In our line of work, supplying goods to finicky and demanding customers, you can't get away with doing anything underhanded. Our reputation is one we've worked for years to build, and we're not about to risk damaging that. If you need to see anything more of our enterprise, by all means, feel free to wander about and look."

"May we?" Penelope leaned forward, her eagerness on full display. For Barnaby's money, that had more to do with her innate curiosity than the case at hand.

The younger Hemingway responded to her appeal. "I'll be happy to take you around and explain anything you wish to know."

"Excellent!" Penelope came to her feet, bringing all the men to theirs. Smiling, she held out her hand to Hemingway Senior. "Thank you, Mr. Hemingway, for being so understanding. I'm sure there's nothing untoward for me to see, but I would like to better understand how you do what you do."

Not even Hemingway Senior was immune to Penelope's charm. He gruffly assured her that she was welcome to explore as she wished.

With Penelope and Hemingway Junior making for the door, Stokes seized the opportunity to tell Hemingway Senior, "I believe the rest of us have seen enough to conclude that the reason Cardwell contacted Roscoe did not arise from anything to do with Hemingways' Linens."

Appeased, the older Hemingway accompanied them to his door. He would have walked them back to the foyer, but Barnaby caught sight of Penelope and Hemingway Junior already deep in the packaging area. Barnaby tipped his head in their direction and, to Hemingway, said, "We'd better keep them in sight."

Stokes had also spotted the pair. He humphed and said to Hemingway, "We might have to step in and rescue your son."

Hemingway barked a laugh, nodded, and waved them on.

With Jordan and Stokes, Barnaby had to step smartly around tables and benches and dance around carts to catch up with his wife. Once they had, Jordan and Stokes slowed to amble a few paces behind. Resuming his customary position at Penelope's side, Barnaby quickly grasped that she wasn't merely satisfying her curiosity, nor was she solely focused on exhausting all possibility that Hemingways' Linens had any association with nefarious activities. Listening to her artful questions, he realized that she was, in fact, interviewing Hemingway as a potential employer for the graduates of the Foundling House.

He should, he acknowledged, have expected that. His wife was nothing if not opportunistic when it came to arranging employment for the foundlings.

It took rather longer than they'd expected to complete their circuit of the Hemingways' business, and when they finally returned to the forecourt, even Stokes was ready to take an oath that there was nothing even remotely nefarious there.

They parted from Hemingway Junior with smiles all around and made their way back to the waiting carriage.

After directing Phelps to return to Mayfair, Barnaby climbed into the carriage and settled beside Penelope. Once the carriage was rolling, he glanced at the others' faces and observed, "It would have been too easy if Cardwell's concern had, in fact, stemmed from Hemingways' Linens."

Penelope hummed, then stated, "Murder is rarely so straightforward."

Stokes glanced at Jordan. "So now we have to hunt for something else

Cardwell recently learned that disturbed him to the extent that he contacted Roscoe for advice." Stokes paused, then ventured, "Nefarious activities. Could Cardwell have inflated some minor matter to that level?"

Instantly, Jordan shook his head. "I only met him three times, yet from what I saw on those occasions, I feel confident in stating that he was a well-grounded man. He knew his business and was naturally cautious and not given to overstatement." He met Stokes's gaze. "Everything I saw of him inclines me to believe that calling whatever he discovered 'nefarious' is more likely to be an understatement than unwarranted hyperbole."

Stokes grimaced. "I have to admit I've yet to meet a successful man-of-business who isn't inherently cautious."

Quietly, Barnaby stated, "Added to that, there's the inescapable fact that Cardwell is now dead."

Jordan returned to Broad Street and Thomas Cardwell's office, first because he'd left Gelman on guard there, lurking inconspicuously and keeping an eye on the premises from the opposite side of the street, and also because that niggling inkling that he'd overlooked something in the ledgers had only intensified.

He found Gelman in an alcove beside the bakery.

Seeing Jordan, Gelman straightened from his slouch. "No activity of any sort over the way. Morgan's inside. He relieved Walsh." Gelman tipped his head. "Anything at Hemingways'?"

"No. As I expected, our visit there was a waste of time, at least as far as the investigation goes."

Gelman followed Jordan's gaze to the office opposite. "So what now?"

"Now…" Jordan debated, then decided and headed for the curb. "I want to take another look at Cardwell's ledgers."

Morgan saw them coming and unlocked the door and let them in.

After advising the constable of the outcome of their jaunt to Battersea, Jordan added, "I just want to take another look at the ledgers."

Leaving Morgan and Gelman standing at the window and looking out at the street, Jordan crossed to the shelves and drew out one of the Hemingways' ledgers he'd examined earlier. He carried the account book to the round table, set the book down, and opened it at random. He placed his palms on the table, on either side of the open book, and leaned on his straightened arms, hanging over the pages displayed.

His eyes immediately scanned the figures, his mind adding and checking, but he knew the arithmetic wasn't the source of his niggle. There was nothing wrong with the numbers or totals. With conscious effort, he forced his mind from its obsession and drew his focus back, away from the details, seeing the page more generally…

The layout was intensely familiar, so what was wrong, odd, strange?

The obvious reached out and, metaphorically, slapped him in the face.

He huffed and straightened, continuing to stare at the page.

Once he saw it, he couldn't unsee it nor understand how he had missed it in the first place.

With a sense of achievement, he shut the ledger and returned it to the shelf, then walked around the office, pulling ledger after ledger from its place and checking each before replacing it.

Every single ledger was in the same hand.

All of Thomas Cardwell's accounts were kept by one person, and that person wasn't Thomas Cardwell.

Of that, Jordan was now supremely sure.

He returned to where Morgan and Gelman were quietly chatting and nodded to Morgan. "We'll leave you to your watch."

Morgan grimaced. "Ah, well—the company's been nice."

Gelman aimed a salute at the constable and followed Jordan out of the door.

Jordan paused on the pavement, then looked at the bakery. "There first, I think."

Gelman kept pace as Jordan crossed the road. "What are we doing?"

"Buying food, to start with."

"Food? Why? We going on a picnic?"

"No," Jordan replied. "But Miranda always takes food when she visits a house that's suffered a bereavement." He paused, then added, "I'm not entirely sure why, so don't ask."

Jordan bought a large fresh loaf at the bakery, then went to the shop two doors down and selected a small wheel of country cheddar. He spotted a lined picnic basket with napkins on one shelf and bought that as well, along with jars of raspberry jam and honey. After settling his purchases in the basket and covering them with the napkins, he set off with Gelman for the corner that would take them to Finsbury Circus.

Just around the corner, they passed a vintner's, and a bottle in the window caught Jordan's eye. Leaving the basket with Gelman outside, Jordan went in and emerged several minutes later with a bottle of sherry.

"That should do it." He slid the bottle in alongside the bread and cheese, then with Gelman shaking his head at him, Jordan headed for the Cardwell house.

CHAPTER 5

When they reached Finsbury Circus, at Jordan's direction, Gelman melted into the trees and bushes in the central park to keep watch just in case anyone had followed them.

Given what he'd realized, Jordan was, in truth, concerned that, at some point, someone might take a less than benign interest in the occupants of Number 29.

He climbed the three steps and, ignoring the swathed knocker, tapped firmly on the door.

The same maid who had opened the door earlier did so again. She looked even more peaky, but recognized Jordan and immediately stood back to allow him to enter.

He did so, then paused, intending to tell the maid not to be so trusting, but the words vanished from his head as Ruth Cardwell appeared in the drawing room doorway.

She blinked in surprise. "Oh. I wasn't expecting…" She looked past him to see the maid shutting the front door. As her gaze returned to Jordan, surprise even more evident on her face, he raised the basket and offered it to her. "I hope this will help in some small way."

Ruth accepted the basket, peeked beneath the checkered napkin, then smiling faintly, glanced at him from beneath her lashes. "Thank you." Her voice was still husky with tears. "That's very thoughtful. Cindy?"

Ruth held out the basket, and the maid hurried to take it from her.

Her hands now free, Ruth clasped them at her waist and turned to Jordan. "I'm afraid Mama is lying down upstairs."

Jordan was aware that meetings between an unmarried lady and a gentleman were usually conducted with someone else present, but Ruth wasn't a *young* young lady, and what he had to say was too important. "Actually," he confessed, "it's you I came to see." When, unsurprisingly, she frowned, he continued, "I've been looking at your brother's ledgers" —he caught and held her gaze—"including those you brought to the office this morning."

She blinked, then her periwinkle-blue eyes widened. "Ah." After a second of searching his face, her lips tightened, and she stepped back and waved him into the drawing room. "In that case, perhaps we do need to talk."

She led him deeper into the room, but didn't halt by the fireplace. Instead, she continued through an archway into what he thought would be termed a garden room. A small chamber with a fireplace sharing the same flue as the drawing room hearth, the room had as its dominant feature a well-positioned bow window overlooking the house's side garden.

Eschewing the twin armchairs angled before the small fire, Ruth walked into the bow of the window and halted, her gaze fixed—Jordan suspected unseeingly—on the vista outside.

He halted beside her, standing more or less shoulder to shoulder with her. When she crossed her arms over her chest and didn't say anything, he ventured, "I work in an unconventional household, and while I keep the ledgers for all my employer's businesses, his wife keeps the accounts for the many charities in which they're involved." He glanced sidelong at Ruth, but all he could see was her profile. "Consequently, I'm very aware that women—ladies, even—are more than capable of accurately managing complex accounts. I'm also familiar with how numbers written in a feminine hand look."

When she still said nothing, he baldly stated what, to him, was now obvious. "You kept most, if not all, of Thomas's accounts."

Finally, her lips twisted, and she turned her head and met his gaze. Then she sighed and closed her eyes. "Yes, I did." Returning her gaze to the garden, she went on, "Thomas was the one who understood business in the wider sense, but I was much better than he ever was with figures. So we worked together. He was the one who dealt with clients, who talked them through any difficulties I discovered and coached them in how to rectify any problems, but I was the one who did the sums and identified those difficulties and problems."

"So you were, in effect, his silent partner."

"Yes." She tightened her hold on her elbows. "I suppose you could describe it that way."

He paused, thinking through what the revelation meant. "So if any of your brother's clients were engaged in any, as he labeled them, nefarious activities, you would know."

She tipped her head consideringly, then pointed out, "I only know what shows in the figures, and it's March, so there's at least two months' worth of income and expenses I haven't yet seen. However, regardless, if some client was engaged in nefarious activities, I would think they'd be clever enough not to put those figures through their official books."

Jordan grimaced. "True. Yet there's no denying that, somehow, Thomas stumbled on something illicit enough to have got him killed." He fixed his gaze on her face. "And if it was one of Thomas's clients who killed him or had him killed, if they believe he discovered their secret through the accounts, and they realize, as I did, that it's you who keeps those accounts, they may feel they need to ensure your silence, too."

When she only frowned, he pressed. "You need to tell the investigators—Stokes and the Adairs."

She shifted to face him so she could frown directly at him. "I find it difficult to believe I'm in any danger. As I just admitted, I know all the clients' accounts, and to my certain knowledge, none contain any evidence of suspicious or illicit activity. And," she continued, when he opened his mouth to argue, "while I'm not personally acquainted with Thomas's clients, I knew Thomas very well. He was a cautious man and very careful in choosing whom he worked for."

Jordan studied her and ended up frowning in reluctant agreement. "He was a very upright character, wasn't he?"

"Very. I've known him to decline to act for potentially lucrative clients because he wasn't sure of the…upstanding nature, if you like, of the business's owners."

Jordan was staring at her face, wondering if he should push for her to speak with Stokes and the Adairs, when they heard the front door open, and the sound of two hotly arguing male voices reached them.

Ruth's eyes flew wide.

Raising his head, Jordan recognized Bobby Cardwell's voice declaring, "It wasn't me who had a yelling match with Thomas only last week."

The sound of the front door slamming cut through a reply that ended with "everyone knows he and I have been at loggerheads for years."

"Yes!" Bobby hissed. "Because you're so intent on being just like Papa. Dissolute, profligate—an infinite drain on the family's coffers."

"As if you're not just as bad, little brother."

"I'm not! It was you Thomas had to do battle with every month, every quarter. I don't know why we need you back here."

"I've only come to see Mama and Ruth," the older voice stated. "You can take yourself off if you wish."

Jordan took a large step back to where he could see through the archway into the drawing room just as an elegantly accoutered gentleman sauntered in from the front hall. In an obvious huff, Bobby Cardwell stalked in at the man's heels.

Jordan's movement shattered the spell that had held Ruth frozen, and she rushed to interpose herself between him and the archway and, beyond that, the drawing room, the newcomer, and Bobby. Walking forward, head rising, she stated with some asperity, "We have a visitor, you two."

Jordan followed her out of the garden room.

Bobby Cardwell recognized him. Bobby's mouth fell open, then snapped shut, and he looked faintly ill.

The other man—a gentleman as much as Bobby and Jordan himself were—watched Jordan approach through narrowing eyes.

The man was wearing a long dun-colored coat and carried a silver-topped cane. His dark hair was elegantly coiffed, and the suit beneath the coat was, to Jordan's experienced eyes, decently tailored and mildly expensive. Most interesting of all, although his coloring was not identical, the man's face bore a strong resemblance to Thomas Cardwell's.

Before the man could demand to know who Jordan was, Ruth stated, "Gibson, this is Mr. Draper, who is assisting Scotland Yard with their investigation into Thomas's murder."

Instantly, the man's aggression ebbed, and he blinked and studied Jordan anew. "He's a policeman?"

"No, I'm not." Jordan didn't offer to shake Gibson Cardwell's hand. "I work for a powerful gentleman whom your brother Thomas asked for advice. However, by the time I reached his office, Thomas had been killed. My employer as well as the police would like to know why Thomas was slain and by whom. Because of that, I'm temporarily seconded to the force."

Gibson frowned and bit his lip.

When none of the Cardwells volunteered anything more, Jordan asked, "I take it you're related to Thomas Cardwell?"

Frowning, Gibson stated, "I'm his older brother."

Jordan glanced at Ruth's face and saw the consternation she couldn't hide. This was what she and her mother—and Bobby, too—had been trying to hide.

Jordan focused on Gibson. "Judging from what I just heard, you and Thomas didn't get along."

Gibson, who had to be somewhere between Ruth's age and Thomas's, plainly looked to Ruth for help. When she pressed her lips tight and didn't oblige, and Bobby simply glowered at him, Gibson reluctantly offered, "We didn't see eye to eye about funds, but that's hardly unusual within a family."

"You don't live here, I take it?" Jordan remembered how Ruth and her mother had replied to the investigators' questions. They'd spoken only of the family members who lived in the house.

"No," Gibson admitted. He looked at Bobby. "Bobby came to fetch me. He told me Thomas had been murdered."

"Indeed?" From Bobby's face, Jordan guessed he'd been ordered to fetch his older brother. "So where do you live? What's your address?"

Increasingly reluctant but getting no support from either of his siblings, Gibson eventually volunteered, "Number fifteen B, Falcon Street. I share a flat with two friends."

Jordan transferred his gaze to Bobby. "It seems you also had an ongoing argument with Thomas. About money?" For a man of Bobby's age, that was much more understandable.

Despite his wariness, Bobby couldn't resist sulking. "He didn't think I needed to do this or that—the usual sort of things gentlemen my age regularly do these days." As if to explain that, he added, "Thomas was a fuddy-duddy—a stick-in-the-mud—in many ways."

Gibson looked about to agree when Ruth cut in.

In a voice tense with anger, she stated, "Thomas was the best of us. Do I need to remind you that it was he who slaved and kept this family afloat after Papa died?" Her tone lashed like a whip. "Have you forgotten that?"

Both Gibson and Bobby looked chastened, Gibson more resentfully so, yet chastened he nevertheless was.

Inwardly, Jordan sighed. While he understood Ruth's reaction, now her brothers would mind their tongues. He wouldn't gain anything useful by remaining, and indeed, his presence was contributing to Ruth's distress.

He turned to her and extended his hand. "Thank you for answering my earlier questions, Miss Cardwell. Please convey my good wishes to your mother."

Ruth gave him her hand, he judged more by rote than intention. After lightly gripping her tense fingers, he half bowed to her, then released her hand and nodded to her brothers.

Ruth stirred and gestured to the front hall. "I'll see you out."

She did. Jordan didn't think he was imagining her relief as she shut the front door behind him.

He paused on the porch, sighed, then started down the steps. In pensive mood, he walked across the carriageway and into the park.

Gelman had been watching and was waiting by a bench. "Anything useful?"

"As matters transpired, yes. You saw the two who arrived—Bobby and the other man?"

Gelman nodded. "I could hear them going at each other from here."

"Turns out," Jordan said, "that the other is an older brother. Older than Thomas, but, I think, younger than Miss Cardwell."

"Huh! That's a turn-up."

"It is, indeed." Jordan glanced back at the prim façade of Number 29. Ruth was safe enough with her brothers in the house. He turned to Gelman. "There's no need for you to remain on watch here, and Stokes's men have the office covered. You may as well head back to Dolphin Square. If anyone asks, I'll be home later. First, I need to report to Albemarle Street."

Gelman nodded, and they set off to walk back to Broad Street, keeping an eye out for an available hackney.

If it had been just himself working on the case, Jordan would have been in two minds over what he should share with the police, but the investigators had invited him in as a full member of their team, and one thing his years working alongside Roscoe had taught him was that teams got the best results when there were no secrets between the members.

Jordan knew what was required of him and accepted that the best he could do for the Cardwells was to convey his newfound knowledge promptly and in as clear a manner as possible. That would serve Ruth Cardwell best, given it was the most direct route to gaining justice for Thomas. Of that, Jordan entertained not a single doubt.

He and Gelman found an idling hackney on Broad Street and climbed aboard, giving the jarvey the Albemarle Street address. Jordan would alight there and leave Gelman to travel on to Dolphin Square while Jordan informed the investigators of what he'd unexpectedly learned.

It was close to six-thirty by the time Jordan reached Albemarle Street, but given the importance of the information he had to impart, he didn't think the Adairs would mind the interruption, and it wouldn't take long to explain what he'd discovered.

He swiftly climbed the steps to the porch and rapped the knocker. The door was opened by the butler, who instantly recognized him and waved him inside. The butler assured Jordan that his master and mistress were available, along with Inspector Stokes, who was also there, then firmly ushered Jordan into the drawing room.

Jordan stepped over the threshold, and the sight that met his eyes—a family situation even more surprising than the one he'd recently witnessed—brought him up short.

Seated back to back on the floor before the fireplace, each with their legs stretched out before them, Stokes and Adair were being assaulted by a platoon of small and very noisy children. While a young boy and girl, both about four years old and entirely sure of themselves, led the charge, flinging themselves at the seated men, a younger boy, perhaps a year old, rendered assistance, mainly by falling over Barnaby's long legs. The rambunctious trio were supported by a tot still crawling, yet plainly intent on being a part of the game.

Completing the picture of domestic bliss, the black-and-white spaniel puppy bounced around the fringes of the group, adding his yaps to the general melee. Stokes and Adair were laughing unrestrainedly and allowing themselves to be tickled unmercifully by the children, who squealed with joy at their fathers' contortions.

Penelope was perched on one sofa, and another dark-haired lady— Jordan assumed she was Mrs. Stokes—sat on the other. Both wore some- what besotted expressions as they watched their families cavort on the rug.

The ladies heard the door shut behind Jordan and looked up.

Penelope smiled warmly. "Jordan! Welcome. Please ignore the rabble and do come in."

She waved him forward and, to the other lady, explained, "This is the gentleman we mentioned—the one Roscoe has delegated to assist us." To Jordan, Penelope added, "This is Griselda, Stokes's wife."

Jordan smiled at Mrs. Stokes and half bowed. "I'm pleased to make your acquaintance, ma'am."

Griselda smiled. "And I'm delighted to meet you, Jordan. But please, just Griselda, at least in this house."

By then, Stokes and Barnaby had realized Jordan was there and were endeavoring to calm their offspring. In doing so, they drew the children's attention to the newcomer, and abruptly deserting their sires, the small group converged on Jordan.

Courtesy of having shared a house with Roscoe and Miranda's now rather older brood, Jordan was unperturbed. He smiled and crouched so that he didn't tower over the tots. "Hello." He met their bright eyes. "I've come to speak with your parents, but what are your names?"

"I'm Oliver Adair," the oldest boy proudly declared.

"And I'm Miss Megan Stokes," the little girl offered in a manner that suggested that being a Miss trumped being just Oliver.

"And this is my younger brother, Pip." Oliver drew the toddler to him, more or less in a headlock, which the younger boy seemed to find intensely funny as he chortled with glee.

The girl bent to hug the crawling child. "My little brother is Oswald, but he doesn't really talk yet."

"Our dog is called Roger," Oliver stated. "We got him from my grandfather's kennels, and he's supposed to be a gun dog, but Roger doesn't like guns."

Jordan nodded sagely. "Most dogs don't. They have to be trained, probably lots, before they become used to the noise."

Penelope approached with Griselda a step behind. "Come along, children." Penelope's smile was indulgent, but her tone was firm. "It's time you went up to the nursery."

"Your papas and mamas need to speak with Mr. Draper," Griselda said.

Two nursemaids came into the room, and Griselda beckoned the pair forward. "Here's Hettie and Gloria. They'll take you upstairs for some cocoa, then they'll tuck you in, and we'll be up to fetch you later."

Jordan rose, and the children and puppy were efficiently herded into the care of the nursemaids.

Within minutes, the drawing room had returned to its normal gracious state, and Barnaby had taken his place on the sofa, beside Penelope, with Stokes and Griselda on the sofa opposite. Penelope had directed the butler to set an armchair at one end of the pair of sofas, and Jordan had subsided into it. From that position, he could see the other four, and they could see him.

"Right, then," Stokes said. "What brings you here?"

"First," Jordan offered, "my apologies for interrupting the play, but I felt you'd want to know what I stumbled on late this afternoon."

"You thought correctly," Penelope said. "Was it something in Cardwell's ledgers?"

"In a way." Jordan explained his realization that Ruth Cardwell kept Thomas's accounts. "I returned to Finsbury Circus and taxed her with it, and she confirmed that she kept the accounts—all of them—while Thomas dealt with the clients and the other aspects of managing the businesses he represented."

Penelope huffed. "I should have realized that she did the books. The figures were neat and precise, and now you've pointed it out, they were definitely in a feminine hand."

"And that," Barnaby said, "explains why she appeared that morning with an armful of ledgers. She and Thomas probably planned to work on them together that day."

"Very likely," Jordan said. "But that Ruth did the accounts was the least of what I learned." He looked at Stokes. "While I was speaking with her, two gentlemen entered the house. One was Bobby Cardwell, and the other was Ruth's and Bobby's other brother, Gibson Cardwell."

"Other brother?" Stokes shifted and hauled out his ever-present notebook.

Jordan nodded. "I think he's older than Thomas, but younger than Ruth. He doesn't live in Finsbury Circus, which, if you think back, means Ruth, Bobby, and Mrs. Cardwell didn't actually lie when answering our earlier questions."

Stokes paused in his jotting, clearly trying to remember.

Penelope supplied, "We asked about the composition of the family, and Mrs. Cardwell replied that it was just the four of them who lived there. She omitted mentioning that there was another member of the immediate family who didn't live there."

"Semantics," Stokes stated, his lips thin. "They deliberately misled us."

"But why?" Griselda turned a puzzled frown on the others.

"As to that," Jordan said, "courtesy of the argument Bobby and this Gibson were having, and them not seeing me or Ruth until Ruth attracted their attention, I learned that Bobby had an ongoing disagreement with Thomas about funds, and Gibson, it seems, had an even more fraught relationship with Thomas, also, it seems, primarily about money."

Penelope was intrigued. "The plot has certainly thickened."

The door opened, and Mostyn appeared, his expression a question Penelope could easily read.

"Thank you, Mostyn." She rose, bringing the others to their feet. "We'll come through now." To Jordan, she said, "Please join us for dinner. I'm sure Roscoe and Miranda can spare you for the evening, and it's our habit to share information, then set it aside while we dine, before returning here, to the drawing room, to reevaluate the situation once any new insights have had a chance to sink in."

"And digest, as it were." Stokes regarded Jordan. "If Roscoe's delegated you to be his eyes and ears in this, best you stay and help us make sense of your recent discoveries."

Obviously curious as to their investigative process, Jordan readily consented to join them in the dining room. As per their stated habit, they eschewed all mention of the Cardwell case and spoke more generally, including sharing views on the recent opening of the Manchester and Leeds Railway, the first railway to cross the Pennines.

Having recently traveled by railway on Roscoe's business, Jordan had much to contribute.

Penelope suspected that, having lived for so long in Roscoe and Miranda's household, Jordan was accustomed to conversation of the style generally found about her dinner table. Indeed, judging by the ease with which he relaxed and became one with the company, it was clear he found their ways familiar.

Once dessert was consumed and the plates cleared, she rose and led the company back to the drawing room.

They settled in the chairs they'd occupied earlier, and Stokes opened the discussion with "I believe we can dismiss any notion of Hemingways' Linens being the source of Cardwell's nefarious activities."

Penelope told Griselda, "The Hemingways themselves run the business, and they seemed distinctly upright men."

"In addition," Barnaby put in, "from Penelope's subsequent inquiries and the extent of their customer list, they've worked hard to gain a reputation it would be folly to put at risk."

"Indeed." Stokes looked at Jordan. "So what can we deduce from your latest discoveries?"

"First," Jordan said, "it occurs to me that if Cardwell was killed because of something he discovered via, in whatever way, one of his client's accounts, then as, in actual fact, Ruth kept the accounts, should the client responsible for Cardwell's murder learn of her involvement, she might be in danger as well."

Stokes was slowly nodding. "That's certainly possible." He scribbled a line in his notebook. "Until we have this murderer by the heels, I'll station a man in the park opposite the house to keep an eye on the place and on her when she ventures forth."

Penelope noted the relief that flitted through Jordan's eyes.

"As for what I learned of the brothers," Jordan continued, "I feel fairly certain the 'something' that we all sensed the three Cardwells—Ruth, Bobby, and Mrs. Cardwell—were hiding was Gibson's existence."

"Hardly surprising," Stokes said, "given he was in active disputation with Thomas."

"More," Barnaby said, "that they so carefully avoided mentioning Gibson Cardwell suggests that they are not certain that Gibson didn't have something to do with Thomas's death."

Penelope mused, "They might not see Gibson as his brother's murderer, but them avoiding all mention of him does suggest that, at the very least, they're wondering if someone connected with Gibson—a creditor, perhaps—might be involved."

Griselda widened her eyes. "You think Gibson might indirectly have caused Thomas to be murdered?"

Barnaby replied, "That seems to be one possibility."

"And," Stokes said, "from what Jordan heard, it appears that the younger brother, Bobby, might also have had reason to wish Thomas ill." He looked at Jordan, then glanced at Penelope and Barnaby. "I believe our next step should be to formally interview Gibson Cardwell and Bobby Cardwell, separately, at Scotland Yard and see what we can shake from them."

"At the very least," Penelope stated, "they each need to explain the basis of their disagreement with Thomas."

"We also need to get a better understanding of the family finances." Barnaby met Stokes's gaze. "Given the facts we've assembled thus far, despite Thomas's letter to Roscoe, it's perfectly possible that Thomas Cardwell's murder is purely a family affair."

Penelope grimaced. "A family argument that went too far and got out of hand."

Stokes had been checking his notebook. "There's nothing to say that our unknown gentleman—the one we believe killed Thomas—wasn't Gibson Cardwell, and Bobby Cardwell, perhaps understandably, is keeping his mouth shut about his older brother being the killer."

Jordan offered, "After speaking with the siblings this afternoon, I came away with the impression that of the three brothers, Gibson is the profligate, Thomas was the serious one, and Bobby…isn't yet sure which of his older brothers he wants to emulate."

Penelope nodded. "Bobby did strike me as being somewhat immature."

"All right," Stokes said. "We'll get both brothers in, but ensure they remain separate. We'll fetch Bobby from Finsbury Circus, and Gibson from…" He looked inquiringly at Jordan.

Jordan smiled, the gesture sharp. "Number fifteen B, Falcon Street. He shares a flat with two friends."

Smiling, Stokes looked down and scribbled the address. "We'll make an investigator of you yet."

Jordan softly grunted.

Stokes sat up and tucked away his notebook, then looked at Barnaby, Penelope, and Jordan. "Shall we say nine o'clock tomorrow morning at the Yard? That'll give my men enough time to roust the pair out of their beds and to the Yard and allow a little time for them to stew in one of the interview rooms."

Barnaby and Penelope readily agreed, then with Stokes and Griselda, looked at Jordan.

He grimaced. "I do work for someone else. I'll report to Roscoe and see what he says. If he wants me to remain on the case—and I'm fairly certain he will—I'll meet you tomorrow at the Yard." He looked at Stokes. "Just please remember to tell the desk sergeant to let me past his gate."

The others laughed, and Stokes assured Jordan his welcome at Scotland Yard was guaranteed.

"In a way, that's what I'm afraid of," Jordan replied, making the others laugh even more.

CHAPTER 6

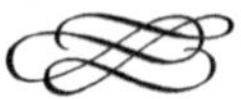

The following morning, Penelope was waiting with Barnaby and Stokes in Stokes's office when Jordan arrived, escorted by a curious constable.

The constable addressed Stokes. "Desk sergeant said as you were expecting Mr. Draper, sir?"

The statement was clearly a question and a skeptical one at that.

Standing behind the constable, Jordan rolled his eyes. As Roscoe's righthand man, he was reasonably well-known among the more experienced members of the force and, given few knew the truth of London's gambling king, consequently distrusted.

Hiding a smile, Stokes nodded. "I was. Thank you, Constable. Mr. Draper is, indeed, here to assist me."

Still looking uncertain, the constable saluted and backed away, allowing Jordan to enter.

He shook his head and walked in. "Good morning. Having already run the gauntlet, I'm hoping the irritation will be worth it."

Penelope and Barnaby smiled, and Stokes assured Jordan, "Your timing is perfect. We just got word that both Cardwells have been brought in and placed in separate interview rooms. I decided it wouldn't hurt for each to see that the other had also been brought in, but they weren't close enough or in sight of each other for long enough to communicate, even via signal."

"I see." Jordan picked up a straight-backed chair from against the wall and set it beside Penelope's.

He sat as Stokes went on, "We were just discussing whom to interview first. You've spoken with both. What's your inclination?"

Jordan tipped his head this way, then that, clearly weighing up the prospects, then decisively stated, "Bobby. He's the younger and much less sure of himself."

Penelope nodded. "That was my thinking, too."

Jordan went on, "That's not to say that I think Gibson is genuinely all that confident, but he's of an age where he'll feel obliged to put on an arrogant face and bluster, deny, and stonewall. Bobby won't. He'll buckle immediately, and we'll get much more out of him without having to play a heavy hand. With any luck, what he tells us will give us pointers on how to approach Gibson."

"A sound analysis," Barnaby said. "I concur."

"Right, then. Our way forward is clear." Stokes rose, and the other three got to their feet. "Let's have at them."

Barnaby, Penelope, and Jordan allowed Stokes to lead the way. They followed him down the main stairs, then around to a second set of stairs descending into the basement.

As he went down the second flight, speaking over his shoulder, Stokes told Jordan, "I'd originally thought to use one of the upstairs interview rooms, the ones we use to interview witnesses rather than perpetrators. But O'Donnell reported that Gibson Cardwell had already got high on his horse over being invited to speak with us, so I thought a touch of reality in less salubrious surrounds might help temper his protests."

"One can but hope," Jordan returned.

"And in order not to show favoritism to either brother," Stokes added, "we put Bobby Cardwell down here as well."

The belowground area was a warren of corridors. Stokes led them along one, then turned a corner and halted before a plain wooden door. Walsh stood beside it. He nodded to Stokes. "Morgan's inside, and O'Donnell's with the other one." Walsh tipped his head along the corridor. "In the last room along there."

"Good work," Stokes said. "Did Bobby give you any trouble?"

"No," Walsh reported. "It was almost as if he was expecting our invitation. I was more concerned about the sister. She wanted to come along as well. It took all of Morgan's charm to make her see sense. Well, that and the young bloke was obviously squirming. I think it was more the latter that swayed her, truth be told."

Stokes's lips quirked. "Very likely." He glanced at Penelope, Barnaby, and Jordan. "Ready?"

When they nodded, Stokes opened the door and led the way into a room that proved to be a spartan space enclosed by four bare walls. A single rectangular table sat in the middle of the floor with a single lamp hanging above it and emitting surprisingly strong light. The better to view the suspect's face, Penelope assumed.

Morgan had been sitting with his back to the door but rose as they entered. He nodded to Stokes and stepped back from the table to take up a stance to one side of the door.

Extra chairs had been brought in so the four of them could sit on the nearer side of the table while Bobby Cardwell sat alone on the opposite side. As Penelope claimed the chair beside the one Stokes commandeered, she thought that Bobby already looked distinctly uncomfortable, even browbeaten, and ready to tell all simply so he could leave the oppressive place.

Once their company of four had entered, Morgan shut the door.

Having watched them come in and sit, Bobby continued to stare at them with some trepidation. Before Stokes could say a word, Bobby, his voice subdued but clear, stated, "I didn't kill him." He drew in a tight breath. "We argued and even fought a bit, but..." His gaze switched to Jordan. "You heard what Ruthie said. Thomas was the one who held us all together. We all knew that, no matter what we said. It was always just words. Words! We never even came to blows, not since we were children." His gaze had fallen to the table, to his clasped hands and clenched fingers. "Killing Thomas...why would anyone want to do that? He was the good one. Without him..." He exhaled, and his voice quavered as he said, "I don't know how we'll all cope."

The sentiment and the emotion investing the words were patently sincere.

Stokes glanced at Penelope and Barnaby, sitting beyond her, then looked at Bobby's downbent head. "If you tell us the truth, all of what you know about that morning, that's arguably the best way you can help your family and gain justice for Thomas."

Bobby raised his gaze, looked at Stokes, and simply asked, "What do you want to know?"

"Start with when you left the house," Stokes suggested. "What time was that?"

"I'm not sure. I just made up my mind that I wanted to speak with Thomas, so I set off—no, wait! I heard the bells pealing for eight when I opened the front door."

"What did you want to speak with Thomas about?" Penelope asked.

A slight flush brought color to Bobby's cheeks. He hesitated, but then replied, "I've been…at loose ends. Casting around, trying to figure out what to do with my life. How to manage so I could stop worrying about having enough money in my pocket when I go out with friends. That was why I've been at loggerheads with Thomas. He managed the purse strings, and although I know he was fair in doling out our allowances, it never seemed enough." Absentmindedly, Bobby tugged at his coat cuff. "Then I heard Ruthie and Thomas talking. This was the day before it happened, in the afternoon. They were in Thomas's room, discussing the business. They didn't know I was on the landing outside, listening."

When Bobby fell silent, his fixed gaze suggesting he was replaying his memories and hearing his brother's voice again, Barnaby gently prompted, "What did you hear?"

Bobby blinked and focused on Barnaby, then replied, "They were debating what to do about several new potential clients. Thomas—well, the business, because Ruthie was half of it—was doing well. All the clients were happy, and several had recommended Cardwell's to acquaintances, and now those acquaintances were wanting Thomas—well, him and Ruthie, although they didn't know about Ruthie's involvement—to take on their accounts. Thomas and Ruthie were already working long hours as it was. They were discussing taking on a clerk to train up and spread the load."

Raising his head, Bobby looked at Stokes and Jordan. "As it happens, I'm quite good with figures. Like Ruthie is. And Gibson as well. It was a joke between us—within the family—that the one who wasn't good with numbers, Thomas, was the one who set up a business that was almost entirely to do with arithmetic."

Bobby sighed. "After hearing that Thomas and Ruthie wanted to find a clerk to help, I tossed and turned all night. Finally, after I came down for breakfast and saw Ruthie working through the ledgers, the ones she brought to the office later, I decided I would do it—that I would ask them to make me their clerk. I wasn't sure if Ruthie would take me seriously, so I decided to go and ask Thomas if he would take me on." Bobby's expression dissolved into one of deep sorrow. "Only when I reached the office, I found him…gone."

Penelope doubted that anyone on her side of the table thought Bobby was their killer, but there was more he could tell them. She let a moment slide past, then said, "We need to know a little more about your family so that we can understand." Deliberately not specifying the required understanding, she continued, "For instance, which of you is the eldest?"

Bobby appeared to gather his resources. "Ruthie. She's the eldest. Then comes Gibson, then Thomas, then me."

"I see. And where did you boys go to school?" It was obvious they'd all been reasonably well-educated.

"The three of us attended King Edward's Grammar in Chelmsford," Bobby replied.

Penelope knew of the school and its excellent reputation. It was also quite expensive and difficult to get accepted into.

As if grasping the direction of her thoughts, Bobby added, "M'father went there, too. Him and his brothers."

That suggested the family was rather higher in the social order than Penelope had thought. She racked her brain for the Cardwell family's connections, then she had it. "You're related to Viscount Mollison."

Bobby nodded. "He's m'father's second cousin." He faintly grimaced. "We weren't exactly told, but we saw enough of Papa to know that he was considered the family's black sheep. He… Well, they called him a profligate, a prodigal spendthrift, and more, and he always spent recklessly— even I remember that. If it hadn't been for Mama squirreling away funds and refusing to let him touch them, I daresay we would have been destitute when he died. As it was, things were difficult for a while, but Thomas held us together, and Ruthie figured out how to make the business work, and…well, up until now, things have rolled along well enough."

Noting that Bobby's answers were coming more easily to the simpler questions she posed, Penelope continued, "We know Gibson and Thomas also fought over money. How long ago did Gibson move out of the family home?"

Bobby screwed up his face, then ventured, "About five—no, six years ago. He left to live with his friends when he turned twenty-five. That was a few years after the pater died."

"And the issue between Gibson and Thomas—was that all about money, too?" Stokes asked.

Bobby grimaced, thought, then said, "Yes in the sense that money was what they mostly fought over—nothing much else. But it seemed to me that Gibs was more angry—resentful—of Thomas becoming the man of the house, so to speak. Gibs left, but even before he did, Thomas was the one we all turned to, even Gibs himself."

"So," Penelope said, "their bickering, if you will, was more about Gibson resenting Thomas taking the familial role that Gibson felt should have naturally fallen to him?"

Bobby's face cleared. "Yes. That's it in a nutshell." Then his face fell. "But don't go thinking that because of that—his resentment of Thomas— Gibs killed Thomas. No matter what either of them felt or said, Gibson and Thomas were close. They are—were—closer in age to each other than either is to Ruthie or me."

Jordan shifted on the chair and, when Bobby glanced his way, asked, "Would it be fair to say that Gibson takes after your father, while Thomas took after your mother?"

Bobby thought for only a second before nodding. "That's a reasonable assessment. Thomas was careful and cautious and serious, always. Gibs can be serious about something, but he's rarely careful or cautious." Bobby paused, then added, "Truth be told, I always felt that having seen what Papa was like and what anxiety that brought to Mama and Ruthie, Thomas had, from early on, decided to be the exact opposite of our father."

They all took a moment to digest that insight.

Eventually, Jordan continued, "You mentioned that Thomas distributed the family's allowances. How were they calculated? As a set percentage for each or…?"

Bobby was already nodding. "A defined percentage of the fund's income for the month." He paused, then added, "As the oldest male and heir, Gibs gets a bit more than Thomas, me, and Mama, and Ruthie gets a bit less."

"That's a common arrangement," Jordan stated. "When was the last payment?"

"A week ago."

"So at the moment, you're all in funds, including Gibs?" Jordan asked.

Bobby nodded. "I expect so. Not even Gibs goes through his allowance that quickly."

"Had Gibson been to the house in the past week?" Stokes asked.

"Only for Sunday luncheon. Mama insists on that, and Gibs always comes. Truth be told, I think his friends are also expected at their parents' houses for Sunday luncheon, so it suits Gibs to oblige Mama and come and eat with us."

Penelope frowned. "On the Sunday just past, two days before Thomas was killed, was there any hint of additional or heightened tension between Thomas and Gibson?"

Bobby frowned, clearly trawling through his memories, then his expression transformed to one of faint surprise. "No. Actually, if anything, it was the other way around. Gibs was in fine form—he can be genial and charming and entertaining when he's in a good mood—and Thomas…" Bobby's frown deepened as he evidently studied some scene in his memory. "It's odd. Now I look back, I can see that over the luncheon table, Thomas was…well, watchful. Watching Gibs, but not in any aggressive way. Just watching and noting, although what Thomas was looking for, I have no idea." Bobby refocused on Penelope. "Thomas never said or made any comment or even dropped a hint about anything being wrong."

Stokes looked at Penelope, caught her eye, and arched a brow.

She shook her head. She couldn't think of anything more to ask Bobby at that point.

When Jordan and Barnaby both responded to Stokes's unvoiced question in the same way, Stokes looked at Bobby. "Thank you for coming and telling us what you know. The information is likely to help us find your brother's killer." With a nod of dismissal, Stokes pushed back from the table and rose. "You're free to go."

Penelope, Barnaby, and Jordan got to their feet.

More hesitantly, Bobby stood and stared at them. "And Gibs?"

Stokes replied, "We'll be speaking with him next. How long he remains here will be up to him."

With that, Penelope led the way from the room. She turned down the corridor toward where they'd been told Gibson Cardwell was being held, then halted. Barnaby and Jordan joined her. Stokes paused to tell Walsh to see Bobby Cardwell out of the building, then Stokes joined the company, and trailed by Morgan, they walked to the room at the end of the corridor.

The room in which Gibson Cardwell sat waiting, a belligerent scowl on his face, was much like the room in which they'd interviewed Bobby—a single rectangular table with four chairs lined up along the nearer side and Gibson seated in the single chair opposite. However, this room was fractionally smaller, and with O'Donnell standing behind Gibson and Morgan taking up a stance by the door, it felt more cramped.

As in the first room, the lamp above the table shone harsh light on the interviewee's face. In Gibson's case, the stark illumination further washed out his wan, pallid complexion. He was dressed in a suit in the latest style favored by rakish gentlemen about town and sported a spotted silk cravat, another fashionable eccentricity.

Gibson watched as they claimed the chairs, with Stokes and Penelope in the middle, flanked by Barnaby on Penelope's right and Jordan on Stokes's left.

Although Stokes paused, unlike Bobby, Gibson made no attempt to offer any spontaneous declaration.

Accepting that, Stokes began, "If you would, Mr. Cardwell, please tell us where you were on Tuesday morning between the hours of seven and nine o'clock."

Dismissively, almost sneering, Gibson replied, "I was in my bed, of course. And at that hour, sound asleep."

His tone uninflected, Barnaby inquired, "Is there anyone who can vouch for that?"

Gibson frowned. "Well, no. Not specifically. But my flatmates were in the flat, too, in their rooms. Usually, none of us stumble out until after twelve."

"So," Stokes said, rather ostentatiously making a note, "there's no one to say that you didn't rise early and leave the flat and return later."

Gibson's frown deepened. "I didn't kill my brother, if that's what you really want to know."

Stokes glanced up and met Gibson's gaze. "You do realize that it's not possible to remove your name from the suspect list purely on your word?"

"Well"—Gibson puffed up with assumed righteousness—"unless you can find witnesses to where I was—namely in my bed asleep—then I can't see that you have any other choice. I will say that I didn't go anywhere near Broad Street that morning."

Stokes continued to question Gibson, shifting from his whereabouts to his knowledge of Thomas's business—little to none—and thence to the family finances. The last topic only caused Gibson to become more blustering and defensive.

Stokes tried again with a wider query, and Barnaby tried two other avenues of approach, but Gibson had his defensive façade firmly in place and wasn't the least bit interested in being helpful.

Finally, Barnaby tried a less pointed question concerning Gibson's intentions regarding the family's future and was met with a blank stare and, eventually, a brusque "That's none of your business."

Jordan shifted, then leaned forward slightly and, in the tone of one who had lost patience, said, "Listen, Gibson. Our only interest in speaking with you—or with anyone else on this matter—is to identify who killed your brother and hand them over to the courts. I would have thought that, if you are innocent of the crime, you would want justice for Thomas." Jordan fixed Gibson with a direct look. "Do you or do you not want that?"

Gibson remained gaze-locked with Jordan for a second, then he swallowed and, with the first hint of emotion in his voice, replied, "Of course I do."

Jordan nodded curtly. "Then just answer our questions as best you can." Jordan glanced at Stokes and Barnaby as if handing the questioning baton back to them, but both gave him encouraging looks, urging him to continue.

Jordan returned his gaze to Gibson. "We know there was tension of sorts—an undercurrent of animosity—between you and Thomas. Why was that?"

Gibson's gaze lowered to the table, then his lips twisted, and he replied, "It wasn't animosity. Nothing to do with hate. It was"—he shifted in the chair—"more like a tussle. Like physically wrestling when we were children, but now…well, we were adults, so the wrestling was done in other ways."

"What were you wrestling about?" Jordan asked.

Gibson shot him a glance, hesitated, then asked, "Do you have brothers?"

Jordan nodded. "Two older."

"After your father," Gibson said, "is your oldest brother considered by the rest of the family as the next senior male? The one who would take over and lead if your father wasn't there?"

Jordan's gaze remained steady on Gibson's face. "Yes."

Gibson sighed and, with the tip of one finger, traced a knot in the table's surface. "Yes, well, that's what Thomas and I fought—wrestled—over. I'm the eldest, but when Papa passed, everyone turned to Thomas, not me. And Thomas accepted the role. I was never given a chance to take it—to step into Papa's shoes."

After a moment during which they all digested that, Jordan said, "With Thomas's death, those shoes are now empty." Carefully, Jordan suggested, "Perhaps killing Thomas was your way of resolving your wrestling match once and for all and taking back what you considered to be yours."

Gibson's gaze lifted to Jordan's face. "What?" For an instant, as the implications of Jordan's words sank in, Gibson's face was stripped of all assumed expression, and something close to horrified revulsion filled his eyes. Abruptly, Gibson sat up and shook his head. "No! No matter how much Thomas and his posturing irritated me, I would never have hurt him." Gibson swallowed, then went on, "And despite everything, inside" —he tapped a fist to his chest—"I never questioned that what Thomas was doing was the very best for the family. That was never the issue."

Gibson seemed to deflate, to sink into himself, and Barnaby felt they were finally dealing with the real man behind the façade as Gibson went on, "Yes, we fought—argued. Over the past year, whenever we met, inevitably one of us would prod the other with some comment, and we'd be at it again. But it was all…fighting between brothers. It was never physically harmful." Gibson paused, then, his voice lowering, continued, "We fought with words and attitudes and emotions. We struck at each other's pride, at each other's sense of self—that sort of thing. But truth be told, I don't think we would have fought at all if we weren't brothers." Briefly, he met Jordan's gaze. "There wouldn't have been any point."

With two older brothers himself, Barnaby understood the observation.

Gibson appeared to collect himself. He straightened on the chair, then looked at Barnaby, Penelope, Stokes, and Jordan, and stated, "Thomas was my brother. Despite how it might appear, we were close. I would never have killed him, and I have no idea who did." His lips turned downward. "Believe me, if I did know who had murdered him, I would already have told you. As I said earlier, I have no real knowledge of Thomas's clients. However, I do know him, possibly better than anyone, even Ruthie. So I can tell you that if one of his clients was involved in something shady—something that didn't meet his standards of the right and proper—he wouldn't stand for it. He would, without question, reveal what he'd learned to the authorities."

A frown slowly formed on Gibson's face, then he grimaced and added, "It would also be just like Thomas to notify his wayward client of what he'd found and that he was about to go to the authorities. He was always one to try to help people. He was idealistic and sometimes rather naive in that way. It's likely he would have suggested that they go to the authorities themselves and confess and put things right, rather than have him tell what he knew."

Gibson paused, then rather sadly said, "Thomas always assumed that if he was doing the right thing and acting as the law dictated, that everything would go his way and work out well in the end. He was one who believed that evil would never triumph."

Penelope murmured, "You sound rather jaded on that point."

Gibson looked at her. "Thomas is dead."

There was nothing anyone could say to that.

After a moment, Jordan ventured, "As you say, Thomas is dead. Now that he is, your family transparently needs someone else to take the helm." He caught Gibson's gaze. "Will you be that man and step up to the mark?"

Barnaby, along with all the others in the room, watched Gibson wrestle with the question.

Eventually, as much to himself as to anyone else, he quietly said, "Will I step into my dead brother's shoes?" Then he squared his shoulders and looked at Jordan. "If the family will have me, then yes. Someone needs to manage the reins overall, and although Ruthie is quietly effective, she needs a man to stand behind while she handles the ribbons."

Penelope smiled. "That's well said." She had to approve, and to her mind, the comment showed that Gibson had a sound understanding of where, within his family, the common sense lay.

Stokes asked when Gibson had last spoken with his brother, and without fuss, Gibson said it had been the previous Sunday at the house in Finsbury Circus, confirming what Bobby had told them.

Stokes shut his notebook and looked at Gibson. "Thank you, Mr. Cardwell. If you should remember or learn anything you believe might be relevant, however tangentially, to identifying your brother's murderer, please send word to me here at the Yard." When Gibson nodded, Stokes continued, "You're free to go."

They all rose and filed out of the cramped room, then stood back and allowed O'Donnell to conduct Gibson back to the street.

With the others, Penelope watched him go. Before he reached the stairs, he returned his top hat to his head. With every step he took, she could almost see him resuming the rakish profligate persona he showed to the world.

Despite that, she now felt there was real hope that Gibson Cardwell would transform into the man his family needed him to be.

Once Cardwell had vanished up the stairs, Stokes waved their company on. "Let's head back to my office and decide where we are now."

They trooped upstairs to Stokes's office on the first floor.

Once they'd settled in the chairs about the desk, Penelope stated, "In all that the Cardwell brothers revealed, I heard nothing that made me think either of them had sufficient motive to kill Thomas."

Jordan nodded. "Gibson could have struck out in anger. He's certainly strong enough and has the stature and coat and hat to pass as our unknown gentleman. But Gibson and Thomas's contentious relationship was long established, and it would have taken something quite dramatic to push Gibson into such an act, and no one's suggested anything even vaguely powerful enough that could have spurred him into acting last Tuesday morning."

"I concur," Barnaby said. "Regarding Gibson, aside from all else, killing Thomas wouldn't have fitted his image—the character of his late father that he has been, at least up to now, attempting to emulate."

"Aha!" Penelope nodded. "Very true."

Stokes had been flicking through his notebook. "For my money, Bobby Cardwell is definitely not our murderer. He might be twenty-something, but he's younger in some ways, and his character is not yet fixed, and it seems he looked up to Thomas and valued what Thomas was doing for the family."

"And," Penelope said, "that's another reason Gibson wouldn't have killed Thomas, either." She looked at the others. "No matter any arguments, from all he let fall, Gibson, too, valued what Thomas was doing to keep the family afloat."

"Indeed." Barnaby, too, looked around at the others. "So where does that leave us now?"

Stokes blew out a breath. "Well, if it wasn't one of the family, and we seem to have accepted that it wasn't, and it also wasn't the Hemingways, then we have to assume that the nefarious activities that moved Thomas to write to Roscoe, which are presumably the reason Thomas was killed, stem from some other client of Thomas's."

"We've heard nothing to suggest that Thomas had recently ventured into some unexpected circle that might have led to such a discovery," Penelope pointed out.

"That suggestion of Gibson's," Jordan said, "that Thomas might have notified the client involved that he was preparing to go to the authorities in the hope said client would do the right thing and rectify the matter themselves, might well have been what happened." He glanced at the others. "Such behavior on Thomas's part fits with the rest of the family's views of his character."

Barnaby stated, "The most likely avenue through which Thomas learned of nefarious activities being afoot is through his work for his clients. That's indisputable. And Gibson's suggestion of Thomas contacting the about-to-be-exposed client also fits the timing of the letter to Roscoe and Thomas's murder."

Stokes was nodding. "Our unknown man presumed to be the murderer is the about-to-be-exposed client."

Penelope straightened on her chair. "We need to check Thomas's ledgers and search for any correspondence—copies of recent letters and so on. There might well be a major clue hidden in his account books."

"I agree," Jordan said.

Stokes frowned. "Wouldn't the murderer—presuming he was this client—have removed any telltale ledger? Surely that will be long gone."

Jordan's brows rose. "Perhaps, but that might be a clue in and of itself." He glanced at Penelope. "There should be a master list somewhere in Thomas's office. And Ruth could well have one, too, given she did all the accounts."

Penelope smiled. "So if we check all the remaining ledgers against the master list and discover some are inexplicably missing…"

Jordan grinned. "That will point to the murderer."

Barnaby, Penelope, and Jordan all looked at Stokes.

He regarded them impassively, then pushed back from his desk. "Right, then. It's back to Cardwell's office to trawl through his files."

Along with his three coinvestigators, Barnaby returned to Broad Street.

On descending from their carriage, they found Gelman chatting to Walsh, who was presently on guard outside Cardwell's office door.

Walsh came to attention and reported to Stokes, "No one's approached, sir. And Morgan said all was quiet overnight."

With a general nod to all, Gelman added, "There hasn't been anyone eyeing the place, either. No attention at all."

"Good," Stokes said, then he grimaced and glanced at Barnaby, Penelope, and Jordan. "I'm not sure if that means the telltale ledger is already gone, but"—Stokes waved them to the door—"let's see if we can locate this master list and work out what's what."

Penelope led the way inside, and the three men followed.

"The master list." Penelope went straight to the desk. "The desk drawers are the most likely place for it."

She started pulling out the drawers on one side of the desk, while Jordan claimed the drawers on the other side.

With Stokes, Barnaby halted facing the desk and waited.

Penelope straightened and held up several sheets pinned together. "Is this it?"

Jordan joined her in scanning the first sheet, then took the collection and flipped through the other pages. His face lit, and he smiled at Penelope. "It is. Good find."

"So now…" She glanced at the shelves and the many ledgers they held.

"Now," Jordan said, separating the pages and laying them across the blotter, "we start at one end of the office and work our way around, checking each set of ledgers against this list until we confirm that they're all here or that one is missing."

Stokes was the least familiar with ledger-keeping, so they installed him at the desk to, with a pencil, mark off each ledger as the others called out the clients' names. Barnaby, Penelope, and Jordan divided the shelves into three sections and started working through them, pulling out the ledgers, checking the name inside the front cover, and calling it out to Stokes before reshelving that ledger and moving on to the next.

As Penelope was so short, she and Barnaby reorganized their allotted area so that Barnaby did the top two shelves over both sections, while she worked through the lower shelves.

As the minutes ticked by, the three worked their way steadily around the office.

Finally, after nearly half an hour, Jordan called out the name of the last set of three ledgers, and Stokes grunted. "That's it." He tossed down the pencil and slumped back in the chair. "It appears all the ledgers are still here."

Penelope dropped into the chair facing the desk. "I suppose it would have been too easy to find that one set of accounts had gone missing."

Stokes frowned at the list with its column of neat ticks. "Perhaps that means the revealing information Thomas found is not, in fact, in any ledger here."

"Or"—Barnaby leaned on the back of Penelope's chair—"that whoever killed Thomas didn't realize it was something reflected in the business's accounts that alerted Thomas to the nefarious activities."

"I still think," Jordan said, halting at one end of the desk and surveying the shelves, "that the financial ledgers remain the most likely source of information about nefarious activities that would have fallen into Thomas's lap."

Stokes pulled a face. "As much as I would like to point to some other source, I can't." He cast an uninspired glance at the shelves. "I believe that means we have to hunt through all the ledgers here until we happen upon whatever it was that signaled 'nefarious activities' to Thomas."

Jordan looked at Stokes, then smiled commiseratingly. "I'll show you a quick way of finding any anomaly in a set of financial accounts."

Stokes sighed. "I suppose you can try."

Penelope, Barnaby, and even Stokes listened as Jordan demonstrated which columns were critical and what to look for.

"We only need to look back over the past six months," Jordan explained, "and if you see any strangely large payments being made or received, bring the ledger to me, and I'll examine it in more detail." He went to the shelves, pulled a ledger at random, and opened it. "For instance, this business is a bookshop. If we look down their income column, you can see the daily sums coming in are of a level that aligns with purchases of books. If you look at the expenses, you can see regular but much larger payments made to various publishers." Jordan paused and looked at the others. "If you came across a large sum, either incoming or outgoing, for say, bakery goods or ironwork or leather work or something that doesn't fit with running a bookshop, that's worth further examination."

He glanced at the ledger in his hands. "This ledger is boringly straightforward. Nothing nefarious going on at Coulter's Books."

"That's easy enough." Penelope bustled to the nearest shelf and started at the end of one row.

Jordan returned the Coulter ledger to the shelf and drew out the next.

Barnaby and Stokes shared a look. Neither was all that fond of scanning figures. Nevertheless, after they both grimaced, they walked to the shelves and took up the task.

Within fifteen minutes, it was apparent that Penelope and Jordan between them were checking and eliminating three times as many ledgers as Barnaby and Stokes.

Finally, Stokes put back the ledger he'd ploddingly checked, hesitated, then turned to the others. To Penelope and Jordan, he said, "You two are better suited to examining the ledgers than Barnaby and me."

"Aside from all else," Barnaby said, also replacing a ledger, "you're both confident of what you're looking for. We"—he met Stokes's gaze—"aren't."

"Exactly," Stokes said. "A better use of my and Barnaby's time would be to hunt for further sightings of our unknown man."

Barnaby nodded. "The likely murderer." He looked at Penelope. "I'm going to find one of the lads and put out an alert through the network. It's possible they might have some useful fact to share."

"An excellent idea," Penelope said.

Puzzled, Jordan asked, "Network?"

Barnaby smiled and described the web of boys and youths they'd started labeling the Lads' Network. "All of them are out and about, virtually every day, and they cover most of the City and the surrounding areas, like Mayfair, Euston, the docks and warehouses, and so on."

"And they're remarkably observant," Stokes put in.

Penelope nodded. "They notice everything that's going on around them far more than adults do."

"That's…intriguing." Jordan's expression mirrored his words. "A novel idea and one I might well steal."

Barnaby grinned. "Feel free. For now, however…" He stepped back and waved Stokes to the door. "We'll leave you two to the ledgers while we search in wider fields."

"We'll return in an hour or so." Stokes saluted Penelope and Jordan and made for the door.

With a smile for Penelope and a tip of his head to Jordan, Barnaby followed.

Together with Penelope, Jordan returned to trawling through the ledgers. It was a thankless chore, for they all seemed to be businesses running along unexceptionable lines, but Jordan accepted that they had to complete their search even if only to convince themselves that there was no clue to be found among the ledgers.

Five minutes later, Gelman looked into the office. "I'm delegated to keep watch here. The inspector has commandeered everyone else to help with their search." Gelman tipped his head, indicating the other side of the street. "I'll be just over there, so no one will see me. If anyone arrives and comes inside, I'll be over in a jiffy."

Jordan nodded. "Good thinking."

Penelope inclined her head absentmindedly, and Gelman left.

Silence settled, broken only by the *shush* as ledgers were pulled out or pushed back onto shelves and the rustle of pages being turned.

Eventually, tired of standing, Jordan collected an armful of account books and settled in the chair behind the desk to go through them. Penelope saw and did the same, stacking a pile of ledgers on the corner of the desk and sinking into the chair facing it.

They worked doggedly on, getting up only to exchange the ledgers they'd checked for a fresh collection.

Jordan had lost all track of time when movement in the front window caught his eye. He looked that way and saw Ruth Cardwell peering into the office. She saw him and hesitated, then her gaze moved on to Penelope, and Ruth froze, then she stepped away from the glass and whisked away.

A minute ticked by, but Ruth didn't reappear. Jordan returned his gaze to the ledger he'd been perusing. Ruth wouldn't have noticed Gelman, watching from the other side of the street. After making a mental note to check with his colleague later as to how Ruth's behavior had appeared to him, Jordan forced his mind back to the task at hand.

Nearly an hour later, Penelope shut the ledger she'd been scanning and heaved a disappointed sigh. "Nothing." She rose, collected her last stack of ledgers, and returned to the shelves to replace them.

"And absolutely nothing here." Jordan shut the last ledger in his pile and tossed it onto the desk. "If anything, all that I've seen convinces me that Thomas Cardwell was very careful regarding which clients he took on."

"Hmm." Penelope came back to the chair and dropped into it as Jordan rose and returned the last of his ledgers to their places. "I got the same impression. The ledgers are also meticulously kept."

"That's Ruth's doing," Jordan said.

"Indeed. But as you say," Penelope went on, "the clients all appear to be rigidly above board, and as I understood things, choosing the clients was Thomas's domain."

"True."

As Jordan returned to the desk, Penelope eyed him, then asked, "In your experience, is that normal? That every client is so transparently doing the right thing?"

Jordan slumped into the chair behind the desk, considered the question, then raised a hand and waggled it. "I would have to say it's a tad unusual—there's always some clients who are inclined to test the legal limits—but from all we've heard of Thomas, he was a careful and cautious man. Also, he valued his reputation, and so I'm not that surprised to learn that none of his clients appear even the least bit shady."

"Hmm." Penelope faintly grimaced. "I'm not sure where that leaves us now."

Jordan didn't have an answer and was grateful that Barnaby and Stokes chose that moment to walk in.

Immediately, Penelope stated, "Jordan and I found absolutely nothing illuminating in Cardwell's ledgers. All his clients appear to be intensely law-abiding."

Taking in Barnaby's and Stokes's expressions, Jordan wasn't surprised when Barnaby confessed that they, too, had learned nothing useful.

"Only one other sighting," Stokes reported. "Just past the last one Morgan turned up, but again, nothing at all to identify the man."

"The washerwoman said he was just another gentleman in that newfangled style of coat and a black top hat." Barnaby smiled rather tiredly at Penelope. "No word from the lads yet, of course, but they're spreading the word, so we can live in hope that they'll turn up something more revealing."

"A distinct and identifying feature would be nice," Stokes said, "but given all we've heard to this point, I'm not holding my breath." He looked at the others, who appeared as disappointed as he. "I vote we close up here, go home for the day, and let all we've seen, heard, and learned distill overnight, then meet after breakfast at Albemarle Street and plan our next move. All in favor?"

They all held up their hands.

"Shall we say nine o'clock?" Barnaby asked.

Everyone agreed.

Stokes called Walsh inside and directed him to remain on guard overnight, just in case there was anyone with an interest in the contents of

Cardwell's office. "Unlikely, I admit," Stokes said, "but better we take precautions rather than realize later that we should have."

Jordan got to his feet. "Just in case there's something we've missed."

"Or," Penelope said as she rose, "something the murderer thinks might still be here."

Barnaby tipped his head her way. "Good point."

Leaving Walsh in the office, they headed outside.

Jordan followed the others onto the pavement. When Barnaby and Penelope offered to take him as well as Stokes back to Mayfair in their carriage, Jordan smiled and declined. He nodded across the street. "I'll pick up Gelman, and then, I believe, we have somewhere else we need to visit."

Assuming, as he'd intended they would, that the somewhere else had to do with his work for Roscoe, the other three parted from him and climbed into the Adairs' carriage.

Jordan remained where he was until the carriage rattled off, then he crossed the street to where Gelman was lounging in the mouth of a narrow alley.

Gelman straightened and stepped out to meet Jordan. "Did you see Miss Cardwell peering in the window?"

Jordan nodded. "I thought she was going to come inside."

"Seemed like," Gelman agreed. "She looked like she was about to step toward the door, then she froze and, a second later, turned and walked straight back the way she'd come."

Jordan looked toward the street that would take them to Finsbury Circus. "I'm going to call at the Cardwells'. Miss Cardwell was about to come in and—I assume—speak with me, then she saw Mrs. Adair and scarpered. I'm curious to learn why."

CHAPTER 7

With Gelman on watch in the central park, Jordan climbed the steps before the door of Number 29. Confronted with the black-crepe-draped knocker, he raised his fist to rap, only to have the door open and Ruth Cardwell step over the threshold.

"Quiet," she warned and, with both hands, shooed him down the steps. Over her shoulder, she called, "I'm just stepping out to take a turn around the park, Mama. I'll be back shortly." She closed the door quietly behind her, then waved Jordan back even more insistently and joined him on the pavement. "Just in case someone looks out, we need to make this look normal." She looped her arm in his and would have towed him to the park if he'd resisted.

Jordan didn't resist but willingly paced beside her as they walked sedately across the street and passed into the park. Although the large trees were not yet in full leaf, there were bushes aplenty to screen them from the house.

Ruth glanced back once, then murmured, "I don't want Mama to hear this—she worries enough as it is."

"About what?" Jordan asked.

"Us," Ruth replied. "Everything to do with the family." She pointed to a bench set in an alcove created by thick bushes. "There will do."

Jordan obligingly directed his steps in that direction.

When they reached the bench, Ruth released his arm and, drawing in her blue-cambric skirts, sat.

She seemed impatient for Jordan to join her, yet once he had, she hesitated as if having second thoughts about what she'd intended to say.

Jordan held his tongue and didn't press. In his experience, sensible women were best left to make up their own minds.

Eventually, Ruth glanced at him, a frown in her eyes. "Did you and Mrs. Adair find anything in Thomas's ledgers to explain why he contacted your employer?"

Jordan couldn't see any reason not to tell her the truth. "No. There was nothing out of the ordinary. Everything seemed to be stultifyingly above board."

To his surprise, she slumped slightly as if that hadn't been the news she'd hoped to hear. He watched as she bit her lower lip, her expression plainly stating that she was wrestling with some momentous decision.

With her conscience, perhaps.

As before, Jordan said nothing and simply waited.

Eventually, her expression cleared. She raised her head slightly, and her chin firmed. "As you already know, I keep the accounts—the actual ledgers—for Thomas's business." She met Jordan's gaze. "I also keep the family accounts—all of them. I go over them weekly, always on a Friday. As usual, I went over them last Friday, and I noticed…" She paused to fortify herself with a restricted breath. "That Gibson hadn't been leeching here and there from the rest of us as he usually does."

Jordan frowned slightly. "Leeching?"

"Gibson is a closet spendthrift—he pretends to get by on his allowance, but he's constantly 'borrowing' from the rest of us to cover his expenses. A crown or two here, ten shillings there, that sort of thing. It usually shows in the individual accounts I keep for each member of the family." She paused, then added, "When my father passed and we realized how financially strained the family truly was, Thomas and I instituted an internal accounting system so that we could keep tight control over the household's and each family member's spending. It was very necessary when we first started doing it, and because of that, we've never really stopped, even though those straitened financial times are behind us."

Jordan nodded his understanding and didn't interrupt.

After a second of staring at him, Ruth continued, "Last Friday, I noticed that we were all tracking as per our expected expenses and, for instance, Mama wasn't down three guineas, those being unaccounted for because she'd slipped them to Gibson when he'd pleaded for help." She sighed. "I'm equally guilty of giving in to his begging, and even Thomas and Bobby sometimes help him out. All on the quiet, of course."

"But last week, nothing?" Jordan asked.

Ruth nodded. "But I've recently seen Gibson with a new silver-headed cane, which he shouldn't have been able to afford. Not without our help. And then there were his new top hat and silk cravats and a new leather wallet to be accounted for. I looked back over the earlier weeks and discovered that I had to go back two full months before Gibson's previous drain on our individual accounts was evident. And there's nothing in his account to explain where he's been getting the cash for his recent extravagances."

Jordan felt increasingly grave. "So you're saying that Gibson has some unexplained source of funds."

"Yes." Ruth clasped her hands tightly in her lap. "I knew asking Gibson outright would be no use—he'd just wave the question aside. So on Saturday, I explained what I'd found to Thomas. I showed him the anomalies—the expenses that weren't turning up in Gibson's account but that we knew should be there. Like that cane."

She drew in a deep breath and rushed on, "Thomas agreed with my conclusion that Gibson had to be getting money—cash—from some-where, but from where and in exchange for what was a mystery. Thomas said to leave the matter to him, that he would find out what was going on."

She paused, then said, "Despite appearances, Thomas was always the closest to Gibson. Even closer than Mama. Gibson was more likely to confess to whatever the situation was to Thomas than to anyone else." She sighed. "So I left the matter in Thomas's hands." She glanced at Jordan. "And now, I have to wonder…"

Wondering, too, Jordan shifted his gaze to the lawn before them.

Ruth rushed to say, "I didn't mention it before because, like you and the other investigators, I assumed that what Thomas had grown concerned over—the nefarious activities—was something to do with one of his clients. But if it isn't that…" She hauled in a breath and, pressing her palms together in her lap, declared, "I will never believe that Gibson killed Thomas. No matter how much they argued, they were brothers, family first and last, and they would have defended each other against the world. Gibson can be difficult to deal with at times, but it's usually pride, not malice, behind his reactions."

That analysis aligned with Jordan's in the wake of the investigators' interview with Gibson.

"So"—Jordan brought his gaze back to Ruth's strained face—"what do you think happened?"

Ruth exhaled. "Well, aside from all else, I don't believe Thomas told Gibson anything about our suspicions. If Thomas had done so, then by now, Gibson would have said something to me about prying into his affairs, and like me, Thomas wouldn't have thought it worth his while directly taxing Gibson, not without first knowing what was going on." She paused, then, her voice firming, continued, "I think Thomas might have been investigating Gibson, as it were, seeking to identify the source of his extra funds." She met Jordan's gaze. "If, in doing that, Thomas stumbled onto some situation…" She hurried to add, "It might not have anything to do with Gibson and his secret funds, but if in seeking the source, Thomas discovered something else…"

His gaze locked with hers, Jordan swiftly reviewed the timing of what Ruth had told him relative to Thomas sending his letter to Roscoe and Thomas's murder. Slowly, he nodded. "I agree that's a possibility." He straightened. "That explanation would also answer the question of why now? Why had Thomas suddenly stumbled onto something he hadn't noticed before?"

After a moment of searching Ruth's large blue eyes, Jordan gently said, "You're going to have to tell the investigators."

She looked down at her clenched fingers, then she heaved a sigh and, after a moment, nodded. "I don't want to, but I know I must." She grimaced and, from beneath her lashes, cast him a swift glance. "I'm going to feel horrendously guilty if me telling Thomas about Gibson's unexplained funds somehow led to Thomas being murdered."

Impulsively, Jordan reached across and closed a hand about her clasped ones. "Don't. You can't blame yourself. You might have warned Thomas about Gibson's extra funds, as in the circumstances you should have done, but from that point onward, Thomas made his own decisions. Sadly, it seems he trusted someone he shouldn't have, but that someone is responsible for his death, not you. Not in any way."

Her half smile was wan, but suggested that she found his assertion comforting.

Jordan lightly squeezed her clasped hands, then released them.

After a moment, she cleared her throat and rather huskily asked,

"How should I approach the investigators? Should I call at Scotland Yard?"

"No need." Jordan smiled at her encouragingly. "We're meeting at the Adairs' house at nine tomorrow morning. If you like, I can call here at eight-thirty and escort you there."

Relief eased the lines in her face. "That would be…helpful." She glanced toward the house. "I don't want to worry Mama or Bobby, so I'll say I'm going shopping"—she returned her gaze, now more at ease, to Jordan's face—"and wait for you here."

Penelope was sitting in her drawing room with Barnaby and Stokes when the front doorbell pealed, and a minute later, Jordan ushered Ruth Cardwell through the doorway.

Along with the men, Penelope bounced to her feet. "Miss Cardwell. Welcome! Do join us."

"Thank you, Mrs. Adair." Ruth nodded gravely to Barnaby and Stokes and exchanged murmured greetings.

Penelope directed Ruth to the sofa opposite the one Penelope and Barnaby habitually occupied, then cast an intrigued and questioning look at Jordan as he moved to sit beside Ruth.

Jordan obliged with "Miss Cardwell has some information that she and I believe you need to hear."

Even more intrigued, Penelope returned to her position on the sofa, and the men sat.

As soon as they had settled, Ruth cleared her throat and said, "I keep the family accounts, and I noticed that Gibson had been spending money and buying things—expenditures I couldn't account for based on his allowance. I mentioned the matter to Thomas, and he looked at the accounts as well, and we both concluded that Gibson had some source of funds other than his allowance. But who was paying him and for what were mysteries, and we weren't sure what to make of it. Thomas told me he'd look into it."

"When was that?" Stokes had hauled out his notebook.

"Last Saturday. But," Ruth said, "I don't know if Thomas had, in fact, made any attempt to discover where Gibson was getting the extra cash."

"However," Barnaby said, "Thomas might have gone searching and, while doing so, stumbled across something that was sufficiently concerning to make him ask Roscoe for advice."

Penelope read Ruth's expression easily enough; that she was torn was obvious. "Regardless," Penelope declared, "we shouldn't leap to conclusions, such as that the something Thomas stumbled upon had anything to do with Gibson and his unexplained income. The connection might have been purely incidental."

"Alternatively," Stokes countered, "the something Thomas uncovered was related to Gibson's newfound source of wealth." He met Ruth's gaze. "We've searched through Thomas's ledgers and accounts and found no hint of any misdeed among his clients. Nothing that would explain him appealing to Roscoe. However, if Gibson was dabbling in some area that gave Thomas serious concern..." He paused, and Penelope felt they all followed that train of thought to the inescapable conclusion.

After a moment, Stokes asked Ruth, "Do you think Thomas would have gone to the authorities over what he described as nefarious activities even if Gibson was in some way, however tangentially, involved?"

Ruth frowned. After a long moment, she confessed, "I really can't say."

Jordan leaned forward, elbows on his knees. "Perhaps that's why Thomas asked Roscoe for advice." He glanced at Penelope and Barnaby. "If Thomas was looking for a route via which to alert the authorities to some illegal enterprise in a way that would keep his brother out of jail..."

Penelope nodded. "Yes. That would make eminent sense."

"And," Barnaby added, "very likely, Roscoe was the only one with the sort of experience Thomas needed that Thomas knew sufficiently well to ask."

They all looked at Ruth and saw her chin firm. She raised her head, met their gazes, and nodded. "Yes. That sounds like something Thomas would do." She paused, then went on, "If Thomas had discovered something illegal—nefarious, to use his word—he wouldn't have been able to let it rest. He would have felt compelled to put it right—to notify the authorities—but if Gibson was involved, then yes, Thomas would have gone looking for some way to alert the authorities while simultaneously hauling Gibson from the mire."

Ruth looked around the circle of faces. "As I've said before, Thomas and Gibson would have defended each other against the world."

Barnaby uncrossed his legs. "From all we've learned of both brothers, protecting Gibson while informing the authorities sounds a much more viable reason for Thomas to contact Roscoe."

Stokes was frowning. "If we ask Gibson where his extra money comes from—"

Penelope leapt in with "Explaining that we believe that uncovering that source might be what got Thomas killed."

"—do you think Gibson will tell us?" Stokes arched a brow at Ruth.

She frowned, clearly uncertain. "That will be a horrible shock, given Gibson has no idea Thomas even knew about his extra funds."

"But," Barnaby said, "asking Gibson will be the most direct route to learning the answer. And if what we now believe is true and Thomas's investigation of the unknown source led to his murder, then we need that answer and as soon as possible."

Penelope glanced at Stokes and Barnaby. "When we interviewed Gibson, once we'd got past his guard, he proved to be a reasonable man."

Stokes and Barnaby inclined their heads, and everyone looked at Ruth, who was plainly still weighing their best course.

Then she raised her head and met their gazes. "You're right. We need to ask Gibson from where he's getting his extra funds. Once he understands that Thomas knew of those funds and that learning of their source might have led to his murder, Gibson will tell us." Her expression set, and her voice strengthened. "I'll come with you and make sure he does and that what he tells us is the truth."

Barnaby assisted Penelope to the pavement opposite Number 15, Falcon Street. Stokes had climbed down first, and Jordan and Ruth were descending from a hackney that had followed the Adairs' carriage from Mayfair.

As the others joined them, Barnaby stood beside Penelope and surveyed the building across the cobbles. Falcon Street lay off busy Aldersgate and had its fair share of through traffic, yet the three-storied town houses that lined the street managed to retain some semblance of quiet dignity. Their red bricks might be darkened by city smoke, and the carved stone pediments and window embrasures, once ivory, were yellowed, yet by and large, the glass in the windows gleamed, and the paint on the front doors was still glossy.

Jordan halted beside Barnaby and looked up at the first-floor bay window. "Gibson said he lived at fifteen B."

Stokes grunted and started across the street. "Presumably the first-floor flat."

According to a small plaque beside the front door, that supposition was correct. The door was unlocked, as was often the case in such shared residences. A narrow stairway led upward, and they climbed to the first landing. In the lead, Stokes rapped on the panel of the door that bore a small brass *B*.

Barnaby halted behind Stokes, with Penelope and Ruth crowding at his back and Jordan waiting on the last stair below the narrow landing. Recalling that during Gibson's interview, he'd stated that he and his flat-mates rarely rose before noon, Barnaby wondered what state of deshabille the three might currently be in.

The door opened to reveal a gentleman of similar years to Gibson. He was tall, black-haired, and a touch heavier than Gibson, with clean-cut, rather aristocratic features in what was, overall, a handsome face. Although his hair was mussed, he was fully dressed.

On seeing their company, the gentleman's eyes widened. "Yes?"

"I'm Inspector Stokes of Scotland Yard," Stokes declared. "And you are?"

"Harrison Moubray. I live here."

Stokes nodded curtly. "We're here to speak with Gibson Cardwell, as well as yourself, and I believe there's another gentleman living here?"

"Josh—Joseph Keeble." Harrison frowned. "Is this about Thomas's murder?"

"Yes," Stokes replied. "I'm in charge of the investigation into Thomas's death." He glanced behind him. "Mr. and Mrs. Adair and Mr. Draper are consultants assisting me." Stokes returned his gaze to Harrison and, from Harrison's expression, saw that he'd spotted and recognized Ruth. "And I believe you know Miss Cardwell."

"Yes, of course." Harrison seemed slightly flustered. He bobbed a half bow, mostly directed Ruth's way. "I say, Thomas getting killed is a deuced shocking thing. My condolences, Miss Cardwell."

Ruth inclined her head. "Thank you, Harrison. I take it Gibson is in?"

When Harrison hesitated and his gaze returned to Stokes, Stokes informed him, "We have a few further questions for Gibson, and it would be helpful if you and Mr. Keeble could join us. If he's in?"

Harrison nodded as he stepped back to allow them to enter. "Yes. Josh is here, too." He waved them past him, through a tiny foyer and into the sitting room beyond. "Come in."

Barnaby followed Stokes into a decent-sized parlor, with the bay window they'd seen from below filling most of the exterior wall. Gray morning light streamed in and illuminated a large, well-worn leather sofa and matching armchair. Low tables at the ends of the sofa and in the center of the space were littered with sporting magazines and similar fashionable periodicals, and a heavy sideboard stood against the side wall.

Gibson Cardwell sat on the sofa, slumped forward and looking rather the worse for wear, although judging by the clearness of his eyes as he raised his gaze to take in the newcomers, his drained expression wasn't due to drink.

On seeing them, Gibson straightened, then noting the ladies, hurriedly stood. Beside him, another gentleman of similar age, presumably the third of the friends, Joseph—Josh—Keeble, also got to his feet. It appeared that Josh—and possibly Harrison before he came to the door—had been commiserating and comforting Gibson.

Gibson's gaze had swung from Stokes to Barnaby, then to Penelope and Jordan and, finally, landed on Ruth. His eyes widened. "Ruthie?"

Barnaby glanced at Ruth in time to see her smile rather tightly at her brother. "Good morning, Gibson." She nodded to Josh. "Joseph."

For Josh's benefit, Stokes repeated the introductions and added in explanation, "We simply have a few extra questions for Gibson and would appreciate Mr. Keeble's and Mr. Moubray's inputs as well."

All three gentlemen looked confused and uncertain, but were too well brought up to question Stokes's authority, let alone deny the likes of Barnaby and Penelope. Instead, all three leapt to rather endearingly organize extra chairs, steering Barnaby, Penelope, Ruth, and Jordan to the oversized sofa and urging Stokes to avail himself of the well-padded armchair while they rushed to fetch straight-backed chairs from the kitchen for themselves.

Subsiding into the armchair, Stokes directed a look at Barnaby that clearly stated, *None of these three could possibly be our killer.*

Barnaby hid a smile. He had to agree. Gibson Cardwell and his two school friends might be around thirty years old, but they'd lived largely sheltered, gentrified lives, and compared to many others Barnaby, Penelope, and Stokes had met—and doubtless contrary to how the three men saw themselves—they were rather naive and gentle souls.

Once everyone else was seated, the three perched on the wooden chairs and, with every appearance of being entirely willing to assist in any way they could, all three fixed attentive gazes on Stokes, their attitudes highly reminiscent of students attending a tutorial.

Stokes undoubtedly saw that but managed to maintain an impassive mien. He commenced by reiterating that it was their investigation into Thomas Cardwell's murder that had brought them there. He inclined his head toward Gibson, sitting beyond the end of the sofa to Barnaby's right. "We spoke at length with Gibson, and we see no reason to suspect him of the crime. At present, what we know of the murder is that some unknown gentleman, wearing a black top hat and a dun-colored coat, was waiting for Thomas at the door to his office when Thomas arrived at eight o'clock on Tuesday morning. Thomas appeared to recognize the man and unlocked the office door and allowed the man to follow him inside. Thomas sat in the chair behind his desk, and the unknown man sat in the chair facing him. We have no idea what was discussed, but at some point, the unknown man seized Thomas's letter knife from where it lay on the desk and stabbed Thomas through the heart."

They hadn't discussed how to broach the matter they wanted to explore, but viewing the three friends' ashen countenances, Barnaby could appreciate that Stokes's tack was wiping out any lingering resistance.

Imperturbably, Stokes continued, "The unknown man then left the office via the rear door and the lane at the rear of the premises. We have subsequent sightings of that unknown man, but as of yet, none have been sufficient to identify him."

Penelope underscored the point. "Not in the slightest."

Stokes paused to regard the three friends, sitting in a line between his armchair and the sofa's end, then went on, "What you might not be aware of is that Thomas had learned of Gibson's new, undisclosed source of funds."

Watching the three friends closely, Barnaby saw all three faces blank, then each of them blinked and blinked again.

Stokes continued, "Thomas had realized that you, Gibson, were flush with cash these past months, and Thomas was intent on learning who was paying you and for what. Consequently, from the Saturday just past, we believe Thomas was actively investigating your movements. He might well have been following you about."

The three looked stunned. They glanced at each other in some consternation. Their expressions were open and ridiculously easy to read. All three were involved in whatever the caper was, and they hadn't expected this and were entirely uncertain how to respond.

No doubt seeing the same, Stokes stated, "In the circumstances, it would be best if you simply told us the answers. Who is paying you and for what?"

All three stared at Stokes, then they shifted to exchange long and meaningful looks with each other.

No one else spoke.

Eventually, after apparently coming to some joint conclusion, still looking at his friends, Harrison shrugged. "I can't see why we shouldn't."

Gibson swallowed. "We promised to keep our lips buttoned, but now someone's murdered Thomas…"

"Exactly." Harrison, who to some extent seemed to be the leader, faced the investigators and said, "We're each getting paid a stipend because we led a gent who had need of a warehouse to one he could use on the cheap."

Josh offered, "Like a finder's fee, but an ongoing one, which as you might imagine, is rather useful to us." He glanced at his friends. "None of us are exactly rolling in funds."

Whatever Barnaby, let alone Penelope, Jordan, and Ruth, had imagined, it wasn't that.

Similarly puzzled, Stokes recommended, "Start at the beginning. Where did you meet this gent, and what's his name?"

Gibson sat forward, his hands between his knees. "We were at one of the pubs we sometimes stop at when we've gone for a drive out of town."

Josh nodded. "The Fox Orsett, north of Tilbury."

Harrison explained, "We were all at King Edward's Grammar in Chelmsford—that was where we met—and sometimes, we drive out that way for the day. Our old turf, you might say."

"We stop at the Fox Orsett on the way back for a bite," Gibson concluded.

"We often stay for dinner and a few pints," Josh elaborated, "before driving back to town."

Gibson glanced at Harrison, somewhat expectantly.

Harrison caught the look, shrugged, and said, "One evening about two months back, we were sitting at our usual table and chatting over our pints when this gent—Cornelius Chesterton is his name—was going around asking if anyone knew of a warehouse available in the locality, somewhere in easy reach of Tilbury Dock." Harrison focused on Stokes. "As it happened, I knew of one. M'father's into buying up land on the outskirts of towns and waiting for builders to come calling. He's been doing it for years, quite successfully. I knew he'd bought this big old warehouse out on Brennan Road, just along from Fort Road, which runs straight to the docks, and I knew he'd left it empty. He said he couldn't be bothered renting it out—said it wasn't worth his time organizing that. So there seemed no reason Chesterton couldn't use the space and pay me, rather than Papa." Harrison glanced at the others on the sofa. "All in the family, as it were."

Barnaby inclined his head. "Quite enterprising of you."

Harrison flashed a grin. "We thought so." He glanced at Josh and Gibson.

Josh cleared his throat and earnestly explained, "Chesterton pays Harrison for using the warehouse, and he pays all three of us an extra stipend, a regular payment every fortnight, because he doesn't want us telling anyone that he's getting the warehouse on the cheap."

The three friends looked at the investigators as if what they'd just said was in no way remarkable.

Jordan broke the momentary silence. "What's Chesterton's business?"

When all three blinked owlishly, Stokes asked, "What is he using the warehouse to store?"

Harrison turned to Gibson and Josh, but from their expressions, neither had any idea. Harrison returned his gaze to the investigators and admitted, "We didn't think to ask, not at first, and then later, we felt... well, we got the impression, at least, that Chesterton thought it best we didn't know."

"I bet he did," Jordan muttered.

Josh blinked, then offered, "Corny—that's what he told us to call him —once, early on, mentioned that he dealt in machinery, and it was all hush-hush because he feared his competitors might come looking and learn of his new designs."

Harrison looked a mite sheepish. "It was a bit of a lark to us, but it didn't seem all that risky. It wasn't as if we had to do anything for Corny."

"And," Gibson added, "the arrangement gave us funds we didn't otherwise have, and Corny using an empty warehouse didn't hurt anyone, it seemed."

"Well," Harrison temporized, "perhaps Papa not getting a cut, but he doesn't care one jot about that warehouse, so it seemed perfectly all right that I got some benefit from it."

Barnaby glanced at Penelope and could tell that she was thinking the same as he—that these three were babes in the woods with very poor survival instincts.

Stokes, who was also regarding the three with faint disbelief, asked, "Did you ever tell anyone about Chesterton and the warehouse?"

All three shook their heads decisively.

"We took Chesterton's money to keep silent," Harrison said. "So we did."

Josh was nodding. "We keep our promises."

Clearly unable to keep silent any longer, Jordan asked, "Didn't it occur to you that Chesterton's payments were, in effect, bribes to ensure your silence?"

From the look on the three friends' faces, that possibility hadn't entered their brains until that moment.

That said, judging by their subsequent expressions, it seemed that the trio were finally starting to connect the dots.

An expression of enlightenment breaking across his face, Harrison said, "Oh! I say…"

Similarly, Josh's expression was one of dawning comprehension—an understanding that was not at all comfortable.

As for Gibson, as the reinterpreted facts slid into place in his mind, he looked increasingly ill.

Deciding it was time to refocus the trio's minds, Stokes asked, "When did you last meet this Chesterton?"

In a dead tone, Gibson replied, "On Monday night."

In stunned fashion, Josh nodded. "At the Fox, as usual."

Harrison hauled in a breath, then said, "We'd actually met him on Sunday evening. That was his usual night to pay us, but this time, he said his shipment had been split, and half of it delayed, and we'd need to come back the next night for our money. So we did—that was Monday night."

Barnaby caught the glance Stokes shot him, then Stokes looked at the three and asked, "Is it possible that on Sunday night, Thomas followed you to the Fox and saw you speaking with Chesterton?"

When all three frowned, plainly trying to imagine the scene, Barnaby added, "Would you necessarily have seen Thomas if he had?"

Penelope put in, "Was the place crowded?"

"And," Ruth added, "it's likely he wore a disguise—like a cap pulled low and an old coat and slouched so he didn't look as tall." She caught Gibson's eyes. "You know how good he was at passing in a crowd."

Gibson sighed. He looked at his friends, then returned his gaze to Stokes. "The Fox of an evening is always crowded. It has one of the best beers in the area and is on the road between Tilbury and town. You can imagine the clientele, and they're always jostling and noisy. If Thomas had been there…if he hadn't wanted us to see him, then we wouldn't have." He tipped his head toward Ruth. "As Ruthie said, he had a knack for passing among others unremarked."

Josh was looking troubled. "We hadn't imagined anyone would be following us, so we really weren't looking about at all."

That was understandable. Taking note of the changes in expressions and attitudes, Barnaby suspected that all three friends were finally realizing that they'd been taken advantage of and that, innocent though it had seemed, their association with Chesterton might have led to a situation that was anything but.

To their credit, all three, now thoroughly sober and serious, didn't give way to helplessness. Rather, their features firmed, and slowly, they sat straighter, literally stiffening their spines.

Then Harrison shook his shoulders slightly as if throwing off some yoke. He looked at his friends, then at the investigators. "I say, if you need to know what Corny is storing at the warehouse, why can't we just go and look? I'm the son of the warehouse's owner. I can't see any reason why I can't take you there and demand entrance."

Josh was nodding. He glanced at Gibson. "Let's go and see." He looked at Stokes with resolution in his eyes. "I think we all need to know what Corny is hiding in that warehouse."

Gibson also nodded. "We do." He looked at Stokes, then at Barnaby and the others. His gaze was haunted, but determination shone through. "Is there any reason we can't go to the warehouse right now?"

None of the investigators had any fault to find with that notion.

Everyone rose, and mere minutes later, they were out on the pavement, piling into the carriage and the hackneys Jordan and Gibson hailed.

CHAPTER 8

Consumed by curiosity, Penelope held Barnaby's hand as, with their expanded group now including Gibson, Harrison, and Josh as well as O'Donnell, Morgan, Walsh, and a bevy of constables Stokes had summoned, they marched up the gravel track leading to the large doors of Harrison's father's rather ramshackle warehouse, set back from Brennan Road.

The constabulary had arrived minutes behind them, having been roused to action by a message from Stokes ferried hotfoot to Scotland Yard by a runner he'd dispatched before climbing into the carriage in Falcon Street.

As soon as the reinforcements had joined them, Stokes had led the company up the short track, with Harrison, Gibson, and Josh flanking him and Barnaby, Penelope, Jordan, and Ruth following, with the uniformed police at their backs.

The warehouse was entirely unprepossessing and appeared to have stood for decades. Its planks were worn gray with the weather, and the roof looked decidedly rickety. Interestingly, a thick chain was looped through the large iron handles on the doors, holding them shut, and the chain was secured with an impressively large and heavy padlock.

Beside one door, a rough shack abutted the front wall. As they neared, a beefy man came out of the shack, his eyes narrowing as he took in their numbers. He settled into a wide-legged stance a few paces before the warehouse doors and, politely enough, bobbed his head. "Can I help ye?"

Stokes halted a yard before the man. "I'm Inspector Stokes of Scotland Yard." He tipped his head toward the warehouse. "You'll oblige me by opening the doors and showing us what's inside."

The man frowned. "I don't rightly know as I can do that. Pretty sure the master wouldn't want me to."

On the words, two even bigger and heavier men came out of the shack. They sauntered closer, but hung back a yard or so behind their mate.

Stokes barely took note of them. Focusing on the first man, Stokes smiled his sharpest, most shark-like smile. "I really don't care what your master thinks, and"—he gestured to Harrison, standing beside him—"this man is the owner's representative. In case you don't know, the owner has a legal right to enter at any time."

Penelope approved of that tack, and it certainly gave the three men arrayed against them pause.

Stokes didn't give them more time to think, much less argue. He called over his shoulder, "O'Donnell."

As the police contingent streamed forward, still addressing the first man, Stokes calmly continued, "I suggest you unlock the door. Then you can wait here with your mates and my constables while the rest of us examine what your master—Mr. Chesterton, I assume—has stored inside."

The man eyed the police gathering around him and his mates, then glanced at the pair of bruisers behind him. After a second, he swung back to face Stokes. "Chesterton didn't say anything about us having to deal with the p'lice, and what's more, he ain't paying us to, so…" He turned and lumbered toward the shack. "Lemme get the key."

While he was fetching it, Stokes delegated six constables to remain with the three men and sent three more to scout around the warehouse.

The watchman returned with a key in his huge hand.

Stokes waved him to the doors.

The man sighed and plodded to the padlock, unlocked it and pulled it away, then unlooped the chains, freeing the doors.

Morgan and Walsh were waiting to step in and haul the heavy doors wide.

Along with the others assembled, Penelope peered into a dimly lit cavern and waited for her eyes to adjust.

Stokes sent the watchman to join his fellows, then led the way into the gloom.

All their company eagerly followed, everyone as keen as Penelope to learn what secrets lay hidden in the warehouse.

They halted a few yards inside. Weak light streamed through the open doorway, but as their eyes adjusted, they could see well enough—well enough to study the stacks of wooden crates that seemed to cover quite half the floor space of the cavernous building.

Each crate was about four feet long and two feet square on the ends.

Penelope bustled forward to examine the nearest more closely.

With his head raised, Barnaby had been doing a quick survey. "I estimate there are something like a hundred crates all told."

Stokes was examining a crate when Penelope exclaimed, "There are marks burned into the sides of the crates—like brands."

Jordan crouched to peer at one such mark, then he whistled and rose. He looked at Stokes, then at Barnaby. "I think these are guns. Rifles. The type that are used by the army."

Harrison's eyes flew wide. "Guns?"

Josh looked equally startled. "But...what would Corny want with guns?"

Gibson was frowning. "More to the point, why be so secretive and hide them away?"

Jordan supplied the answer. "These have to be contraband." He looked at Stokes. "Legal gun trading is done via the government docks, not Tilbury."

Barnaby said, "Tilbury Dock is primarily used by merchant shipping." He met Stokes's gaze. "Almost certainly, these are en route to be smuggled out of the country."

"Are they made here?" Penelope was still studying the burned-on marks. "Or are they imported and being sold on?"

"An excellent question," Stokes said.

"Sir," Walsh called from deeper in the warehouse. "There's an open crate here and another way in. You might want to take a look."

They found Walsh and Morgan waiting by the rearmost stack of crates.

Walsh pointed at the wall toward the rear corner of the warehouse. "The rear door's been forced, then put back to look like it's still secure."

"Presumably," Stokes said, "that's how Thomas got in."

"Most likely he came to this stack," Morgan said. "It's the closest." He gestured at the uppermost crate, which was open. "The lid was loose. Lifted right off."

Lying inside on a bed of straw were six rifles.

Barnaby reached into the crate and lifted one out. Stokes and Jordan did the same.

Almost immediately, Stokes grunted. He pointed to a small plaque affixed to the base of the rifle's stock. "These are Enfields," he growled.

Upturning the rifle he was holding, Barnaby squinted at its plaque. "From the Royal Small Arms Factory, no less."

"That's not what the crates say," Jordan pointed out.

"And that," Stokes informed them all, "means that these are not official production."

Unclear on the implication, Barnaby ventured, "So these are unofficial production...meaning they've been diverted from the proper channels?"

Grimly, Stokes nodded. "Sadly, there are always those who think to make a quick quid on the side."

"Well"—Penelope spread her arms and turned, gesturing to the crates all around—"this certainly qualifies as a nefarious activity. Thomas was perfectly correct in labeling it that."

Stokes shook his head, then turned away and started giving orders to his men to arrest the three watchmen and take them to the Yard.

That done, Stokes faced the three younger gentlemen. "You said Chesterton expected a part of his delivery on Monday?"

All three nodded. "That's what he said," Harrison confirmed.

"And," Gibson added, "he met us on Monday evening, all bright and chipper, and paid us with a smile on his face."

Obviously, Gibson now saw through Chesterton's cheery demeanor.

Jordan offered, "That sounds as if someone connected with the delivery paid him. Presumably for the storage and watchmen and possibly for arranging transport to Tilbury Dock."

Barnaby was eyeing the crates. "That also makes it likely that Chesterton will move this lot on soon."

Stokes grunted. "Let's see what the watchmen have to say."

Along with Stokes, Jordan, and the three younger gentlemen, Barnaby walked out of the warehouse. Penelope and Ruth trailed behind, quietly discussing what their discovery might mean.

Outside, the three deflated and slightly bruised watchmen were having their hands tied behind their backs. All three looked thoroughly disgusted.

Stokes halted before the group and addressed the man who'd first approached them. "When is this lot"—Stokes tipped his head toward the warehouse—"scheduled to be moved on?"

Through narrowed eyes, the watchman studied Stokes, then glanced at his mates.

One lifted his heavy shoulders in a shrug. "Chesterton's done us no good. This was supposed to be no trouble, yet here we are."

The other nodded. "Tell 'im. No 'arm to us either way, I'm thinking."

"Sound advice," Stokes said. "If you cooperate, I'll put in a good word with the magistrate."

The watchman pursed his lips, then nodded. "Fair enough. Chesterton's set it up for tonight. It's all arranged. The drays arrive about half after nine. He's usually here by then, counting the crates."

Jordan asked, "Did you ever hear the names of any of those in charge of the deliveries or managing the transfer to the docks?"

The three men shook their heads, and the watchman said, "We were told to stay in the shack at such times, which suited us."

One of his mates added, "With crews of that sort, we didn't really want to know more 'n we had to."

Jordan grimaced and met Stokes's eyes.

Stokes dipped his head to the three men. "Thank you." To the constables, he said, "Take them away."

The constables obliged and, after prodding the men to get them started, accompanied them down the track to where a police wagon waited on the street.

With the captives dealt with, Stokes turned to the younger gentlemen. "Now, as for you three, you need to avoid this area entirely and make sure you don't run into Chesterton. We'll be here tonight in force, and hopefully before midnight, we'll have him in our tender care."

"Will we be called into court to give evidence?" Josh asked.

Stokes waggled his head. "That depends on how sensible Chesterton is, but it's possible none of you will be called as witnesses." He glanced at the rest of their company. "We have more than enough respectable witnesses without dragging you three in."

Josh appeared intensely relieved, but Harrison and Gibson weren't as forgiving.

Harrison looked hopefully at Stokes. "Can't we help you catch him?"

Barnaby stepped in to save Stokes from issuing an adamant "No," instead pointing out, "Given he's been paying you to keep his secret, that might not be wise."

Jordan elaborated, "We can't be sure who else might turn up, so best if you three stay far away."

"Amen," Stokes muttered.

Harrison and Gibson exchanged disappointed glances, but reluctantly agreed that they would return to Falcon Street and remain there until the following day.

"We may as well be off, then." Gibson looked at Harrison and Josh. "Gun running." He shook his head. "Even in my wildest dreams, I would never have imagined it was that."

When no one encouraged them to remain, the three nodded to all and started to trudge down the track. Then Gibson paused and looked back. "Ruthie?"

Jordan glanced at Ruth, standing beside Penelope, and called to Gibson, "I'll see Miss Cardwell home."

When Gibson arched a brow at Ruth, she hesitated, then nodded. "I'll be fine. Go—and keep your head down."

Barnaby didn't need to see his wife's expression to know what she was thinking.

They watched the three men walk to the street where several hackneys, having delivered passengers to the out-of-the-way address, had loitered, hoping to secure fares to take back to town.

Once the three had climbed into a hackney and it had turned and rattled off, Jordan looked at Ruth. "We should probably head off, too. There's nothing we can accomplish by staying, and your mother must be wondering where you are. Your shopping trip has taken hours."

"Oh! Yes—I'd forgotten." Ruth turned to Penelope. "I really better go."

"Of course." Penelope squeezed Ruth's hand and beamed at Jordan. "No doubt we'll be following you shortly."

Stokes looked up from dealing with his constables. "I'd appreciate it if both of you would join us at Albemarle Street tomorrow morning at nine. Barnaby and I will need to share what we learn from Chesterton's arrest tonight and combine that with what we've already gleaned before we formally interrogate the man."

Ruth glanced at Jordan, then both readily agreed.

Jordan waved Ruth down the track. "Let's grab one of those hackneys before they get tired of waiting and take off."

Barnaby smiled as Ruth and Jordan made their farewells. Then

Barnaby watched his wife stare intently at the pair as they walked close beside each other, rather studiously not touching, all the way to the street.

~

Jordan led Ruth to the best-looking hackney of the three lined up on the verge. It was the same hackney he'd hailed in Falcon Street and had proved to be well sprung.

He handed Ruth into the carriage and called to the jarvey, "Finsbury Circus."

The jarvey smiled and saluted with his whip, entirely willing to embark on such a lengthy trip. The instant Jordan had climbed aboard and settled beside Ruth on the padded bench, the jarvey's whip snapped, and his horse stepped smartly out. In seconds, they were bowling through Tilbury, then swung north onto the London Road.

They'd traveled that far in silence, both no doubt thinking of the recent discoveries and their implications. But as they left Tilbury behind and the horse's pace picked up, Ruth said, "I own to being rather surprised by the inspector's invitation to join the meeting tomorrow."

Jordan shot her an amused glance. "You shouldn't be. You're by far and away our best source of insight into Thomas's thoughts and likely reactions." He paused, then facing forward, added, "Being able to judge with some degree of confidence how he might have acted in a given situation—for instance, discovering those guns—will be crucial to figuring out what he did next." *And presumably, that was what led to him being killed.*

A faint frown in her eyes, Ruth glanced at him. "I'm fairly certain that what he did next was send that letter to your employer asking for advice."

Jordan conceded, "That seems likely. He sent the letter on Monday, so it must have been on the Sunday night that he followed Chesterton to the warehouse."

"Oh, look!" Ruth leaned forward, staring to the right. "There's the pub."

They were crossing Orsett Heath, and separated from the road by a decent-sized yard, a squat, whitewashed building with multiple bay windows beneath a steeply sloping roof sported a sign across the front labeling it "The Fox." There appeared to be two main doors, one at either end of the almost triangular façade.

"That's a good size," Jordan remarked, "and close to Tilbury but not within the town. I imagine that on any given night, it would host a large and varied crowd."

Ruth nodded. "Judging by the windows, it looks to have multiple public rooms inside." She sat back as the pub fell behind. "A crowded place with adjoining rooms. Thomas wouldn't have found it difficult to follow and watch Gibson without being spotted by Gibson, Harrison, or Josh."

A second later, she heaved a deep sigh. "I miss Thomas." She looked out to the side. "He was…always there. The steady rock the rest of the family leaned on. I might be the eldest, and Gibson after me, but Thomas was our anchor, and with him gone, the family—all of us—feel…adrift."

Jordan waited in silence. There was little he could say.

After a moment, her gaze still on the passing landscape, Ruth went on, "Bobby is still immature, and as you saw today, Gibson is also naive in many ways. He and Bobby seem to have not quite grown up—our father was like that, too. Gibson and Bobby take after him, while Thomas and I take after our mother. We're the responsible ones, while the other two are…not bad-hearted at all but flighty. Difficult to rely on."

We need to find another anchor.

Jordan heard the words she didn't say. He clasped his hands firmly against the compelling urge to reach out and close his hand about hers and tell her he was willing to audition for the part.

That he felt such an impulse—heard the words ready-formed in his brain—was something of a shock. A development startling enough to make him pause and think—and then firmly set aside the issue for later examination. Regardless of what he might actually want, now was not the time to make any sort of advance.

Keeping his gaze fixed forward, he racked his brain for some innocuous topic of conversation to fill the minutes to Finsbury Circus.

Barnaby crouched beside Stokes behind a stack of crates in the dank, dark confines of the old warehouse. They'd found a spot along the front wall where the planks had warped enough to allow them to peer out and watch the track and view any activity in the yard in front of the doors. Else-where in the warehouse, several groups of Stokes's men were likewise waiting in the dark.

They'd moved into position half an hour ago, along with the rest of the sizeable force Stokes had assembled and deployed, and the warehouse was now effectively surrounded while they waited for Chesterton and his drivers to arrive.

The night sky was cloudy with the moon well screened, which was a blessing. The land around the warehouse was relatively flat, with only the occasional bushes and clumps of vegetation dotted about. Nevertheless, those delegated to remain outside had found somewhere to crouch out of sight, and as timepieces ticked past nine o'clock, all were alert and growing increasingly impatient.

Barnaby glanced at Stokes, a shadowy presence in the darkness, then grinned to himself. At Penelope's suggestion, Griselda, Stokes, and their family had joined the Adairs for dinner, arriving early enough so that the four children could take their meals together as well. After presiding over that event in the nursery, the adults had left their offspring to play and returned to the peace downstairs. They'd dined at half past six, and Penelope and Griselda had waved Barnaby and Stokes off at a quarter past seven. It had been transparently obvious that both Penelope and Griselda had wanted to come—to be there to see Chesterton captured—but they'd reluctantly accepted their lot and consented to remain in town and await the men's return.

In truth, the only reason for Barnaby's presence was the possibility that someone else would arrive with Chesterton, someone who might be Chesterton's coconspirator, and legally speaking, having a reliable and unimpeachable non-police witness might be a very good thing.

Other than observing, there was little for Barnaby to do. Stokes and his men were, by now, experts in staging successful traps. In addition to those inside the warehouse, ready to witness and deal with whatever transpired, the bulk of the force had spread to right and left of the building, in position to close in once their quarry had halted before the doors, hemming them in with a ring of blue.

O'Donnell had taken on the role of primary watchman, the one with the key to the padlock on the chain securing the doors. It would be largely up to him to string Chesterton along until the drays arrived. The Commissioner wanted the entire crew taken up, not just Chesterton.

Stokes suddenly shifted, leaning closer to the wall as he peered through a chink between two planks. Following Stokes's lead and staring out through a gap a little farther along the wall, at first, Barnaby could see nothing, then a horse materialized out of the gloom shrouding the track and came plodding toward the warehouse.

An average-sized, solidly built man swayed slightly in the saddle. Oblivious to the many eyes watching him, he rode into the yard before the warehouse doors. He halted his mount near the wall on the other side of the doors to the shack and dismounted. Dropping in rather ungainly fashion to the ground, he looped the reins through a ring set into the wall, then turned toward the shack. "Willis! Where are you, man?"

O'Donnell, garbed in civilian clothes that had seen better days, came out of the shack and stared at the man. "Be you Chesterton, then?"

Chesterton frowned. "Yes. Who the devil are you?"

"I'm Willis's cousin." O'Donnell came forward, pulling the padlock key from his pocket. "He's been taken ill—the whole family, really—and he begged me to stand in for him. Just for tonight, mind. He'll be back tomorrow."

Chesterton huffed, but was clearly uninterested in his hireling's health. He waited with reined impatience as O'Donnell made a performance of freeing the doors, then Chesterton seized one handle and, together with O'Donnell, hauled the doors wide open.

After kicking a stone into place to hold the door in position, Chesterton walked toward the gaping maw of the warehouse. "The drays should be along any minute. Get them to line up out here, wagon parallel to the doorway. That way, we can be quick about loading. The drivers know the drill."

O'Donnell tugged his forelock. "Aye, sir."

With all arranged to his liking, Chesterton strode into the warehouse.

With Stokes, Barnaby remained crouched by the front wall, screened from Chesterton's immediate sight by a stack of crates.

They listened as Chesterton went straight to a shelf on the other side of the front wall. A lamp had been left there, along with a box of matches, and within a minute, Chesterton had the lamp burning. He picked it up, turned, and walked to the nearest crate.

Peering out from their hiding place, Barnaby and Stokes saw Chesterton smile and affectionately pat the crate on top of the first stack, then hoisting the lamp, he started walking slowly down the central aisle, counting the crates in the stacks along one side.

Chesterton was halfway down the central aisle when the sound of rattling wheels reached through the gloom, followed by the unmistakable clop of hooves and the jingle of harness as horses were reined in, then O'Donnell could be heard directing the drivers as to where to halt their wagons.

Seconds later, two hefty men in long coats came striding into the warehouse.

Watching from their hiding spot, Stokes and Barnaby tensed.

"Good. You're here." Chesterton raised the lamp and pointed to the line of crates. "All of these are to go. Load them up and take them to the dock. By the time you get there, *The Viscount* should have come alongside and be waiting to take them on board."

"Right you are, sir." One of the men saluted, then the pair moved to pick up the crate on top of the nearest stack.

Shouts and yells erupted outside.

The three in the warehouse froze, then swung to face the door.

For several seconds, disorientating sounds of pandemonium rolled through the open doorway.

Then Chesterton cursed and, with his two helpers, turned to flee or possibly hide, only to come face-to-face with Morgan, Walsh, and several other constables, all with truncheons in their hands and grim expressions on their faces.

The pair of drivers immediately halted and held up their hands in surrender.

With rather more to lose, lamp still in hand, Chesterton whirled to flee through the doorway, possibly thinking to slip away through the melee engulfing the yard outside.

Instead, he found himself facing Stokes with Barnaby at his side. They stood squarely blocking the aisle, and with his crates of illicit guns piled on either side, Chesterton had nowhere to run.

No way to escape.

Barnaby could see that realization dawn on the man, and Chesterton's shoulders slumped.

"Damn!" he muttered and let the lamp hang.

Stokes stepped forward, took the lamp from him, handed it to Barnaby, and arrested Chesterton for gun running. "And," Stokes added with grim relish, "who knows what other crimes we'll find you guilty of?"

Barnaby saw confusion pass across Chesterton's face, but then Morgan came up and took him in charge, and together with Stokes, Barnaby walked outside to see what had transpired in the yard.

Six drays had turned up. The drivers and their helpers, at least two for every wagon, had all been captured and were being corralled in the center of the yard. O'Donnell was in charge of taking names and, once the prisoners' hands had been securely tied, sending them off in the care of a constable, to be loaded into the police wagons that had been summoned from where they'd been waiting in concealment farther up Fort Road.

The next half hour and more went in organizing the prisoners, and they also had to return the horses and drays to Tilbury. Stokes had decided that the wisest course was to order constables to drive the horses and wagons to the drivers' families, but that meant sending a police coach along to ferry the constables back to Scotland Yard.

Barnaby stood to one side of the yard and watched, listened, and thought.

Finally, Stokes was free and came to join him, pausing only to beckon to Morgan and Walsh to bring their principal prisoner out of the warehouse.

The yard was largely empty when the constables, each holding one of Chesterton's arms, marched him out into the light of the waning moon.

Chesterton looked slightly rumpled, but appeared defeated and, if anything, puzzled.

When the trio halted before Stokes and Barnaby, Chesterton shook his head and looked at them. "This was such a sweet operation. What gave us away?"

Barnaby glanced at Stokes and sensed the swift internal debate Stokes waged before he replied, "Killing Thomas Cardwell."

Chesterton's bafflement was undeniably genuine. "Who?"

Having shut and locked the warehouse doors and left the key with the four constables who would remain on guard until more wagons were sent from London to remove the crates of illegal guns, O'Donnell came up and saluted. "All locked tight, and the others are all away."

Stokes looked at Chesterton, then said, "We can discuss Cardwell's demise tomorrow. For tonight, sleep well in your cell."

Stokes nodded to his men. "Take him away."

Standing beside Stokes, Barnaby watched as Chesterton was led to a police wagon reserved solely for him. The constables loaded him into the closed coach, and Walsh followed, then Morgan took the reins and, with O'Donnell beside him on the box, sent the coach rumbling down the track before turning for London.

Relieved by how well the evening had gone, with their hands sunk in their pockets, Barnaby and Stokes strolled slowly down the track to where the Adair carriage with Phelps up top waited in the street.

Barnaby glanced at Stokes. "Chesterton has absolutely no idea who Thomas Cardwell is."

Stokes grunted, but didn't disagree. Several paces on, he offered, "Chesterton has no idea, but someone connected with this not-so-little enterprise might have realized the threat Cardwell posed. And no, I don't know how, but before we go much farther, we need to find some concrete evidence that Cardwell did, indeed, follow his brother to the Fox on Sunday night and that, after seeing Chesterton with Gibson, Thomas followed Chesterton here, to the warehouse."

His gaze on the ground before his feet, Barnaby nodded. "If Cardwell never made it here and never saw the guns, then the gun running wasn't the reason he turned to Roscoe for help."

"Exactly." Stokes grimaced. "As much as I don't want to think it, there's a chance that Cardwell's reason for contacting Roscoe was something else. However, arguing against that, if ever there was a reason for someone of Cardwell's limited experience to consult Roscoe over how to alert the authorities to a nefarious activity, then this caper surely fits the bill."

Barnaby huffed. "Nefarious activity. Cardwell was right in labeling it that."

CHAPTER 9

When the investigators gathered the following morning in Albemarle Street, together with Jordan and Ruth, Penelope found herself hanging on Barnaby's and Stokes's every word as they described the events of the previous night.

She hadn't heard the details before. She'd been sound asleep when Barnaby had returned, and this morning, given that they expected to be out for most of the day, they'd devoted their breakfast hours to the children.

Stokes ended the recitation with the unexpectedly glum admission, "However, when I mentioned Thomas and his death, Chesterton plainly had no idea who I was talking about."

Barnaby glanced at Ruth. "He truly didn't seem to know who Thomas was."

"Let alone how Thomas's death led us to him and the warehouse," Stokes said. "Chesterton couldn't figure out how we'd rumbled his scheme. He was genuinely puzzled and confused."

"Well, then." Penelope sat straighter and looked at Ruth and Jordan. "I, for one, am keen to view Chesterton for myself and try my hand at teasing more information from him."

Everyone was of similar mind, and in short order, Penelope, Barnaby, and Stokes were in the carriage and rolling over the cobbles, with Jordan and Ruth following in a hackney.

They arrived at Scotland Yard and congregated in the foyer while

Stokes arranged to have Chesterton brought up from the cells to one of the ground-floor interview rooms. Once Chesterton had been installed, Stokes returned and escorted their small group through the corridors to a door toward the end of one wing. Stokes opened the door and led them in.

Penelope followed, eager to get her first view of Chesterton. Her gaze fell on the ruddy-faced man in a rumpled suit who was seated in the lone chair on the opposite side of the simple table. The man's features were fleshy, and his suit was made of plaid in a bilious shade of mustard.

Her eyes widening, Penelope stared as she trailed Stokes to the line of chairs set along the table's nearer side. Stokes and Barnaby had described Chesterton as being in early middle age, stocky and solidly built, and he was definitely all that, but what neither had mentioned was Chesterton's shock of wiry carroty-red hair.

Bountiful orange curls, thick and dense, covered his head, and it was instantly apparent that no hat could ever be made to sit securely upon such a springy cushion.

Chesterton had been sitting slumped, his gaze on his manacled hands, but as they entered, he heaved a sigh and glanced up and was clearly surprised to see Penelope and, behind her, Barnaby, Ruth, and Jordan.

As they all filed in and claimed seats, Chesterton sat back and stared. Once they'd settled, a puzzled frown in his eyes, he asked, "What's all this, then?"

Stokes replied, "The Yard has several consultants assisting us with this case." He then proceeded to read out the charges the Crown intended bringing against Chesterton, namely gun running and smuggling. Stokes fixed Chesterton with a direct look. "We caught you red-handed with the guns and, what's more, attempting to move them on. We also have your accomplices in the cells, and they've informed us that they're willing to trade information for leniency."

Chesterton made a sound of disgust, but from his expression, it was clear he didn't doubt Stokes's assertion.

"Now," Stokes continued, "as to the reason for our consultants being present this morning, they're here because the brother of one of your unsuspecting dupes—the three you paid to keep quiet about you using the warehouse—was murdered on Tuesday morning, and our information is that the killing happened shortly after he—the brother—followed you from the Fox to the warehouse and, apparently, discovered what you were storing there. It seems the brother worked out what you were doing and planned to take steps to bring the matter to the authorities' attention."

Chesterton's confusion had only grown as he attempted to follow Stokes's reasoning. "You think that the brother was murdered because he'd learned about the guns?" He frowned. "But…by whom?"

Stokes looked at him pointedly. "We were assuming by you."

Chesterton's jaw dropped, then he snapped it shut and blustered, "Me? I don't even know who this geezer is! How could I have killed him?"

Barnaby asked, "You didn't see him following you from the Fox or, later, slipping inside the warehouse and finding the guns and think to follow him home?"

"No!" Chesterton paused, then grudgingly added, "I had no idea anyone had followed me back to the warehouse. I didn't have a clue that anyone who shouldn't have known had learned about the guns." He stared at them as if trying to force them to believe him, then his face cleared. "Well, obviously, I had no clue, because if I had, I would have moved the guns straightaway, and I wouldn't have walked so blindly into your trap last evening, would I?"

Studying Chesterton, Barnaby said, "You might have left the guns where they were if you thought you'd killed the man before he'd had a chance to pass on the information."

Chesterton swore beneath his breath. "You've got that wrong—I never even knew someone had rumbled my patch."

A moment passed, then Chesterton transferred his gaze to Stokes. "Look. My business runs on secrecy. That means the fewer people who know anything about what I'm doing, the better. That's why I paid off those three likely lads. They were easy to appease and never asked difficult questions—dupes, just like you called them. But killing anyone, no matter what threat they might pose, is guaranteed to bring the rozzers sniffing around, and that's the last thing I'd ever want. Like I said, if I'd known someone had found the warehouse and the guns, I would've moved the lot quick smart and set up somewhere else. I wouldn't have wasted time trying to hunt down some geezer I'd never met." He glanced curiously at Jordan and Ruth. "I don't even know which of the likely lads' families this brother belonged to."

To Penelope, Chesterton sounded a touch desperate, but his arguments were reasonable and, therefore, convincing. And to her eyes, at least, he was never going to be confused with a gentleman, and with that shock of hair, he'd never be able to wear a top hat, let alone pull off a disguise.

To drive home the point, she asked, "Do you wear a hat? Ever?"

Chesterton started to raise a hand to his curls, then was reminded of the manacles and stopped. "No. No hats for me. They just won't stay on my head."

Penelope glanced at Barnaby, then at Stokes. Both faintly grimaced. Regardless of his involvement in the gun-running scheme, Chesterton wasn't Thomas Cardwell's murderer.

Jordan leaned forward and asked, "You say you value secrecy highly, so think back to Sunday evening. If someone in the Fox had been watching you interact with those three likely lads, could that someone later have followed you to the warehouse?"

From Chesterton's expression, it was plain to all that he—or rather, his pride—wished he could dismiss the suggestion. Eventually, however, he admitted, "I suppose it's possible. I hadn't thought that anyone might follow me from the Fox. The clientele there generally keeps its nose out of other people's business, so I wasn't on guard. I'd had a few pints as well, so..." He shrugged. "I can't say that couldn't have happened."

Jordan glanced at Stokes, then sat back.

Penelope judged that, all in all, Chesterton had been truthful, at least in what he'd put into words.

Apparently thinking they'd learned all they would, Stokes asked Chesterton, "Is there anything more you'd like to tell us?"

Chesterton regarded Stokes levelly, then stated, "You've got me to rights with the gun running and smuggling. I even gave you the ship's name, not that I meant to, but still. All that admitted to, I swear on my mother's grave that I've never killed anyone." His gaze flicked to Jordan and Ruth. "And I never met this brother who was killed, either."

Stokes studied Chesterton for a moment, then nodded. "Duly noted." He signaled to the constables that they could take Chesterton back to the cells, then rose and led their small band out of the room.

Stokes paused in the corridor and, once they'd all come through the door, suggested, "Let's go upstairs to a more congenial setting and decide what to try next."

◁◦▷

Minutes later, they settled into chairs in Stokes's office.

"First," Penelope said, "can we all agree that Chesterton is definitely not our unknown gentleman-cum-murderer?"

Barnaby grimaced. "Not with that riot of hair. It wasn't as evident last night, in the poor light."

"Let alone that he wouldn't easily pass for a gentleman," Stokes said. "His posture, the way he walks and talks—that observant baker wouldn't have mistaken him for a gentleman, even if he'd donned the right sort of coat."

"And," Jordan added, "Thomas might have recognized Chesterton, but he wouldn't have readily unlocked his office door and invited him inside."

Stokes tipped his head, conceding the point. "I also can't see Chesterton being in a position to hire an assassin who would pass for a gentleman, either."

"I thought," Barnaby said, "that he made a convincing argument that if he had known someone had learned about the guns, then the first thing he would have done was move them." He looked at the others. "The guns must represent a considerable amount of money to Chesterton."

Jordan nodded. "Even if he later thought to kill Thomas, however he could bring that about—which isn't easy to see—regardless, he would have moved the guns. They wouldn't have been in the warehouse for us to find. I can't see any self-respecting smuggler leaving his goods sitting in a hidey-hole after he suspected someone unexpected had learned they were there."

Stokes grunted in agreement. "So where does that leave us on this gray March morning?" He looked at the others expectantly.

Penelope stated, "It all comes back to our unknown man—our suspected murderer. Who is he?" She looked around the circle of faces. "If not Gibson or Chesterton, who else could he be?"

Jordan grimaced. "Theoretically, our murderer could be Harrison or Josh." He glanced at Ruth. "Thomas knew both, I take it?"

She nodded. "Thomas was a year behind them at King Edward's, so they all knew each other from their years there, and of course, they were Gibson's friends, so Thomas met them when they occasionally visited with Gibson."

"So," Stokes mused, "if it had been one of them, Thomas would have readily invited them into his office."

Penelope wrinkled her nose. "I really can't see it being either of them."

"I can't, either," Ruth said. "From all I saw, Harrison and Josh were always quite friendly toward Thomas." She paused, then added, "I think that, like Gibson, they were a bit in awe of Thomas, in that he was a year younger but had established a successful business, and they hadn't yet accomplished anything in that vein."

Stokes huffed. "Let's not overcomplicate things. We have an unknown gentleman and have yet to discover who he is. All we actually know is that Thomas appeared to recognize him well enough to invite him into his office."

Jordan was frowning. "I think we should accept that the coat and hat weren't any sort of disguise. Our unknown man didn't enter Thomas's office expecting to kill him. He used Thomas's letter knife to do the deed. He hadn't come prepared with a knife of his own."

Barnaby nodded. "An excellent point. Our unknown man isn't any type of hired killer. However, he is a gentleman—that much is certain."

"So what other gentleman could be involved in this case?" Penelope asked.

No one leapt to answer, then Ruth cleared her throat and said, "I did wonder… Well, I realized Gibson had more money than I could account for and told Thomas, and he went looking—" She broke off, drew in a breath, then went on, "What if Harrison's or Josh's mother or father realized the same thing—that their son was spending more than he should have had?"

"Another excellent point." Stokes pulled out his notebook. "Do you happen to know who Moubray's and Keeble's parents are and where they live?"

"Sir Ulysses Moubray is Harrison's father," Ruth said. "He and his wife live in a house in Frederick Street—number twelve, I think. And Josh's father is Mr. Earnest Keeble. He's a widower and has a house on the north side of Myddleton Square."

Both addresses were of gentry areas of similar social status to Finsbury Circus.

"Thank you." Stokes looked at Barnaby and Penelope. "You two are unquestionably our best choice for interviewing the Moubrays and Mr. Keeble. You might use the pretext of informing them of their sons' apparently unwitting involvement in the gun-running scheme. You can assure them that their sons are not suspects and are viewed as innocent dupes in the matter, but we felt that they should be informed, just in case the news sheets inadvertently learn of the incident. That should give you an opening to gauge their reactions to the news."

Penelope was nodding. "And get some idea whether the existence of the warehouse and the guns is, in fact, news to them."

"Indeed." Stokes added, "No need to mention Thomas's murder unless it suits you."

Barnaby said, "Even if one of the families had learned about the guns, it's difficult to see why that would lead either father to—in an impulsive act—kill Thomas. Both Harrison and Josh denied ever mentioning the scheme to their parents, and having once been a younger gentleman, I believe them."

Beneath her breath, Penelope muttered, "You were never that young."

Fleetingly, Barnaby smiled, then went on, "However, I agree it's best that we're thorough and investigate all possibilities."

"Especially as," Stokes grumped, "in this case, we seem to have so few of them." He glanced at the others. "I'm going to be tied up here for several hours—probably the rest of the day—dealing with Chesterton and his associates and the ensuing reports."

Penelope stated, "We'll interview the Moubrays and Keeble, then head back to Albemarle Street."

"Meanwhile"—Stokes looked at Ruth and Jordan—"can I leave you two to inform the Cardwells of the current situation? You can tell Mrs. Cardwell that I believe that our three dupes are unlikely to be named in court, but as with the Moubrays and Keeble, the family needs to be aware of the potential exposure and be prepared to weather it."

Ruth nodded and glanced at Jordan.

He met her gaze, then turned to Stokes. "I'll help Ruth with the explanations, then"—he switched his gaze to Barnaby and Penelope—"I'll drop by Albemarle Street to learn how your interviews played out."

Barnaby and Penelope nodded.

Stokes shut his notebook. "Right, then. I'll be around there as soon as I get free. I, too, am curious as to what you might learn, and by then, I'll be sorely in need of some light relief."

Penelope stood beside Barnaby as he rapped the handsome brass knocker that hung on the door of the Moubray residence. It was one of a row of terrace houses in a style common to the area. Every house in the row was neat and well-kept, and the front stoops were scrupulously scrubbed.

A small weeping tree graced the handkerchief-sized plot between the wrought-iron fence and the front door. The short, paved path that led from gate to door looked freshly scrubbed as well.

The door was opened by a footman in standard attire. "Yes, sir?"

Barnaby replied, "Mr. and Mrs. Adair. We're assisting the Metropolitan Police with a particular case and would like to speak with Sir Ulysses and Mrs. Moubray."

Understandably, the footman blinked. He hesitated for a moment, then pulled the door wider. "Please, come into the drawing room, and I'll inform Sir Ulysses and the mistress that you're here."

Good. They're at home. Penelope looked about her with unfettered interest as they were shown into a slightly fussy drawing room where the upholstery was all flowered chintz. At least, Penelope thought, it was in one pattern only, and the apricot and peach hues blended well with the warm tones of the woodwork. A vase on a small round table placed before the window held a profusion of daffodils and other early blooms.

All in all, the room gave the impression of being sunny and airy despite not being well-endowed with windows.

She sat on the sofa, and Barnaby took up a stance before the fireplace, and the footman whisked off to notify his employers of their arrival.

Three minutes later—long enough to appear not to have leapt to respond—Sir Ulysses Moubray walked into the room. An imposing older gentleman of fifty-something summers, he possessed an impressive mane of steel-gray hair and a harsh-featured face with a distinctly square jaw. From beneath wiry beetling brows, shrewd blue eyes regarded Barnaby and Penelope with curiosity and a touch of suspicion.

Sir Ulysses's military past showed in his bearing, in the way he held his shoulders and kept his spine ramrod straight regardless of his age and the natural tendency in one so tall to stoop. He was dressed in a fashion best described as studiously conservative—expensive attire that sought to never draw attention to the wearer.

The same attitude of seeking to blend into the background might, with accuracy, have been applied to his wife. A short, slightly dumpy lady with mousy-colored curls and soft features, she entered at Sir Ulysses's heels. As she was garbed in a gown of muted peach twill, it would have been easy to overlook her presence, but after taking in the lady's bright brown eyes and wide-awake expression, Penelope had to wonder if Mrs. Moubray going unnoticed was more by design than accident.

The notion piqued Penelope's interest, but she had no time to further dwell on it as Sir Ulysses came to a halt before them and stated, "I'm Moubray. You're the Adairs, I take it."

Barnaby gracefully inclined his head and introduced them and explained their connection to Scotland Yard and Stokes.

Penelope added, "We assist in investigations that require a broader understanding of society." She shifted her gaze to Mrs. Moubray, and as if reminded, Sir Ulysses gruffly introduced his wife.

Penelope offered her hand, and she and Mrs. Moubray pressed fingers.

Retrieving her hand, Mrs. Moubray waved at the sofa and armchairs. "Please, do sit."

Penelope sank onto the sofa, and Mrs. Moubray claimed the other end while Barnaby and Sir Ulysses settled in the twin armchairs.

"Now," Sir Ulysses commanded in a sergeant-major bark, "what's this about, heh?"

"Somewhat indirectly," Barnaby replied, "we're here in relation to the murder of Thomas Cardwell."

Along with Barnaby, Penelope took in the shocked expressions on the Moubrays' faces.

A hand rising to her throat, in a horrified whisper, Mrs. Moubray asked, "Gibson's brother?" She looked at her husband. "You remember, dear. We met Thomas at various school functions. He was a year younger than Gibson, Harrison, and Joseph."

A frown had taken up residence on Sir Ulysses's face. Slowly, he nodded. "I thought he—Thomas—was the sensible one." He looked at Barnaby. "Went into business as an agent, as I recall."

Barnaby said, "He was killed in his office last Tuesday morning."

"Good Lord!" Sir Ulysses's expression darkened. "What is the world coming to?"

"Indeed," Barnaby went on, "but the reason we're here is because, entirely unexpectedly, Thomas had stumbled on a gun-running scheme and was in the process of notifying the authorities of it when he was killed."

"Good gracious!" Mrs. Moubray cast a quick glance at her spouse. "So it wasn't anything unlawful that Thomas was involved in that got him killed."

"No." Penelope noted Mrs. Moubray's glance and had a fair notion of the reason for it. "If anything, one might argue that Thomas died a hero, for Crown and country as it were."

Sir Ulysses nodded, but his suspicion was deepening. "His death is certainly regrettable, but I fail to see why the police have sent consultants to notify us of Cardwell's passing. It's not as if we had much interaction with the young man."

"True," Barnaby said. "However, we're here because of the gun-running enterprise Thomas uncovered. He stumbled upon it because he'd noticed that his brother, Gibson, was rather more flush with cash than could be readily accounted for."

Watching Mrs. Moubray, Penelope saw that lady fractionally nod as if Thomas's observation matched her own, and her interest in Barnaby's revelations noticeably sharpened.

In an even tone, Barnaby continued, "We've now determined that a man by the name of Chesterton had been searching for a place to store crates near Tilbury and, by sheer luck, had approached your son, who at the time was in the company of Gibson Cardwell and Joseph Keeble. Harrison knew of the abandoned warehouse east of Tilbury that you, Sir Ulysses, own, and a deal was struck such that Chesterton paid Harrison for the use of the warehouse and also paid all three—Harrison, Gibson, and Joseph—for keeping silent about said deal."

Aghast, Mrs. Moubray stared at Barnaby, then switched her gaze, almost pleading, to Penelope. "You—the police—can't possibly think that Harrison, or Joseph or Gibson, murdered Thomas."

"No," Barnaby firmly stated. "The police have established that the three gentlemen were not involved in the killing, and that regarding the gun-running scheme, they were unwitting dupes. They knew nothing about the guns or Chesterton's scheme, nor were they aware that Thomas had followed them and discovered the source of their recent wealth."

Sir Ulysses's cheeks had taken on a purplish hue, and his expression was thunderous. "You're talking about my warehouse in Brennan Road?"

"Yes," Barnaby replied and left it at that.

Watching Sir Ulysses's ire build, Penelope stated, "We came to inform you of the circumstances of your son's involvement with the gun-running scheme."

"Also because," Barnaby put in, "you own the warehouse used to store the guns."

"And," Penelope went on, "while the police do not anticipate your or your son's names being mentioned in open court, it was thought advisable to warn you of the connection, as there is always a risk some news sheet might learn of the association."

Sir Ulysses's features had grown progressively stormier. "Damned puppy!" His delivery was just short of a suppressed explosion. "I offered to buy him a commission in my old regiment, but would he take it? No!" He thumped the arm of his chair. "He had to go off and join his friends in living an existence—I wouldn't go so far as to call it a life—as a 'gentleman about town.' Whatever that is!"

Mrs. Moubray had grown decidedly anxious. Shifting forward, she fixed wide eyes on Penelope. "Mrs. Adair, perhaps we should leave the gentlemen to discuss these matters while we take tea in the conservatory."

Deciding that she would learn more from the observant Mrs. Moubray than she would from her spouse, especially if they were private, Penelope readily agreed. "Thank you. Tea would be most welcome."

They rose, and the gentlemen came to their feet as Mrs. Moubray ushered Penelope to the door. Looking back at Sir Ulysses, Mrs. Moubray asked, "Would you like me to send in a tea tray, dear?"

Sir Ulysses gave vent to disgusted sound. "Don't bother. I need something stronger after learning of Harrison's latest idiocy, and I daresay Adair won't say no to joining me, even if it's early in the day."

Barnaby inclined his head in acquiescence.

As, with Mrs. Moubray close behind, Penelope went through the doorway, she heard Sir Ulysses growl, "I always kept a tight rein on Harrison's funds. Didn't want him going off the rails. But it seems he's managed that anyway."

A few minutes later, Penelope was ensconced in a well-padded sofa, again covered in flowered chintz, in a sunny room that looked out over a pleasant side garden.

The footman, carrying a properly stocked tray, had followed her and Mrs. Moubray into the room, and after settling into an armchair opposite Penelope, Mrs. Moubray expertly poured, then handed a cup and saucer to Penelope.

She accepted it, sipped, gently smiled, then set the cup on the saucer and said, "I couldn't help but note that you weren't surprised on learning that Gibson had shown signs of having unexplained funds."

After taking a no-doubt-revivifying sip of her tea, Mrs. Moubray met Penelope's gaze and admitted, "I'd had much the same thoughts of Harrison. A new hat, new gloves, and a very nice silver-headed cane. And he had a different air about him—as if he no longer had a care in the world and wasn't concerned about what his father thought of him." She rested her cup on its saucer and looked into it for a moment before saying, "Sir Ulysses served on the Subcontinent. He was knighted for bravery under fire. He always hoped that Harrison would follow in his footsteps, and when Harrison refused, as you might imagine, that caused something of a rift." She raised her cup and took another sip, over the cup's rim meeting Penelope's encouraging gaze. Lowering the cup, Mrs. Moubray went on, "Naturally, therefore, Ulysses didn't approve of Harrison's decision to set up camp, as Ulysses terms it, with his two closest friends and, for that reason, kept Harrison's financial reins rather short."

Feeling her way, Penelope ventured, "Am I correct in thinking that Sir Ulysses's dislike of Harrison's chosen lifestyle extends to Harrison's friends?"

Mrs. Moubray faintly grimaced. "I would have to say that even during their schooldays, Ulysses was in two minds about Harrison's friendships with Gibson and Joseph, although for different reasons. The Cardwells are an old established family, and even though Gibson's father was regarded as a black sheep, a ne'er-do-well, he was nevertheless well born. However, Gibson's attitudes were much the same as Harrison's, and Ulysses couldn't approve of any situation that bolstered Harrison's defiance. As for Joseph, well, Keeble Senior is the son of a merchant who moved up the social ladder by marrying into the gentry. Sadly, even though Keeble paid to send Joseph to King Edward's Grammar, courtesy of his family's connections or rather lack thereof, Joseph will never meet Ulysses's standards for being a close associate of Harrison's."

"I see." Penelope was forming a much clearer view of Sir Ulysses Moubray. Her gaze on Mrs. Moubray's face, she asked, "Do you share your husband's reservations regarding Gibson and Joseph?"

Mrs. Moubray frowned. "Well, no. I've always found the pair entirely unexceptionable, and in my view, no matter one's station in life, friends are critically important. And those three have remained close ever since they met in their very first year at King Edward's."

Penelope threw her net of questions wider and learned that Harrison was the Moubrays' only son and their eldest daughter was married and settled, while the youngest, Nettie, was still at home. Apparently, neither daughter encountered any difficulties with Sir Ulysses and his often-rigid views.

"Coming from years in the army, Ulysses likes to believe he's in charge and in control," Mrs. Moubray confided. "As long as one allows him to think so, he remains content, and really, as long as one pauses to think and organize a trifle, my daughters and I have always found him easy enough to manage."

Penelope had no difficulty believing that. But in considering the image of himself Sir Ulysses plainly held, she had to wonder... "If Sir Ulysses had wished to speak with one of the younger gentlemen, would he have gone to meet them at their home?"

"Oh no." Mrs. Moubray shook her mousy curls. "He would have summoned them to speak with him here, in his study, or at his club." She paused, then said, "I'm fairly sure he hasn't met with any of them recently. He does tend to ramble about everything that happens in his day, and he hasn't mentioned the lads for the past two weeks. Not since Harrison, Gibson, and Joseph last dropped in to see me and Nettie."

Penelope smiled to herself. She was prepared to take everything Mrs. Moubray said of her husband and son as well-nigh gospel. Mousy, she might be, but she understood the characters of those close to her.

Mrs. Moubray asked about Penelope's children, and she was happy to switch tacks and describe the imps.

Then the footman arrived and announced that Barnaby was ready to leave.

Penelope drained her teacup, placed cup and saucer on the tray, then rose and smiled at Mrs. Moubray. "Thank you for the tea and the conversation."

Mrs. Moubray waved a hand. "It was entirely my pleasure, Mrs. Adair."

Together, the ladies—both of them, Penelope suspected, entirely satisfied with the outcome of their private chat—left the conservatory and went to join their husbands.

Half an hour after leaving Scotland Yard, Jordan found himself sitting beside Ruth on the sofa in the Cardwells' drawing room with Mrs. Cardwell in an armchair closer to the fireplace and Bobby and Gibson in the armchairs opposite.

Both Cardwell males looked haggard, as if they'd barely slept since learning of Thomas's death. As for Mrs. Cardwell, to Jordan, she epitomized the image of a lady sunk in grief over the death of a child—as if she'd lost all hope and all that anchored her to the world.

Experience suggested that her grief would eventually ebb to manageable levels, and with three other children to steer through life, she would come around.

Jordan wasn't so sure Gibson would ever put his brother's death behind him. There was a degree of guilt and self-blame in Gibson's demeanor that, Jordan felt, went well beyond the deserved. He hadn't expected to feel any sympathy for the older of Ruth's brothers, but as he and Ruth, aided by Gibson, explained to Mrs. Cardwell and Bobby the situation Gibson had unwittingly become involved in and how that had, the investigators believed, led to Thomas being killed, Jordan came to the firm conclusion that the sooner the murderer was identified and taken up the better. He didn't want to have to start constantly watching Gibson to ensure he didn't take it into his head to wander down to the river.

Were Gibson to commit suicide over his role—however unintentional —in Thomas's death, the remaining Cardwells would be shattered.

Jordan didn't question why he felt that at least some of the responsibility for ensuring such an event didn't occur now rested on his shoulders.

While they described the gun-running scheme and how they believed Thomas had stumbled across it, Mrs. Cardwell stared blankly at her surviving sons. But when Jordan finished relating the tale of Chesterton's capture and his subsequent interview at Scotland Yard and the charges he was facing, Mrs. Cardwell's gaze focused on Gibson, then, her expression filling with dawning horror, she swung to look at Jordan.

Seated between them and accurately reading her mother's thoughts, Ruth rushed to explain, "The police have absolved Gibson—and Harrison and Josh—of any crime. They are not going to be charged with anything—"

"Well," Gibson muttered, "other than stupidity."

Ruth threw him a chiding look and continued, her voice firm with conviction, "The three of them will not be going to jail."

Jordan added, "In the eyes of the police, Gibson, Harrison, and Josh ended up assisting the authorities. The information they provided was vital in allowing the police to shut down the scheme, arrest Chesterton, and prevent the latest consignment of guns from leaving our shores."

Mrs. Cardwell fixed her faded-blue eyes on Jordan. She considered him as if weighing his assurances, then she nodded. "Thank you, Mr. Draper."

The young maid appeared in the doorway and bobbed a curtsy. "Luncheon's on the table, ma'am."

"Thank you, Cindy." Mrs. Cardwell looked at Jordan. "Please join us,

Mr. Draper." The vestige of a smile edged her lips. "If nothing else, your presence will ensure our good manners don't allow us to sink into maudlin silence."

Jordan suspected that prediction was accurate. He dipped his head. "I will stay on the condition that you call me Jordan."

Again, Mrs. Cardwell studied him briefly, then her lips curved more definitely. "Jordan, then." She rose, bringing everyone else to their feet. "Now, to the dining room. Regardless of the circumstances, we all must eat."

Jordan offered Mrs. Cardwell his arm, and pleased, she took it, and they led the group to the dining room, which lay on the opposite side of the hall, toward the rear of the house.

He ushered Mrs. Cardwell to what was plainly her seat at the head of the oval table.

Settling into the carver, she waved him to the chair on her right, while Ruth moved to the next chair along, and Gibson and Bobby took the chairs opposite Jordan and Ruth.

The table was set with a cold collation comprising platters of cold meats, cheeses, and fruit plus a basket of buns and slices of fresh crusty bread. They all helped themselves, and in the occasional comment made by one or other participant, Jordan detected a note of customary family banter, subdued by the circumstances though it was.

Gibson sat directly opposite Jordan and was the quietest of those at the table.

Jordan had ample opportunity to study Gibson's expression while they ate, and it would have been obvious to the meanest intelligence that Gibson was blaming himself for Thomas's untimely demise.

A glance at Ruth confirmed that she, too, was seriously worried by the apparent direction of Gibson's thoughts. Prompted by he wasn't sure what, Jordan stated, "One of the issues within this case on which all the investigators—the Adairs as well as Inspector Stokes and myself—have unequivocally agreed is that none of the Cardwells, or Harrison Moubray or Josh Keeble, are in any way to blame for Thomas's murder."

At that, Gibson, who had been staring, apparently unseeing, at his plate, glanced up.

Jordan caught his gaze and went on, "It might seem emotionally correct to imagine"—he threw Ruth a swift glance—"that Ruth setting Thomas on the trail of Gibson's newfound income or"—Jordan switched his gaze to Bobby—"Bobby going to see Thomas or"—he returned his gaze to Gibson—"Gibson's arrangements with Chesterton, or Harrison's or Josh's, in some way contributed to Thomas's murder, but such thinking only serves to downplay the role of the man guilty of the crime. *He* was the one who met Thomas, went into Thomas's office as a friend of sorts, then seized Thomas's letter knife and stabbed Thomas."

Jordan glanced at Mrs. Cardwell. "I apologize for such plain speaking, ma'am, but the only person who needs to feel deep and consuming guilt over Thomas's death is that man."

Mrs. Cardwell met his gaze and graciously inclined her head. "Thank you, Mr. Draper—Jordan. I believe that needed to be said." Her gaze passed over the faces of her surviving children, then she stated, "To take on undeserved guilt is not a virtue, especially as, in this case, doing so denies the part Thomas himself played in the matter. We shouldn't forget that he was seeking to bring about the best possible outcome for this family—that was forever and always his aim—while also doing right by the country, and we shouldn't, by denying his responsibility for his own actions, diminish that."

Those sentiments clearly gave her children pause.

Briefly reviewing the state of the investigation and considering what else he might share, Jordan realized there were several connections yet to be corroborated. Recapturing Gibson's gaze, he said, "In fact, looking at where the investigation stands at this time, we've yet to prove that Thomas ever saw Chesterton or followed him to the warehouse and learned about the guns. At present, that's all conjecture—simply the best explanation we've thus far stumbled on to explain Thomas's action in appealing to my employer for assistance in contacting the authorities. It's possible that what moved Thomas to make that appeal—the knowledge that actually led to his murder—was something else entirely."

Gibson frowned. "So it might not be the gun-running scheme at all?"

"As I understand things"—Ruth threw Jordan a questioning glance—"what got Thomas killed might just as easily be something he learned about one of his clients or even someone else."

Jordan nodded in agreement. The point called to mind the possible threat to Ruth herself.

Plainly curious, Bobby asked Jordan about how he came to work with the investigators.

Answering that question brought the issue of working for Roscoe into the open. Jordan glanced at Ruth, then at Mrs. Cardwell. "Although it's not common knowledge, Roscoe was born to the nobility. My father was

—still is—the man-of-business to Roscoe's family, and when Roscoe left to come to London and establish himself here, I left my father's practice and became Roscoe's man-of-business. I'm responsible for keeping all his accounts—much as Thomas did for his clients."

Gibson was frowning, following the tale. "But you have just one client."

Jordan nodded. "Roscoe's enterprises are extensive, and then there are all the other businesses that contract to his."

"Like Hemingways' Linens, who Thomas represented," Ruth said.

Jordan continued, "Normally, day to day, I'm kept very busy, but in this instance, Roscoe decreed that I spend my time helping the investigators. Roscoe doesn't approve of violence, especially perpetrated on someone he knew, even if his acquaintance with Thomas was through me." Jordan paused, then with a faint smile added, "While I'm chasing the murderer, Roscoe's lady is filling my shoes and keeping the books up to date."

"His wife does accounts?" Mrs. Cardwell looked surprised.

Jordan nodded. "Usually, she handles the accounts of all the charities she and Roscoe support, but she's perfectly capable of filling in for me for a time." He glanced at Ruth. "That's how I realized that Thomas's accounts were actually kept by Ruth."

Gibson's and Bobby's expressions conveyed their understanding.

Jordan's tale had provoked Bobby's curiosity, and the younger man asked several questions about Jordan leaving his father's practice and striking out on his own and about what was actually involved in being a man-of-business.

Soon, Gibson joined in, and Jordan got the impression that, while matters were still at an early stage, as all the remaining Cardwells were, apparently, good with figures, the notion was slowly blossoming in all their minds of continuing Thomas's business with Gibson and Bobby dealing with the clients and Ruth actually keeping the accounts.

Jordan was pleased that he'd managed to shift their thoughts from Thomas's death, at least for a while.

Shortly after, having cleared the platters, the company rose, and Jordan took his leave of Mrs. Cardwell, Gibson, and Bobby, and Ruth offered to walk him to the door.

They approached the portal, and Jordan slowed, then halted. Turning to Ruth, he said, "We mentioned it earlier, but it bears repeating. Because you were the one who actually kept the accounts, if whoever killed

Thomas realizes that, it's possible they might view you as a threat as well. Stokes and the Adairs share that concern, so until we have Thomas's murderer by the heels, please don't go out alone."

Stokes had said he would arrange a watch, but Jordan didn't know if that had actually been done.

Ruth faintly grimaced but reluctantly inclined her head. "Very well. If I need to leave the house, I'll take one of my brothers or a footman."

Jordan smiled. "Thank you. That will be a load off my mind."

His words hung between them, an admission of sorts.

Then he turned to the door. "I've just enough time to return to Dolphin Square and report to Roscoe before I convene with the investigators at Albemarle Street."

Ruth moved past him and opened the door. Then she met his eyes and smiled. "Your employer sounds fascinating and his lady even more intriguing."

Jordan's smile deepened. "Perhaps one day, I'll take you to meet them."

Ruth held his gaze. "I would like that."

With a dip of his head, Jordan dragged his eyes from hers and walked out of the door—before he uttered something it was entirely too soon to say.

*L*ater that afternoon, after returning to Albemarle Street and consuming a leisurely luncheon, Barnaby escorted Penelope up the short path that led from the front gate of the Keeble residence to the house's front door.

The house was one in a line of detached two-story dwellings that filled the north side of Myddleton Square. The square played host to St. Mark's Church, which faced the western boundary, with the rest of the area within the square's wrought-iron fence given over to trees and lawns with the occasional stone bench inviting pedestrians to sit and rest in the quiet and shade.

Myddleton Square lay to the west of the Moubrays' house and was considered to be a desirable address for the upper gentry.

On reaching the black-painted door, Barnaby lifted the knocker and beat a commanding *rat-a-tat-tat*.

A minute later, the door was opened by a footman. "Yes?"

"The Honorable Mr. Barnaby Adair and Mrs. Adair to see Mr. Keeble." Barnaby didn't feel any need to say more, and sure enough, the footman showed them into the drawing room and left them there while he consulted his master.

A quick survey of the room—leather sofa and armchairs with gentlemen's sporting periodicals scattered on the low table between—found no evidence of a woman's touch.

Penelope murmured, "Definitely a widower's house."

To Barnaby's eyes, it wasn't simply a gentlemen-only abode. Every included feature—like the thermidor half full of fat cigars and the well-stocked tantalus by one wall—appeared to signal wealth and the ability to indulge expensive tastes.

Before he could comment, the footman returned and conducted them to Keeble's study.

With an expression of hopeful curiosity infusing his face, Keeble rose from behind a large ostentatious mahogany desk. "Good afternoon, Mr. and Mrs. Adair. What brings you to my door?"

Barnaby inclined his head. "Mr. Keeble."

Keeble was a stocky, rather rotund man of average height, with a paunch that pulled his coat tight across his body. He was garbed in a brown suit of conservative cut, the hue of which matched his wavy brown hair, now amply streaked with gray. His features were undistinguished and unremarkable, and his round brown eyes regarded them from beneath straight brows. His complexion was faintly ruddy, and his hands were soft, the short fingers pudgy.

On hearing the study door shut behind them, Barnaby continued, "My wife and I occasionally act as official consultants to Scotland Yard in cases where a broader experience of society is desirable."

Keeble's eyes widened. "Indeed?" After a fractional hesitation, he waved Barnaby and Penelope to the twin velvet-upholstered armchairs facing the desk. "Please sit and tell me how I may assist you."

"As to that," Penelope said, drawing in her skirts and sinking onto one chair, "the shoe is somewhat on the other foot."

Having resumed his seat in the chair behind the desk and set his clasped hands on his blotter, Keeble faintly frowned. "How so?"

"First, if we may," Penelope continued, "we understand that your son, Joseph, shares a flat with two friends—Gibson Cardwell and Harrison Moubray—both of whom he met while at King Edward's Grammar School. Is that correct?"

Clearly puzzled by her direction, Keeble affirmed, "That's right. I made sure Joseph had every advantage to move up in the world. His mother would have wanted that. She hailed from a very good family, you see, and I believe it's incumbent on me to ensure Joseph lives up to her expectations."

Penelope had told Barnaby that Sir Ulysses considered that, having risen from humbler beginnings, Keeble and his son were socially inferior to the Moubrays and Cardwells. Consequently, Barnaby wasn't surprised when his wife baldly asked Keeble, "What are your thoughts on Joseph's choice of friends?"

The unexpected question made Keeble blink. "Well…" He drew out the word, then collected himself and replied, "I've always encouraged Joseph's connections with the Moubrays and the Cardwells. Both families are established in society, and I was and continue to be pleased that Joseph has chosen his intimates so well."

Keeble's statements held the ring of a devoted social climber, which was, very likely, what had most ruffled Sir Ulysses's feathers.

Penelope nodded as if Keeble's answer was entirely satisfactory and glanced at Barnaby, passing the metaphorical baton to him.

Accepting it, he stated, "As to why we are here, Keeble, we regret to inform you that Joseph has unwittingly been caught up in a gun-running scheme that was recently uncovered by the police. Harrison Moubray and Gibson Cardwell were also unsuspecting dupes in the matter. The details will be of little interest to you, but of greater significance is the likelihood that Thomas Cardwell, Gibson's brother, had, we believe, stumbled upon the scheme and was on the point of contacting the authorities when, last Tuesday morning, he was killed."

Keeble's eyes had widened, and his face had paled to a ghastly hue. "Good gracious me!" He swallowed. "Killed, you say?" His voice rose to a near squeak. "How? Where?"

"As to where," Penelope stated, "he was attacked in his office, and as to how, he was stabbed with his own letter knife."

"Oh, dear me!" Keeble looked quite ill. "And Joseph is somehow caught up in this?"

"No," Barnaby was quick to reassure him. "Joseph—and Harrison and Gibson—are not considered suspects in the murder investigation."

"And in the matter of the gun-running scheme, the authorities view the three as more unwitting victims than perpetrators," Penelope added. "No charges will be laid against them. Indeed, our purpose in calling on you is to inform you that, at present, the police do not expect any of the three gentlemen to be named in open court. However, of course, there is always the risk of some news sheet getting hold of the information and seeking to scandalize the public with some extravagant story."

Keeble continued to look shocked and almost panicked.

To further reassure him, Barnaby explained, "That said, it's unlikely your son's involvement will ever become public knowledge, and even if it does, the story will be cast as Joseph and his friends having assisted the police in apprehending the villains involved."

That seemed to do the trick, and the tension in Keeble's shoulders started to ease, notch by notch.

"From the three young men's point of view," Penelope went on, "very likely nothing more will come of the situation, but the police felt that you and the Moubrays needed to be forewarned in case some connection to the scheme is inadvertently made."

Instantly, Keeble's worried frown returned. "Inadvertently made?"

Penelope gestured vaguely. "Via the news sheets discovering the link, but again, that's highly unlikely."

Judging by Keeble's expression, relief only slowly overcame his apprehension. Eventually, however, he nodded. "Yes. I see. Thank you for the warning. It's reassuring to know that the police are satisfied that the three young men were innocent and merely misled."

Penelope smiled. "Is Joseph your only child?"

"Yes." Keeble's pride in his offspring was evident. "He did exceptionally well at King Edward's, and I hope that, in time, he'll find a suitable calling. Perhaps he'll join me in my firm. I handle the finances of several large investors."

Penelope widened her eyes. "I see. Have you had any thoughts of steering Joseph toward marriage?"

Keeble's faint frown made it clear he had considered the question. "Not yet, I think. In my opinion, he and the other two have some maturing to do before being ready for that commitment."

From what they'd seen of the three younger men, neither Barnaby nor Penelope would dispute that conclusion. Of more interest was Keeble's lack of urgency in pushing his son toward the altar. That suggested that while Keeble was a social climber, he was a cautious and sensible one. He would go step by sure step up the social ladder, rather than leap for the top.

Considering that Penelope had gained sufficient information regarding Keeble's social aspirations, Barnaby asked, "Had you met Thomas Cardwell? He was a year younger than Gibson and also attended King Edward's Grammar."

Keeble nodded. "Yes, I believe I met him several times during school events." Unexpectedly, he added, "I'm aware his office is in Broad Street. It would be hard to miss as, being a financier, I'm often in that area."

"Did you ever interact with Cardwell professionally?" Barnaby asked.

"Oh no!" Keeble smiled and spread his hands. "Well, why would I? As a financier with my own office—and if I do say so myself, I've done rather well over the years—I have no reason to engage the services of another man-of-business."

Barnaby inclined his head in understanding and glanced questioningly at Penelope, but it seemed his wife had learned enough. At least for now.

She smiled at Keeble and rose. "Thank you for your time, sir."

Springing to his feet, Keeble assured her, "No, no, dear lady. It is I who must be thanking you and your husband for calling and informing me of the current situation. And, of course, of the grave news of Cardwell's death." He paused, then shook his head. "Such a waste. He was still so young."

"Indeed." Barnaby extended his hand, and Keeble promptly grasped and shook it, the courtesy clearly pleasing the man.

"Come." Keeble waved them to the door. "I'll see you out."

Penelope made an effort to project a patience she didn't feel while she waited with Barnaby in the drawing room for their coinvestigators to join them.

She'd had Mostyn bring in the tea tray and endeavored to distract herself by pouring cups of tea for herself and Barnaby and sampling Cook's freshly made scones and her latest batch of blackberry jam.

At last, the front doorbell heralded Stokes's arrival. He walked in, studied them for a moment, then admitted, "I could do with a scone or two myself."

Penelope waved him to a chair and poured him a cup of tea while Barnaby passed the scones and jam. "I suppose," she said, setting down the teapot, "that we should wait for Jordan before sharing our findings." She glanced toward the door.

"Probably best," Stokes mumbled around a scone, "unless you want to repeat everything."

Barnaby caught her gaze and smiled understandingly.

She pulled a face and raised her teacup, then to her relief, the doorbell pealed again.

A second later, Jordan walked into the room. "My apologies. After leaving the Cardwells, I realized I should report to Roscoe, and the traffic wasn't helpful getting back and forth. However"—Jordan subsided into the armchair Penelope waved him to and, with obvious gratitude, accepted a teacup and saucer and a plate with a scone and a dab of jam— "I'm glad I made the effort. Roscoe had an insight that, I suspect, will prove very helpful, but first." Jordan eyed Barnaby and Penelope as he raised the scone toward his lips. "What did you two learn?"

"We called on the Moubrays first," Penelope said, "and that was quite enlightening."

"Both Moubrays—Sir Ulysses and Mrs. Moubray—were at home and received us," Barnaby said. "Both seemed genuinely shocked by the news of Thomas Cardwell's murder."

"Indeed," Penelope affirmed. "And Sir Ulysses was even more thunderstruck to learn of Harrison's connection with the gun-running scheme and the use that his warehouse on Brennan Road—"

"Which he admitted was his," Barnaby interjected.

"—had been put to." Penelope added, "Sir Ulysses served in the army on the Subcontinent, and I suspect he's one of those military types who find civilian life a touch incomprehensible."

Barnaby nodded. "That was my reading of the man, too. But in all he said and in his reactions to our revelations, I detected nothing to suggest that he might have been involved in Cardwell's murder. In truth, I doubt he would have remembered Thomas if his wife hadn't jogged his memory."

"I entirely agree," Penelope said. "Although rather mousy and outwardly retiring, Mrs. Moubray is significantly more observant than one might think. She and I managed a private interlude, and her descriptions of Sir Ulysses and Harrison and, indeed, the other two young men were, I judge, very close to the mark. As Ruth had with Gibson, Mrs. Moubray had noticed Harrison's recent displays of unexplained wealth. However, she didn't mention the matter to her husband as she didn't want to exacerbate the rift between them."

"Rift?" Stokes asked.

Barnaby explained, "Sir Ulysses had fond hopes that Harrison—the Moubrays' only son—would follow Sir Ulysses's footsteps into the army, but Harrison has refused to have any truck with that, opting instead to live the life of a gentleman about town, which endeavor is largely outside Sir Ulysses's comprehension."

"I can imagine that." Jordan glanced at Penelope. "Did the observant Mrs. Moubray have any further light to cast?"

Penelope nodded. "She remembered Keeble, whom she and her

husband have met but only through the link between Harrison and Josh. From her comments, I gather Sir Ulysses rather looked down on Keeble as, it seems, Keeble's father was a merchant. Sir Ulysses had not encouraged Harrison's friendship with Josh Keeble, but he entertained fewer reservations about Gibson, given the Cardwells are an old, established gentry family."

"So," Stokes dryly remarked, "Sir Ulysses is high in the instep."

"Palpably so," Barnaby replied.

"One particular and relevant insight that arises out of that observation," Penelope said, "is that, as Mrs. Moubray stated, if Sir Ulysses had wanted to speak with Thomas, Sir Ulysses would have summoned Thomas to attend him either at his home or at his club." Penelope looked at Barnaby, Stokes, and Jordan. "From all we learned about Sir Ulysses, that rings very true."

Stokes frowned. "So if Sir Ulysses had learned about the gun running and wanted to speak with Thomas…"

"Exactly." Penelope nodded. "For a start, why would Sir Ulysses think to speak with Thomas about the gun running? But assuming that for some reason he did, then Sir Ulysses is not the sort to go calling at a younger man's office. He's regulation army—he would expect the junior man to come to him."

Stokes slowly nodded. "Yes, I can see that." He raised his gaze to Penelope's and Barnaby's faces. "So what did you learn about Keeble?"

Barnaby glanced at Penelope, then at her urging, commenced, "He's a widower, and he's devoted to steadily ascending the social ladder."

"Rung by sure rung," Penelope put in. "I sensed his campaign in that regard is very carefully constructed and executed." She looked at Jordan and Stokes. "For instance, I asked if he'd thought about Josh marrying, and he replied, 'Not yet.' It's clearly a step in his overall plan to socially advance himself and Josh—they're the only two in the family—but Keeble Senior isn't the sort to rush into anything. It's all very calculated."

"To me, it seemed that he uses his late wife's higher social status as an excuse," Barnaby said, "in that, had she lived, it would be what she would have wanted."

Penelope nodded. "That's true. However, with respect to the gun-running scheme and Thomas being killed, Keeble appeared truly shocked. Rattled and even distressed."

"It took some effort to reassure him that Josh's name is unlikely to be made public," Barnaby said.

"I suppose," Penelope said, "that given his plans to advance the family socially, the prospect of having their name feature in some news sheet in association with gun running and murder would, indeed, be upsetting."

Her mock-earnest tone made Stokes and Jordan smirk.

"Interestingly," Barnaby said, "when we inquired if he knew Thomas, while Keeble gave a similar answer to the Moubrays—having only encountered Thomas at school events—Keeble added that he knew Thomas's office was in Broad Street."

"Oh?" Stokes perked up.

Penelope smiled at him and shook her head. "Keeble pointed out that as he's a financier and, therefore, often in the area, Thomas's office would be hard to miss."

"Hard to claim not to have been aware of it," Barnaby said. "But Keeble denied ever interacting with Thomas professionally, having an office of his own and no need of the services of another man-of-business."

Penelope looked from Stokes to Jordan. "That's all we learned from Keeble and the Moubrays. So"—she arched her brows at Jordan—"what useful insights did Roscoe offer?"

Jordan set down his empty plate and took a sip of his tea.

"Before we get to Roscoe," Stokes said, "was there anything of note at the Cardwells?"

Jordan shook his head. "No. Nothing that seemed pertinent, just the family trying to band together and get through this terrible time."

Barnaby had been mulling over the facts they'd collected thus far. "So was it learning about the guns that sealed Thomas's fate, or was it something else entirely?"

Stokes pointed out, "The gun running certainly qualifies as Thomas's 'nefarious activities,' and little else we've come across fits that bill. However, I agree that we need to prove that Thomas did, in actual fact, learn about the guns. Until we have solid proof of that, we're trying to stitch together a story with unconnected threads."

Jordan nodded. "We need to get to the bottom of this—identify the reason that Thomas was killed—not least for the Cardwells and, perhaps strangely, most of all for Gibson Cardwell."

Stokes regarded Jordan shrewdly. "Having an attack of the guilts, is he?"

"Very much so."

Penelope was frowning. "The only place that Chesterton and Gibson, Harrison, and Josh met was at the Fox." She looked at the men about her. "So the Fox is the only place where Thomas could have spotted Chesterton and picked up his trail and followed Chesterton to the warehouse and found the guns."

Stokes grimaced. "We need to find someone who saw Thomas following Chesterton away from the Fox. That's the very least we need." He jotted in his notebook. "I'll send Morgan to ask at the Fox. Depending on how good Thomas's disguise was, someone there might have noticed him."

Jordan's expression stated that he was mentally surveying the sequence of events they were endeavoring to construct. "For the sake of our case, let's say that Thomas did see Chesterton at the Fox with Gibson and subsequently followed Chesterton from the Fox to the warehouse. That had to have been on the Sunday night—thirty-six hours before he was murdered—because on Monday, Thomas sent his letter to Roscoe, and Thomas was killed on Tuesday morning."

Barnaby nodded. "That's Thomas's timetable as we know it to this point. And assuming we do, indeed, find sound evidence that Thomas followed Chesterton and learned about the guns, given the timing, that makes the motive for Thomas's murder his knowledge of the gun-running scheme." Barnaby looked at the faces about him. "Presumably, that knowledge made Thomas a threat to someone."

Jordan glanced at Penelope, then looked at Barnaby and Stokes. "That's the perfect opening to reveal Roscoe's insights. When I told him about Chesterton and the gun-running scheme, Roscoe's immediate question was 'Who are Chesterton's backers?'"

Staring at Jordan, Stokes slowly sat up.

On the sofa, Barnaby and Penelope straightened.

Noting their reactions and the dawning comprehension in their expressions, Jordan continued, "Roscoe contends that, for an operation of such size and scope, Chesterton wouldn't be the one filling the purse. He's just a middleman enabled by the syndicate providing the cash. And given the nature of the scheme and the amounts involved, it's all but certain the members of that syndicate are wealthy and potentially powerful gentlemen."

Stokes grunted. "And if anyone would understand such a setup, Roscoe would."

"If you think about it," Barnaby said, his tone enthused, "all those guns would have cost a pretty penny."

"More," Stokes stated. "Significantly more because of being illegally sourced."

In the tone of one summing up, Penelope stated, "So Chesterton must have had backers, and whoever they are, Thomas learning about the gun running and being intent on informing the authorities would have featured as a definite and very likely highly significant threat to them."

Stokes shut his notebook with a snap. He glanced at the clock, then looked at the others. "First thing tomorrow, we interview Chesterton again."

CHAPTER 11

They all arrived at Scotland Yard bright and early the next morning. Jordan was just approaching the steps when Barnaby and Penelope drew up in their carriage, and Stokes strode up a moment later.

"I set things in motion yesterday evening," Stokes informed them. "Chesterton should already be languishing in the interrogation room, so we can head straight downstairs."

They did and walked into the bare interrogation room with its single glaring lamp to find Chesterton sitting at the rectangular table, staring morosely at his clasped hands. Quiet and watchful, O'Donnell and Morgan stood unobtrusively against the wall behind Chesterton's chair.

As they filed into the room, Chesterton raised his gaze and watched them claim the chairs on the table's opposite side. Judging by the expression in his eyes, he was curious as to what they wanted with him and also a trifle wary.

Once the four of them had settled, Stokes looked directly at Chesterton and stated, "We're interested in learning from where you got the funds to pay for the guns."

Tellingly, Chesterton's eyes widened. He waited, but when all four investigators simply stared back and said nothing more, he ducked his head and mumbled, "All a part of the arrangements."

"Arrangements with whom?" Barnaby asked, his tone flat.

Chesterton wrestled with his answer and eventually offered, "The bods who thought it was a good idea."

Sourness colored his voice.

Stokes shifted tacks. "Obviously, you have backers. Don't you think they'll grow concerned when they learn you've been nicked?"

Jordan elaborated, "Concerned about what you know and what you might tell us?"

"Sadly," Barnaby observed, "accidents do happen in Newgate."

As if helpfully clarifying the point, Penelope said, "That's where you'll be heading shortly."

The look in Chesterton's eyes confirmed that he was genuinely worried. His expression suggested he was tempted to reveal the names, but after several moments of considering his options, he shook his head. "I can't—I won't. It's not worth my head. If you don't go after them, they'll know I never told you anything, and they'll let me be, so thank you all the same, but I'll take my chances."

Jordan sighed. "I was hoping we wouldn't need to do this the hard way."

"Heh?" Alarmed, Chesterton reared back. He looked at Stokes, then glanced at O'Donnell and Morgan. "What's that supposed to mean?"

"First," Stokes said, "I should mention that yesterday, Constable Morgan"—he tipped his head Morgan's way—"checked the address you gave when you were formally taken into custody." Stokes caught Chesterton's gaze. "Consequently, we know that the flat in Lambert Street is, in fact, your current home."

Chesterton was plainly wondering if he should have given a false address. "So?"

"So," Jordan said, "now, we'll go there and turn the place upside down until we find your account book."

Chesterton's eyes slowly widened, his growing apprehension clear.

Jordan nodded. "Just so. Of course you've kept a reckoning, because when dealing with the likes of your backers, you knew you would need to be able to answer for every single pound. I imagine there'll be a register of the payments made to you, and even if you used a bank—and considering the amounts that must have been involved, I would wager you did—there'll be a record, a trail if you will, that those who know about such things will be able to follow all the way to your backers."

Stokes smiled in anticipation. "And then we'll have them as well as you." He arched his brows at Chesterton and mildly asked, "Sure you don't want to get in our good books by giving us their names and saving us the legwork?"

Chesterton's eyes had narrowed on Jordan and Stokes. He studied them for several long minutes, then said, "You're having me on. I was told it's really hard to trace payments made through a bank, so if it's all the same to you, I'll keep my trap shut and take my chances."

Jordan beamed. "Thank you."

Confused, Chesterton blinked at him. "What for?"

"For telling us that somewhere, there's a bank account in your name," Jordan said, "and that we'll find the account details hidden somewhere in your rooms. Once we find those details—and trust me, we'll find them— we'll be able to do as I said and follow the trail to your masters."

Still smiling, Stokes pushed back his chair and rose. "On that note, Chesterton, allow us to bid you a good day."

Caught between disbelief and fear, Chesterton watched them file out of the room.

Stokes paused in the doorway and looked at O'Donnell. "Take him back to the cells." Stokes transferred his gaze to Morgan. "Meanwhile, you can fetch Walsh and join us in the foyer."

Both sergeant and constable snapped off salutes, and Stokes followed the others into the corridor and on toward the stairs.

Once in the foyer, Stokes went to the front desk and returned with a large, old-fashioned key.

Barnaby eyed the key. "I think Lambert Street runs south from Whitechapel."

"That's what Morgan said." Stokes turned as Morgan and Walsh came striding up.

Both saluted, and Morgan hopefully inquired, "You wanted us, guv?"

Constable Morgan was one who liked to be doing.

"Indeed," Stokes said. "I want the pair of you to go down to the Fox— that pub on the Tilbury Road where Chesterton and the three gentlemen used to meet. We need to find evidence that Thomas Cardwell was there last Sunday night. He might have been in disguise, but I can't imagine it was all that good. See what the staff can tell you—if any of them remember a bloke who could have been Cardwell and, most especially, if anyone happened to notice Cardwell following Chesterton when Chesterton left."

"The staff must know Chesterton," Barnaby pointed out. "By all accounts, he's been a regular there for at least the past few months."

"The three gentlemen are also regulars, even more so than Chesterton," Penelope said, "so the staff will definitely remember them. As for Chesterton, all you need to mention is that shock of carroty-red hair. The staff are sure to remember that."

Morgan grinned and saluted again, this time to the entire group. "Right you are, sirs, ma'am. We'll head down there immediately. They should be just opening up when we arrive, and that's a good time to chat, before they get too busy."

Stokes grinned. "You're the expert." He tipped his head toward the street. "Off you go."

With jaunty nods, the pair strode for the doors.

Stokes turned to the others. He weighed the heavy old key in his palm, then slid it into his pocket. "Right, then. Let's head to Lambert Street and see what we can find."

~

Half an hour later, Stokes used the old key to open the door of Chesterton's flat above a bakery on Lambert Street.

The scent of freshly baked bread permeated the space as the four investigators walked into the small parlor and looked around.

"There." Jordan tipped his head at a simple desk set between two windows. He walked across and drew out the wooden chair set before it. "I'll search here, but he might have had the sense to hide his account book in some unlikely place."

"I'll help with the desk." Penelope dragged a second chair over to the side of the desk before one window. "The light's better here."

Stokes humphed. "I suppose that leaves Barnaby and me to search all the unlikely places."

When the two already pulling out the drawers of the desk made no comment, Stokes exchanged a wry look with Barnaby, and together, they moved to examine the few other pieces of furniture in the room.

Penelope helped Jordan gather all the notebooks and loose sheets stuffed into the desk drawers and poked into the double row of pigeon-holes above it. They piled their finds on the blotter, amassing a considerable stack.

Once they'd gathered every last shred of paper, Jordan studied the pile. "Right. Let's have at it."

"You take half"—Penelope suited the action to the words and divided the pile roughly in two—"and I'll take the rest."

They started by examining the notebooks.

"Household accounts," Penelope declared in a somewhat intrigued tone. "I'm surprised a single gentleman keeps track."

Jordan threw her a smile. "Not all gentlemen are hedonists with no interest in what they spend their blunt on."

She huffed to indicate she doubted that and laid the account book aside.

Jordan paused to stare at the discarded notebook, then said, "It's wise to check the back of the book. Sometimes, sensitive accounts are hidden by using the book in reverse."

Penelope dutifully retrieved Chesterton's household accounts and flicked to the pages at the end of the small volume. Then she gave vent to an excited sound, turned the notebook upside down, and peered more closely at the page.

Jordan was watching her. "What is it?"

"I believe we've struck gold." She stared at the figures for a moment more, then handed him the notebook. "What do you think?"

Jordan set aside the notebook he'd been perusing and eagerly took the one she offered. He quickly scanned the entries, then flipped further on in the book. After a minute during which she kept her eyes on his face and held her breath, he smiled, raised his gaze, and met her eyes. "This is it! Well done!" He swiveled on the chair and called, "Stokes. Adair!" The pair had vanished into the bedroom. "We think we have it."

Stokes came striding out. "That was quick."

Jordan waggled his head. "If you think about it, Chesterton must have needed to access this account frequently." He waved the notebook. "The first entry is dated more than two years ago, and"—he flicked through the pages, studying the neat script—"the financial activity seems to have been reasonably constant." He kept flipping pages, then finally stopped at one. "This is the end of the record—Chesterton's most recent withdrawal. Judging by its size, it's most likely the payment for the latest consignment of guns."

Stokes had halted by Jordan's side. He nodded at the notebook. "What else can you make from it?"

"Give me a moment." Jordan settled to carefully scan page by page through the entries.

Penelope exchanged an impatient look with Barnaby, who smiled at her.

Stokes settled his weight evenly on his feet, and they waited.

"All right," Jordan eventually said. He glanced up and met their eyes. "There's a pattern. Three people—or, I should say, three separate bank accounts—are regularly paying amounts into this account."

"Are the amounts of the order one would expect for a gun-running enterprise?" Stokes asked.

"Oh yes," Jordan stated. "There's no doubt about that." He paused to study several pages, then said, "For instance, over the past three months, there's been more than ten thousand pounds moved in, and Chesterton's taken virtually all of it out in cash." He glanced at Stokes. "As you might imagine, illegal sellers always want their payments in cash. Likewise the drivers of the drays transporting the guns from Enfield to the warehouse and from the warehouse to the ship."

"If this has been going on for more than two years, then previously, Chesterton must have been using somewhere else to store the guns," Barnaby pointed out.

"It's likely," Jordan said, "that prior to recent months, he wasn't using Tilbury at all but some other port. Harwich or Bristol or even Manchester. I suspect a wise gun runner will change his routes frequently, and by this account"—he waved the notebook—"Chesterton's succeeded in his chosen profession for at least two years."

"What about money returning?" Penelope asked. "From the sales of the guns, presumably to Chesterton, who, one assumes, would then repay his backers their initial investment plus a healthy amount of interest."

Jordan shook his head. "That's not done via this account. In fact, I'd be surprised if all such payments weren't made solely in cash, possibly via the smuggling ship's captain to Chesterton and, from him, directly to his backers, and there'll be no accounting kept of them anywhere."

Barnaby grunted. "Making it far more difficult to prove the backers are profiting from this scheme."

"Exactly." Jordan held up the notebook. "With this, we're essentially looking at only half the business—the outgoing expenses, not the incoming return."

Stokes tipped his head at the notebook. "So which bank is this account held in?"

Jordan flipped to the first page and squinted. "There's a scribbled name at the top of the page, but it's smudged." When Penelope waggled her fingers before him, he surrendered the notebook. "I think it says Moreton's."

Penelope had drawn a small magnifying glass from her reticule. Through it, she examined the scribble. "Yes. It's Moreton's." She glanced at Barnaby. "That's one of the larger private banks, isn't it?"

Barnaby nodded. "It used to be a public bank, but recently shifted to private clients only." Eyes narrowing, he paused, then said, "I wonder if using such an august institution was Chesterton's idea."

"Or," Penelope added, her eyes gleaming behind her spectacles, "was Moreton's the bank his backers preferred to use?"

"Because they have accounts there, too?" Jordan considered the point, then shrugged. "Could be." He glanced at the notebook, still open to one page, and amended, "Could very well be." He looked at the others. "Moving money solely within one bank makes the transfers much easier and, theoretically at least, means there's only one record in one bank of any of the transactions." He pointed at the notebook. "The only reason Chesterton had to keep his own account is because he deals entirely with cash payments."

Stokes nodded in understanding. "So from the backers' point of view, there's only one record, and I can imagine wealthy, powerful gentlemen feeling much safer if that single record was kept within an institution such as Moreton's."

"Indeed." Barnaby was smiling. "However, having only one bank also means that we have only one bank manager to convince to give us those wealthy gentlemen's names."

Jordan frowned. "Given the bank is Moreton's, that might not be an easy task."

Barnaby's smile deepened. "Luckily, we have resources we can call on for assistance." He glanced at Stokes. "I suggest that, before heading to Moreton's, we consult Montague. He may have—is very likely to have—connections that will smooth our way."

Penelope was quick to state her approval of that plan, and Stokes readily agreed.

Studying the others' faces, Jordan grinned. "I've only sighted Montague on a few occasions, always at a distance, but he's a legend in my field, and learning at the feet of such wisdom should never be disdained."

Penelope laughed.

Grinning, Stokes reached out and took the vital notebook. "To Chapel Court, then. Let's see what the great man says."

~

Over the years, Montague, sometimes with the aid of his wife, Violet, had assisted Stokes, Barnaby, and Penelope with various investigations. On entering Montague's chambers, they were met by his longtime head clerk, Mr. Slocum.

"Good morning, Slocum." Barnaby smiled at the dapper, earnest man who stood behind his raised desk on the other side of the waist-high barrier that divided the foyer from the area where Montague's clerks and juniors labored. "Is Mr. Montague available?"

"Mr. Adair. Mrs. Adair. And Inspector Stokes." Slocum bowed, cast a curious glance at Jordan, then, his expression bright, Slocum stated, "If you'll wait here, I'll check, but I daresay Mr. Montague will wish to see you immediately."

Slocum hurried down a short corridor, tapped on the door at the far end, then whisked through, only to reappear moments later, his smile even more firmly entrenched, and with Montague himself at his back. Slocum hurried to open the gate in the barrier and wave them through.

Montague was waiting to greet them, an expectant expression on his face. He held out his hand to Barnaby. "Dare I hope you come with a problem, preferably knotty, with which I can assist?" Releasing Barnaby's hand, he grasped Stokes's. "I have to inform you that compiling the same accounts year after year, however satisfactory the profit, does grow somewhat dull."

Stokes grinned and waved at Jordan. "We've brought you an admirer."

Jordan blushed faintly and grasped the hand Montague offered. "Jordan Draper. I'm Roscoe's man-of-business."

"Indeed?" Montague looked intrigued. "I've always wondered how he manages, but if you work solely for him…?"

Jordan nodded. "I do."

"Then that would explain it." Montague's eyes twinkled. "I'm well aware of the broad scope of your master's empire."

It was Jordan's turn to grin.

"And last but certainly not least"—Montague turned to Penelope, took both her offered hands in his, leaned in, and bussed her cheek—

"how are you, my dear? Violet's out shopping—she'll be desolated to have missed you."

"As I am over missing her." Penelope smiled. "Do remember to tell her I said so."

"Of course. Of course." Montague looked from her to Barnaby, then to Stokes and Jordan. "But come into my office and tell me your tale and how I might assist."

He ushered them down the corridor to the pleasant office at its end.

Once they were settled in the comfortable chairs arranged before the desk, Montague resumed his seat behind it and looked at them hopefully. "So, do tell."

At Stokes's nod, Barnaby briefly outlined the critical details of Thomas Cardwell's murder, from his letter to Roscoe to the finding of his body.

"Cardwell?" Montague frowned. "A younger practitioner, I think, but from memory, he's quite well thought of in the profession."

"That fits with what we've heard from others," Stokes said. "So it's perhaps unsurprising that we've found no evidence of any nefarious activities among his clients. That caused us to cast our net wider, and the long and the short of it is that we now believe Cardwell stumbled upon a gun-running scheme. That was the nefarious activity to which he referred. Consequently, we captured the gun runner himself, along with the latest batch of guns. However, the description of the unknown gentleman who we believe killed Cardwell in no way matches the gun runner, Chesterton."

"A gentleman, heh?" Montague glanced at Penelope as if asking if this was the point where his expertise came into play.

She obligingly explained, "While Chesterton could not be the unknown gentleman, we realized that he must have backers." She glanced at Stokes. "When we questioned him, he more or less confirmed their existence."

Montague was nodding. "Given Chesterton's station, it's hard to see where he could have got the money otherwise. Guns are not cheap, and illegal wares are even more expensive."

"Exactly," Stokes said. "Consequently, we searched Chesterton's rooms and found his account book. With Jordan's help, we established that Chesterton used a bank account for receiving his backers' funds. Given the sums involved, that's hardly surprising."

Stokes drew Chesterton's notebook from his pocket and held it out to Jordan. "Best you explain what you found."

Jordan took the small book, rose, and circled the desk to stand beside Montague, who promptly perched a pair of pince-nez on his nose.

After opening the notebook, Jordan flattened it on Montague's blotter. "If you look at the entries here"—he pointed—"and here, you can see that the same three bank accounts regularly feed funds into this account."

Intrigued, Montague picked up the notebook and studied the figures more closely.

"If you look backward and forward in time," Jordan continued, "you'll see that every time payments are made, they're always from those same three accounts, and every time such payments are made, each of the three accounts pays a similar amount into Chesterton's account."

Studying the figures, Montague huffed. "And it appears this Chesterton withdraws the lot in cash."

"For the guns and the transport and storage of them, we suppose," Penelope said.

Montague flicked through the pages. "In which bank is this account held?"

Jordan showed him where the name was scribbled. "We think that says 'Moreton's.'"

Montague studied the name, then looked at the account numbers and nodded. "Yes, it's Moreton's." He glanced at Stokes and Barnaby. "And from the account numbers, I can tell you that, as well as Chesterton's account, all three crediting accounts are with the same bank."

Stokes inclined his head. "That's what Jordan thought. We were hoping you might be able to assist us in convincing the manager at Moreton's that, in this instance, it would be right and proper to supply us with the identities of our three mystery account holders."

"Well, plainly, you need to identify them, and yes, of course I'll lend my voice to your chorus." Montague paused, clearly thinking, and they waited to hear the outcome. Eventually, he refocused on Stokes and Barnaby and explained, "However, Moreton's is now the private arm of the New Union Bank, and while I haven't had any recent dealings with New Union or Moreton's myself, I know of someone who has, and I'm sure he'll be delighted to add his considerable weight to mine in persuading the bank manager to divulge the details you require."

Barnaby grinned. "Thomas Glendower?"

Montague nodded. "He dropped in earlier to discuss another matter, so I know he's at Drayton's today."

"Well, then." Stokes slapped his palms on the chair's arms and pushed to his feet. "Let's get around there and rope him in."

Barnaby ushered Penelope into the corridor, and the others followed.

In the foyer, Montague paused to pick up his hat and inform Slocum, "I'll be out, possibly for up to an hour, Slocum." Setting his hat on his head, Montague smiled at the investigators. "How long depends on how resistant to seeing sense the manager of Moreton's proves to be."

"Indeed, sir," Slocum replied. "We'll hold the fort here."

The company trooped out of the office and onto the pavement, then proceeded around the corner into Threadneedle Street. A little way along, Barnaby and Penelope, in the lead, turned in to a narrow building indistinguishable from its neighbors. They climbed the stairs to the first floor, then made for the front of the building, where a pair of half-glazed double doors gave access to the prime suite that overlooked the street.

The name "Drayton and Company" was etched in simple gold lettering on the doors, and the wide, light-filled room beyond was crammed with staff, all busy doing this and that. The middle-aged receptionist seated behind the counter-like desk facing the door looked up, a pleasant and welcoming smile on his face.

He recognized them, and his smile brightened. "Mrs. Adair, Mr. Adair, Mr. Montague, and Inspector Stokes, too." He was already rising and reaching for the gate in the waist-high barrier. "Please, come through."

"Mr. Glendower isn't expecting us, Minns," Montague stated. "But I suspect he'll be glad to see us."

"Indeed, sir." Minns waved them through the gap. "He doesn't have anyone with him, and I'm sure he'll be glad of your visit."

Penelope led the way to the unmarked door set in the paneled wall that formed one side of the office.

She paused before it, and Barnaby reached around her and, after a single rap on the panel, set the door swinging wide.

Penelope swept into the room with the words "Good morning, Thomas. We come bearing gifts—namely, an adventure and a challenge."

From his position behind his imposingly large and neat desk, Thomas Glendower looked up, took in the people invading his private space, then set aside the pen he'd been holding and smiled charmingly. "Excellent, my dear Penelope. Investing has been rather dull of late, and I could use a distraction."

Thomas rose and greeted Penelope warmly, raising her hands to his lips and bussing her knuckles, then he shook the men's hands. Barnaby introduced Jordan by name only. Jordan appeared a trifle wide-eyed as he clasped the legendary investor's hand.

True to the expectations of Barnaby, Penelope, and Stokes, Thomas narrowed his eyes at Jordan, then said, "Ah yes. You're Roscoe's man."

Jordan was surprised to have been recognized as such. Hesitantly, he asked, "Have we met previously, sir?"

Thomas smiled. "No, no. I just make it a habit to keep abreast of such things."

Barnaby shared a smirking glance with Penelope, then they drew up chairs and sat in a half circle before the desk, while Thomas resumed his seat behind it.

"So"—Thomas leaned back and folded his hands across his waistcoat—"what is this challenge?"

Stokes ran through the details of the murder and how that had led them to the gun-running scheme and Chesterton, then Montague took over and explained what they'd discovered in Chesterton's account book.

Barnaby concluded with "So now we need to identify the holders of those three crediting accounts."

Thomas nodded. "That should certainly be possible. Forbes is the manager we need to see at Moreton's. He'll be easy enough to convince"—Thomas dipped his head toward Stokes—"especially with Scotland Yard's finest making their presence felt."

Stokes dryly replied, "I'll do my best to loom large."

Thomas and Montague laughed, then Thomas rose, and the others did, too, and he waved them to the door. "No time like the present. New Union is just around the corner in Leadenhall Street."

They walked out of Thomas's office, and Thomas stopped to have a word with the helpful Minns before following the others out of the main office, down the stairs, and onto the street.

On the pavement, the company reorganized, then with Montague and Thomas in the lead, set off, striding along. At the end of the short street, they turned south on Bishopsgate, then at the next intersection, walked west along Leadenhall Street.

Penelope had taken Barnaby's arm and was walking behind Thomas and Montague. Bringing up the rear with Stokes, Jordan paced behind her.

As they made their way along Leadenhall, Jordan leaned forward and murmured to Penelope, "Even though I've only just met him, Glendower reminds me strongly of Roscoe."

Penelope arched her brows. She was rather intrigued that Jordan had so quickly detected the very real similarity between the two men. Not many would have noticed the subtle signs of their birthright that, despite their long years out of society, both Roscoe and Thomas still carried.

She glanced fleetingly at Jordan, then smiling to herself, whispered back, "Your instincts are sound. There is a definite commonality and, indeed, on more than one plane."

Jordan frowned faintly, but she offered no further explanation of her enigmatic comment, and as they were nearing the New Union Bank, there was no time for him to press her for more.

With expectation building, on Barnaby's arm, Penelope followed Thomas and Montague through the impressively polished doors of the New Union Bank.

Inside, the recently refurbished black-and-white-tiled foyer was abuzz with people queuing to speak with the cashiers stationed behind their long counter. Every piece of wood in sight was richly finished, and every sliver of brass was polished to a gleam. The New Union Bank was clearly intent on projecting the image of a successful and trustworthy repository of customers' money, and the subtle hum of commerce filled the air.

Apparently unimpressed, Montague and Thomas drew their party to one side of the foyer, close to one wall, where two large palms in brass pots gave an illusion of privacy.

In response to Penelope's questioning look, Thomas replied, "Now we wait."

She wondered for what, but before she asked, a dapperly dressed man came hurrying out of a discreet door at the rear of the foyer. From his pomaded hair to the starched stiffness of his collar and the excellent cut of his suit, he was plainly a higher-level employee.

The man made straight for their party—or rather, with an ingratiating smile affixed to his face, he hurried to present himself before Thomas and Montague. On reaching them, he halted and bowed. "Mr. Glendower, sir. And Mr. Montague!" The man smiled hopefully. "To what does More-ton's owe the pleasure of your presence?"

Penelope noticed that Jordan, standing beside her, was struggling to hide a too-revealing grin.

"As to that, Forbes"—Thomas waved to include the rest of them—"we are here on a legal matter."

"I see." Forbes's gaze drifted over Barnaby and Penelope, but then fixed on Stokes, and his manner grew wary.

Noting the change, Thomas explained, "We need to identify three account holders."

His tone a touch supercilious, Montague added, "It seems they've been involved in a quite dastardly—indeed, one might even say treasonous—crime."

"Good heavens!" Forbes darted glances at Penelope, Barnaby, and Jordan, clearly wondering about their roles in the matter. "Well, of course," he somewhat hesitantly said, "if it's in my power…"

"Oh, it definitely is," Thomas informed him.

"If it weren't," Montague added, "we would hardly be here, wasting our time as well as yours."

Forbes flushed. "No, of course not. I…that is…" He glanced at the crowd in the foyer, then stepped aside and waved their group to the door through which he'd entered. "Please, come through to my office. You can show me the details, and I'll see what I can do."

Penelope was the first through the door and found herself in an even more opulent foyer. Unsure which way to go, she paused to one side of the space. She'd noted that Jordan was paying close, indeed, rapt attention to every aspect of Thomas's and Montague's actions. When Barnaby and Jordan joined her, as Forbes was bringing up the rear and was still in the outer foyer, she seized the moment to whisper to Jordan, "Taking notes?"

He flashed her a grin, then dipped his head and murmured back, "I'm never loath to learn from the masters." He glanced at Thomas and Montague as the pair walked toward them. "And these two can plainly teach me a trick or two, or even three."

She chuckled, then Forbes came through the door, closed it behind him, and hurried to lead them on and into a large, luxuriously furnished office with ample seating for their company.

Thomas grasped the moment as they moved deeper into the office to perform the introductions. To say that Forbes's wariness escalated on learning Stokes was an inspector with Scotland Yard and, despite their station, Barnaby and Penelope acted as official consultants to the Metropolitan Police would be a severe understatement.

The man wasn't foolish and could plainly see the pressure that would be brought to bear on him and his bank should he not promptly accede to the group's request.

Learning that Jordan was Neville Roscoe's man-of-business and also assisting in the present investigation effectively eliminated any lingering resistance Forbes might have harbored.

He urged them to avail themselves of the comfortable chairs, but he chose to remain standing before his large desk. Once they'd settled, he cleared his throat and, plainly unsure whom to address, eventually looked at Thomas and Montague. "If I understood the matter correctly, you wish to identify the owners of several accounts for which, I presume, you have the relevant numbers."

Thomas nodded, and Montague replied, "Indeed. That is what we require in a nutshell. Three accounts with, very likely, three individual owners."

Forbes hesitated, then glanced at Stokes. "Might I inquire what manner of case the identification of these three account holders relates to?"

He wanted to be assured that breaking the seal of confidentiality any customer of Moreton's would expect him to preserve could be justified. However reluctantly, Penelope had to approve of Forbes's caution.

With every evidence of patience, Stokes explained about the gun-running scheme. "Such a scheme, of course, qualifies as treason. The account holders we seek to identify were, in effect, the financiers behind the scheme."

"Without them," Barnaby stated, "the scheme could not have existed, and we believe it's been active for at least two years."

"We might have stopped one shipment," Jordan put in, "but others went out over previous months."

Forbes's eyes had rounded. "Good Lord. Treason, you say?"

"Indeed," Stokes replied. "And I should add that the trail that led us to the gun runner started with a murder."

"We believe it's possible," Barnaby said, "that the murder of a man-of-business in his office not far away in Broad Street was committed by or at the behest of one of the three backers of the scheme."

"Good heavens!" The news caused a dramatic change in Forbes's demeanor. He looked from Stokes to Montague and Thomas. "You said you have the account numbers?"

Stokes drew out Chesterton's account book, and Montague and Thomas rose. Montague took the book from Stokes and waved Forbes to his chair behind the desk. "Sit, and we'll show you what we need."

Forbes did as he was bid, sat in his chair, and Montague opened the notebook and set it on the blotter before Forbes. Coming to stand on Forbes's other side, Thomas pointed to the relevant entries. "These three accounts are the ones we wish to trace."

Frowning, Forbes studied the entries.

Thomas calmly went on, "The notebook details payments into and out of an account held by Moreton's. Consequently, the easiest way to identify the holders of the three crediting accounts, each of which presumably comes from some other bank"—Thomas flicked a glance at the others, warning them not to correct that statement—"will be to compare this accounting with your official registers, which will detail which bank each payment came from and also confirm the account number."

Vaguely, Forbes nodded. "Yes. I see. And of course, you're right." He glanced at Stokes. "This is not an account I handle personally. If you will permit, I'll fetch the account ledger, and we can see what that reveals."

Stokes inclined his head in acquiescence, and looking greatly troubled, Forbes jotted down Chesterton's account number, then taking the number, rose and left the room.

Montague and Thomas exchanged knowing glances, then returned to their chairs.

In a bare two minutes, Forbes was back, carrying a large ledger and wearing an even deeper frown. He shut the door, then faced the company. "This account—the account whose details are in that notebook—was opened by a member of the public about two years ago, when Moreton's was still a public bank." Forbes looked at Stokes and Barnaby. "Consequently, those of us currently at Moreton's, which is now solely for private clients, are not familiar with the holders of these older public accounts."

"We know who that account belongs to," Stokes replied. "One Cornelius Chesterton."

Forbes looked at the front page of the ledger he held. "Oh. Yes. Quite right."

The banker was plainly rattled—more rattled than he had been before.

Noting that, Montague waved Forbes back to his chair behind the desk, and as he sat, Thomas mildly suggested, "Let's concentrate on those three crediting accounts." He waited while Forbes opened the bank ledger and flicked through the pages to locate the entries relating to said accounts. Once he had, Thomas asked, "First point of interest—from which bank were those deposits transferred?"

Forbes ran his eye down the ledger page, checking as he went against Chesterton's notebook. Then his finger paused. He stared at the ledger, then looked again at the notebook, and his face paled. He sat back, his gaze locked on the ledger entries. Faintly, he said, "Oh, I say..."

Montague shared a vindicated look with Thomas, then Thomas regarded Forbes and gently prompted, "I take it that all three crediting accounts are held by Moreton's?"

Forbes swallowed and, his complexion quite pasty, nodded. Then he gathered himself and looked up. "Yes. All three." He glanced at Stokes. "And now I've looked more closely, I believe I recognize the accounts."

Calmly, Stokes drew out his notebook. "Who owns those three accounts?"

Forbes's lips pressed tight. He was clearly torn.

Penelope stated, "Mr. Forbes, we are hunting a murderer and dealing with three men known to be behind the smuggling of treasonous contraband. Any law-abiding person, no matter their rank or occupation, should assist the police in whatever way they can."

Forbes regarded her, then slowly nodded. "Indeed, ma'am. You're right." He looked at Stokes. "But please let me check the account numbers before I give you the names. I don't want to make any mistake in such a serious matter."

Stokes nodded his acquiescence, and Barnaby added, "That's entirely understandable."

Forbes rose and crossed to a handsome brass-and-polished-wood filing cabinet that stood against the wall. He pulled out the top drawer, reached inside, and straightened with a long list in his hand.

As Forbes returned to the desk, his gaze going to the ledger, Thomas said, "It would be helpful, Forbes, if you would write down the names alongside the account numbers." When on resuming his chair, Forbes glanced at him, Thomas smiled and added, "This will become official evidence, after all—best you do all the police need you to do at once so the inspector or his men don't need to return again later."

That wasn't quite a threat, yet it served to focus Forbes on delivering what they needed. He drew out a clean sheet of headed notepaper, picked up his pen, dipped it in his inkwell, then working from his account list yet also crosschecking Chesterton's ledger and the account book to make absolutely sure, he started to write.

"It would be helpful," Stokes murmured, "if you would sign the list once it's complete."

"And add your official title," Penelope said.

Forbes glanced briefly at them, then returned to his task.

Three minutes later, he sat back, stared at what he'd written, then blotted the sheet and picked it up. His hand shook slightly as he held the list out to whoever wished to take it. "These are the names of the three gentlemen who own the three accounts that made regular deposits into Mr. Chesterton's account."

Being closest, Thomas took the sheet. He scanned the names, and his brows rose. He looked at Montague and handed the list to him.

Montague took it, read it, and his expression also changed to one of mild surprise tinged with intrigue.

Thomas looked at Forbes, who was clearly shaken. "Thank you, Forbes. By readily rendering such vital assistance to Scotland Yard in such a fraught case, you've solidified my confidence in you and Moreton's."

Forbes looked relieved, and a hint of color returned to his pale cheeks. "I…I'm pleased to have been of help."

Montague had passed the sheet to Penelope. She angled it so Barnaby and Stokes could read it, too, and Jordan rose and, over their shoulders, scanned the list.

On seeing the names associated with the three accounts, Barnaby understood Thomas's and Montague's reactions. Also Forbes's uncertainty. The Honorable Mr. James Winter, Mr. Claude Haverstock, and Mr. Herbert Huxtable were not names one would have expected to be allied with gun running.

Montague turned to Forbes. "You've done the right thing, Forbes, and I'm quietly impressed. I must come in and speak with you soon about what services Moreton's can offer my clients."

That declaration made Forbes brighten even more.

Barnaby heard Jordan, standing behind him, softly swear. When Stokes and Barnaby glanced up at him, Jordan rather grimly stated, "I know all three names."

That was curious. Barnaby resisted the impulse to ask why, as did Stokes. Right time, wrong place.

Stokes took the list from Penelope, who was, predictably, frowning. He folded the sheet, tucked it into his notebook, then came to his feet. He nodded to Forbes. "Thank you for your assistance, Forbes. We'll leave you to get on with your day." Stokes glanced at the others. "For our part, we clearly have avenues to pursue."

With the rest of their company eager to comply, with good wishes all around, they parted from Forbes, who showed them out into the main foyer.

When the unmarked door to Moreton's closed quietly behind them, Thomas waved them into the palm-delimited alcove they'd occupied earlier.

As they clustered around, Montague declared, "I've heard of all three gentlemen—Winter, Huxtable, and Haverstock." He met Stokes's gaze. "The rumors are that all three appear to have grown unexpectedly wealthy over the past few years."

Thomas nodded. "I've heard the same. And in the men-of-business world, unexpectedly means unaccountably." Thomas looked at Jordan. "The last I heard, all three were claiming they'd simply been lucky at the tables."

His expression serious, Jordan shook his head. "They have been playing the tables, but they haven't been lucky." Shifting his gaze to Stokes, he explained, "All three have been frequenting the boss's establishments over the past few years. But the thing is—and this is why I know their names—none of the three are the usual gamblers. They never come in expecting to win. Instead, they amble in, risk a little, inevitably lose it, then they hang about. It seemed to us that they were making sure they were seen by others. Then after a time, they amble out again. Because their rather strange behavior has been repeated many times, our staff noticed and reported it. Roscoe, Mudd, Rawlings, and I have been wondering what the three are about—whether there was something going on beneath our noses of which we were unaware."

Stokes huffed. "Unlikely, but I see your point."

"How often do they visit?" Penelope asked.

"Every few months, they'll be in for several evenings over a few weeks," Jordan replied. "Then we won't see them for several months, then they reappear, do the same thing, then vanish for another few months."

Barnaby was frowning. "It seems as if they're using Roscoe's tables as a smoke screen. Enough people see them gambling so when others notice their newfound wealth, they can believably claim to have had a lucky run."

Penelope nodded. "That no one ever sees them win doesn't matter. Everyone assumes that must have been on some other night when the particular observer wasn't present." Penelope looked at Thomas and Montague. "Speaking of their inexplicable newfound wealth—the sums Chesterton must have paid them—is there any way at all to trace that?"

Thomas and Montague grimaced, and both shook their heads.

"If they have any brains at all," Thomas said, "and it seems they do, they'll be keeping their ill-gotten gains as cold, hard cash, and there won't be any trace of it in any account of any stripe."

"It's likely," Jordan said, "that Winter, Huxtable, Haverstock, and Chesterton agreed on some simple formula for his payments to them. For instance, that once the smugglers pay Chesterton for the guns—which will always be in cash—he gives each backer three times whatever they'd put in for that shipment."

Thomas was nodding. "Such an arrangement would be easy for all four to calculate and keep track of, and that also leaves Chesterton with whatever was left over as his slice, which is a sound incentive for him to get the best price possible over and above covering the repayments."

Montague added, "I wouldn't expect to find any telltale trail to follow with respect to the money returning to the backers. They would certainly see that as a potential threat to them. However, when it came to making the initial payments to Chesterton, I suspect they simply found using Moreton's all too convenient. Luckily for us, as it transpires."

Jordan put in, "Whether by luck or design, they all had accounts at Moreton's, and as I said earlier, moving money within a single bank leaves minimal records and, therefore, fewer chances of anyone stumbling over the connection between Chesterton and the three."

"All of that," Stokes said, "the visits to the gambling clubs, the single bank account, and only cash going back to them, speaks to them knowing they needed to conceal the sums they've been raking in from the sales of the guns."

Barnaby nodded. "There's no chance that they were unaware of the illegality of what Chesterton was doing on their behalf."

Penelope huffed. "Not with all the steps they've taken to conceal their involvement."

Thomas tipped his head toward Stokes's pocket. "You have the list of names and account numbers, and you have Chesterton's private account book listing those same accounts. That should be all you need."

"Indeed." Stokes looked around the group. "So I'm for the Yard. I need to see the Commissioner about getting arrest warrants for these three."

CHAPTER 12

After parting from Montague and Thomas in Leadenhall Street, Barnaby beckoned to Phelps, who'd trailed them with the carriage. After the carriage drew up beside them, Barnaby handed Penelope up and, with Jordan and Stokes, followed her in, and as instructed, Phelps set the horses for Scotland Yard.

Once they arrived, Stokes left Barnaby, Penelope, and Jordan in his office and, taking the evidence of Forbes's list and Chesterton's account book, strode off to beard the Commissioner.

While they waited, Barnaby, Penelope, and Jordan reviewed the facts of the case as they knew them to that point and discussed which questions would best serve their cause in the upcoming interrogations.

Ten minutes after he'd headed off, Stokes returned with a smile of triumph wreathing his face. "Success! I've permission to bring in all three gentlemen. The Commissioner agrees we've evidence enough to hold them. I'm off to organize the arrests."

"Don't forget," Penelope said, "to do your best to make the arrests simultaneous."

Stokes paused in the doorway to add, "I'll also arrange that they don't see each other. Best to keep each of them guessing as to whether the others are speaking with us as well."

With that, he headed for the stairs.

"Well," Barnaby said, "it seems that we'll shortly be interviewing

Winter, Huxtable, and Haverstock." He looked at the other two. "So what do we know about each gentleman? I know all three are family men."

"As I recall," Penelope added, her tone disapproving, "they all have young children."

"They're what?" Jordan asked. "In their late thirties?"

"Something like that," Barnaby said. "More pertinently, all three hail from minor branches of long-established aristocratic families. None are close to any major title, but their arrests are sure to cause a stir."

Somewhat less than half an hour later, Stokes came back, an even greater smile splitting his face. "We have Winter downstairs, and Huxtable and Haverstock are on their way."

"That was quick!" Penelope sat up and eagerly asked, "Can we start with Winter?"

Stokes grinned. "I can't see why not." As she, Barnaby, and Jordan rose and joined Stokes in the doorway, he added, "Incidentally, you'll be meeting Inspector Mann. I'm handing the gun-running charges to him so that I can concentrate on pursuing Cardwell's killer."

"Excellent!" Penelope led the way to the stairs. "I admit I'm keen to hear what Winter says. He's always struck me as a straightforward, sensible sort, but obviously, social appearances are, in his case, deceiving."

They filed down to the main interrogation room in the basement. As they descended below ground, the atmosphere grew faintly claustrophobic, and the bare stone walls were cold and uninviting.

A tall, thin plainclothes policeman was waiting in the corridor opposite the main interrogation room door, his head bent as he studied the file he held open in his hands. He looked up as their group neared, then closed the file and straightened, a pleasant and plainly intrigued expression on his face.

Penelope smiled and stated, "Inspector Mann, I take it."

Mann smiled back and half bowed. "Mrs. Adair, I assume."

The riposte appealed to Penelope's sense of humor, and she grinned.

Stokes stepped forward and completed the introductions.

Mann shook hands with Barnaby and Jordan. "I've heard about you— well, the Adairs—of course. All the force has." His gaze on Jordan, he added, "Not so many have had the pleasure of meeting Roscoe's right-hand man, but most would know your name."

Jordan's lips quirked. "I'm not sure whether to be flattered or insulted by that."

Mann laughed. "Definitely flattered."

Stokes, who'd been conferring with O'Donnell, who was standing to one side of the interrogation room door, returned. "According to O'Donnell, Winter was taken completely by surprise at finding Scotland Yard on his doorstep, but as soon as he heard what the charges were, he gave every evidence of being eager to get here and clear his name."

"Interesting," Penelope mused.

Stokes waved at the door. "Let's see what he has to say."

He opened the door and led the way in.

With her curiosity concealed behind a censorious mask, Penelope followed.

Winter was sitting at the standard bare rectangular table with a constable Penelope didn't know at his back. Winter's gaze had been fixed on his hands, clasped on the table before him, but as their party entered, he raised his head and, with an angry frown on his face, watched them file in.

Then he recognized Penelope and, somewhat uncertainly, rose to his feet.

He was a large man, tall and broad shouldered and heavy with it. Penelope knew Winter as the third son of a minor viscount. She and Barnaby had been aware of his existence, although he didn't move in their more exalted circles. That said, he was nevertheless very much of the ton, and that showed in his expensive suit, his styled hair, and in the air of confidence and arrogant privilege he exuded.

As Barnaby followed her into the room and Penelope moved to claim one of the five chairs lined up along the nearer side of the table, the one to Stokes's right, she noted that Winter recognized Barnaby as well.

To her eyes, there was definite tension in Winter's shoulders, an aggressive tautness signaling hostility, and at the sight of her and Barnaby, that tension had only increased.

Then Winter's gaze fell on Jordan, and Winter's confidence noticeably ebbed.

Mann followed Jordan in and claimed the remaining chair on Stokes's left.

They all sat, including Winter.

The instant the chair legs ceased to scrape, Winter locked his gaze on Stokes and protested, "This is outrageous! Your men came blathering about some illegal scheme, and rather than arguing at the front door, I agreed to come here." His contemptuous gaze swept the cold, bare room, and he raised his hands, revealing that his wrists were manacled. "I didn't expect to be treated like a common criminal."

Stokes arched his brows and mildly replied, "I suggest you get used to it. From here, the ambience only gets worse."

"Indeed." Mann laid his folder on the table. He regarded Winter with an intensity that, to Penelope, called to mind a lepidopterist studying a recent find.

Winter scowled. "What is this nonsensical talk of gun running?" Fleetingly, he glanced at Penelope and Barnaby. "Why on earth am I here?" Manacles clanking, he spread his large hands. "I've done nothing wrong."

Ignoring that outburst, Stokes calmly introduced himself and the others, ending with Jordan, seated beyond Mann. Stokes described Jordan as Neville Roscoe's righthand man.

"What's he doing here?" In the manner of a dog unsure if he should cower, Winter scowled blackly at Jordan.

Stokes smiled thinly. "You may not realize it, Winter, but Roscoe values his business's reputation very highly, and he's quite protective of it. Consequently, Roscoe isn't a fan of illegal enterprises that in any way cross his path, and by all accounts, you and your coconspirators have been repeatedly doing so over the past two years."

Winter's gaze narrowed, and he seemed to draw back.

Imperturbably, Stokes continued, "With regard to this case, Roscoe has delegated Mr. Draper to assist with our investigation. Now"—Stokes glanced at Mann—"as to our case and the evidence we hold..."

Mann took over. "We have a gun runner and smuggler, one Cornelius Chesterton, in custody. We caught him in the act of transporting illegally acquired guns to Tilbury Dock." Mann met Winter's darkening gaze. "You will, no doubt, be interested to learn that Chesterton refused to name his backers."

"Well, then." Winter, who had paled slightly on hearing of Chesterton's arrest, resumed his belligerent attitude and flung a challenging glare at Stokes. "Again, why am I here? I have no idea who this Chesterton is and no connection with him."

Stokes smiled, and the tenor of the gesture had Winter easing back in his chair. "I was hoping you'd say that."

Winter swallowed. "There is no evidence. You can't possibly tie me to Chesterton."

"What about," Stokes asked, "the money you and your two coconspirators paid into Chesterton's account to fund his purchases of the guns?"

Winter almost asked, "What of it?" but caught himself just in time. He blinked twice, then ventured, "There's no evidence…"

"Only there is." Barnaby leaned forward. "Chesterton had to keep a running account for his own purposes. We found that, and from it, learned the account numbers of the bank accounts that paid Chesterton the funds to run the gun-smuggling enterprise."

"Someone," Penelope said, "had told Chesterton that tracing the owners of bank accounts from the account numbers—in effect, via the banks themselves—wasn't possible." She smiled tightly at Winter. "But in thinking that, that someone erred."

"You see," Stokes said, "the banks themselves have reputations to uphold and operating licenses to protect. When Moreton's was shown the evidence that certain account holders had been using their Moreton's accounts to fund a treasonous scheme, the bank was quick to provide us with the names of the three account holders involved."

Stokes had placed Chesterton's notebook and the signed statement from Forbes on the table. Now, he opened the notebook, found one of the relevant pages, and set it, open, on the table, facing Winter. "This is Chesterton's running account." Stokes pointed to three specific lines. "These three entries show payments into Chesterton's bank account, held in Moreton's, from three other accounts also held in Moreton's. One of those three account numbers is…" Stokes picked up the notebook and rattled off, "Six-seven-two-three-five-seven-two."

Stokes set down the notebook and picked up Forbes's statement. "And this is a signed statement from the manager of Moreton's bank, listing the owner of that account as"—Stokes looked at Winter—"you."

Winter stared at Stokes. On the table, his hands gripped tight.

After a moment of silence, Stokes sat back and asked, "Regarding the charges brought against you, do you have anything to say?"

Winter's earlier angry color had faded entirely. Pale and plainly out of his depth, he stared at the damning evidence resting on the table before Stokes and wrestled with his options in a situation he'd never thought he would face.

Eventually, Penelope took pity on him. "Trust me, Winter, it will go much better for your family—especially your sons and daughter—if you stop trying to cling to the façade of innocence and, instead, confess and assist the police."

Winter had glanced up at her mention of his family, and her comment about his children clearly struck home. After staring at her for a moment more, he slowly straightened, then he drew in a long breath and looked at Stokes. "What more do you want to know?"

Stokes, with Barnaby assisting, led Winter through the details of the scheme, including how it came about.

"That was purely by chance," Winter explained. "Chesterton came seeking backers at a race meeting in Doncaster. He fell in with us, and after realizing we might be open to the idea, he explained how his scheme would work. He'd already put together a crew of disgruntled workers at the gun factory who were ready to supply him with guns. For a price, of course, but it was easy to see that massive profits could be made by selling the guns overseas."

"Purely out of interest," Mann said, "did Chesterton tell you how the workers got the guns out of the factory?"

Winter paused, lightly frowning as he dredged his memories. "He said that there was always a pile of guns set aside as faulty. Those were the guns the workers were proposing to supply Chesterton with, I suppose on the grounds that they'd be least missed. He didn't say how they would get them out of the factory, but the impression we got was that they'd be smuggled out one by one, under men's coats, that sort of thing."

Jotting in his file, Mann nodded. "I assume that's the reason for the irregular gaps between Chesterton's runs. He had to wait for the factory workers to smuggle out enough guns to make a run worthwhile."

Glum and deflated, Winter shrugged. "I suppose so. That just seemed to be the way it worked."

Now leaning back in his chair, Stokes asked, "So what happened with Cardwell?"

Winter looked at Stokes, and his brow slowly furrowed. Eventually, he asked, "Who?"

Watching Winter, Penelope nearly groaned. *He doesn't have a clue who Thomas is.*

Confirming that, still frowning in an apparent effort to recall the connection and failing, Winter shook his head. "I don't know any Cardwell. Where does he fit into this?" He looked from Stokes to Barnaby and Penelope. "If he was a part of Chesterton's organization, then we—the three of us who supplied the funds—never met anyone but Chesterton himself. Everyone felt it was safer that way."

While answering their questions regarding the scheme, Winter's defensive façade had fallen, and his expression had grown increasingly easy to read.

It was obvious he truly knew nothing of any Cardwell.

Accepting that, Barnaby explained, "Last Sunday evening, a man named Thomas Cardwell stumbled upon the cache of guns Chesterton had stored in a warehouse near Tilbury. Less than two days later, before Cardwell could notify the authorities as he intended, he was stabbed to death, apparently by a gentleman wearing a fashionable dun-colored coat and a black top hat."

Penelope arched a brow at Winter. "Do you own a black top hat and a dun-colored coat, Winter?"

Winter blanched. "Of course I do—along with half the gentlemen in the ton." He looked at Stokes and Mann, then apparently came to a decision. "Look, I might own the right sort of hat and coat, but I have no idea who this Cardwell person is. As I said, we—the three of us—never had anything to do with Chesterton's arrangements or the people he employed. That was his side of the business, and we didn't want to know anything about it." He paused as if hearing how that sounded, then shook his head impatiently and continued, "So we know nothing about any warehouses. Until you mentioned it, I didn't know he used such places—I never thought about how he managed things at all. That wasn't our part of the bargain to meddle with, and as for Cardwell, until you mentioned him, I'd never even heard his name."

Penelope would wager that not one of the investigators thought Winter was lying. He truly knew nothing about Thomas Cardwell or anything of the circumstances that had led to his murder.

"For the record," Barnaby said, "where were you on Tuesday morning between the hours of seven and nine?"

Frowning, Winter thought back. "Tuesday morning? I would have been at home at that time. Breakfast is served at eight—I usually get down a trifle earlier and start reading the news sheets, then my wife and daughter arrive, and lastly, my sons come down. They're just old enough to join us. On Tuesday…I didn't leave the house until close to noon, when I went to my club to meet with friends." He glanced at Stokes. "The entire household can vouch for that."

Stokes held Winter's gaze. "The friends you met for lunch—were they the same friends who joined you in supporting Chesterton's scheme?"

Winter shook his head. "The three I met were not in any way involved in that."

After a moment studying Winter, Stokes nodded. "All right." He glanced at Mann, who'd been taking notes beside him. "We'll leave you to the tender mercies of Inspector Mann, who is taking over the gun-running case."

The door at the investigators' backs opened, and a young constable came in. He walked to Stokes and Mann, halted between their chairs, and bent to whisper some message.

When the constable finished speaking and straightened to attention, Mann met Winter's gaze. "I'm sending you to the cells for the moment. It seems we have your coconspirators in custody. I'll see you after we learn what they have to say."

With his shoulders slumped and looking defeated, Winter glumly nodded. From his expression, the reality of what his future was to be was inexorably sinking in.

With the other investigators, Penelope left the room.

Stokes and Mann paused in the corridor, and after a quick word, the pair dispatched sergeants and constables to Winter's, Haverstock's, and Huxtable's residences to question their wives and staff as to the men's alibis for Tuesday morning.

"Best we get those nailed down." Stokes grimaced. "It would be nice if Haverstock or Huxtable didn't have an alibi, but I think we're more likely to get the same result as we got from Winter."

Barnaby huffed. "Let's not count chickens either way."

"Indeed." Stokes waved them on, and they proceeded to another interrogation room farther down the narrow stone-walled corridor. There, they found Haverstock waiting behind a wall of bluster.

His resistance quickly faded when Stokes laid out the evidence against him, Winter, and Huxtable.

As with Winter, Haverstock was too intelligent to continue protesting and denying his complicity, and once again, Penelope's mention of his young family eradicated the last of his defiance.

The tale he told of how the three gentlemen had fallen in with Chesterton matched Winter's in every respect.

Also like Winter, his puzzlement and confusion as to who Thomas Cardwell was rang true.

After Mann sent Haverstock to the cells, they moved on to interrogate Huxtable, with a near-identical result.

At that point, the men sent to question the three households regarding Winter's, Haverstock's, and Huxtable's alibis returned with the unsurprising news that all three gentlemen were vouched for as being at home on Tuesday morning not only by their wives and older children but also by their staff.

With Huxtable on his way to the cells, the investigators trudged up the stairs to the foyer.

Through the interviews, Mann had grown increasingly alert. He turned to the others. "Unless you need me, Stokes—and I can't see why you would—I'll leave you to your endeavors. I need to get my crew up to speed so we can head up to Enfield first thing tomorrow."

"To the Royal Small Arms Factory?" Barnaby asked.

"Indeed." Mann's smile was one of anticipation. "I plan on spending the rest of this afternoon leaning on Chesterton for a list of his contacts there. Whoever they are, we have to put a stop to this caper as soon as we possibly can." He tipped a finger to his forehead in a salute. "Wish me luck."

With smiles and good wishes, they watched him stride away.

His expression sobering, Stokes faced the others. "Let's head to my office and take stock and think again about the Cardwell case."

As soon as they were seated, Penelope, Barnaby, and Jordan in the chairs before Stokes's desk and Stokes in his usual chair behind it, Penelope stated, "While I'm faintly disappointed that none of those three are guilty of Thomas's murder, I always suspected Chesterton's backers would prove too distant to be the killer."

"Distant?" Jordan asked, beating Stokes and Barnaby to it.

"Hmm," she said. "Just stop and think of the timing. Thomas was killed just over a day after learning of the guns. Sunday night to Tuesday morning—that's the time span we're working with. So how did the three backers—or any one of them—discover that Thomas knew about the guns and intended to alert the authorities, all within that relatively short period of time?" She looked at the others. "I just can't see it, can you? If Chesterton didn't know—and given he didn't move the guns, he didn't— then how could his backers have learned about Thomas?"

Stokes pulled a disgusted face. "Even though each of them is a gentleman and possesses the required hat and coat of the right sort, their denials were beyond believable, and their alibis are far too sound. Cardwell's murderer isn't one of them."

"About the murderer being a gentleman," Jordan said. "I had a word with Mudd and Rawlings about the possibility that the murderer wasn't actually a gentleman but a hired assassin dressed for the part." He grimaced. "They laughed. Apparently, the assassin who might pass for our unknown gentleman simply doesn't exist. According to them, assassins are highly secretive—obviously—but also are not the sort who would know how to pass for a gentleman, hat and coat or not."

"Regardless," Penelope said, "a hired killer means premeditation—meaning the person came to the office intending to kill Thomas. The killer would have come prepared with his own knife, not trusted to find a likely implement on Thomas's desk. A hired killer would have used his own knife and taken it away with him."

Stokes nodded. "The use of the letter knife argues that the killing was spontaneous, not planned. It was an opportunistic crime driven by a spur-of-the-moment decision."

"We also mustn't forget," Barnaby said, "that Thomas recognized the man and knew him well enough to let his killer follow him into his office." He looked at the others. "Whoever killed Thomas wasn't a complete unknown, so not a hired killer or any of Chesterton's backers."

Stokes sighed. "Excellent points, all." He looked around their circle. "So where does that leave us?"

"More specifically," Penelope said, "*who* does that leave us? Whose name is, however unconfidently, still on our list?"

Stokes's office door slammed open, startling Penelope as well as Barnaby, Stokes, and Jordan.

They swung around to see Morgan clutching at the swinging door.

"Sorry, sorry!" Belatedly, the young constable rapped his knuckles on the wooden panel while the huge grin on his face grew. "But you'll all want to hear this!"

At Stokes's nod, Morgan bounded into the room, closely followed by Constable Walsh. Both were beaming fit to burst.

Stokes was struggling to find a frown. "Close the door, Walsh." As Walsh obeyed, Stokes looked at Morgan. "All right. Out with it. What have you found?"

Barnaby held up a staying hand. "In the interests of our understanding, start at the beginning rather than the end. You were sent to the Fox to see if you could find witnesses to confirm that Thomas Cardwell was there on Sunday evening and followed Chesterton when he left for the warehouse."

Morgan was nodding. "And we found our witnesses, right enough.

Both the barmaid and the barman remember Thomas being there on Sunday evening. They're an observant pair—I suppose they have to be with a clientele like that. They're always on the lookout for troublemakers. That's why Cardwell caught their attention, not that they knew it was him. Apparently, he was wearing an old frieze coat with a cap pulled low on his forehead, and he was slouching back in the darkest corner and watching the three regulars who were talking with Chesterton. It was Cardwell's focus on that table that triggered the barman's and barmaid's instincts, but Cardwell simply watched, so they let him be."

"Then," Walsh said, "the three gents up and left, but Cardwell remained in his corner, watching Chesterton."

"And then," Morgan took back the telling, "Chesterton finished his pint and left. Cardwell watched him go, then came to the bar and asked the barman if he had a hack for hire. Just for a few hours, maybe the night."

"And?" Penelope demanded. The constables' excitement was infectious.

"And," Morgan replied, "the Fox does hire horses, and the barman fitted Cardwell up with one. That's when the barman got a better look at Thomas's face, and without us saying anything, the barman said he thought he looked like the brother of one of their regular gents."

"Excellent!" Stokes looked up from his notes. "That's going to make life easier."

Morgan grinned. "We haven't got to the good bit yet."

Barnaby waved him on. "Stick to the what-came-next, or you'll lose us."

"Right." Morgan paused for a second to gather his thoughts. "Anyway, the barman watched Thomas ride off. The land's very flat there—well, we all saw that when we went to the warehouse. The barman said Thomas rode out onto the road, but seemed to pause and cast about, then he rode off southwestward across the fields."

Jordan's eyes had narrowed as he envisaged the scene. "In the direction of the warehouse." He met Morgan's bright eyes. "So as we thought, Thomas followed Chesterton, almost certainly to the warehouse."

"Another point ticked off." Stokes made a note in his book.

Walsh added, "The barman said that Thomas brought the horse back a bit over an hour later. They were still open, but about to shut up for the night."

"Good." Stokes looked up. "Is that it?"

"No!" Morgan's blue eyes were alight. "There's more! I thought to ask the barman and barmaid if they saw anyone unusual—not a regular—around on the next night. The Monday night when we know Chesterton came in again and paid the three gents. And both barman and barmaid described another man—a different geezer. This one was tightlipped, not as tall as the first—Cardwell—and in the barmaid's words, looked to have borrowed an old coat and cap from some poorhouse, but she noticed his linen and waistcoat were much better quality. And this second geezer was watching Chesterton and the three gents, too. And to cap it all, when Chesterton left, this second bloke also hired a hack from the house and, as far as the barman could tell, followed Chesterton."

"The barman said it was like a sideshow," Walsh put in, "all following Chesterton."

Morgan nodded. "The barman said as the second man also brought the hired horse back before they shut for the night. I asked whether he—the barman—saw any resemblance to the three gents, and he said that night it was too dark to see much, but from what he did see, he didn't think so."

Stokes looked at Morgan—who had all the appearance of a puppy who had just delivered a bone to its master—then Stokes transferred his gaze to Walsh, who was merely looking hopeful, and nodded. "That is one excellent piece of detective work on both your parts."

Both constables all but preened under the rare but well-deserved praise.

Barnaby leaned forward, drawing Stokes's attention. "So there *was* another man who learned about the guns." Barnaby looked at Penelope and Jordan, then back at Stokes. "Who was he?"

"And was he the man who killed Thomas Cardwell?" Penelope mused. "If so, why?"

Jordan was frowning. "What led this other man to follow Chesterton?" He met Penelope's eyes. "Was it the same reason that prompted Thomas to follow Chesterton—meaning because of our gentlemen dupes and their unexplained additional income?"

"That," Barnaby said, "would make the second man either Sir Ulysses or Keeble."

"Or someone sent by one or the other to follow their son," Morgan volunteered.

Penelope felt as if they were literally spinning, juggling facts and conjecture.

Stokes broke the momentary silence. "The essential question still before us is this: Who was the gentleman who met Thomas Cardwell on Tuesday morning at his office door—the man Thomas recognized enough to greet, then allow to follow him inside? The man who, a little while later, departed the office via the rear door and, in between, left Thomas Cardwell stabbed to death with his own letter knife."

Stokes glanced around, clearly inviting comment.

After a moment, Penelope asked, "Have we been approaching the murder—the motive for it—from the wrong angle?" She glanced at Barnaby, then looked at Stokes. "What if it's not about the guns *per se* but about the exposure of the gun-running scheme? We know Thomas intended to alert the authorities to the existence of the scheme."

Barnaby frowned. "I think you're right, but regardless, that's a valid way forward motive-wise. So who does the exposure of the scheme threaten?"

They batted possibilities back and forth, but inevitably returned to the three gentlemen dupes and Sir Ulysses and Keeble.

"But," Penelope said, "if we're now on the right track as to motive, then the killer can only be someone who knew about the guns. By that reasoning, it can't be the three dupes because, naive as they are, they never knew about the guns. We all agree on that."

Barnaby nodded. "If they didn't know about the guns, they couldn't have known there was any threat hanging over them." He looked at Stokes. "Based solely on motive, that leaves us with Chesterton, Winter, Haverstock, Huxtable, and this other man who followed Chesterton and learned about the guns."

Stokes humphed. "And we know it can't be Chesterton, and we've just proved his three backers were otherwise engaged at the time of Thomas's murder."

"We have an unknown gentleman who followed Thomas into his office and killed him," Jordan said, "and another unknown man—according to the observant barmaid, likely a gentleman as well—who followed Chesterton from the Fox on Monday night and, we assume, learned about the guns." Jordan looked at Barnaby and Penelope. "What are the chances we have two unknown gentlemen—one who learned about the guns and one who, for some other reason entirely, killed Thomas?" Jordan shook his head and answered his own question. "Those odds are too long. I think we need to accept that the man who followed Chesterton on Monday night is the same man who, on Tuesday morning, met Thomas at his office and killed him."

"We mustn't forget," Penelope put in, "that our unknown man—and I agree there can be only one—didn't go to see Thomas expecting to kill him. He went to see Thomas to…well, we don't know what they discussed, but clearly, something Thomas said caused the man to seize the letter knife and stab Thomas to death."

"But," Stokes said, tapping his blotter with his pencil, "if we agree we have only one unknown man, then that argues that the motive for Thomas's murder is, indeed, the threat posed by the exposure of the gun-running scheme."

"More," Barnaby said, his voice growing firmer, "that also means that the unknown gentleman came to see Thomas because he had reason to at least wonder if Thomas knew about the guns."

"By that reasoning," Penelope stated, "Sir Ulysses Moubray and Mr. Keeble are now at the top of our suspect list."

Stokes nodded. "The easiest first question for us to tackle is whether each has a solid alibi for Tuesday morning between seven-thirty and eight-thirty."

Barnaby was nodding. "Also, if we're down to two prime suspects"— he glanced at Morgan and Walsh, who had been quietly standing by and avidly listening to the discussion—"regarding the man who followed Chesterton on Monday night, can we push further and see if the barman or barmaid of the Fox might be able to identify him?"

Stokes looked at Morgan and Walsh and nodded. "It's worth a try."

As it was too late for Morgan and Walsh to travel to Tilbury and return that day, Stokes told the pair to check with him first thing the next morning. "Depending on what we learn this afternoon, you'll likely be heading down to the Fox to employ your persuasive talents."

Morgan and Walsh grinned and chorused, "Yes, guv."

Stokes waved them off, then turned to Barnaby, Penelope, and Jordan. "Should we beard our prime suspects this afternoon or leave it until tomorrow?"

"This afternoon," Penelope stated. "It's not even four o'clock, and between four and five is not a bad time to call if we want to be sure our suspects are at home."

The men agreed, and they left the building and climbed into the waiting carriage, and Barnaby directed Phelps to the Moubrays' house in Frederick Street.

This time, with Stokes and Jordan accompanying Barnaby and Penelope, they were shown directly into Sir Ulysses's study. Mrs. Moubray was not present nor was she summoned to join them, and it was very clear from the first curt word of greeting that Sir Ulysses was not at all happy to see them.

Good manners, however, prevented him from saying so.

Barnaby performed the introductions, and after waiting until Penelope subsided into the armchair the butler set for her, Sir Ulysses waved the gentlemen to the remaining chairs before his desk and resumed his seat behind it.

Sir Ulysses regarded Stokes from beneath beetling brows. "Inspector." The word was all but barked. "What can I do for you, sir?"

Ignoring the hostility Sir Ulysses was directing his way, Stokes explained that they were, they believed, closing in on Thomas Cardwell's murderer. "However," Stokes continued, "as part of our investigation, it's become necessary to eliminate every gentleman potentially connected with Thomas Cardwell. Consequently, we need to inquire as to your whereabouts between the hours of seven-thirty and eight-thirty last Tuesday morning."

Sir Ulysses huffed in a disbelieving fashion. "You expect me to give an account of my movements?" His tone suggested the request was the height of inappropriate rudeness.

Imperturbably, Stokes inclined his head. "If you would, sir."

Sir Ulysses huffed again, even more incensed. He turned his gaze to Barnaby. "Surely, Adair, this isn't necessary?"

His expression impassive, Barnaby replied, "I assure you, Moubray, that answering the inspector's question is the fastest route to seeing the back of us."

Penelope leaned forward and assured the man, "Truly, Sir Ulysses, we have no wish to cause the slightest difficulty. However, the inquiry is a valid one and will likely be judged as crucial to the outcome of the inquest."

Barnaby hid a grin as his wife artfully paused to allow the specter of a public hearing to fully bloom in Sir Ulysses's mind before she added, "The simplest way to avoid any unnecessary attention is to tell us and the inspector where you were at that specific time."

Sir Ulysses's demeanor had undergone several subtle changes during Penelope's speech, denoting, Barnaby suspected, a horrified cringe at the thought of being called to the dock at Thomas Cardwell's inquest. After staring at Penelope for several seconds, Sir Ulysses huffed again, but this time in defeat. He shifted his gaze to Stokes and gruffly stated, "At that time on Tuesday morning, I was out walking. Taking my constitutional, as I do every morning, weather permitting."

After showing them in, the butler had remained in the room, unobtrusively standing back against the bookshelves. Barnaby thought Sir Ulysses had forgotten the man was even there. However, in this instance, that proved helpful, as the butler was nodding in ready and instinctive confirmation of his master's statement.

Penelope couldn't see the butler, so asked, "I take it, sir, that your staff will vouch for that being your habit?"

"Of course they will." Sir Ulysses's color heightened. "Because it is."

That Sir Ulysses didn't glance at the butler confirmed Barnaby's supposition that the master had forgotten the servant was there.

Stokes had been jotting in his ever-present notebook. "As I recall, last Tuesday morning was reasonably fine."

Sir Ulysses replied, "If it was, then I was out strolling the streets, and before you ask, I didn't encounter anyone I know who might vouch for that. At that hour, I rarely meet any acquaintances."

That's likely why you walk so early, Barnaby thought.

It was clear that Sir Ulysses was no one's fool, and his prickliness over accounting for his movements on the fateful morning was because he understood why the investigators had asked their question, and by being out of the house and unable to offer any corroborating testimony as to his actual whereabouts, he would, inevitably, remain on their suspect list.

Penelope smiled on Sir Ulysses as if congratulating him on being so forthcoming. "Can you recall where you strolled on your constitutional last Tuesday?"

Sir Ulysses primmed his lips, then consented to reveal, "If you must know, I always take a turn around Regent's Square. It's not far—a few blocks away—and I pause and take note of the trees there." On seeing Penelope's brows rise, he gruffly added, "I grew up in the country, and the trees in the square remind me of the trees around my old home in Shropshire."

"I see. How lovely." Penelope flashed the old soldier an understanding smile, then looked brightly at Stokes. "Do we have any further questions?"

Stokes shut his notebook and stated, "For the moment, that will do."

They rose, and Penelope voiced her hope that Sir Ulysses would remember her to his lovely wife, then Stokes and Jordan exchanged nods with their host, and Barnaby shook his hand, and they allowed themselves to be ushered by the butler out of the study and out of the house.

They paused on the pavement beyond the gate.

"I don't think it's him," Penelope stated. "He didn't want to tell us where he was at the critical time because he feels the revelation is too personal. That it reveals too much about him emotionally in that he still misses his childhood home."

Stokes was nodding. "I agree, but to my mind, even more telling is that he made no attempt to concoct an alibi. If he was the murderer, he would have fabricated something believable by now."

His hands in his trouser pockets, Jordan stated, "Making up something to deflect police interest is an instinct that's extremely difficult for a guilty person to ignore."

Stokes shot Jordan a grin. "Just so."

"That's true enough," Barnaby said, "but in terms of confirming Moubray's alibi, despite his obliviousness, others will have seen him out walking." He caught Penelope's eyes. "I'm going to set the lads onto finding people who saw Sir Ulysses on his morning ramble about Regent's Square. Given the area, even at that time, someone will have been out and about and aware of him. He's large and, with his striking mane and carriage, rather hard to miss."

Penelope stated, "If he was walking around Regent's Square and not anywhere east of Frederick Street, heading toward Broad Street, I believe we can cross him off our list."

"But not," Stokes insisted, "until we have confirmation of his alibi." He nodded at Barnaby. "Get going and find some of your lads and put them on the case. The sooner we can prove that Sir Ulysses is not our man, the sooner we can concentrate solely on Keeble."

After a short discussion, they decided to go straight on to Myddleton Square and interview Keeble before Barnaby set off to find his lads and set them searching.

They gathered on the pavement before the Keeble residence, and Penelope turned to Stokes. "Keeble has a footman acting as butler, and at this hour, the chances are that, like Sir Ulysses, Keeble will be in his study and will choose to see us there. Might I suggest that you and Barnaby have the footman take you to see Keeble while Jordan and I"—

she included Jordan with a glance—"go to the kitchen and question the staff?"

Stokes regarded her with interest. "You think the staff know something useful."

"I think they'll tell us where Keeble was on Tuesday morning without any roundaboutation," Penelope stated. "And if we want a corroborated alibi for the man, then his staff are likely our best source."

"I agree," Barnaby said. "So we'll tackle Keeble while you interview his staff." He grinned at Stokes. "Seems a sensible division of labor."

Stokes grunted in agreement and led the way through the gate to Keeble's front door.

As Penelope had predicted, the door was opened by the footman she and Barnaby had encountered before. The footman remembered them and, after Stokes had introduced himself, admitted their party to the house. He left them in the drawing room while he informed his master of their presence. Penelope sat on the sofa, but the men remained standing as Stokes and Jordan looked around curiously. Then the footman returned, intending to show them to the study where Keeble awaited them.

Penelope smiled at the footman. "You may take the inspector and Mr. Adair through to Mr. Keeble, then please join me and Mr. Draper in the kitchen. We have a few questions for the staff before joining the gathering in the study."

Her confident delivery—that of a hostess well-accustomed to managing staff—had the footman falling in with her directives without hesitation. He paused only to show her the way to the kitchen before leading Stokes and Barnaby to Keeble.

Penelope waited until the door to the study shut, then walked quickly down the corridor to the kitchen.

Amused and curious, Jordan followed at her heels.

They walked through the archway that gave onto the kitchen to discover a maid, a tweeny, and an older woman who was clearly the cook standing about a central deal table. The three were engaged in preparing the evening meal, but froze at the sight of the unexpected intruders.

Penelope smiled understandingly. "My husband and I called yesterday as part of an ongoing police investigation. We simply have a few questions we believe you can assist us with. This won't take much of your time."

Jordan stepped aside as the footman returned, eager curiosity in his face. He nodded respectfully to Penelope. "Ma'am. You said you have questions for us?"

"Just a few simple ones." She glanced at the cook, maid, and tweeny. "Is this the entire staff?"

"Yes, ma'am." The cook wiped her hands on her apron. "Now Mr. Josh has gone to live with his friends, there's only the master to see to, so we manage well enough."

"I see. Well, that should make this easy." Penelope glanced at the footman. "Inspector Stokes, who together with my husband is currently speaking with your master, and myself and Mr. Draper here are trying to establish where Mr. Keeble was last Tuesday morning, during the hour between seven-thirty and eight-thirty."

With a reassuring smile, Penelope went on, "You see, asking Mr. Keeble for his movements is one thing, but of course, what he says cannot be taken as proof. For that, we need the testimony of others, which is why we've come to speak with you. So"—she looked around brightly—"what are your recollections of what your master did last Tuesday morning?"

The cook frowned, then hesitantly offered, "Well, I serve breakfast at a quarter of seven. He likes it early—always has."

Penelope nodded encouragingly. "So at seven or so, he was seated at the breakfast table?"

Both maid and footman nodded.

"Very well," Penelope said. "At what time did he rise from the table?"

The footman's face cleared, and he turned to the maid and cook. "Tuesday last—that was the morning he went out early." He looked at Penelope. "Quite took me by surprise, but he sent me to fetch his hat and coat and left at barely seven-thirty." Suddenly looking conscious, the footman added, "I'm sure of the time because it was so odd for him to go out at that hour that I checked the clock in the hall."

"Excellent," Penelope said.

"So he doesn't usually go out in the morning?" Jordan asked.

"Not until after eleven, normally," the cook stated.

"I can't think of when he last left the house before ten," the maid added.

"Did he happen to mention what caused him to leave so unexpectedly?" Penelope asked. "Did he drop a hint of where he was going or why or what he planned to do?"

Again, the four shook their heads.

"Not one to share his business with the staff," the footman said, "if you know what I mean."

Penelope inclined her head. She and Jordan exchanged a glance, then Penelope turned to the staff. "Thank you. You've been quite a help." She looked at the footman. "I believe it's time Mr. Draper and I joined the discussion in the study."

"Yes, ma'am." The footman half bowed, turned, and led her and Jordan from the kitchen.

On reaching the study, the footman opened the door, announced Penelope and Jordan, and stood back to allow them to enter.

She and Jordan walked into the study, and it was plain from the look on Keeble's face that their arrival had caused him to startle and stumble and break off whatever he'd been saying.

Then the three gentlemen got to their feet, Keeble almost springing upright.

The footman, perhaps wisely, had slipped out of the room and drawn the door closed.

Penelope went forward, a calm smile on her face. "Good afternoon, Mr. Keeble. We meet again. Mr. Draper and I have just been securing corroboration of your whereabouts from your staff."

Jordan set a chair for her beside the one Barnaby had occupied, and she sat, allowing the gentlemen to resume their seats. Once they had, she turned to Barnaby and Stokes and inquired, "So, have you gentlemen established where Mr. Keeble was on Tuesday morning?"

Evenly, Stokes replied, "Mr. Keeble has assured us that, as usual, he remained at home for the entire morning."

Penelope widened her eyes in exaggerated surprise and turned her gaze on Keeble. "That's strange…"

Keeble all but squirmed, then he cleared his throat and focused on Stokes. "Actually, Inspector, now I think of it, I believe Tuesday morning might have been the morning on which I felt rather queasy, and I went out for a brief walk to clear my head."

"Is that so?" Stokes responded. "So you weren't here between seven-thirty and eight-thirty?"

"Not in the house, no." Keeble hurried to assure them, "But I was nearby."

"Oh?" Barnaby said. "Where did your walk take you?"

Now he'd made his confession, Keeble seemed to calm. "Not far at all —just around the square. I sat on one of the benches on the other side of the church, on the south side of the square, and when, eventually, I felt rather better, I came home."

Stokes had been taking notes. "I see." He looked at Keeble. "Is there anyone—a neighbor or acquaintance—with whom you spoke while you were out?"

Keeble frowned, then grimaced and shook his head. "No. I'm sorry. I'm afraid I wasn't paying much attention to anything beyond my stomach."

Stokes glanced at Barnaby and Penelope, then looked at Jordan. When all three looked back and said nothing, Stokes returned his gaze to Keeble and nodded. "Thank you, Mr. Keeble." Stokes stood and tucked his notebook away as the others got to their feet. "At the moment, I think that's all we need to know."

Keeble fussily assured them that he was only too happy to help, then ushered them out of his study and to and through the front door.

As the door shut behind them and they strolled up the short path to the pavement, Barnaby murmured, "He was so very happy that we were leaving."

Penelope glanced at the house. "He was very relieved to see the back of us."

"Indeed." Stokes halted on the pavement and looked at Penelope and Jordan. "So what did the staff have to say?"

"They seemed entirely straightforward in answering our questions," Penelope stated. "And they were very surprised that, on Tuesday last, Keeble left the breakfast table at close to seven-thirty, called for his hat and coat, and quit the house. He doesn't normally walk in the mornings, not like Sir Ulysses, so they were taken aback when he unexpectedly up and left."

"Note," Jordan said, "the mention of hat and coat. He was definitely wearing both when he left. No saying if they're the right sort, but we at least know that much."

Barnaby grimaced and glanced around their circle. "We need to be careful about leaping to conclusions."

Stokes nodded. "At this point, based on the facts as we know them, either Sir Ulysses or Keeble could be our man. Neither has an alibi for the time of Cardwell's murder, so logically, both must remain on our list."

Jordan glanced at the other three. "But only Keeble tried to hide his lack of an alibi. Sir Ulysses was reluctant to tell us, but he didn't try to pretend he wasn't out of the house, ambling, at the critical time." He looked from Penelope to Stokes. "Sir Ulysses was honest about where he went, while Keeble tried to dissemble."

Stokes pulled a wry face. "Sadly, we've had too many cases where, when faced with an apparently straightforward question, the innocent dissemble, and more often than not, it's for some reason entirely unconnected with the case."

"And," Barnaby added, "all too often, the guilty appear brazenly innocent."

Penelope had been staring at the pavement. She raised her head and looked at Barnaby. "Perhaps you should put your lads onto finding sightings of Keeble, as well."

Barnaby nodded. "I'll do that. There's no saying what they might turn up." He looked northeastward toward the busy intersection where Pentonville Road met City Road. "I should be able to find some of the crew nearby." He looked at the others. "Why don't you head back to Albemarle Street? I'll see who I can find to get the word out that we need sightings of Sir Ulysses and also Keeble on Tuesday morning, then I'll join you there."

The other three agreed, and while they piled into the waiting carriage, Barnaby slid his hands into his trouser pockets and, eyes scanning the streets for any likely lads, strolled off toward City Road.

CHAPTER 13

When Barnaby returned to his house, he found Penelope entertaining Stokes and Jordan in the drawing room. A late tea tray bearing a platter of Cook's buttered crumpets had been brought in, and with small plates in their hands, Stokes and Jordan were looking distinctly replete and content.

Penelope smiled at Barnaby and leaned forward to pour him a cup of tea.

Barnaby claimed his usual position beside her on one of the long sofas, and she handed him the cup.

He'd just taken his first sip when the doorbell pealed, and half a minute later, Mostyn opened the drawing-room door and ushered Ruth Cardwell in.

The men rose, and smiling rather nervously, Ruth approached. "I pray you'll excuse the intrusion, but I came hoping to learn if you've made any progress in the case." She hesitated, then added, "The family are keen to know."

"Of course." Penelope waved Ruth to the opposite sofa. "Do sit down and let me pour you some tea." She shifted to do so. "Barnaby's just arrived, and we were about to review what we know to this point and plan our next moves, so your arrival is opportune."

Once Ruth sank onto the sofa, the men resumed their seats.

"It's entirely reasonable for the family to seek updates," Barnaby assured her.

"Indeed." Stokes set aside his empty teacup and, for Ruth's benefit, briskly recapped. "This morning, we reinterviewed Chesterton and subsequently identified, arrested, and interrogated his backers, of which there were three."

"Three gentlemen of the ton," Penelope interjected.

Stokes went on, "While the three will be charged over their part in the gun-running scheme, we do not believe they had anything to do with your brother's murder."

"They didn't even know who Thomas was," Jordan put in.

"However," Stokes continued, "we then learned that, in the same way as Thomas had followed Chesterton on Sunday night, on Monday night, some other gentleman, presently unknown to us, surreptitiously observed Chesterton's meeting with Harrison, Gibson, and Josh and subsequently followed Chesterton from the Fox, presumably to the warehouse."

"We have to assume that the as-yet-unidentified gentleman also learned about the guns," Penelope said.

"Also," Barnaby added, "that he, too, had some reason to find out what Chesterton was up to, presumably linked to the reason that took him to the Fox in the first place."

"And he wore a disguise," Jordan said. "And on the Monday evening, after the delivery had been completed, the warehouse would have been full of guns."

"Just as we found it on Thursday." Stokes paused, then went on, "Now we know that some other gentleman had also learned of the guns and, it seems, Harrison's, Josh's and Gibson's involvement in Chesterton's scheme, our attention has, unsurprisingly, turned to the two gentlemen who, it could be argued, had a vested interest in whether information concerning the gun-running scheme was conveyed to the authorities."

Ruth had been following their revelations closely. She frowned. "You mean Sir Ulysses and Mr. Keeble?"

"Exactly." Penelope focused on Ruth. "Are you acquainted with them?"

"I wouldn't say acquainted," Ruth replied. "We've only ever met at ceremonies or events at King Edward's Grammar, and even then, it was only in passing." She met Penelope's eyes. "I'm afraid I can't tell you anything specific about either man."

Jordan shifted. "Would Thomas have recognized Sir Ulysses or Keeble Senior?"

"Oh yes." Ruth was clearly confident about that. "Thomas was only a year younger than Gibson, so Thomas knew Harrison and Josh at school and definitely knew who their fathers were, certainly well enough to recognize them."

"Hmm," Penelope said. "We had interviewed Sir Ulysses and Mr. Keeble earlier, but we reinterviewed them this afternoon, seeking to establish if either or both had alibis for the time of your brother's murder. Sadly, neither did."

"Well, not satisfactory alibis, at any rate," Stokes explained. "Both were out walking at the time."

"We're hoping," Barnaby said, "that informants on the ground will help us verify where both men were over the critical period."

"That," Stokes declared, glancing at his fellow investigators, "has to be the first task on our revised list—confirming the whereabouts of Sir Ulysses and Keeble Senior between seven-thirty and eight-thirty on Tuesday morning."

Brisk footsteps in the hall ended with a rap on the door, and when Barnaby called, "Come," Mostyn walked in. The majordomo halted and, to Barnaby, reported, "One of the lads—Julian—is here with information regarding your recent inquiry."

Jordan blinked. "That was quick."

Barnaby smiled. "Our network can be surprisingly effective." He nodded to Mostyn. "Send Julian in."

Mostyn retreated and, mere seconds later, ushered in a young lad of about thirteen. He was dressed neatly enough and, by his cap, presently grasped tightly in his hands, was one of the errand boys who haunted the city's streets, looking to serve those who wished to send messages faster than the penny post.

Smiling, Barnaby leaned forward and beckoned the lad closer. "Julian. Mostyn says you have news?"

Clearly overawed by the company, Julian shuffled a trifle closer and stiffly bowed. Then he fixed his bright eyes on Barnaby's encouraging face and said in a rush, "That cove you wanted to know about—Sir Ulysses. He always takes a stroll around the streets every morning. Regular as clockwork, he is. I live not far away, and I often see him of a morning. I was curious, so I took note—as you always say as might be helpful. I know he leaves his house at seven-forty-five on the dot, then he goes across to Regent's Square and walks around it, always clockwise, and he looks at the trees. He walks slowly all the way around, then he returns to his house, and he's going in the door at eight-thirty. Every day, even Sundays, unless it's raining cats and dogs. You could set your watch by him—he's as good as listening to the bells."

Stokes was busy jotting. "And Sir Ulysses—how do you know the man you see every morning is him?"

"That head o' hair," Julian replied. "And he struts like an old military man, and he lives in a house halfway down Frederick Street."

Stokes nodded. "And Sir Ulysses was definitely out walking his usual route on Tuesday last?"

"Yessir." Julian bobbed his head. "It was fine all the mornings this week, and I know he was there because I'd've noticed if he wasn't, if you take my meaning." Julian paused, then said, "I know I saw him every morning this past week, if that helps?"

Stokes grinned, raised his gaze to Julian's face, and nodded. "It does, yes. Thank you. You've done excellently well."

Julian's chest puffed up, and his smile grew wide.

Barnaby smiled approvingly. "Thank you for coming so promptly, Julian." He tipped his head toward Mostyn, who had waited by the door. "Go with Mostyn, and he'll give you your reward. You've earned it."

Thoroughly chuffed, Julian bowed again, then turned and went to Mostyn, who ushered the boy out and shut the door.

Deeply impressed, Jordan turned to Barnaby. "Your Lads' Network is inspired. I'm definitely stealing the idea."

Barnaby laughed. "By all means."

Penelope looked at Stokes. "It seems Sir Ulysses is struck off our list."

Barnaby leaned back against the sofa. "That means our trail of evidence leaves us looking at Keeble Senior as the murderer."

Stokes grunted. "Agreed." He looked around the circle of faces. "Now how can we prove it? Knowing he could have committed the murder isn't enough. We need evidence that he did."

The company fell silent, everyone going over what they knew and what they didn't.

Eventually, Stokes said, "We can see if the barman and barmaid of the Fox can identify Keeble as the second man who followed Chesterton on Monday night."

Barnaby nodded. "That's one point in the chain of events that we should make every effort to nail down."

"Keeble had to have learned about the guns," Jordan said, "or the rest —killing Thomas—doesn't make sense."

Penelope shifted on the sofa. "Tomorrow's Sunday. Given Keeble's social ambitions, I'll eat my best bonnet if he doesn't attend the church in Myddleton Square. He's so careful of his image, he's sure to be at the service."

"The rest of the square," Barnaby said, "well, at least beneath the trees, is more or less open ground." He looked at Stokes. "If we can get the barman and barmaid up from the Fox, we should be able to set up a viewing." Imagining it, he arched his brows. "Most likely at the conclusion of the service when the congregation files slowly out of the church."

Stokes nodded. "I'll send Morgan and Walsh to use their best efforts to bring the barman and barmaid up to town. Assuming they succeed— and as it's Sunday and the Fox will be shut, there's a decent chance they will—we can arrange to have the pair there, at the right time and in position to view Keeble as he exits the church."

Jordan had been mulling over something. He looked up and said, "The killer must have—or have had—a dun-colored coat and a black top hat."

Penelope perked up. "An excellent point!" Bright-eyed, she regarded Jordan. "I propose that, tomorrow morning, once Keeble leaves his house for the church"—she shifted her gaze to Ruth and smiled encouragingly —"Ruth, Jordan, and I should call at the Keeble residence and ask his staff about his wardrobe."

Jordan was nodding. "The staff struck me as pragmatic people and not the sort to be blindly loyal."

"I don't think Keeble Senior is the sort to inspire blind loyalty," Penelope observed.

Jordan said to Ruth, "There are four staff members all told. A cook, a maid, a tweeny, and one footman."

Stokes sat back. "I think we can agree that those two avenues—identifying Keeble as the man who followed Chesterton from the Fox on Monday night and confirming that he possessed the required style of coat and hat—are the most viable paths for us to pursue tomorrow."

No one argued.

After a moment, Jordan ventured, "I've been trying to work out why Keeble killed Thomas. What drove him to such an act?" He looked at the others. "It doesn't seem to fit with his character."

Barnaby frowned. "I think we have to start by assuming that, like Thomas, Keeble learned about the guns."

"That was on Monday night," Penelope pointed out. "He couldn't, at that point, have known that Thomas knew about the guns, much less that Thomas planned to alert the authorities to the scheme."

"No, he couldn't have known," Stokes said. "But what if that's why he went to see Thomas? To find out if Thomas—like Keeble himself—had grown suspicious enough to follow Gibson and had subsequently learned about the guns. Remember, Keeble—if our unknown gentlemen is he—was waiting impatiently outside Thomas's door that morning. For some reason, Keeble felt he had to learn the answer right away—and that sort of reaction does fit his character."

Barnaby narrowed his eyes, as if imagining the scene in Thomas's office. "So Keeble goes to see Thomas to find out if Thomas knows of the guns—"

"And Thomas told him he did and also that he, Thomas, planned to go to the authorities." Penelope looked around the circle of faces. "Thus far, I can see all that happening."

"So can I," Jordan said, "but what I can't see is why Keeble then seizes the letter knife and stabs Thomas."

Everyone frowned as they tried to work out a plausible motive to account for that event.

Eventually, Stokes said, "We know that Thomas would have recognized Keeble and not balked at having Keeble come into his office."

He cocked a brow at Ruth, and she nodded. "Thomas would have recognized Keeble Senior and wouldn't have seen him as any threat."

"And," Penelope stated, "we already know, because Keeble told us so, that given he was in a similar business, he had no need of Thomas's services, so there was no professional connection between them."

When Penelope also looked to Ruth for confirmation, Ruth stated, "Thomas never mentioned having any dealings with Keeble, and he most definitely would have if such an interaction had occurred."

Penelope nodded. "So there was no business connection, and the only reason Keeble could have had for killing Thomas was the guns...or rather, the threat of the gun-running scheme being brought to the attention of the authorities." She tipped her head and regarded Stokes, then looked at Barnaby and Jordan. "So the question is, was there a reason that Keeble saw Thomas notifying the authorities of the gun-running scheme as a fundamental threat?"

Frowning, Ruth admitted, "I, too, can't imagine why, on learning that Thomas knew about the guns and was about to contact the authorities, Keeble wouldn't have agreed and worked with Thomas to mitigate the effects of any revelation on Josh, as well as Gibson and Harrison. That was surely Thomas's intention. That had to be what drove him to write to Roscoe."

Stokes nodded. "I agree. Both Keeble and Thomas had the same reason for attempting to approach the authorities in the best way, namely to protect their son and their brother respectively. And given Keeble's dedication to climbing society's ladder, doing the right and proper thing and notifying the authorities is exactly what one would have expected him to do."

"That's why Thomas was so surprised." Jordan glanced at Ruth. "I'm sorry if speaking of Thomas distresses you, but…"

Ruth shook her head. "Better to speak of him and find his murderer. Trust me, that's what the family wants."

Jordan nodded and looked at Stokes. "Let's try the sequence of events again. Keeble learns about the guns, and as soon as he possibly can, he goes to see if Thomas knows, too. He learns that Thomas does know and intends to notify the authorities."

"We shouldn't forget," Barnaby cut in, "that Keeble didn't go to see Thomas intending to kill him."

Penelope picked up the thread. "But something Thomas said caused Keeble to panic, pick up the letter knife, and kill Thomas."

Stokes stirred. "We keep circling the point of Keeble having some unknown but deeply compelling reason for not wanting Thomas to contact the authorities." He looked at the others. "What could such a reason be?"

Jordan offered, "Because he wanted to protect Josh?"

"But Thomas was already doing his best to protect Gibson, Harrison, and Josh," Stokes said. "I can't believe that in telling Keeble he intended to alert the authorities, Thomas didn't make that part of his plan plain."

Penelope nodded. "Just think of how that discussion must have gone. If Keeble balked on the grounds of protecting Josh, Thomas would have tried to calm his parental concerns by explaining what he hoped to achieve." She paused, then went on. "I would be more inclined to think that Keeble feared that any revelation would fundamentally undermine, even fatally damage, his long-standing efforts to socially elevate the family."

Stokes thought, then grimaced. "That's possible, but in truth, neither of those motives—protecting Josh or protecting the family's social status —feel strong enough, compelling enough, to have panicked a man like Keeble into committing murder."

Barnaby was slowly nodding. "The reason, whatever it is, must be powerful enough to inspire a degree of panic sufficient to make Keeble lash out—unexpectedly and, in many ways, uncharacteristically."

They all pondered the situation, then Jordan glanced at Stokes. "Perhaps we can approach this from a different angle. If Thomas hadn't been killed but had proceeded as he'd planned and notified the authorities, what would have happened?"

"Specifically," Penelope said, "what would have happened to Keeble Senior?"

Stokes frowned. "The guns would have been seized, as, in fact, they have been. Chesterton would have been arrested and interrogated"—he glanced at Jordan—"and I hope we would have eventually hauled in his backers as well. Our three innocent dupes would have been interviewed— as they were." Stokes paused, then went on, his voice growing firmer, "And to prove that the three gentlemen's claims of being dupes was, in fact, the truth, and they or members of their families hadn't been taking a larger slice of Chesterton's pie, we would have looked into their finances…" Stokes met Jordan's eyes. "And the finances of their families."

Jordan pointed at Stokes. "There it is. That's what Keeble feared. He's not unintelligent. He realized it was likely that if the gun-running scheme was exposed and Josh's part in it investigated, that would have led to his books being examined."

"He told us he was a financier." Barnaby straightened. "That he handles the finances of several large investors."

Stokes smiled wolfishly. "I think we've finally seen the light. Keeble's motive in killing Thomas Cardwell wasn't anything to do with the gun-running enterprise *per se* but had everything to do with keeping the authorities away from Keeble's own business."

His eyes narrowed, Jordan said, "Most financiers wouldn't want the authorities poring over their ledgers, yet the threat of that happening wouldn't drive any to murder."

Stokes nodded. "So there's something illegal—possibly highly illegal —that Keeble Senior is a part of."

"And" Penelope said, "don't forget Keeble's lifelong devotion to ascending the social ranks. He's devoted his entire life to struggling further up—"

"So the prospect of his illegal business dealings being exposed and bringing his social house of cards crashing down around his ears..." Barnaby looked at Stokes. "*That's* a powerful enough motive to compel a man like Keeble to murder."

Penelope sat back and declared, "Keeble was living in a glass house. He couldn't afford any stones to be thrown, and Thomas was preparing to launch a brick."

Stokes had been thinking. Raising his head, he looked at the others. "As we aren't arresting Josh Keeble, until we can arrest Keeble Senior, we can't barge in and examine his accounts. That said, I agree that the answer to what got Thomas Cardwell killed lies there. So our immediate task is to find sufficient solid evidence to make our case against Keeble Senior. Once we can arrest him, his accounts are the first place we'll look for the reason he killed Thomas."

All agreed, and they settled to make firm plans for the following morning in their push to gain the evidence necessary to arrest Earnest Keeble.

That Sunday morning at a few minutes before ten o'clock, accompanied by Jordan and Ruth, Penelope sat waiting in her carriage, which was parked along the side of Myddleton Square that faced the rear of the church and the bulk of the trees and lawns.

From his position on the box beside Phelps, Penelope's footman-cum-guard, Connor, had a clear view of the Keeble residence across the corner of the square. Connor had been delegated to keep watch and inform his mistress the instant Keeble Senior departed his abode.

When Connor dropped to the pavement, opened the door, and announced, "He's just left his gate. He's striding along the pavement toward the front of the church," Penelope felt thoroughly vindicated in her prediction that Keeble would attend the morning service.

"Excellent." She held out her hand and allowed Connor to help her down the steps to the pavement.

Jordan joined her and handed Ruth down.

Penelope cast a glance over the pair, then tipped her head toward

Keeble's house on the north side of the square. "He'll be out of sight by now. Let's go."

She set off walking briskly for the gate, and Jordan and Ruth hurried to keep pace.

Penelope paused before the gate to allow Jordan to open it, then sailed through and up the path to the door. She glanced along the street and confirmed Keeble was no longer in sight, having presumably rounded the corner of the church, making for the front door, then she lifted the knocker and rapped a demanding tattoo.

The footman opened the door and showed only mild surprise at finding her and Jordan and Ruth on the doorstep. "The master's just left for church, ma'am."

"I know." Penelope waved the footman back, and he obligingly retreated, allowing them into the house. "It's you and the rest of the staff we're here to speak with."

"Oh?" The footman looked more curious than apprehensive.

Penelope nodded decisively and gestured for him to shut the door. As he did, she informed him, "The police have a few more questions, and we're here to ask them."

When the footman dithered about whether to show them into the drawing room, Penelope pointed toward the kitchen. "We're not here to cause trouble. The kitchen will do."

She determinedly led the way and walked under the archway into the kitchen's warmth to find the cook and maid sitting at the table, nursing cups of tea. A plate with slices of raisin cake sat in the table's center, and the tweeny was replacing the kettle on the stove.

All three women stared, then the cook and maid leapt to their feet.

"Ma'am." The cook cleared her throat. "Could I offer you a cuppa and a slice of cake?"

Penelope smiled reassuringly. "No need to trouble yourselves. We won't keep you long." She glanced at the footman and beckoned him to join the group at the table. "As I mentioned to…"

She arched her brow at the footman, and he dutifully supplied, "Phillip, ma'am."

She nodded and continued, "As I just told Phillip, the police have a few further questions for you, the first of which is does Mr. Keeble have a long, dun-colored coat, the sort that's currently all the rage among gentlemen of the ton?"

Penelope put forward the question generally, but brought her gaze to rest on Phillip, who, as the only male member of staff, she assumed also acted as Keeble's gentleman's gentleman.

Phillip cleared his throat and replied, "He did have such a coat, ma'am, but after his walk last Tuesday morning, he came home in one of his fusses and stripped off the coat and bundled it up and declared it was damaged beyond repair." Phillip glanced at the maid. "Sally was passing, and the master gave the coat to her and told her to get rid of it."

Along with Ruth and Jordan, Penelope shifted her gaze to Sally, who blushed under the attention.

As if this was some story game, Penelope smiled encouragingly at Sally. "So you took the coat. What did you do with it?"

Sally cast a glance at the cook, then at Phillip, before looking at Penelope and admitting, "I did take the coat, ma'am, but when I got it in here and shook it out, I couldn't see what Mr. Keeble was on about. Lovely coat it was—expensive material and silk lining, too. It seemed perfectly fine to me, so I gave it to my beau. He was thrilled to have it."

Penelope couldn't keep the delight from her face. "And who is your beau?"

Sally's expression dimmed. "He's not in any trouble, is he? Because of the coat?"

"No," Penelope assured her. "Not at all. If anything, it's quite a relief to know the coat is in safe hands." She paused, head tilting as she thought, then added, "We might need to borrow the coat for a short time, but I'll make sure he has it back."

"But," Jordan said, "we will need to know who he is."

"No trouble of any sort will come to him," Penelope declared. "You have my word on that."

Sally read the truth of that statement in Penelope's face and, reassured, revealed, "Jimmy is Lord Monteith's footman. His lordship has the house at number twelve, just around the square."

"Thank you." Penelope inclined her head to Sally. "That's very helpful, and I assure you no difficulty will arise for you, your beau, or any of you"—she included the rest of the staff with her gaze—"due to answering our questions." She looked around the circle of staff again. "Now, does Mr. Keeble have a black top hat?"

Phillip nodded. "He wore it to church this morning, ma'am."

"Excellent." Penelope could verify with Connor that Keeble was wearing the hat, and of course, the others would see Keeble when he emerged from the church. She allowed her smile to brighten and swept an approving gaze over the staff. "That's all we came to ask." She inclined her head to the group. "Thank you for your help. I should also add that there's no need whatsoever to inform Mr. Keeble of this visit."

"Yes, ma'am" was a chorus as the maid, cook, and tweeny curtsied, and Phillip, rather surprised, moved to lead them out.

Penelope followed Phillip along the short corridor and into the front hall, her mind busy imagining how to explain her need to speak with his footman to Lord Monteith, with whom she and Barnaby were acquainted.

Ruth and Jordan followed her. Their presence during the short interview had been primarily by way of bearing witness so that the staff wouldn't need to be called on to testify in court.

On reaching the front door, Phillip set his hand on the latch and paused. Then he turned and looked at Penelope, who had halted behind him, then raised his gaze to Ruth and Jordan, who stood at her back. "This is about that morning, isn't it?" Phillip asked. "Last Tuesday, when the master went out so unexpectedly—which was strange enough—and then came home in a flat-out fluster."

Penelope regarded Phillip with sudden interest. "Anything you can tell us regarding that morning will be much appreciated."

Phillip hesitated, then offered, "The master's fluster wasn't just about his coat being ruined. He'd also lost his gloves. He definitely had them on his hands when he left, and it's strange because he rarely takes them off, not when outside the house. They were a lovely pair, too—soft, buttery leather. He was truly upset and said he must have forgotten them somewhere."

"What color were these gloves?" Jordan asked.

"Tan," Phillip replied. "Very soft, top of the range. Monogrammed, too."

From Jordan's expression—and Ruth's—both were thinking furiously.

Penelope hid her surging expectation and smiled as mildly as she could at Phillip. "Thank you. That information might prove useful."

Vital, even.

Phillip bowed and swung open the door, and Penelope led the way out of the house. She made straight for the gate and the pavement and kept walking, drawing Jordan and Ruth in her wake.

Penelope stopped only when they'd reached the carriage. She swung and faced Ruth and Jordan as they halted facing her. "Right," Penelope said. "What are you two thinking?"

The pair exchanged yet another glance, then Ruth looked at Penelope. "The gloves. If Keeble was wearing them when he stabbed Thomas, they'll be bloodied."

"That's why Keeble had to get rid of them before coming home," Jordan said. "More, he probably had to get rid of them as soon as he got into the lane."

"They could very well still be in the lane," Ruth said. "Not many people use it, and there are hidey holes between the stones. We should search and see if we can find them."

"And they're monogrammed, of all things." Jordan shook his head. "How ironic if it's Keeble's vanity and trying to mimic his betters that contributes to his downfall."

"Indeed." Fire flared in Ruth's eyes, and determination infused her tone.

Penelope looked from Jordan to Ruth and had to wonder if that was how she and Barnaby appeared and sounded to others when they were in the throes of a shared investigation. "Well," she said and refocused on the task at hand. "I suggest the pair of you find a hackney and go to Broad Street and see if you can find those gloves. Meanwhile"—she turned to survey the houses along that side of the square—"I'll go and beard Lord Monteith and have a word with his footman regarding his new coat."

Excitement had taken hold, especially for Jordan and Ruth. The pair readily agreed, and Ruth took Jordan's arm.

"Whatever you find," Penelope reminded them, "don't forget that as soon as we've completed our missions for the morning, we're reconvening at Scotland Yard to share all we've gleaned."

Jordan nodded. "We'll go and look and meet you there."

Buoyed by fresh expectations of success, the three parted and determinedly embarked on their separate missions to track down the critical elements of Keeble's wardrobe.

At the time Penelope knocked on Lord Monteith's front door, Barnaby was standing with Stokes, O'Donnell, Morgan, Walsh, and their two witnesses—the barman, Stan, and the barmaid, Lottie, from the Fox Orsett public house—waiting for Earnest Keeble to emerge from the church.

They'd taken up a position just inside a tiny back alley off Chad

Street. Ten yards or so away, the eastern end of Chad Street joined the street that formed the western boundary of Myddleton Square at a point directly opposite the main door of St. Mark's Church. From the corner of the alley, their witnesses would have a clear and unobstructed view of the members of the congregation as they filed out of the church.

Considering the position's advantages, Barnaby felt moved to compliment O'Donnell. "This is an excellent site for our purposes. Neither too far away for sure identification nor so close that anyone exiting the church is likely to notice us watching."

"Aye," O'Donnell said. "Bit of luck Walsh being familiar with the area and knowing about this spot."

His gaze trained on the closed double doors of the church, Stokes observed, "Presumably, Keeble will turn toward his house. That should give our witnesses a clear view of his face and, as he walks along on the pavement, of his profile and his movements."

O'Donnell nodded. "Couldn't be better, really."

A few yards along the alley, Morgan and Walsh were standing with Stan and Lottie and keeping the pair from the Fox amused while they waited for the service to end, the congregation to emerge, and their moment to arrive.

Minutes ticked past, then the large wooden doors of the church were pushed wide, and the strains of the organ playing a processional spilled into the street.

"This is it." Stokes waved to Morgan and Walsh, and they guided their witnesses to the corner.

Barnaby and Stokes fell back along Chad Street and watched as the constables, overseen by O'Donnell, directed their witnesses in where to look and what to watch for.

A species of expectant excitement crackled in the air as they waited.

The minister emerged and took up his stance by the door, and his flock started filing out, pausing to shake the minister's hand and exchange a few words before moving on and allowing others to take their place.

A bevy of older ladies came first, followed by several older couples.

"Looks like a decent-sized congregation," Stokes murmured.

Barnaby nodded. "Still, we know he's in there. He'll eventually appear." After a moment, he added, "It's to our benefit that they all move so slowly. When Keeble eventually emerges, our witnesses will have time to take a good look."

Almost on the words, Keeble appeared in the front archway. He had to wait for another minute before the old and obviously well-to-do couple before him greeted the minister and moved on, then Keeble stepped forward, a smile on his face, and shook hands with the minister.

Barnaby looked at their witnesses, who were being kept separate enough that one's reaction wouldn't signal the other. Nevertheless, it was instantly apparent from the way both had stiffened that each had independently recognized Keeble.

Keeble exchanged a few words with the minister, which kept Keeble in full view, then he half bowed to the minister, set his top hat on his head, and stepped away, onto the pavement.

An elderly gentleman hailed Keeble, and he stopped to chat, all the while in perfect view of the witnesses at the corner of the alley.

Finally parting from the old gentleman, Keeble turned and walked on around the square toward his house.

The instant Keeble turned the square's corner, Stan, the barman, swung to face Stokes and O'Donnell. "That was him. The gent as just walked away was the man who hired a hack from me last Monday night."

Lottie nodded. "It was definitely him as was watching Mr. Chesterton that evening."

"Thank you." Stokes exchanged a look with O'Donnell and Morgan, then returned his gaze to Stan and Lottie. "Would you be willing to testify to that—that he's the man you saw on Monday night at the Fox—in court?"

Barnaby wasn't surprised when both barman and barmaid looked alarmed and hurriedly disclaimed any willingness to appear before a judge.

Stan shook his head. "Won't do me business any good were that to come out—and it always does, doesn't it? Once that happens, people will wonder if I'm keeping tabs on them, and they won't come in."

Looking rather frightened, Lottie was nodding in adamant agreement.

Stokes regarded both, not without sympathy, then asked, "Instead of appearing in court, would you be willing to sign a statement saying that you believe the man you just saw, who we know to be Mr. Earnest Keeble, is the gentleman who came to the Fox last Monday evening, watched Mr. Chesterton, and then when Chesterton left, Keeble hired a hack and, apparently, followed Chesterton?"

Stan and Lottie exchanged a long look, then Stan asked Stokes, "Will the statements be read out in court along with our names?"

Barnaby sensed Stokes stifle a sigh, then Stokes said, "I'll give you my word that your statements won't go anywhere outside Scotland Yard. They won't be tendered to any court or seen by any judge. Just the Commissioner of Police."

Again, Stan and Lottie communicated wordlessly, then Lottie asked Stokes and Barnaby, "This geezer—Keeble—you're saying he murdered the other gent, the younger one who came in the night before?"

His expression grave, Barnaby replied, "That's what we believe."

"That," Stokes explained, "is why we need your statement. So that we can arrest him for the murder of Thomas Cardwell, the younger gentleman you saw the evening before."

"The one as was a brother to one of our three likely lads?" Stan asked.

Barnaby and Stokes nodded.

Stan and Lottie exchanged another long look, then Stan faced Stokes. "All right, then—but just a statement for the police."

Relieved to have got that much, Stokes readily agreed and handed the pair to Morgan and Walsh to escort to the Yard, take the statements, then return the pair to the Fox as the constables had promised.

After watching O'Donnell and the constables usher Stan and Lottie away, Stokes shared a glance with Barnaby, then they started walking toward the main street in order to find a hackney.

"At least," Barnaby said, looking ahead, "we can now feel sure we're on the right track."

Stokes grunted. "Maybe so, but let's hope the others have had more luck in securing some admissible evidence."

Penelope was waiting in Stokes's office when Barnaby and Stokes walked in.

The instant they appeared, she beamed triumphantly, sat up, and shook out the long dun-colored coat she'd retrieved. "Exhibit number one, I believe."

His gaze on the coat, Stokes rounded the desk. "Is that Keeble's?"

"Yes." Penelope surrendered the coat to a curious Barnaby. "When he returned to the house on Tuesday morning, Keeble was all a-fluster, apparently. He declared the coat ruined and gave it to his maid and told her to get rid of it."

"Did he, indeed?" Stokes sat in his chair.

"Obviously," Barnaby said, examining the garment's labels, "the maid didn't burn it."

"She couldn't see what was wrong with it," Penelope said, "so she gifted it to her beau, who happens to be Monteith's footman."

Barnaby threw her an amused look. "You enjoyed asking Monteith to speak with his footman on secret police business, didn't you?"

Her lips pressed tight in a vain attempt to mute her grin, Penelope nodded. "He was so consumed with curiosity, but he served me tea and biscuits, and the footman surrendered the coat willingly, although he would like it back."

"I'm not surprised," Stokes said, eyeing the garment. "It appears to be an expensive piece."

"From one of the best tailors," Barnaby confirmed. "It has the tailor's label sewn in, and I'm sure he'll be able to confirm that Keeble was the customer for whom he made this."

Stokes frowned and looked at Penelope. "But why did Keeble declare it ruined?" He looked at the garment hanging from Barnaby's hands. "Is it damaged in some way?"

"Not so anyone would readily notice." Penelope leaned forward, caught the skirt of the coat, and held up the inside hem. "Here, see? A smear of blood. Almost certainly, Keeble got that when he crouched beside Thomas to check that he was dead."

Stokes's smile grew wolfish. "Excellent."

"And I can also confirm that he has the right sort of top hat," Penelope said. "You will have seen it yourself when he left the church."

Barnaby and Stokes nodded. "We did," Stokes said.

The sound of footsteps pattering along the corridor reached them, then the door was flung open, and Jordan and Ruth rushed in, their faces alight with determination.

"Good," Jordan said. "You're all here."

Ruth reached into her large reticule and drew out and brandished a pair of bloodied gloves. "We found Keeble's gloves, and they're covered in blood." Her voice broke. "Thomas's blood."

Barnaby handed the coat to Stokes and reached across and gently took the gloves from Ruth. "Where did you find them?"

"And how did you know to look for them?" Stokes asked.

Penelope explained about the information they'd unexpectedly received from Keeble's footman. She looked at Barnaby. "Once Keeble is in custody, we must go back and reassure his staff. They've been nothing but honest and sensible and helpful."

Barnaby nodded. "We can speak with Josh about what to do about them."

"He seemed a good sort," Penelope said. "Hopefully, he'll keep them on."

Jordan stepped up to explain how, reasoning that the gloves would have been very bloody and that Keeble would have disposed of them as soon as he possibly could, Jordan and Ruth had combed the alley behind Thomas's office, unfortunately in vain, but then an urchin had asked what they were looking for. "When we told him, he directed us to one of the local beggars. He had the gloves. He'd found them stuffed into a crevice in the wall just along from the rear door of Thomas's office. For a fee, he surrendered the gloves and was happy to show us exactly where he found them."

By then, Ruth had recovered her equanimity. "And best of all, they're monogrammed." She pointed to the gloves.

Barnaby turned them over and found the embroidered initials. "EK. Earnest Keeble." He checked for a label and found one. "The glover's label is here, too, so we won't have any difficulty proving these are Keeble's gloves."

"His entire household knows those gloves," Penelope said. "And almost certainly, Josh will, too."

More footsteps had them all looking at the open doorway.

O'Donnell and Morgan arrived and, with satisfied expressions on their faces, nodded to everyone, then approached the desk and handed Stokes two formal-looking sheets.

"The signed statements from Stan and Lottie, sir," O'Donnell said.

Morgan added, "By the time we reached here, both were a bit torn over not testifying in court, it being a murder case and all, so they signed these readily enough."

"Walsh has gone with them to see them off back to the Fox," O'Donnell reported.

"Good." Stokes rose, gathered the statements, the coat, and the gloves, then surveyed the crowd in his office. "An excellent morning's work all around. I'm off to see the Commissioner to get permission to act on this evidence."

Stokes moved toward the door, and the others made way for him to leave the office.

Once he had, O'Donnell and Morgan eagerly asked about what Penelope, Jordan, and Ruth had found, and the company spent several minutes trading stories of the morning's events.

Then Stokes was back, his expression caught between a satisfied grin and a frown. When everyone looked at him, he grunted. "The verdict is that, yes, we can arrest Keeble for the murder of Thomas Cardwell. The caveat is that, today being Sunday, we can't do so until tomorrow."

Barnaby thought, then waggled his head. "The delay shouldn't be an issue."

"No," Stokes admitted, "but the other point the Commissioner made, once he'd taken a gander at our evidence, is that he feels the case, while being strong on the physical evidence, is weak when it comes to motive."

Penelope pursed her lips. "He's right about that." She glanced at Jordan. "As we concluded yesterday, Keeble must have an extremely powerful motive we've yet to uncover."

Jordan nodded. "And that motive has to derive from his business, and any evidence of it will be buried in his ledgers."

Barnaby considered that, then looked at Stokes. "We need to catch him off guard so he has no chance of destroying that evidence."

Stokes nodded. "We should plan to have his arrest and a major search occur virtually simultaneously."

"We need," Jordan stated with a glance at Ruth, "to learn what fact was powerful enough to spur a man like Keeble to kill to hide it."

Barnaby looked at the faces around him. "We're almost there, and it's Sunday. Given our enforced hiatus, I suggest we should take the time for a pre-celebratory luncheon at Johnson's."

Johnson's Steak House was an eatery nearby of the sort where O'Donnell, Morgan, and Walsh could join the party.

Penelope smiled and rose. "I agree." She took Barnaby's arm. "And after enjoying our well-deserved reward for all our hard work thus far, we can make our plans for tomorrow and discuss how best to ensure we learn all of Keeble's secrets."

~

After enjoying the camaraderie about the shared luncheon table, Jordan hailed a hackney and escorted Ruth home to Finsbury Circus.

After descending from the carriage, Ruth glanced at the house, then looked at the park and tipped her head toward the walks beneath the trees.

"Can we sit in the park for a little while?" She blushed. "If you have time, that is."

"I have time." Jordan reached for her hand and wound her arm in his and turned their steps across the cobbles.

As they passed into the cool shade beneath the trees, many now bursting into leaf, Ruth sighed. "I feel so…discombobulated. Uplifted by the news that we know who the murderer is, then I think of Thomas—" She broke off, then went on, her voice softer, "It's so strange. I feel like he's still here, and in my head, I'm turning to tell him…about his murderer."

Jordan glanced at her face, then steered her to an unoccupied bench.

She sat, and he sat beside her, and as they looked out at the well-tended lawn, he closed one of his hands about one of hers. Gently. In support.

She didn't seem to mind.

After a moment, she shifted her hand and lightly returned the pressure of his fingers. "Learning why Thomas died is important to me and the family. We can't put his death behind us—can't come to any sort of terms with it—without knowing why."

She paused, then went on, "I'm also concerned for Gibson, and Harrison and Josh. Josh… He's never shared his father's avidity regarding social status. Because of his mother, Josh was, in a way, born to a higher rank than his father. She might have died when he was young, yet she's clearly had a lasting impact on how Josh sees himself. He's not obsessed with social climbing at all."

Jordan nodded. "I've only met him in passing, but he didn't strike me as thinking in such terms." He glanced sideways at Ruth. "He didn't seem at all like Keeble. Not fussy or particular or trying to show he's special in some way."

She was silent for a moment, then said, "I hope that Gibson and Harrison will stand by Josh."

Jordan gently squeezed her hand. "If they do, you can be there for them. All three of them. They'll need others to stand beside them."

Ruth turned her fine blue eyes on him. "Will you?"

Jordan blinked.

Ruth smiled wistfully. "They look up to you, you know. You're the much older brother who knows what he's doing with his life, and they don't. They still haven't worked that out, but interacting with you, they realize that they can and, eventually, must."

"And will," Jordan said. "They're not silly, any of them. They'll find their way if they search for it."

"I rather think," Ruth said, "that Fate has decreed that knowing you will be a pivotal point on their journey."

"You give me too much credit," Jordan said, feeling faint heat in his cheeks.

"I don't think I do." Ruth sighed. "But I'm dillydallying over what I wanted to ask you."

Surprised, Jordan looked at her. "Ask away. I told you earlier—and I meant it—that with anything, anything at all, all you have to do is ask."

"In that case"—a small smile played across Ruth's lips—"I wanted to ask if you would…stay." She met his eyes. "Stay and see this through with me. Stay…and see where this leads." She glanced down at their linked hands, then raised her gaze to meet his. "I don't know what might come of this"—with her free hand, she waved between them—"but I do know that I want to find out."

"As do I." Jordan raised her hand to his lips and brushed a kiss across her knuckles, then raised his eyes to hers. "I will stay. Gladly. Like you, I don't know what might be, but I am very certain that I want to learn what the future could hold."

The rattle of a carriage's wheels had them turning to watch as a hackney drew up before the Cardwells' house. Gibson stepped down, paid the jarvey, then head hanging, shoulders slumped, walked up the steps and went inside.

Ruth looked at Jordan. "Will you come inside and help me explain what the investigators have found?"

Jordan nodded. "I'll help, but we'll need to hold back on the identity of the murderer for now." He met her gaze. "It would be unfair to burden Gibson with the news that it was Keeble, his best friend's father, who murdered Thomas. And we don't want any whisper of suspicion to reach Keeble at this point."

Frowning, Ruth nodded. "You're right. And there's no telling what Gibson would do or let fall to Josh between now and tomorrow."

"Much less what Josh might feel compelled to say or do." Jordan enclosed her hand between both of his. "So let's work out what we can tell them—your mother, Bobby, and Gibson—how much of the story we can share without revealing that Keeble is the murderer."

They sat in the weak sunshine and planned for more than ten minutes, then with their agreed tale firmly fixed in their minds, rose, walked out from beneath the trees to the house, and went in to report to her family.

CHAPTER 14

The next morning, at a few minutes after nine o'clock, Barnaby stood beside Penelope in an alley off White Cross Street. The group intending to support Stokes and his men in searching for Keeble's motive had agreed to gather in that spot prior to approaching Keeble's office, which lay opposite the end of the alley on White Cross Street itself.

Keeble had arrived ten minutes before, opened the office door, and gone inside. No one else had appeared, and the office seemed too small to accommodate more than one desk.

Barnaby and Penelope had been joined by Jordan and Ruth, which had been no surprise, as they'd arranged the rendezvous at the steak house the previous day.

What did make Barnaby's eyes widen was the foursome who suddenly turned in to the alley and, smiling broadly, walked to where they stood.

Penelope, too, stared. "This," she murmured to Barnaby, "is going to be quite a crowd for that small office to accommodate."

"Don't worry," Roscoe said, bending to buss her cheek. "We'll leave Mudd and Rawlings outside. They can glower and steer away anyone who finds our activities interesting."

Miranda clasped fingers and touched cheeks with Penelope. "Jordan told us the whole story, and we want to help." After greeting Barnaby, she shifted to stand beside Penelope. "And if it's accounts you have to pore over, the more educated eyes the better."

Penelope inclined her head. "Very true." She knew Miranda's talents in that sphere were equal to her own. "We have no idea how many clients, ledgers, and account books Keeble has in there. Who knows how long our search will take?"

The steady tromp of footsteps neared, then another two couples abruptly turned into the alley.

Amazed to see Montague, Violet, Thomas, and Rose, Barnaby and Penelope laughed.

Taking in the crowd now thronging the narrow alley, the four newcomers looked a trifle sheepish, but assuming his most haughty tones, Thomas declared, "We didn't feel it was fair that you had all the fun."

Penelope laughed again, and smiling, Barnaby shook his head. "Only you four would describe the chore of poring over an untold number of ledgers and accounts as fun."

Most there knew each other well enough to mingle without any introductions, the sole exception being Ruth, who Jordan quickly made known to those she hadn't previously met.

Then heavy, regimented footsteps approached the alley, and Stokes, backed by O'Donnell, Morgan, and Walsh, turned in to the alley mouth and came to an abrupt halt.

Stokes took in the waiting company, then met Barnaby's eyes and shook his head. "Keeble won't know what's hit him."

"That, I suspect," Roscoe said, "will be to your advantage."

Stokes inclined his head. "One can hope. Now"—he surveyed the crowd—"as to where we are at present." Briskly, aided by Barnaby, Stokes went over the case against Keeble as it currently stood and elaborated on what they hoped—and needed—to find in Keeble's office.

"Without a clear and believable motive, we're going to be relying solely on the physical evidence," Stokes said, "and while that's damning enough in our eyes, any good solicitor is going to protest that even the gloves belong to someone else and Keeble was never anywhere near Thomas Cardwell's office last Tuesday morning."

"As Keeble's appearance in coat and hat is indistinguishable from half the ton's gentlemen," Penelope said, "we're never going to be able to place him at the scene of the crime via any witness."

Thomas nodded. "So you need to find the evidence that ties everything together—the reason Keeble killed Cardwell—and that will, of necessity, be something weighty and compelling."

"Exactly." Stokes glanced at Penelope. "As instructed, we called at Keeble's house after he'd left and confirmed that there are no ledgers or accounts kept there. We searched his monstrosity of a desk, and the drawers were next to empty. Not even a diary."

Penelope nodded. "I thought the surface was too neat for it to be a working desk."

Violet, who served as Penelope's occasional secretary, smiled at her fondly. "And as to that, you would know."

Penelope's lips twitched as she nodded decisively. "Indeed."

Stokes glanced around the company one last time. "Right, then." He tipped his head across the street. "Let's go." He turned and led the way. "O'Donnell, Morgan, and Walsh—you're to remain outside and keep a general watch on the place. The rear as well."

From a few people behind Stokes, Roscoe said, "Rawlings and Mudd will join your men, Stokes. Neither has any head for figures."

"Good with our fists, good with our eyes," Mudd rumbled. "We'll keep watch, too."

Stokes dipped his head in agreement and continued across the street.

White Cross Street was not as close to the financial hub of the City as Broad Street, and overall, Keeble's office was considerably less impressive than Thomas's. That said, the row of shops and offices in which Keeble's office was located was neat and respectable and altogether unremarkable.

Penelope, who was trailing Barnaby, who, in turn, was following Stokes, poked Barnaby's arm. "There's not much of a sign. Just his name in small letters on the glass of the door."

"True." Barnaby considered the façade. "For someone so desperate to be recognized, that's strangely self-effacing."

Keeble's office was wider than Thomas's, with a larger bay window facing the street, but on entering the premises through the single door located to the left of the window, Barnaby saw that Keeble's workplace was less deep. However, the ceiling was significantly higher, and the number of ledgers, account books, and file boxes stacked on shelves that rose all the way to that elevated ceiling was nothing short of daunting. Barnaby darted a glance at Penelope, at his shoulder, and saw her grimace at the sight.

Keeble had been sitting behind a decent-sized and predictably ostentatious desk. "Empire-style," Penelope whispered. "Shades of Napoleon."

To Barnaby's eyes, there were other touches of wealth readily detectable in the quality of the two client chairs set before the desk and the lamps and implements Keeble had artfully displayed on the desk and on the deep windowsill.

At the tinkling of the bell above the door, Keeble had looked up with a welcoming smile, but on taking in Stokes and those who followed him inside, Keeble slowly rose, his features shifting as he tried to decide on the most appropriate reaction.

Barnaby thought he saw a flicker of fear pass through Keeble's eyes.

Then Keeble plastered on a polite but faintly surprised expression and inquired, "Yes, Inspector?" Keeble's gaze shifted to the stream of people coming in through his door, and his eyes fractionally widened. "What can I do for you…and your friends?"

Stokes glanced back and confirmed that Roscoe, bringing up the rear of their company, had closed the door and flipped the small sign on it to Closed.

Stokes returned his gaze to Keeble. "Earnest Keeble," Stokes intoned in his most formal voice, "I'm here to arrest you for the murder of Thomas Cardwell."

Keeble's face drained of all color.

To Barnaby's eyes, the reaction was as good as a confession. Keeble didn't look surprised, shocked, or confused. Instead, he looked…frightened. Shaken and deeply scared.

Stokes rolled on, "The Crown will attest that on the morning of Tuesday last, you were waiting for Cardwell when he arrived at his office, that you accompanied him inside and subsequently seized his letter knife and stabbed him through the heart. You left him dead and exited the office through the rear door."

While Stokes had been speaking, Keeble's attention had wandered to the people now filling his office. Most, he didn't recognize and didn't know why they were there, but the situation of having a well-heeled audience jolted him back into his usual persona. As soon as Stokes paused, Keeble blustered, "What nonsense! That's ridiculous!" He glimpsed Ruth, standing beside Penelope, and faltered for a second, but then he spread his hands and, with increasing fervor, protested, "Why on earth would I kill Thomas Cardwell?"

Stokes bestowed on Keeble his most shark-like smile. "That, Keeble, is what we're here to find out."

Stokes glanced at the others, then shifted his gaze to the walls—to the ledgers, account books, and file boxes. "Have at it."

Penelope, Ruth, Jordan, and Miranda put their heads together, and a second later, they were joined by Violet, Montague, Thomas, and Rose. While they planned how best to tackle the task before them, Stokes, Barnaby, and Roscoe circled the desk, dragged chairs around, and corralled Keeble into one corner.

All but pushed into his chair, Keeble spluttered, "This is an outrage!" But his gaze was fixed on those advancing on his records, determination in their faces.

Noting that, Stokes grunted and sat in the chair directly opposite Keeble. "The thing is, Keeble, we know you did it. What we've yet to understand is why."

From his position in the chair on Stokes's right, Roscoe suggested, "It would be best all around—for you as well as us—if you simply told us why you killed Cardwell."

Watching Penelope direct the searchers, Barnaby added, "It would certainly be less fraught all around." He returned his gaze to Keeble and met the man's bulging eyes. "They will find it, you know. When it comes to accounts—of all stripes—the collective knowledge in this room is second to none."

Keeble looked faintly horrified, but no matter how Stokes, Barnaby, and Roscoe framed their questions, Keeble refused to engage. Indeed, he appeared almost paralyzed as he watched the ruthlessly thorough inspection of his files unfold.

They tried subtle threats as well as encouragement, but increasingly, Keeble barely heard them. He sat with his gaze locked on the searchers as if praying they wouldn't find what they were looking for and, at the same time, terrified they would.

As the investigation continued apace, with each experienced searcher methodically examining every ledger, account book, and file box in the office, Stokes sat back in his chair and, in a murmur that failed to impinge on Keeble's utter focus on the searchers, observed to Barnaby and Roscoe, "Telling, don't you think, that his attention is all for them and not us?"

Barnaby had been studying Keeble intently. "Thomas Cardwell's murder isn't important to him, but what's in his files assuredly is."

Roscoe snorted softly in agreement.

It was obvious that, had it not been for the three of them hemming him in, Keeble would have sprung from his chair and accosted the searchers. Even attempted to beat them off. He was tense and constantly shifted in his chair, his gaze darting from one searcher to another. He started to gnaw on one nail.

Then the tension gripping Keeble abruptly intensified.

Barnaby looked at the searchers and saw Ruth standing clear of the shelves and frowning at a ledger she held open in her hands. Then she looked up, located Montague and Thomas, and walked across to show them what she'd found.

"No," Keeble whispered. His gaze locked on the trio, he started to shake his head. "No, no…"

Stokes and Barnaby exchanged glances.

Then Thomas said, "Ah. I see."

Montague was still frowning. "Well, I don't."

"You will." Thomas raised his head and looked toward their corner. "Roscoe? If you would take a look at this and see if it strikes you as it does me? Jordan—you as well. You likely have more knowledge of this sort of caper than we do."

"No," Keeble whispered again. He shrank into his chair, his hands clasped tightly to his chest and his arms tucked protectively close.

After noting that reaction, Roscoe rose and walked across to join the growing knot of searchers gathered around Ruth, Montague, and Thomas. Barnaby and Stokes couldn't see past Roscoe's shoulders, but everyone seemed to be studying whatever was in the ledger and trading comments and observations.

Then Penelope made some remark that clearly struck a chord with the others and sent her, Ruth, Violet, Rose, and Jordan back to hunting through the shelves. They found other ledgers and ferried them to Montague, Thomas, and Roscoe. The group conferred, comparing ledgers, looking from one to the other with increasing excitement in their voices.

Unable to hear the comments clearly, with mounting impatience, Barnaby and Stokes watched and waited.

Finally, Montague, Thomas, Roscoe, and Jordan, with the ladies at their backs, came to stand before Barnaby, Stokes, and the now faintly whimpering Keeble.

After glancing at Keeble, Jordan waved to the shelves crammed with account books. "Most of the accounts held here are innocuous. Small businesses trading day-to-day, month-to-month. Nothing startling or out of the ordinary."

His expression grave, Montague held up the thick ledger they'd all been studying. "This account is very different." Keeble's answering whimper was audible to all. Imperturbably, Montague went on, "There are large sums—large by Thomas's and my standards—coming in from four different sources. In cash. That money is then expended in one of two ways—either to buy outright and subsequently fund small businesses or to make loans to such businesses."

Thomas waved a hand at the shelves. "Many of the businesses for which Keeble does the accounts are connected in one or another way to this central account."

Roscoe explained, "Those small, entirely legitimate enterprises are either owned by this account and pay all their profits to it, or they have loans from this account and make repayments to it." His gaze rested on Keeble. "And Keeble takes his cut on every payment."

"And then," Jordan said, his tone portentous, "every six months, the funds accumulated within this account are dispersed equally to four closed trusts."

Barnaby frowned and looked at Montague. "Closed trusts?"

Grimly, Montague nodded. "They're a style of account where it's very difficult to trace ownership. Even for Thomas or me. Each closed trust has its own bank account, but tracing the owners, as we did for the accounts linked to Chesterton, will be well-nigh impossible."

Thomas nodded. "All trails will loop back on themselves and, ultimately, lead nowhere."

Stokes's eyes had narrowed as he thought through the implications. Now, he suggested, "Proceeds of crime put to work in a legitimate way?"

Roscoe tipped his head in agreement. "So that subsequently, the returns appear legitimate. That's what this looks like." He transferred his gaze to Keeble, who was now sitting silent and still in the manner of a man dazed. Roscoe went on, "The one question we can't answer from this ledger is who the four owners of this enterprise are. The names are in code."

Along with all there, Stokes returned his attention to Keeble. "Are you willing to give us the code? Or more to the point, the names of the four owners of the enterprise represented by this ledger?"

Keeble boggled at Stokes. After a second, his voice weak, he warbled, "I don't know what you're talking about."

Stokes sighed. "All right. Let's revisit the situation. We now know why you needed to make sure Cardwell didn't report the gun running to the authorities. It wasn't to protect your son or even to protect the social rank you've worked all your life to achieve. You needed to ensure that the police didn't come here and search through your files to confirm your business wasn't in some way profiting from Chesterton's scheme."

"As it turns out," Barnaby said, "you weren't involved in Chesterton's scheme. You were involved in something much larger."

In a censorious tone, Jordan stated, "You killed Thomas Cardwell to ensure that the police never came to your door."

Keeble looked ashen, but now they'd uncovered his secret, he seemed to be almost resigned. Woodenly, he raised his gaze to Jordan's face and said, "No. You have it all wrong."

There was little force behind the words. Nevertheless, Stokes reached into his pocket and drew out the pair of bloodied gloves. "So these gloves," he said, "that were found in the alley behind Cardwell's office aren't yours?"

Keeble shrank back in the chair, his horrified gaze locked on the gloves.

"You see," Stokes continued, "these gloves are monogrammed. EK—not common initials. And they're made to measure, too. I'm sure the glover will remember which customer he made these for. They're relatively new, after all, and his label is sewn inside."

"We already know," Penelope said, "that you had these gloves on your hands when you left home on Tuesday morning."

Keeble blinked at her, then swallowed and shook his head. "I don't know how they got there."

"Or whose blood stains them?" Stokes asked skeptically.

Keeble started gnawing on one nail again while slowly shaking his head.

Barnaby leaned back and studied the man, then quietly said, "If I were you, Keeble, I'd start to worry about the police being here"—he tipped his head toward the street—"with uniformed constables at your door, because inevitably, people will talk, and others will hear about that."

Keeble looked at Barnaby, then as the words sank in, horror—pure horror—seeped into Keeble's face.

Roscoe pressed. "You killed an innocent man to ensure your crimes—

or rather, your role in concealing the proceeds of the untold crimes of your four masters—never came to light. But it has anyway, precisely because you killed Thomas Cardwell."

Keeble appeared to be mentally reeling. He started swaying slightly, his gaze fixed, unseeing, ahead of him. "I didn't mean to." His voice was barely a whisper, and the company edged closer the better to hear as, tearfully, he looked at Stokes, then Roscoe, and went on, "I thought if Cardwell had learned about the gun running, he'd want to keep quiet about it to protect his brother." His gaze lowering, he whispered, "But instead…"

His tone flat but not aggressive, Jordan filled in, "Instead, Thomas told you about the gun running and that he'd sent to an acquaintance to inquire how best to go about informing the authorities in a way that would cast his brother—and your son and Harrison Moubray—in the best possible light. Isn't that so?"

Keeble suddenly sat upright, startling the onlookers, and all but hissed, "Yes! The silly blighter thought he could pull that off, but…"

When he trailed into silence, Thomas suggested, "But that wasn't the point, was it? Not for you."

Keeble made an attempt to gather himself, then he looked around the circle of faces and, as if pleading for understanding, said, "I had to stop him. Don't you see?"

When no one responded, Keeble went on, "They tricked me into being their man-of-business. I didn't know they were crooks and villains, not at first. They had funds that needed investing, and I needed the business, and it all seemed so perfect. It was more than a year before I realized who they were and what they did and where their money was coming from, and by then, it was too late. I tried to resign as their representative, and they laughed. They said…" Keeble closed his eyes. "They said the only way to resign from their service was to die! And I believed them! You would have, too." He swallowed and opened his eyes. "They were very convincing."

Penelope wasn't surprised to learn that Keeble's vanity and his desire for wealth to bolster his social standing had been a weakness ruthless men had seen and exploited.

"So I was stuck," Keeble said. Everyone else in the room remained silent and still and listened as he went on, "And then I learned about the gun running. I told myself that no one else would think to investigate from where the lads were getting their new funds, but then I thought of Thomas and wondered if he might notice, and once I'd thought of that—

of someone else knowing and possibly alerting the police—I couldn't rest until I'd learned if Thomas knew or not. So I went to his office on Tuesday morning, and I didn't even have to mention the guns—he told me and explained what he intended to do..."

Penelope thought that, in their minds, the entire group stood in Thomas's office and watched Keeble sitting in escalating panic before the desk.

Morosely, Keeble shook his head. "I tried to steer him away, to suggest we shouldn't act precipitously, but he told me he'd already made discreet inquiries regarding how to go about it." Abruptly, Keeble looked up, his expression pleading. "I had to do it. He gave me no choice. He wasn't going to listen to reason! I had to stop him before he went any further—before he spread the secret any further!" Keeble's gaze locked on the ledger in Montague's hands. "If you knew the four men behind that business, you would understand."

"So tell us who they are," Barnaby said. "If you want us to understand why you killed Cardwell, why you felt such an overwhelming compulsion to do so, then tell us who you fear."

Keeble's eyes rounded, his expression aghast. "I can't! They'll kill me!"

"Keeble," Penelope gently said, drawing his anguished eyes to her. She captured his gaze and held it. "You're going to hang for Thomas Cardwell's murder. If, as you claim, your fear of these four men drove you to it, then shouldn't they pay as well?"

Keeble stared at her and continued to stare as, clearly, her words sank in.

They were all holding their breaths when the office door opened.

The entire company turned, surprised and prepared to be annoyed at the interruption.

Grim-faced, Walsh stepped inside, turned, and held the door wide as Morgan manhandled a rough-looking man into the office. A second scrawny, disreputable specimen followed, propelled inside by O'Donnell.

Mudd and Rawlings brought up the rear, and Rawlings closed the door.

Mudd dipped his head at the pair struggling in O'Donnell's and Morgan's grips. "Saw them eyeing the front of the place, then they headed around the back and checked along there before coming around to the front again."

"We saw they were lugging this." Rawlings held up a large battered canvas bag and grinned. "All the goods one needs to set a place alight."

Stokes and Barnaby rose.

Stokes looked at the men, who had finally realized the futility of struggling and were standing half slumped in O'Donnell's and Morgan's holds.

Before Stokes could speak, O'Donnell said, "We already asked." He tipped his head toward Mudd and Rawlings. "Seemed sensible to take advantage of the situation we found ourselves in."

Stokes arched a brow. "I see. And?"

"And it seems they have orders to torch the place and make sure Keeble dies in the blaze," O'Donnell reported.

"In their words," Morgan added, "they were to make sure Keeble went up in smoke along with his records."

"Oh, dear Lord," Keeble whispered. Although he, too, had got to his feet, he was hidden from the newcomers by the searchers.

Staring at the floor, the man in O'Donnell's grip shook his head. "We was paid to do it—didn't seem all that bad. The geezer as paid us said this joker Keeble had double-crossed his boss."

Stokes turned his head and looked at Keeble. "You're right about your masters arranging your demise. If you leave them unnamed, they won't let you live long enough to meet the hangman."

In a pensive tone, Penelope observed, "Burning to death is said to be a terrible way to die."

"Who knows what they'll try next," Barnaby said. "Poison?"

"If you tell us their names," Stokes said, "they'll be too busy trying to save themselves to worry about visiting any horrific retribution on you."

Peeking between the intervening bodies, Keeble fastened his gaze on the men sent to kill him.

It took a good minute for his resistance to completely crumble, but eventually, he looked at Stokes and, in an utterly defeated tone, said, "Toby Mavenpick, Edgar Wallace, Gordon Conroy, and Elias Mitchell."

As if saying the crime bosses' names aloud had released some of their hold on him, in a firmer voice, Keeble told Stokes, "I don't want to die in some horrible way—hanging will be bad enough. Just get the four of them and their lieutenants behind bars, and I'll explain everything about that ledger and throw myself on the mercy of the court."

Barnaby nodded. "An excellent decision. It's the best and really only thing you can do."

Stokes had whipped out his notebook and was jotting down the names. "That and pray that the judge hearing your case understands your reasoning, for I think it's safe to say"—he looked at the faces of the searchers gathered all around—"that ultimately, we do not."

Stokes raised a hand and beckoned Walsh to him.

When the constable approached, Stokes nodded at Keeble. "Take him and them"—he pointed to the men in O'Donnell's and Morgan's charge—"to the Yard."

~

Stokes followed his men to Scotland Yard to arrange for Keeble and the two others they'd apprehended to be put into the cells.

Meanwhile, the rest of the triumphant company made for Johnson's Steak House. Barnaby organized a private room, and they sat and drank and waited for word from Stokes.

Eventually, Stokes strolled in, with O'Donnell, Morgan, and Walsh at his heels.

The company sent up a cheer, and uncharacteristically beaming with delight, Stokes sat and informed them, "There were inspectors in other departments who've been after those crime bosses for years and couldn't believe their luck. I left them poring over Keeble's ledger, and they'll speak with him soon, but I've been able to pass off that side of the case entirely to them." He glanced around the group. "And in the matter of Thomas Cardwell's murder, we've reached the end and solved the case."

Stokes looked along the table to where Ruth was sitting next to Jordan. "Miss Cardwell, I know that nothing—no amount of kudos—will ever fill the hole in your family left by your brother's death, but please know and let the other members of your family know that, through Thomas's insistence on doing the right thing—namely, insisting to Keeble that the authorities had to be informed of the gun-running scheme—even though that action led to Thomas's death, his integrity resulted in not only the gun runners being arrested, Chesterton as well as his three backers, but also brought about the fall of four of the most notorious crime bosses currently operating in the capital." He paused and inclined his head to Ruth. "The Commissioner asked specifically that I convey his regards to you and your family, and his condolences on Thomas's death along with his commendation for Thomas's action that ultimately led to the downfall of so many villains."

"Hear, hear!" echoed around the room, and everyone raised their glasses.

"To Thomas Cardwell," Barnaby said. "He might be gone, but he will not be forgotten."

"He left his mark," Penelope stated with a grateful nod directed at Ruth.

Ruth blushed a trifle under their regard. "Thank you. I will let the family know."

The serving girls arrived to take their orders for food and more drinks, and the company settled to eat, slake their thirsts, and relive various parts of the case. Montague, Violet, Thomas, and Rose had yet to hear of all the twists and turns—of the Fox Orsett and the warehouse outside Tilbury, or the guns illegally sourced from the Royal Small Arms Factory, or Penelope's interviews with Keeble's staff—and were eager to hear the whole tale.

Later, as the talk turned to other subjects, Penelope overheard Jordan tell Ruth, "Thomas sounded like the sort of man who would have taken comfort in knowing that his death wasn't in vain, that it led to so many serious villains being brought down." Jordan paused, then went on, "I only met him on three occasions, but I suspect he believed that, ultimately, justice rules the world, and what's happened has proved him right."

Ruth squeezed Jordan's hand and nodded. "That's exactly how Thomas would see it." She looked into Jordan's eyes. "And it's a comforting thing to be able to tell Mama, Bobby, and Gibson that Thomas has been avenged, his murderer caught, and that, because of Thomas and his honesty, justice has been served."

Penelope decided she couldn't have put it better and turned her attention down the table, leaving Jordan and Ruth to their own devices.

After the meal, Roscoe, Miranda, Mudd, and Rawlings, along with the Glendowers and Montagues, departed for their respective homes.

"A lovely little interlude filled with excitement and satisfaction," Thomas said with a smile. "But now, it's back to real life and the daily grind of investments calling my name."

The others all laughed, and those leaving waved and walked off to find hackneys to ferry them to their destinations.

With Stokes and his men, Barnaby, Penelope, Jordan, and Ruth returned to Scotland Yard.

Barnaby had never seen that venerable institution so abuzz with excitement. The speculation and expectations generated by the impending arrests of four major crime bosses flooded the corridors with an atmosphere of enthusiasm, hope, and determination.

Their party settled in Stokes's office and waited to hear the news as the arrests were carried out.

It wasn't long before the inspectors who had taken on the connected cases started to drop by with verbal reports for Stokes.

The first to look in was Mann. He paused in the doorway and beamed at them all. "We got the whole crew. All those at the factory who had decided to indulge in a little dealing on the side. One of the supervisors was involved, too. Getting all the rotten ones out, more or less in one fell swoop, is a major feather in our caps. Those higher up the management ladder had no idea they were losing guns, and the commendations are flowing freely."

Stokes grinned. "Excellent. A good result for the Yard."

Mann nodded. "The Commissioner is more delighted than I've ever seen him, but I hear that might have even more to do with the other unexpected outcomes of your case."

"One can only hope," Stokes replied. "However, not all our foxes have as yet been caught."

But they were. One after another, the reports from the other inspectors came in. London's underworld was reeling with not just the four bosses taken up but quite a few of their underlings as well. The praise freely heaped on Stokes's head and directed at his team was unstinting.

The inspector who'd overseen the arrest of Toby Mavenpick observed, "I never thought they'd trip themselves up in such a way— through an account ledger!" He leveled a look at Stokes. "Not but that they weren't very clever, setting up that business as they did. Just lucky for us that the one weak link in their chain happened to fall into your hands for another reason entirely."

Penelope smiled at the inspector. "Fate moves in mysterious ways."

"It does, indeed, ma'am." The inspector bowed to her, then saluted Stokes. "I'm off to interview Mavenpick, who, apparently, is spitting chips. I'll let you know how it goes."

Eventually, they received confirmation that all four crime bosses had been incarcerated in the cells below the building.

Penelope, Barnaby, Ruth, and Jordan were about to leave Stokes to wind up his highly successful day when the Commissioner arrived.

"Stokes, well done!" The Commissioner bowed to Penelope, then shook hands with Barnaby. They were acquainted socially through Barnaby's father, who remained one of the peers overseeing the Metropolitan Police. "Excellent work all around."

Stokes introduced Jordan and Ruth, and the Commissioner grew serious and shook their hands and asked Ruth to convey his best wishes to her family and his condolences on Thomas's death.

Then the Commissioner swung to face Stokes, Barnaby, and Penelope. "I understand that finding the needle in the haystack of Keeble's accounts and, even more, understanding what the critical account actually meant was a group effort. Please pass on my sincere thanks to all those who helped."

Penelope hid a smile while Barnaby assured the Commissioner that his approbation would be conveyed to all the appropriate quarters.

"Now, I must away!" The Commissioner clapped his hands together and beamed upon them all. "Thanks to you all, I've an untold number of charge sheets to authorize before evening."

Once he was gone, Penelope looked at Jordan. "'All appropriate quarters' includes the crew from Dolphin Square."

Grinning, Jordan nodded. "And I can guarantee that Roscoe will flaunt that commendation like a feather in his cap for years to come."

Everyone was laughing as they made for the door.

Following them to the stairs, Stokes observed, "Today has been one of those rare days that's been an unrelieved good day all around."

Jordan escorted Ruth home to Finsbury Circus. After descending from the hackney, she took his hand, and he made no demur when she led him to the house and inside.

There, Ruth called not just her mother, Bobby, and Gibson to the drawing room but all the staff as well. "You all knew Thomas," she told them. "You all valued him, in your own way, so you should all hear the truth of what happened."

She told them the story, all of it, simply and without any undue embellishment.

Her mother wept, and Bobby and Gibson surreptitiously wiped their eyes.

When the murderer was revealed as Keeble, Gibson spontaneously exclaimed, "Oh God! Poor Josh."

Jordan felt that said a lot about Gibson's true character.

After relating the unexpected outcome of so many well-deserved arrests, Ruth passed on the Commissioner's condolences and commendation.

Jordan had remained silent to that point, but felt compelled to add, "In the end, by taking such a principled stand over the gun-running scheme, Thomas, through his death, was instrumental in bringing down multiple villains, all of whom would otherwise have escaped the police's net. In many ways, by many measures, Thomas died a hero."

Ruth sent him a watery smile, and Mrs. Cardwell reached across and gripped his hand tightly.

It took several moments for the family and the staff to compose themselves, then the staff slipped away, and Mrs. Cardwell drew in a breath and raised her head. She looked at Ruth and smiled, then turned that smile on Jordan. "You have both brought me comfort. Losing Thomas is hard—very hard—but at least I know it wasn't in any way his fault and that, ultimately, much good came from his death." Her gaze shifted to Gibson, who was looking somber and serious. "And it wasn't Gibson's fault, either."

He grimaced and raised his head. "Except for me being a stupid dupe."

"You didn't know," Jordan said. "And in following you, Thomas made his own decision. You cannot and ought not take that burden onto your shoulders—that would, in a way, be diminishing what Thomas did."

Gibson frowned, unconvinced but also uncertain.

Mrs. Cardwell rapped her chair's arm. "Now, I know Cook had the dinner almost ready. You will stay to dine, won't you, Jordan?"

He looked at Ruth, saw encouragement and hope in her eyes, and smiled, then turned the gesture on Mrs. Cardwell. "Thank you, ma'am. I'd be honored."

Jordan hadn't consciously made any decision to guide Gibson or Bobby, but over the course of the meal, he found himself gently steering the younger men. He was relieved to learn that the pair had been talking to each other about taking on the responsibility for the family that previously Thomas alone had shouldered and rethinking the direction in which each wished to steer their life. Jordan readily encouraged them to pursue their tentative notion of keeping Thomas's business running.

As Ruth had told Jordan, both Gibson and Bobby had inherited the same facility with numbers that she possessed. In addition, Gibson was quite good with people, yet clearly doubted his capacity to step into Thomas's shoes with the clients his brother had dealt with.

"I'll be happy to help," Jordan finally said. "I deal with business owners all the time. I could…I suppose the right phrase would be to mentor you as you pick up the reins."

The offer was embraced with copious thanks all around.

Later, when he was taking his leave of the family, Mrs. Cardwell gripped his hand and looked into his eyes. "Thank you for all you've done for our family, Jordan. Please be assured that you will always be welcome in this house whenever you wish to call."

"Thank you, ma'am." Jordan darted a glance at Ruth. *Me calling here will, with any luck, happen quite often.*

He shook hands with Gibson and Bobby and instructed them to send word to Dolphin Square if they had need of his advice.

Then he turned to Ruth, and she smiled and linked her arm in his. "Come, I'll see you out." Ignoring the interested looks from her family, she started for the front hall.

There, she amended, "In fact, I rather fancy a turn about the park." Her laughing eyes met Jordan's. "Will you please escort me, sir?"

His smile deepened. "I would be happy to, Miss Cardwell."

They walked beneath the trees, now burgeoning into full leaf. Ruth looked up at the sky, then said, "Thomas's life was cut short. Unexpectedly and unavoidably. If his death has taught me anything, it's that the future is uncertain and always unknown."

Jordan halted and turned to face her and took both her hands in his. "I feel the same." He looked into her blue eyes. "And because of that, I intend to make the best of what life has placed in front of me—what it's offering me now. I intend to enjoy life as it presents itself to the fullest." He smiled. "As Penelope would say, there really is no other viable, sensible, logical choice."

Ruth laughed softly.

Lost in her dancing eyes, Jordan drew in a deeper breath and asked, "Will you, Ruth Cardwell, live that life—life lived to its fullest—with me?"

She sobered, but still smiling, searched his eyes. "What, exactly, are you asking, Jordan?"

He took a moment to think, to find the right words, then said, "Until I met the Cardwells, I didn't know I was looking for a family. I come from a close family, I've always been a part of a family, but I thought my family—the one I needed—was made up of Roscoe, Miranda, their brood, and Mudd, and Rawlings, and theirs." He shook his head. "But it's not. I'm close to them all, but as my forever family, that group doesn't quite hit the mark."

He looked into her eyes—fell into the blue—and spoke from his heart. "Fate has shown me—life has shown me—that the family I need is one that needs me. Like the Cardwells. So I'm asking if you will allow me to become a part of your family, to stand beside you and them. If you wish it, I'll be there."

She searched his eyes one last time, then a smile of great sweetness broke across her face. "Yes," she simply said. "I would like—I would love—that."

Jordan blew out a breath. "Good."

She laughed again and stepped close, and he gathered her in, and they kissed soft and sweet under the shade of the trees in Finsbury Circus.

Dear Reader,

Jordan Draper, righthand man to London's gambling king, first appeared in *The Lady Risks All,* and since that time, has made cameo appearances in quite a few of my novels. His was always a different character, on the fringes of society and with different aspirations, so writing his story held a certain appeal and was merely a matter of time.

With Jordan being from a different level of society, albeit closely connected with the ton and our investigators, I seized the chance to explore some areas of early Victorian life and business that hadn't fallen within the scope of any previous story. The story also gave me the opportunity to draw in other members of the Adairs' and Stokes's investigative circle, as this case proved to be one in which all of them could contribute. I hope you've enjoyed venturing into slightly different fields in this latest installment in the continuing adventures of Barnaby, Penelope, Stokes, and friends.

As for what's coming next, in *The Curse of Ill-gotten Gains* (October 16, 2025), we return to the social whirl and a select summer house party where Richard Percival discovers the young lady he is supposedly at the party to court standing over the murdered body of their host.

Information about earlier volumes in THE CASEBOOK OF BARNABY ADAIR series—*Where the Heart Leads, The Peculiar Case of Lord Finsbury's Diamonds, The Masterful Mr. Montague, The Curious Case of Lady Latimer's Shoes, Loving Rose: The Redemption of Malcolm Sinclair, The Confounding Case of the Carisbrook Emeralds, The Murder at Mandeville Hall, The Meriwell Legacy, Dead Beside the Thames, and Marriage and Murder*—can be found following.

Barnaby, Penelope, Stokes, Griselda, and their friends and supporters continue to tackle the solving of crimes with undimmed enthusiasm. I hope they and their adventures solving mysteries and exposing villains will continue to entertain you in the future just as much as they do me.

Enjoy!

Stephanie.

For alerts as new books are released, plus information on upcoming books, exclusive sweepstakes and sneak peeks into upcoming novels, sign up for Stephanie's Private Email Newsletter http://www.stephanielaurens.com/newsletter-signup/

Or if you don't have time to chat and want a quick email alert, sign up and follow me at BookBub https://www.bookbub.com/authors/stephanie-laurens

The ultimate source for detailed information on all Stephanie's published books, including covers, descriptions, and excerpts, is Stephanie's Website www.stephanielaurens.com

You can also follow Stephanie via her Amazon Author Page at http://tinyurl.com/7c3e9mp

Goodreads members can follow Stephanie via her author page https://www.goodreads.com/author/show/9241.Stephanie_Laurens

You can email Stephanie at stephanie@stephanielaurens.com

Or find her on Facebook
https://www.facebook.com/AuthorStephanieLaurens/

COMING NEXT:
THE CURSE OF ILL-GOTTEN GAINS
The Casebook of Barnaby Adair #12
To be released in October, 2025.

Richard Percival has bowed to familial pressure and agreed to attend a tonnish house party at Patchcote Grange, for which the primary aim is to introduce eligible gentlemen to suitable young ladies. Two of Richard's elderly aunts assure him that Miss Rosalind Hemmings will make the perfect wife for him, and after meeting Miss Hemmings over dinner on the first evening of the party, Richard is sufficiently intrigued to be willing—indeed, he's even looking forward—to learning more of the unusually direct young lady. But on coming downstairs the following morning, he hears an anguished scream for help. On racing outside to the orchard from whence the scream came, he finds his possibly-intended standing over the very dead body of their universally well-regarded host. This is clearly a matter for Scotland Yard, and Richard wastes no time in summoning Barnaby and Penelope to his, Rosalind's, and the company's aid. For very soon, it's blatantly apparent that the murderer is one of presently residing at Patchcote Grange.

Available for pre-order by July, 2025.

RECENTLY RELEASED:
The tenth volume in
The Casebook of Barnaby Adair mystery-romances
MARRIAGE AND MURDER

#1 NYT-*bestselling author Stephanie Laurens returns with a puzzling case in which her favorite sleuths must untangle a slew of secrets to expose a coldblooded murderer.*

When a middle-aged spinster is found strangled in her country cottage and scurrilous gossip implicates Henry, Lord Glossup, he appeals to Barnaby and Penelope Adair along with Inspector Stokes to unravel the mystery of who killed Viola Huntingdon.

Henry, Lord Glossup, arrives on Barnaby and Penelope Adairs' doorstep and begs their aid—and that of Stokes—in identifying the murderer of Viola Huntingdon, a middle-aged spinster who lived a largely blameless life in a country cottage in a tiny village close to Henry's home. As Stokes has already been tapped to take the case, the investigators travel to Salisbury and thence to Ashmore village and throw themselves into the case.

While initially Henry was touted as a suspect, he is quickly eliminated, and with the help of the victim's sister, Madeline, the investigators set out to discover all they can about the victim and who might have wished her ill. In such a small village, with a commensurately small population, the list of possible suspects is short, but the existence of Viola's 'secret admirer, H' has everyone stumped. First, how could Viola, living in such a small community, have had a secret visitor, a man no one saw except at a distance? And who on earth is he, this H?

As the investigators piece together the clues of missing jewelry and sightings of H and follow the leads generated by opportunistic thieves, dodgy jewelers, and local moneylenders, a picture emerges that points to only one conclusion. But in small villages, things are rarely as they seem. Have the investigators got the right man in their sights, or have they been led astray?

A historical novel of 82,000 words weaving mystery and murder with a touch of romance.

The ninth volume in
The Casebook of Barnaby Adair mystery-romances
DEAD BESIDE THE THAMES

#1 NYT-bestselling author Stephanie Laurens returns with a confounding case that sees her favorite sleuths acting to save a friend wrongly accused of murder.
When a detested viscount is found murdered by the banks of the Thames

and Charlie Hastings becomes the prime suspect, Barnaby and Penelope Adair join forces with Stokes to discover the real story behind the unexpected killing.

Charlie Hastings is astonished to find himself accused of murdering Viscount Sedbury. Admittedly, Charlie had two heated altercations with Sedbury in the hours preceding the man's death, but as Charlie is quick to point out to Stokes – and to Barnaby and Penelope – there are a multitude of others in the ton who will be delighted to learn of Sedbury's demise.

As Penelope, Barnaby, and Stokes start assembling a suspect list, Charlie's prediction proves only too accurate. Yet the most puzzling aspect is who on earth managed to kill Sedbury. The man was a hulking brute, large, very strong, and known as a vicious brawler. Who managed to subdue him enough to strangle him?

As the number of suspects steadily increases, the investigators are forced to ask if, perhaps, one of their suspects hired a killer capable of taking Sedbury down. With that possibility thrown into the calculations, narrowing their suspect list becomes a futile exercise.

Their pursuit of the truth leads them to investigate the many shady avenues of Sedbury's life, much to the consternation of Sedbury's father, the Marquess of Rattenby. Rattenby does not want Sedbury's distasteful proclivities exposed for all the world to see, further harming the other family members who Sedbury has taken great delight in tormenting for most of his life.

In the end, the resolution of the crime lies in old-fashioned policing coupled with the fresh twists Barnaby and Penelope bring to Scotland Yard's efforts.

And when the truth is finally revealed, it raises questions that strike to the very heart of justice and what, with such a victim and such a murderer, true justice actually means.

A historical novel of 62,500 words interweaving mystery and murder with a touch of romance.

**The eighth volume in
The Casebook of Barnaby Adair mystery-romances
THE MERIWELL LEGACY**

#1 NYT-bestselling author Stephanie Laurens returns with her favorite sleuths to unravel a tangled web of family secrets and expose a murderer.

When Lord Meriwell collapses and dies at his dining table, Barnaby and Penelope Adair are summoned, along with Inspector Basil Stokes, to discover who, how, and most importantly why someone very close to his lordship saw fit to poison him.

When Lord Meriwell dies at his dining table, Nurse Veronica Haskell suspects foul play and notifies his lordship's doctor, eminent Harley Street specialist Dr. David Sanderson. In turn, compelled by a need to protect Veronica who is at Meriwell Hall as David's behest, David calls on his friends Barnaby and Penelope Adair for assistance.

However, as the fateful dinner was the first of a house party being attended by the local MP and his family, the Metropolitan Police commissioners also consider the Adairs' presence desirable, and consequently, Barnaby and Penelope accompany Stokes to Meriwell Hall.

There, they discover a gathering of the Meriwell family intended to impress the visiting Busseltons so that George Busselton, local MP, will agree to a marriage between his daughter and Lord Meriwell's eldest nephew, Stephen. But instead of any pleasant sojourn, the company find themselves confined to the hall and grounds while Stokes, Barnaby, and Penelope set about interviewing everyone and establishing facts, alibis, and the movements of those in the house.

To our investigators' frustration, while determining the means proves straightforward, and opportunity reduces their suspect list, motive remains elusive, and their list of suspects stays stubbornly long.

Then the killer strikes again, but even then, the investigators are left with the same suspects and too many potential reasons for the second death.

What did the killer hope to gain?

More importantly, will he kill again?

At last, the investigators stumble on a promising clue, yet following it requires sending to London for information, and their frustration builds. As the clock ticks and they doggedly forge on, they uncover more and more facts, yet none allows them to identify which of their prime suspects is the murderer.

Will they get the breakthrough they need, one sufficient to exonerate the innocent?

When the answer arrives, they discover that the Meriwell family legacies are more far-reaching than anyone realized, and that the crimes involved and the motivation for the murders is far more heinous than anyone imagined.

A historical novel of 78,000 words interweaving mystery and murder with a touch of romance.

PREVIOUSLY RELEASED IN THE CASEBOOK OF BARNABY ADAIR NOVELS:

Read about Penelope's and Barnaby's romance, plus that of Stokes and Griselda, in
**The first volume in
The Casebook of Barnaby Adair mystery-romances
WHERE THE HEART LEADS**

Penelope Ashford, Portia Cynster's younger sister, has grown up with every advantage - wealth, position, and beauty. Yet Penelope is anything but a typical ton miss - forceful, willful and blunt to a fault, she has for years devoted her considerable energy and intelligence to directing an institution caring for the forgotten orphans of London's streets.

But now her charges are mysteriously disappearing. Desperate, Penelope turns to the one man she knows who might help her - Barnaby Adair.

Handsome scion of a noble house, Adair has made a name for himself in political and judicial circles. His powers of deduction and observation combined with his pedigree has seen him solve several serious crimes within the ton. Although he makes her irritatingly uncomfortable, Penelope throws caution to the wind and appears on his bachelor doorstep late one night, determined to recruit him to her cause.

Barnaby is intrigued—by her story, and her. Her bold beauty and undeniable brains make a striking contrast to the usual insipid ton misses. And as he's in dire need of an excuse to avoid said insipid misses, he accepts her challenge, never dreaming she and it will consume his every waking hour.

Enlisting the aid of Inspector Basil Stokes of the fledgling Scotland Yard, they infiltrate the streets of London's notorious East End. But as they unravel the mystery of the missing boys, they cross the trail of a criminal embedded in the very organization recently created to protect all

Londoners. And that criminal knows of them and their efforts, and is only too ready to threaten all they hold dear, including their new-found knowledge of the intrigues of the human heart.

FURTHER CASES AND THE EVOLUTION OF RELATIONSHIPS CONTINUE IN:

**The second volume in
The Casebook of Barnaby Adair mystery-romances
THE PECULIAR CASE OF LORD FINSBURY'S DIAMONDS**

#1 New York Times *bestselling author Stephanie Laurens brings you a tale of murder, mystery, passion, and intrigue – and diamonds!*

Penelope Adair, wife and partner of amateur sleuth Barnaby Adair, is so hugely pregnant she cannot even waddle. When Barnaby is summoned to assist Inspector Stokes of Scotland Yard in investigating the violent murder of a gentleman at a house party, Penelope, frustrated that she cannot participate, insists that she and Griselda, Stokes's wife, be duly informed of their husbands' discoveries.

Yet what Barnaby and Stokes uncover only leads to more questions. The murdered gentleman had been thrown out of the house party days before, so why had he come back? And how and why did he come to have the fabulous Finsbury diamond necklace in his pocket, much to Lord Finsbury's consternation. Most peculiar of all, why had the murderer left the necklace, worth a stupendous fortune, on the body?

The conundrums compound as our intrepid investigators attempt to make sense of this baffling case. Meanwhile, the threat of scandal grows ever more tangible for all those attending the house party – and the stakes are highest for Lord Finsbury's daughter and the gentleman who has spent the last decade resurrecting his family fortune so he can aspire to her hand. Working parallel to Barnaby and Stokes, the would-be lovers hunt for a path through the maze of contradictory facts to expose the murderer, disperse the pall of scandal, and claim the love and the shared life they crave.

A pre-Victorian mystery with strong elements of romance. A short novel of 39,000 words.

The third volume in
The Casebook of Barnaby Adair mystery-romances
THE MASTERFUL MR. MONTAGUE

Montague has devoted his life to managing the wealth of London's elite, but at a huge cost: a family of his own. Then the enticing Miss Violet Matcham seeks his help, and in the puzzle she presents him, he finds an intriguing new challenge professionally…and personally.

Violet, devoted lady-companion to the aging Lady Halstead, turns to Montague to reassure her ladyship that her affairs are in order. But the famous Montague is not at all what she'd expected—this man is compelling, decisive, supportive, and strong—everything Violet needs in a champion, a position to which Montague rapidly lays claim.

But then Lady Halstead is murdered and Violet and Montague, aided by Barnaby Adair, Inspector Stokes, Penelope, and Griselda, race to expose a cunning and cold-blooded killer...who stalks closer and closer. Will Montague and Violet learn the shocking truth too late to seize their chance at enduring love?

A pre-Victorian tale of romance and mystery in the classic historical romance style. A novel of 120,000 words.

The fourth volume in
The Casebook of Barnaby Adair mystery-romances
THE CURIOUS CASE OF LADY LATIMER'S SHOES

#1 New York Times *bestselling author Stephanie Laurens brings you a tale of mysterious death, feuding families, star-crossed lovers—and shoes to die for.*

With her husband, amateur-sleuth the Honorable Barnaby Adair, decidedly eccentric fashionable matron Penelope Adair is attending the premier event opening the haut ton's Season when a body is discovered in the gardens. A lady has been struck down with a finial from the terrace balustrade. Her family is present, as are the cream of the haut ton—the shocked hosts turn to Barnaby and Penelope for help.

Barnaby calls in Inspector Basil Stokes and they begin their investigation. Penelope assists by learning all she can about the victim's family, and uncovers a feud between them and the Latimers over the fabulous shoes known as Lady Latimer's shoes, currently exclusive to the Latimers.

The deeper Penelope delves, the more convinced she becomes that the murder is somehow connected to the shoes. She conscripts Griselda, Stokes's wife, and Violet Montague, now Penelope's secretary, and the trio set out to learn all they can about the people involved and most importantly the shoes, a direction vindicated when unexpected witnesses report seeing a lady fleeing the scene—wearing Lady Latimer's shoes.

But nothing is as it seems, and the more Penelope and her friends learn about the shoes, conundrums abound, compounded by a Romeo-and-Juliet romance and escalating social pressure…until at last, the pieces fall into place, and finally understanding what has occurred, the six intrepid investigators race to prevent an even worse tragedy.

A pre-Victorian mystery with strong elements of romance. A novel of 76,000 words.

The fifth volume in
The Casebook of Barnaby Adair mystery-romances
LOVING ROSE: THE REDEMPTION OF MALCOLM SINCLAIR

#1 New York Times bestselling author Stephanie Laurens returns with another thrilling story from the Casebook of Barnaby Adair…

Miraculously spared from death, Malcolm Sinclair erases the notorious man he once was. Reinventing himself as Thomas Glendower, he strives to make amends for his past, yet he never imagines penance might come via a secretive lady he discovers living in his secluded manor.

Rose has a plausible explanation for why she and her children are residing in Thomas's house, but she quickly realizes he's far too intelligent to fool. Revealing the truth is impossibly dangerous, yet day by day, he wins her trust, and then her heart.

But then her enemy closes in, and Rose turns to Thomas as the only man who can protect her and the children. And when she asks for his help, Thomas finally understands his true purpose, and with unwavering commitment, he seeks his redemption in the only way he can—through living the reality of loving Rose.

A pre-Victorian tale of romance and mystery in the classic historical romance style. A novel of 105,000 words.

The sixth volume in
The Casebook of Barnaby Adair mystery-romances
THE CONFOUNDING CASE OF THE CARISBROOK EMERALDS

#1 New York Times *bestselling author Stephanie Laurens brings you a tale of emerging and also established loves and the many facets of family, interwoven with mystery and murder.*
A young lady accused of theft and the gentleman who elects himself her champion enlist the aid of Stokes, Barnaby, Penelope, and friends in pursuing justice, only to find themselves tangled in a web of inter-family tensions and secrets.

When Miss Cara Di Abaccio is accused of stealing the Carisbrook emeralds by the infamously arrogant Lady Carisbrook and marched out of her guardian's house by Scotland Yard's finest, Hugo Adair, Barnaby Adair's cousin, takes umbrage and descends on Scotland Yard, breathing fire in Cara's defense.

Hugo discovers Inspector Stokes has been assigned to the case, and after surveying the evidence thus far, Stokes calls in his big guns when it comes to dealing with investigations in the ton—namely, the Honorable Barnaby Adair and his wife, Penelope.

Soon convinced of Cara's innocence and—given Hugo's apparent tendre for Cara—the need to clear her name, Penelope and Barnaby join Stokes and his team in pursuing the emeralds and, most importantly, who stole them.

But the deeper our intrepid investigators delve into the Carisbrook household, the more certain they become that all is not as it seems. Lady Carisbrook is a harpy, Franklin Carisbrook is secretive, Julia Carisbrook is overly timid, and Lord Carisbrook, otherwise a genial and honorable gentleman, holds himself distant from his family. More, his lordship attempts to shut down the investigation. And Stokes, Barnaby, and Penelope are convinced the Carisbrooks' staff are not sharing all they know.

Meanwhile, having been appointed Cara's watchdog until the mystery is resolved, Hugo, fascinated by Cara as he's been with no other young lady, seeks to entertain and amuse her...and, increasingly intently, to discover the way to her heart. Consequently, Penelope finds herself juggling the attractions of the investigation against the demands of the Adair family for her to actively encourage the budding romance.

What would her mentors advise? On that, Penelope is crystal clear.

Regardless, aided by Griselda, Violet, and Montague and calling on contacts in business, the underworld, and ton society, Penelope, Barnaby, and Stokes battle to peel back each layer of subterfuge and, step by step, eliminate the innocent and follow the emeralds' trail…

Yet instead of becoming clearer, the veils and shadows shrouding the Carisbrooks only grow murkier…until, abruptly, our investigators find themselves facing an inexplicable death, with a potential murderer whose conviction would shake society to its back teeth.

A historical novel of 78,000 words interweaving mystery, romance, and social intrigue.

**The seventh volume in
The Casebook of Barnaby Adair mystery-romances
THE MURDER AT MANDEVILLE HALL**

#1 NYT-bestselling author Stephanie Laurens brings you a tale of unexpected romance that blossoms against the backdrop of dastardly murder.

On discovering the lifeless body of an innocent ingénue, a peer attending a country house party joins forces with the lady-amazon sent to fetch the victim safely home in a race to expose the murderer before Stokes, assisted by Barnaby and Penelope, is forced to allow the guests, murderer included, to decamp.

Well-born rakehell and head of an ancient family, Alaric, Lord Carradale, has finally acknowledged reality and is preparing to find a bride. But loyalty to his childhood friend, Percy Mandeville, necessitates attending Percy's annual house party, held at neighboring Mandeville Hall. Yet despite deploying his legendary languid charm, by the second evening of the week-long event, Alaric is bored and restless.

Escaping from the soirée and the Hall, Alaric decides that as soon as he's free, he'll hie to London and find the mild-mannered, biddable lady he believes will ensure a peaceful life. But the following morning, on walking through the Mandeville Hall shrubbery on his way to join the other guests, he comes upon the corpse of a young lady-guest.

Constance Whittaker accepts that no gentleman will ever offer for her —she's too old, too tall, too buxom, too headstrong…too much in myriad ways. Now acting as her grandfather's agent, she arrives at Mandeville Hall to extricate her young cousin, Glynis, who unwisely accepted an invitation to the reputedly licentious house party.

But Glynis cannot be found.

A search is instituted. Venturing into the shrubbery, Constance discovers an outrageously handsome aristocrat crouched beside Glynis's lifeless form. Unsurprisingly, Constance leaps to the obvious conclusion.

Luckily, once the gentleman explains that he'd only just arrived, commonsense reasserts itself. More, as matters unfold and she and Carradale have to battle to get Glynis's death properly investigated, Constance discovers Alaric to be a worthy ally.

Yet even after Inspector Stokes of Scotland Yard arrives and takes charge of the case, along with his consultants, the Honorable Barnaby Adair and his wife, Penelope, the murderer's identity remains shrouded in mystery, and learning why Glynis was killed—all in the few days before the house party's guests will insist on leaving—tests the resolve of all concerned. Flung into each other's company, fiercely independent though Constance is, unsusceptible though Alaric is, neither can deny the connection that grows between them.

Then Constance vanishes.

Can Alaric unearth the one fact that will point to the murderer before the villain rips from the world the lady Alaric now craves for his own?

A historical novel of 75,000 words interweaving romance, mystery, and murder.

ABOUT THE AUTHOR

#1 *New York Times* bestselling author Stephanie Laurens began writing romances as an escape from the dry world of professional science. Her hobby quickly became a career when her first novel was accepted for publication, and with entirely becoming alacrity, she gave up writing about facts in favor of writing fiction.

All Laurens's works to date are historical romances, ranging from medieval times to the mid-1800s, and her settings range from Scotland to India. The majority of her works are set in the period of the British Regency. Laurens has published over 80 works of historical romance, including 40 *New York Times* bestsellers. Laurens has sold more than 20 million print, audio, and e-books globally. All her works are continuously available in print and e-book formats in English worldwide, and have been translated into many other languages. An international bestseller, among other accolades, Laurens has received the Romance Writers of America® prestigious RITA® Award for Best Romance Novella 2008 for *The Fall of Rogue Gerrard.*

Laurens's continuing novels featuring the Cynster family are widely regarded as classics of the historical romance genre. Other series include the *Bastion Club Novels,* the *Black Cobra Quartet,* the *Adventurers Quartet,* and the *Casebook of Barnaby Adair Novels.*

For information on all published novels and on upcoming releases and updates on novels yet to come, visit Stephanie's website: www. stephanielaurens.com

To sign up for Stephanie's Email Newsletter (a private list) for heads-up alerts as new books are released, exclusive sneak peeks into upcoming books, and exclusive sweepstakes contests, follow the prompts at http:// www.stephanielaurens.com/newsletter-signup/

To follow Stephanie on BookBub, head to her BookBub Author Page: https://www.bookbub.com/authors/stephanie-laurens

Stephanie lives with her husband and a goofy black labradoodle in the hills outside Melbourne, Australia. When she isn't writing, she's reading, and if she isn't reading, she'll be tending her garden.

www.stephanielaurens.com
stephanie@stephanielaurens.com